THE GREAT WALL OF BALLYGALL

THE GREAT WALL OF BALLYGALL

Seamus Boshell

RESOURCE *Publications* • Eugene, Oregon

THE GREAT WALL OF BALLYGALL

Resource Publications
An Imprint of Wipf and Stock Publishers
199 W. 8th Ave., Suite 3
Eugene, OR 97401

www.wipfandstock.com

PAPERBACK ISBN: 979-8-3852-7059-0
HARDCOVER ISBN: 979-8-3852-7060-6
EBOOK ISBN: 979-8-3852-7061-3

Contents

… And what rough Wall,
its hour come round at last,
rises from Ballygall to be born.

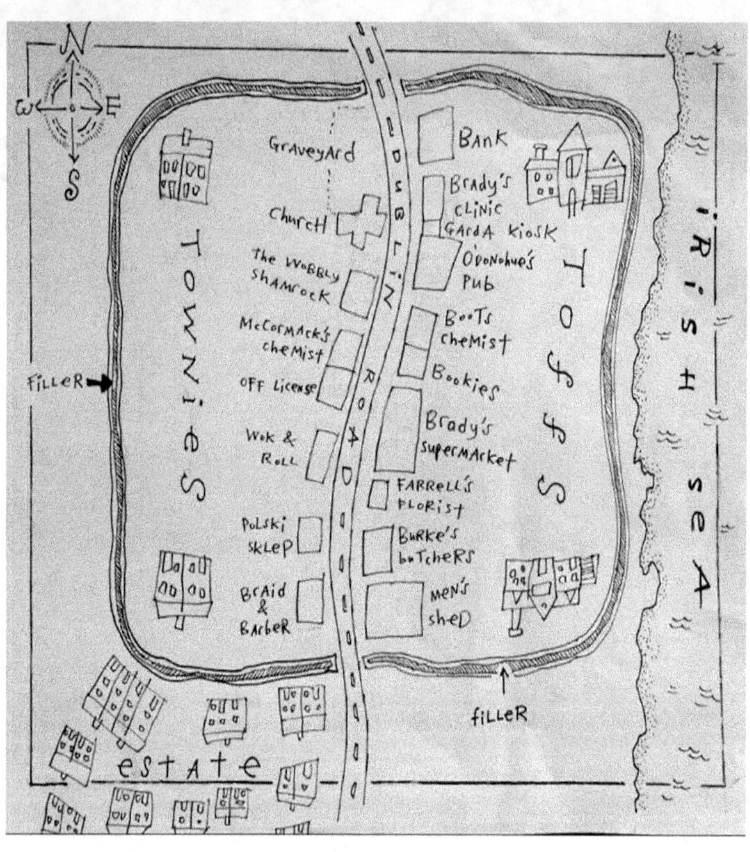
N
W
E
S
Graveyard
Church
The Wobbly Shamrock
McCormack's chemist
Off License
Wok & Roll
Polski sklep
Braid & Barber
Townies
Dublin Road
Bank
Brady's clinic
Garda kiosk
O'Donohue's Pub
Boots chemist
Bookies
Brady's supermarket
Farrell's florist
Burke's butchers
Men's shed
Toffs
Irish Sea
Filler
filler
estate

To Jennie, Eamon, and Molly, of course.

To my teachers, of course:
Maxine Rodburg, Phil Gambone, Susanne Berne, Tom Perotta, Tony Ardizzone, Dana Johnson, Jonathan Ames, Ray Hedin, Mary Otis.

To my colleagues, of course:
Jane Cavanagh, Martin Rogers, Joe O'Farrell, Bashir Otukoya, Sarah Banse, Carin Aquiline, Susan Finch, Danit Brown, David Trimble, Nico Hart.

To Ronan Gibney, who got me started.

To Damon Burnard, who drew the map.

To Lola, our Bernedoodle, who walked the walk with me.

And to all those scribblers I've met along the way.

A Proper Burial

A couple of strong drinks after midnight, we gathered at my father's grave, equipped with shovels, pickaxes, and a screwdriver, all arranged on an orthopedic stretcher, despite the fact that my poor, mistreated father had been dead a month. Liam, my younger and medically-inclined brother, and Professor Conor O'Reilly, a renewed acquaintance of my mother's, took a shovel each, reserving the pickaxe for me, Brendan 'Finn' McCormack, the eldest son, barely a year out of college. We stood stiff and reluctant in our Sunday clothes, though it wasn't Sunday. I felt shaky, incapable, avoiding their eyes.

From the far reaches of the graveyard came the caterwaul of cider drinkers, a medley of song and slur, hopefully too intoxicated to notice us or our idling pharmaceutical van, *McCormack's Chemist*, parked darkly on the central path of this country graveyard. Their fire, sparkling beyond the lamppost light, reeked of thick, fat tires. Conor glanced, tempted I'm sure to whisper another professorial objection but didn't. Beside him rose a leviathan angel, made of marbled white, its outspread hands unable to diminish its vengeful aspect, its wings flexed, its alabaster face predatory. In its anomalous scale and intricate design, it seemed to have descended from the heavens themselves, an intervention made incarnate, sent not to rouse the sinners but to restrain them, to exile them to their purgatorial graves forever.

But not my father.

"Jaysus' sake, come on," said Liam, agitating his flashlight at me, stamping his anxiety into Murphy's grave. Conor standing opposite on Young Akinfenwa's.

From the stretcher, I took a pickaxe, unsure whether a shovel would prevail on the dry, hard summer ground. "You sure, Liam, everything's grand?"

Liam had prepared everything — the body, the coffin, the shallow grave — for our clandestine purposes, and so naturally I worried at what apparition would confront us. Something worse than the hollowed shell relinquished by that murdering, negligent hospital? Something worse than decay? Something worse than worms? Maybe a smell? Maybe the ridiculous prospect of survival — my dad, suddenly awake and obstreperous, up gallivanting across the graves for a fire-warmed cider? But then the simple, undeniable fact of the clay, humped and mounded, tucked at its dark corners, weeds already at its fringes. On my flight from Boston that morning, pried yet again from my new emigrant life, I had girded myself against this clay, imagining instead a gardening chore, a repotting, made necessary by the betrayal of the Catholic Church of Ballygall, Dublin. Though our hometown graveyard was ancient and no longer used, they had promised to make an exception for my father and allow his burial there. Until they reneged, the bastards.

"Here, I can do it," said Liam, with a gentleness that infuriated me.

I reared the pickaxe in an exaggerated arc above me. My suit rose tight under my arms, the knot of my tie pressed against my neck.

A sudden and sodden chorus from the distant cider drinkers, "I fought the law, and the law won …"

"Shallow," shouted Liam. "Jaysus, it's shallow."

Conor recoiled backward, a little, plastic fence crackling under his Sunday brogues.

"Told ya, ya dope, barely a Jaysus foot," said Liam, grabbing a shovel, throwing another at Conor.

Wanker, but he was right. The coffin had been buried barely a foot below, ideal for easy retrieval. So, knees bent, back bent, I pick-pocked the length of the grave, manically loosening the ground for our spade work, me at the head, Liam in the middle, and Conor at the feet. Shoulder to shoulder, spades clashing, we sifted in parallel across the width of the grave, gradually uncovering the coffin. But not the scrape of wood I expected. Plastic. A whole swirl of it. What was this? With bubbles. Bubble-wrap. A whole lump of it. What the Jaysus?

Liam stood up, nodding to himself. "First layer of defense. Bubble wrap." Leaning on his shovel, a look of grim satisfaction.

Just bubble wrap?

I bent to look, relieved to see a coffin beneath the bubbles, suspended within, it seemed. All snug and swaddled. Its length partitioned by fat loops of silver duct tape. Possible, since only Liam and the undertaker

Podrowski had attended my father's descent into this distant Wicklow graveyard.

"Hurry," said Conor, glancing up at that monstrous angel.

I didn't. I stood, admiring Liam's effort. "Fair play to ya, Liam." My fears of decay, of worms and worse, receding. It was my idea after all to do this, to honor my father's last and oft-repeated request.

"That's nothing," Liam said, but said contritely, without his usual arrogance. On his hunkers, he applied a glinting, surgical scissors lengthwise, releasing, with an incongruity of celebratory pops, the bubbled skin.

There it was. The simple, wooden lid of my father's coffin. Free now to feel the summer breeze, seasoned with bonfire smoke.

I knelt opposite to Liam, pulling the bubbled sheets toward me as if unwrapping a giant, unwanted present. Unsullied, unscratched, not even a bead of moisture on the coffin. It was plain, unadorned by cross or dove, flat not domed. Four wooden handles. A fittingly dreary receptacle for such a fittingly temporary place. I leaned and touched the lid, to calm myself, to inoculate myself against the rest of the night. The wood cool but not cold.

Conor trundled the stretcher closer, alongside the grave. He seemed agitated, his pillowy cheeks puffed and reddened. He was tall and pale, his beard wispy, his gray hair linty, almost ghostly beside the brawn and summer brown of Liam, his black hair long like my father's, his nose blunt — the invidious image of my father, whereas I, with my pale skin and blue eyes, resembled our mother, and yes, my chipmunk cheeks, and from an agricultural ancestor a set of cow licks, the twin sources of my inescapable nicknames, 'Munk' and 'Sls-upp, Sls-upp.'

Liam bent to the coffin, screwdriver in hand. Yes, a glance at me, the eldest, but, daunted, I let him proceed. The courage of my earlier Jamesons was fading.

He was brisk, but left the last screw to Conor, who, to my delight, had trouble. His bony hands feckless against the recalcitrant screw.

"Jaysus' sake, Conor," said Liam, smiling, loosening his black tie a little.

Conor, his pillowy cheeks blowing, finally skittered it out.

The lid was loose.

We waited.

We held our breath if not our ground, but nothing emerged. No banshees, no ghouls. Nothing sprang from its white, oddly white interior.

We reapproached.

A corner each, we removed the lid with a shaky reverence, placing it on the ground, like a cold night's blanket. We took a collective breath. Glanced beyond at that still sparkling fire, before turning, looking, peeking down into —

Jesus.

The body was wrapped in gray bandages. Tightly looped. Its full length. Face too. The feet unshod but bandaged. Gauze covering the ears. At various and unpredictable junctures, thickets of silver duct tape.

"Bandages, elastic type, helps preservation," explained Liam.

"And those?" said Conor, pointing at the aura of small white packages arranged around the body. Hundreds of them.

"Sweets?" I asked. Our family had a sweet tooth. Maybe Krowki, those Polish caramels my father loved so well?

"No," said Liam. "Silica gel, packets. Desiccation. I took them from Downstairs."

'Downstairs' being our downstairs of commerce, *McCormack's Chemist*, Upstairs being our home, a small, two-bedroomed flat.

"Ordered them. Wholesale."

From a very early age, my father had called Liam 'My Wee G.P.,' his doctor, his Hippocratic consultant. Liam conducted a daily checkup, vigilant on the vital matters of pulse, temperature, heartbeat, and the rest. A practice never missed, never neglected; well, until a month ago.

"Weird," I said.

"Such a Yank already," said Liam, mocking my diction. "Take the feet. Just us."

Conor stepped back, wrapping his long arms around himself.

Liam leaned, leveraged, lifted the body up slightly. I took my dad's feet, shins, the stiff knees. Up we lifted it, together, the brothers McCormack, for once united, and up the body rose, the bandages loosening, trailing, a sudden downpour of sachets. So loud. Somehow louder than the bubble wrap.

Laterally, a couple of quick steps, then with a cautious almost hammocky motion, we swung and settled my poor dad on the stretcher, which rocked, which wheezed, which steadied.

"Well done," said Conor.

Liam nodded.

Applause too from the cider heads, but for themselves, still singing, their fire higher now, bending and crackling upward.

We blessed ourselves before turning back to the grave, to the empty coffin, its interior now only bearing the impress of my father. His disgraceful, unmerited purgatory was finished. "Let's get him to Ballygall," I said to Liam.

"Yep," he replied, with unusual succinctness.

I shoveled a great pile of clay into the coffin. Such an unearthly sound, the clay on those shiny, shrill sachets. We re-buried the empty coffin, working fast, silently.

Quickly into the van, Liam scissoring the bandages, which reeked of Old Spice. Liam's steady, glinting dexterity reminded me of a ship, an ice breaker, breaking a shallow path through the white surface, showily effective but useless against the deeper, silent depths.

He cut, then unwrapped. Beginning at the legs. Efficient but tender.

My father was slowly revealed, dressed in his favorite digging jeans and his blue Dublin G.A.A shirt. Liam removed the blue eye shades, saying, "Brace yourself, Brendan."

Liam used my real name, Brendan, often refusing to acknowledge my father's nickname for me, 'Finn,' a truncation of his own nickname, Fionny, Ciaran 'Fionny' McCormack.

Nothing grotesque, just the unsettling sight of my dad's right eye open. Only his right. A startlingly brown.

"The Evil Eye," explained Liam, as perfected by Finn McCool, the Irish warrior my father had claimed as a fictional ancestor. (If unacquainted with all things McCool, see Appendix I.)

"The Evil Eye," I said, wincing. It seemed to convey surprise, shock, the temerity of his premature passing.

We stood up to gain a better view.

It *was* our dad.

Pale, tumid, apprehended by some inner petrification, but it was him. Full blunt nose, like Liam's. A crescent-shaped scar. Mischievous pointed chin. Full, jaunty lips. Long black hair, which seemed longer than usual, and brushed, as if recently brushed. And that eye closed. Pinched. Painful looking.

"Like he's winking, isn't it," said Liam.

Which I liked. "A rogue to the last, wha."

From our Tesco bag of keepsakes, I prepared him (per instructions) for his journey into the afterlife. A twenty Irish punt into his right pocket. And into his left a wee bottle of Chianti. And something to read, *The*

Boyhood Deeds of Fionn McCool, tucked into his shirt. And something to listen to, his ancient radio, a mess of loose wires, nudged into his neck.

We drove back to Ballygall. Quickly. Silently. Only slowing to marvel at the growing army of builders now encamped outside the town. Assembled by the Northern Irish Billionaire, Hugh O'Neill, known far and pejoratively as The Toll Queen, to build The Great Wall of Ballygall. Charmed into action by my father.

Ah, Ballygall, the town I once left so well. Situated south of Dublin, south of the affluence of Killiney, a small clot on the coastal road, a bank, church, and cemetery at its north, two pubs at its middle, and a Nigerian hairdresser's and a Polish shop at its south.

On reaching its slumbering center, I slowed to a funereal pace, an almost stillness, which bitterly evoked the thwarted spectacle of our planned funeral procession. My father had been particular and detailed about his funeral. A lifelong obsession. He had wanted a crowd. He had wanted a horse-drawn bier, preceded by a band of local troubadours, with drums, fiddle, and pipes, superseded by a troupe of Ullalloos, keeners, professional grievers, announcing the unwelcome, premature interruption of death. An authentic Celtic burial in the ancient graveyard of Ballygall, beside the saint he discovered, St. Palladius, allegedly the first and better St. Patrick.

All fucking thwarted by the Church, which had posthumously prohibited him. So we had buried him in Wicklow. No wake, no Mass, no funeral, no Ullalloos, nothing that would exonerate the treachery of the Church. The poor town, mystified, and indignant. A non-invite to a non-funeral.

At the graveyard, in front of the main door of our Not-So-Small-Church, congregated my mother, Maeve McCormack, and Professor Aedeen O'Reilly, wife of Conor, both of whom I expected, but between them stood the welcome partition of a small, rotund woman. Unrecognizable until I remembered: Caitlin Diarmada, a professional ululator (keener), discovered by my father and still employed in Donegal. A red-faced, vivacious woman, with a thick throat, a full mouth, and shoulders broad enough to bear the intrusion of death.

Each of them wore black dresses and dark shawls against the night. A pitiful number of mourners really, six when there should have been hundreds. And at the dead skulk of night when it should have been dusk, the beginning of the Celtic day. And a clear, traitorous sky when it should have been rain and thunder, meteorological protestations against his premature passing.

My mother also wore a cardigan, a sleeveless jacket, a couple of scarves, her ancient wax jacket, a wooly hat, a couple more scarves — her usual forty layers.

Professor Aedeen O'Reilly was as alluring as ever. Elegant in her sleeveless dress, her black hair short and styled, but wearing her monkey boots, identical to my father's. In reverential honor, I suppose. For years she had led the DIG, mining the religious riches of Ballygall's graveyard, my father beside her, colleague, confidant, acolyte, who had daily chosen that clay over our chemist.

We parked in front of them, dousing the lights then the motor. Everything quiet. Ours was a town that enjoyed its sleep, lulled by the susurrating sea, the salty, soothing breeze, its rigmarole of routine.

The security fences surrounding the graveyard were open if not inviting.

Me and Liam removed the stretcher from the van. Conor and Aedeen, barely a word between them, and separated by Caitlin, proceeded to the grave, allowing us a family moment. Just our own family, when it should have been our extended families, my mother's from the north, my father's from the west.

My mother, pulling her layers about her, bent and looked at him. "Och, ridiculous as ever, so he is," scowling, but a lone tear in her eye, which she fisted away. "For God's sake, that stupid wink. But, aye, good work there now, Liam. And Finn too." Another glance down, another scowl, irritated anew by the theatricality of it, a subterfuge she might never have acceded to but for the intransigency of the Church. She loved a good fight, or 'barney' as my father would say. The ecclesiastical standoff had radicalized her and aroused an unexpected fidelity to my father's wishes, even allowing her nemesis, Aedeen, to orchestrate the Ballygall burial.

"Och, better get on," she said, eyeing the street, wary.

We conveyed the stretcher and the shovels to the graveside, located at the rear of the graveyard, behind the alleged grave of St. Palladius, his remains removed months ago to be verified by the Catholic Church. Enthused, and well-funded, Aedeen had continued the DIG.

She had arranged a ring of standing lights, a not unusual archaeological illumination that would not draw suspicion. The plot was square-shaped, unusually and noticeably small, a postage stamp slightly elongated.

"Could we place Fionn on hallowed ground?" said Caitlin. Her voice was clear, high, like a windswept hill.

We removed him from the stretcher and laid him at the head of the grave, where the ground had been smoothed, tilted, an incline to assist us, his feet now dangling over the edge of the grave.

A couple of sachets tumbled from the empty stretcher but were ignored.

He lay beneath a disrespectfully clear sky. Where was the thunder and lightning?

"Now," said Caitlin, who took a nip of something before addressing my father directly. "Ciaran 'Fionny' McCormack, husband of Maeve, father of Liam and Finn. Pray attend to us now."

A reverential pause.

"Were you a handsome man?" Which she answered. "You were." A quick smile.

"Were you a man of wit and sophistication?"

"A man of brawn and strength?"

"A man of unequaled wisdom and unmatched elegance?"

My father's words, of course.

"You were," said Caitlin. Continuing. "Were you an honest man?"

She nodded to us, to join in, to take our part in the responsorial psalm according to Fionny McCormack.

"He was honest," we answered. Mostly.

"Were you a man of work, a man of diligence?"

A collective hesitation, until Aedeen said "Yes," which seemed appropriate, given his daily preference for clay over commerce.

"Were you an honorable neighbor? A force for the town?"

As originally planned, there would have been multiple, alternating Ullaloos (Keeners). A raucous inquisition, with assertions, allegations, and rebuttals, with rumors and ruminations, and heckling, surely there would have been heckling. And an insult or two. Testimonies! Tears! Lamentations from our many creditors. It would have been wonderful.

Instead, Conor, in his puffy, pillowy voice, replied, "He was, most certainly was." Gazing at my mother, across the small patch of grave.

"Was he the bold discoverer of the real patron saint of Ireland, St. Palladius?"

"Yes!" said Aedeen.

Caitlin was waved on by my mother.

"A succor to the poor and powerless?"

"Och, give it all away if he'd be let," said my mother.

"Was it he who discovered the famous Wall of Ballygall? "The Great Wall of Ballygall," I said, though I had discovered it.

"A Wall to save and secure the poor town of Ballygall."

My father's words again, delivered precisely.

Then Caitlin, knowledgeable, astute, seemed to improvise, asking, "Will this good man's discovery be in vain? Will it not be re-built?"

"It will," I said, loudly.

"Will it forever enclose the venerable town of Ballygall?"

"It will," I replied.

"The Great Wall of Ballygall," said Caitlin. A nod for us to repeat. Serious.

"The Great Wall of Ballygall," we intoned.

Except my mother, who said, "Och, Caitlin, is it all night we'll be?"

"We should hurry," said Liam, evincing his usual antipathy to the Wall.

"Fionny McCormack, were you an honorable father?" Sternly.

"He was," I answered, echoed by Liam.

"Are your sons dutiful?"

"They are," answered Conor.

How would he know?

"Is the family well provided for?"

Silence. Half-a-home and half-a-business, probably insolvent.

"Aye," said my Mum. "We're rolling in it, so we are."

"Was he a loving husband?"

Jesus! Perhaps Caitlin wasn't so knowledgeable, so astute.

A chastening glance from Liam, which prompted from Caitlin a summary, an ending. "A fair, faithful wife. Brave, courageous sons. The respect of your neighbors. The gratitude of your town. Then why did you die, Fionny? Why did you leave us?"

"Murdered," said my mother.

"That arrogant-patronizing doctor," said Liam. "That negligent fucking hospital. In a corridor." My mother reached, soothed him.

Quicker now. "Ciaran 'Fionny' McCormack, you have all you need. You have been praised, feted, and provisioned by your family. Everything you shall need yonder is at your disposal. We commend you to the sacred soil of Ireland."

"And more importantly," I said, "the soil of Ballygall."

"Yes," said Liam.

"Rest in Peace," said my mother, with an amen from Conor and Caitlin.

A pause.

The sea wind strengthening.

A nod from Caitlin to Aedeen.

The worst part.

The burial.

Originally, it was to have been a large pit into which, held by myself and Liam, my father would have been stood. Then, the town, with individual handfuls of clay, would have filled the grave, my father held by his sons until he had taken root. What a spectacle that would have been. Buried like a chieftain of old, standing, watching over his town, with its great Wall, and his treasure, the grave of St. Palladius.

"Boys, crouch behind him, don't touch 'til I say." Aedeen whispering, supervising.

I can't really describe the burial. We basically pushed him feet-first into the small, square grave, his descent cushioned by cardboard boxes placed at its bottom. I held him upright while Liam shoveled, pelting me at times, the ground rising up to take him. Such a shock when I was able to let him go. His steadiness, his rootedness, his terrible permanency.

We then shoveled to completely secure him. From the rear, from the side, but not from the front. There he stood, as if participating in a strange, nocturnal excursion to the seaside. The radio nudged into the crook of his neck.

We shoveled.

I didn't look. Neither did Liam. We shoveled until Aedeen said stop.

Which she did.

Twice.

The grave was covered.

My father gone.

Just a mound that needed to be flattened. A grave, but secret. No headstone, not even a cross.

But there, I tried to remind myself. Standing. In Ballygall. Like his beloved Palladius. And soon with the protection of The Great Wall.

"A wee prayer," said Caitlin, incantating it softly, a short panegyric, cast in ornamented Gaelic, the bulk of which I could not understand — *Ar dhèis Dè go raibh a anam* — or the quick tears it prompted.

But then.

My mother interrupted. “Och, enough, rest in peace, Fionny.”

She left.

She actually left.

Jesus.

Liam trotting after her. An apologetic glance back to me.

I forced a smile. “Please finish,” I said.

Caitlin stood stupefied. On her tippy toes. Looking. Waiting for them to return.

“Not coming back,” I said.

Caitlin finished the prayer, her high voice a little shaken, nodding at our collective ‘Amen.’

Everyone left. Hugging but hurrying.

Even Caitlin. Speeding away in her old black Mercedes.

I stood there with my dad for a bit. Closed my own left eye. Promised myself. Promised him. The Great Wall would rise from the earth to save Ireland, and more importantly, Ballygall. And that I, Finn McCormack, son of Fionny McCormack, descendant of that great fictional warrior, Finn McCool, would build it.

Or at least help.

My Mother the Murderer

A few evenings later, I installed myself on my father's throne on our back stairs, the thirteen unlucky steps that connected our Downstairs of commerce, McCormack's Chemist, to our half-a-home Upstairs. To my father it was The Giant's Causeway, or more colloquially, The Causeway, and to my mother it was the Not-So-Giant Causeway. It connected the two giants of our house, my Finn McCool dad, and his nemesis, my mother, whom he called Benandonner, McCool's enemy, who clashed there daily, to the easy eavesdropping delight of our customers.

Like my father, I arranged myself sideways on the bony, middle stair, my monkey boots protruding through the broken banisters. A pillow for my neck, a good book, an embezzled supply of crisps-chocolate-coke and a cup of tea left to cool.

Cozy, tenebrous. Partially lit from the light from Upstairs and the light from Downstairs. No intrusive windows. No upper or lower doors.

My mother initially aghast. Shouting at me. But I stayed. Shook my dad's huge bunch of keys at her and stood, or sat, my ground. Her parting words, "Och, credit to yourself, you are, lying there like a dirty amadhàn," her chipmunk cheeks roaring red.

On the wall opposite me, fluttered an assortment of newspaper articles, arranged in no apparent order. Palladius, of course. Bearded, cloaked, and austere. A *Times* article proclaiming, "*Discovery of Palladius, The First St. Patrick, in Ballygall*". And print-outs of other celebrated walls, Derry, Dubrovnik, Lugo, but mostly Monteriggioni, which my dad loved and would have visited but for our insolvency. Then that weird article on the poisoning of a Boston College professor. From my parents' time in Boston. Obviously tons of fun. And that poster of Finn McCool, of course, jockeying the Salmon of Knowledge.

I took a good bite of my own thumb of knowledge. A sup of tea.

We were a strange, divided family.

My parents, graduates of Trinity College, emigrated to Boston in time to confer US citizenship on me, their eldest. By all accounts, they had a wonderful time in Boston, but on compassionate grounds, they returned to Ballygall to care for my ailing grandmother, Tasy, who sadly died, which was expected. What was not expected was their decision to stay in Ballygall, this parenthetical town, and furthermore, to conduct their marriage in this half-a-home and half-a-business.

Life meagered along, my mother Upstairs, my father on his Causeway, Janowski in the shop.

Until that day.

The town awash. The wind howling. I discovered a wee stone which suggested a wall, which suggested a town important enough for a wall. I was six-ish. Life became exciting, purposeful. A Christian wall, it was, originating from the time of St. Patrick. So, naturally, my father resolved to rebuild it. To restore the town's importance. Mobilizing the pro bono burghers of Ballygall to build it east and west of the town. Nothing south and nothing north. A parenthesis for an already parenthetical town. But great craic. Great camaraderie. Great expense. Until a recession scuttled us back to normal. The ravines, however, remained, scarring the town east and west. The Wall un-built.

So, my father turned his restless attention to the town's graveyard. Encouraged by His Holiness Father Seamus O'Shaughnessy, our parish priest. Which became the DIG. With Professor Aedeen O'Reilly. I was not allowed to join. Too dangerous, somehow.

Our lives continued. Our business wilted. I attended Trinity College. Liam took to medicine (and music), agreeing to yoke himself to our family shop. Then. A holy miracle. Me dad and Aedeen found St. Palladius. The first St. Patrick. Buried not in Scotland, but in Ballygall. Our town lifted to instant importance.

Regardless, I announced my intention to emigrate to Boston. Yes, feeling a bit left out. The publicity, the excitement. Even attracting the interest of the billionaire Toll Queen.

The site flourished. My father always at DIG. In all types of weather. In all types of health. And barely a year later, dead, mistreated, neglected, in a hospital corridor.

And now, barely a week after his proper burial, at my mother's insistence, a communal dinner, two families, the O'Reillys, without the matriarch, Aedeen, who hadn't been invited, and us, the McCormacks, without the patriarch, who couldn't be invited.

I offered to cook, to showcase the one worthy accomplishment of my challenging and lonely year of emigration but my mother ordered a take-away from The Wok and Roll.

What?

A take-away?

My mother strictly forbade outside food, assembling a perimeter of three daily meals to keep us safe, the prevalence of food poisoning seemingly rampant.

Up the Causeway came Tommy 'Teddy Boy' McDermott, atop his black, suede, brothel-creeper shoes, with bags of The Wok's finest. Nodding. Smiling. Saying, "Sls-upp, Sls-upp," my nickname. "Taking your dad's spot, lad." Handing me the bags. Already paid.

My Mum had a debit card?

Turning back. His ear buds blasting Northern Soul music. Leaving. Nodding to the incoming Professor Conor O'Reilly, who helped me with the bags of food. "A feast," said Conor the Comforter. My scornful nickname for him.

We arranged the feast on our huge dinner table, which dwarfed our half-a-home, really just a narrow rectangle, with two bedrooms separated by a bathroom on the right, the sofa and TV on the immediate left, the counter and kitchen beyond that.

Conor was about to – but I sat at the head of the table. The Jaysus cheek of him. But I let it go. I took my poor father's pew, his sideways perch at our prescribed meals together. A fussy eater but only when it suited him.

In waltzed my mother. Suddenly youthful. Her hair, once long, once thick, weaved and coiled, was now cut. Not just cut but quartered, the length lopped, abbreviated to a bob, not a long, shaggy bob, but short, well lifted from her bared shoulders. Unseen for decades, her neck was now a fierce shade of pale, like a bright pane of sun-simmered glass.

"Och, smells grand," she said, bringing plates and cutlery. She seemed to have ordered the whole menu, including the king prawn fried rice, my dad's favorite, which she left on the kitchen counter. Strange.

My mother the stranger.

She had dressed up for the occasion. Earrings, new brown leather boots, a blouse low enough to show the suggestion of an actual, inaugural tan, and a lemon-yellow skirt high enough to reveal the unsuspected existence of a symmetrical set of knees.

My mother had knees?

Slender, small-boned, well-capped, but bulbous and bruised from her years of kneeling in our Not-So-Small-Church, their skin raised and reddened — her own set of prayer bumps, hard and horned, which, over the coming weeks, would ominously heal.

"The windows," she said, opening them, west and even east, forcing them wide, the paint cracking and crackling. "Och, bit of fresh air."

Our windows opened?

And in rushed the foolish air, oblivious to the hermetic danger. A sea breeze, salty, seasoned with the sound of the fiddle from The Wobbly Shamrock next door.

Yes, we lived next door to a pub. So Irish.

Everyone sat.

"Lovely evening," my mother proclaimed, her bare arms lifted, as if they might carry her into song. *Ballygall is alive with the sound of music.* Opening a bottle of really good Chianti, from my dad's collection.

Curiouser and curiouser.

We engaged in small talk. About Liam. His impending exams, his Leaving Cert., after which he would yoke himself to our Downstairs chemist. Forever! Talked about his daily Hippocratic rounds, checking on the ailing burghers of Ballygall, drumming up business for our chemist. But no. Done. Stopped. No interest in medicine now. Even purged his side of the bedroom, lowering the Order of Malta flag, trashing the arsenal of medical supplies.

My brother the scholar?

No. The musician. Constantly at the church organ a few doors north.

And wearing, Jesus, wearing my dad's wedding ring. Who wears their father's wedding ring, with his mother still alive?

She was alive and alert. Asking me not about Boston or the Great Wall or The Toll Queen, but about money: to have a look at the chemist's financials, or lack thereof. And even more surprising, a longer look at our VAT returns, those fraudulent inflows! And Jesus, the loan, the Bank of Ballygall, and other loans, the good burghers of Ballygall. My father practiced an inverted form of philanthropy by bestowing on our many creditors the generosity of our needs.

We ate. Ravenously. My mother particularly. As if she hadn't eaten for decades. And guzzling the wine.

My mother drank wine?

Suddenly chatty. The old days, the different times, a bitter sort of nostalgia.

"Living here, so he was, Fionny, when we met. Trinity. Och, embarrassed."

I understood that embarrassment, having suffered the same domestication while at Trinity College myself. Sandwiches stuffed into my bag. Curfew calls. An apocryphal address in Killiney.

"Such kids we were, Conor. Dreams of fame and tenure. Changing the world, or at least the border. His mother didn't take to me. Aye, no chatty enough. And from the North. But it was his scholarship, not mine, that took us off away there to Boston. Brighton. Such a house. Wood. A basement kept you cool for the summer. So many rooms. What was it, a sun room? A professor on sabbatical. Och, the snow. Feet of it. And flying home. Like a film star. Back and forth. Until. Was it Rory's wedding that time?"

I could smell the king prawn fried rice still unopened on the counter but didn't want to interrupt or antagonize her. I was enjoying her garrulousness. So rare.

"What were the Yanks like?" asked Liam. Sincere, actually interested. Sitting up sideways out of his customary slouch. His thick, black hair reared back, like my father's.

"Och, that crowd, our crowd, so right wing, fascist almost, over there. Capitalists. Money." Her chipmunk cheeks aglow. "But Fionny loved it all. A shower, was that the name? At the college. Gifts for the baby, little Finn. But before he was born. Aye, made me queasy. Jinx ourselves. T'was lovely though."

I was an American citizen, a fact not disclosed to me until my thirteenth birthday or thereabouts. But I began, that very day, to prepare for my life as an American. I flossed. I drank Americanos. I watched (interminable) American football. I withdrew from the piffling minutiae of my poor friends, doomed to spend their life in Ballygall, Ireland, England, or Australia.

"Och, a great life, so it was, Conor, until, that business, had to, middle of the night so it was. Back to Ballygall. Derry and that not an option. Too dangerous. Sure, Ballygall, lovely wee town. I was the one for staying. Safe as kittens. No one would think, here. Though of course Dirty Doherty found us."

Dirty Doherty, neighbor, friend of my father, professional tunneller.

She lifted her hand into her hair, surprised at its shortness, surprised at her bare neck. "Och, fair to say, Conor, God forgive me, ruined it for Fionny. His studies. Boston College. Never forgave me, so he didn't."

Ruined? Middle of the night? Safe? Kittens? What had happened? Hadn't America merely convened an argument between them, my mother for Ireland, my father for adventure.

"The mother, Tasy, passed, and west we would have went, if he hadn't found that there Wall. Delighted."

Except I found it.

Conor poured her another glass. Just her. And then himself. Intent. Listening.

"Kept us, Conor, its discovery, in the town so it did. Kept us together, no argument there. And sure didn't it bring along my wee boy Liam here."

Liam reddened.

Was there no limit to the powers of The Great Wall? A protector of the faith, a binder of families, an aphrodisiac that prompted my little brother into the little world of Ballygall.

"Och, Liam, so it did." Her syrupy glance at our Maestro Liam. Never before advanced in public.

I felt jealous. His nativity now inscribed in fourth century stone. His fate entwined with the Wall, perhaps their slings and arrows reciprocally felt, to rise and fall in tandem …Wanker. Not only was he the spit of my father, but that procreative sparkle, it had originated from the Wall, from history itself. How unfair was that?

"But took away too, that Wall. When was he ever, always running away. Then the DIG, then that there saint."

Her voice hardening, tensing, the sea breeze suddenly stalled at the street window. Our collective breath held. Her glance northward, to the graveyard, to my father. Remembering perhaps our appointment, the next week, at that so-called hospital, our non-binding, exploratory, sure-just-a-chat, just yourselves and our fifty solicitors.

"Och, Conor, wasn't I a widow anyway. Left with the boys. Left with Downstairs. A grown man digging in the dirt." Her cheeks now as red as Liam's.

Again that glance northward. Maybe not the grave, but toward that remaining Digger, Aedeen the Grave Licker. Livid. A gaze into the future not the past. Revenge perhaps.

I leaned away. An early lesson. Lean away. When the fires are flowing, when her cheeks are blowing, lean away, boys, lean away. Or if you're Liam, lean in, lean all the crazy way in. "Wall is one thing, but don't for a second believe all that Palladius shite. All her St. Paddy malarkey." Liam's voice rising.

"This here town, Conor," she said, loudly. "Full of half-wits, half-truths, sure no one would give you a straight face." She lifted herself, stretched, perhaps trying to rise out of her disturbing past. "Ah, boring these young pups, so am I. Away with ye. Liam, to the church, keep the practice going. Brendan, I mean Finn, take that there prawn thing to Aedeen. That God-awful DIG of hers."

Liam did not hesitate. He hurried down and out. To the church. To play. Jesus, was he doing any study for his Leaving Cert.?

My mother closed the street window, then the back window, the poor sea breeze caught, captured, doomed to stultify and stale.

I stayed. Eager to hear more.

But she handed the king prawn to me. "Here, for Grave – for Aedeen. Keep ye going through the night."

Curioser and curioser.

She was dispatching her eldest son to that same reviled woman, to that same despised graveyard, her dead husband standing only feet away? Sending me with my dad's favorite dish?

Why?

To be alone with her Comforter?

Not aloneness, I think, but the lack of togetherness, keeping Conor and Aedeen apart. Her revenge. Settling scores.

She stood over me. Stared. Did not move.

I yielded. Took the dish. And the offered bottle of wine.

Down our Causeway I went, through our small chemist, opening then slamming the front door, and then creeping my way back to the bottom of the Causeway, to its lower rungs, lying down, outstretched, extending my better eavesdropping ear upward.

Listening, for a fidget of minutes, about to leave when my name, Finn, descended down in diminuendo from my mother. Not a calling, but a conversation. My name again, my birth, in America, an incitement.

"That, with the wee boy growing inside, Och, Conor, you didn't grow up in Derry. How could I not? All that there truth came back to me. My child coming into the world. Shouldn't I do what I can, take on The Cause once more. Ay, once more. It's true. I'll hold nothing back. But shouldn't I prepare the way for the child somehow."

Her voice sounded plaintive, defensive, strained in justification of something I had missed. And walking, my mother actually walking, the modest length of Upstairs. I extended my ear a creak further up the steps.

"That there Northern apartheid. A child into that world, how could I not do something?"

She ebbed away, toward the sea, her boots like a small boat, bashing on the floor. I strained beneath, deafened by her distance. My breath stopped, held itself. But she returned, flowing back, her voice re-surfacing.

"Thirty-two. No peace without a price, so there isn't."

I understood. Back then, enclosed in the womb, curled and comfy, I was made to make room, to accommodate another creation, another developing thing, my mother's love for a united Ireland. A love worth sacrifice, risk, and, danger. A love worth a mother's commitment. Lying on those stairs, I conceived a resentment, a competitive enmity against the struggle for a united Ireland, a movement since separated and abstracted from my mother's involvement but whose progression, which I peacefully support, has come to mean only deprivation for me. A rivalry, an insecure son against an incomplete nation.

"I'll not mince, so I won't. Physical force. Active service. Are you with me, Conor?"

Seaward, she bumped away, but I rose and wriggled after her, between the aisles, my ear poked toward the surface, her muffled mumblings, but indiscernible.

Defeated by the depth, I treaded back to the stairs.

Conor, a tone of alarm, an exhortation to sit, to be still.

She acquiesced with a name, "Tim McGregor. Professor. BC," before returning to that inaudible sea.

BC. Boston College. That anomalous news story on our Causeway! Facing me. BC professor poisoned. Irish American. Brilliant, forthright, swashbuckling. Unknown assailant. Unknown motive. Disgruntled student? Envious competitor? His murder half a year into my young life.

Above me, consternation. Conor now standing, now striding toward my mother. Together, walking, a choppy momentum, two boats bashing back into her murderous past.

Up another stair I advanced, and up bobbed a name, familiar, dreadful.

"Dirty Doherty. Poisoned him."

Dirty Doherty. The poisoner. That was Doherty? That was Doherty and my mother? Was my father involved? Why would he hang such an article on the wall? Facing it every day?

"We poisoned him," she said. Crying now, at first audible but soon muffled by her Comforter. "It's only fair that, now, to tell, Conor, so it is," she said.

Though unseen, I could imagine her righting herself, raising herself, settling her new shortened hair, calming her clothes, composing her breath. Straightening her still welted knees.

Jesus, Doherty had poisoned him. The professor in that article.

Murdered him.

With my mother's assistance, it seemed. And she, a new-born mother, daring and conniving. My young life besmirched, bloodied. The siren call of her incomplete nation. What if she had been apprehended? Jailed? Injured? Me just a baby. Such risk. Such recklessness. Such, Jesus, murder.

The sofa bore their shared silence.

A pause.

Shock?

Regret?

Relief?

I allowed my breath its ragged procession. What to do? What to do? Should I, Finn the eldest, rise up, confront, demand an explanation, a more benign interpretation? Silence still. For a matter of minutes. But then small talk, a segue, to king prawn fried rice of all things, its chewy, tough, waxy awfulness. Their laughter. The clink of the wine bottle. Then the distant sound of Liam, playing the church organ. So beautifully, they agreed. Such a wonderful lad. Maturing. And on they went, rhapsodizing about our amazing Maestro.

I left.

Walked slowly. Past The Wobbly Shamrock. To the –

But the graveyard was padlocked. I tried the small key from my father's huge bunch of keys, but no, nothing. It was a new padlock. A new fence too. Sturdy. No sign of Aedeen. A sign, No Trespassing. Dangerous Terrain. Had the DIG been canceled?

I sat on the steps, the prawn dish beside me.

Tired.

Wondering.

Was she lying to him? Wasn't he a professor of Irish History, especially The Troubles, The IRA. Her way of keeping him away and estranged from Aedeen? But mentioning Dirty Doherty? Why would she do that? Especially if Conor were to write about it?

Jesus, my mother the murderer.

The Toll Queen Lands at Ballygall

The next morning, my mother woke me, shook me. Pulled back my sheets. Even pulled the pillow from under me. She was dressed in her churchly best though it was well past Sunday. A black skirt, a cream blouse, shoes of a modest elevation, her newly shorn hair brushed, shined it seemed, her blue eyes bright. And makeup! Her chipmunk cheeks rouged. And warm encouragement. "Och, great surprise for you, Finn. Come on out and meet *him*. Put on yer old trousers." Which were hung for me on the door. In the bunk bed above, a snuffling, snoring Liam, exempted from this prestigious introduction.

I did as I was told. More out of surprise than compliance. Bewildered at the dissonance of meeting him but in my old ratty trousers. Wrecked, still on Boston time.

From the morning kitchen, music, a medley of Chopin.

Unheard of.

But there he was. Sitting at our table, the chair pipsqueak beneath him.

The Toll Queen himself. Hugh O'Neill. Alleged great, great etc. grandson of The Great O'Neill. Earl of Tyrone. Scourge of the English until he scarpered off with the other great earls.

An obliterated breakfast in front of him. A fry-up. A pot of tea. A dram of Jameson. A rubble of toast. Before dawn she must have got up.

"Fionny McCormack," he thundered, rising, his monstrous handshake merely a preliminary to a gigantic hug, my mother beaming behind him.

"Finn," said my mother," "not Fionny." Her smile tight, which ebbed, but tightened again, obviously resisting the introduction of my real name, Brendan.

"Give us a look at you, nauuw."

Said in his best Derry accent, 'nauuw' not 'now.'

We took a look at each other.

Definitely bigger than I imagined, and older, early forties, chubby, big pored, a once celebrated physique that had captained Tyrone's football team before his migration to London. A vision in red, he wore the beginnings of a new red beard, well tugged, badly tufted. His skin was reddened, lightly freckled, cast from paleness by a foreign sun. Long red hair, cut with a straight and severe fringe, which proceeded in wavy terraces to his neck, which he habitually threw back, just like my father. Hard, pale, blue eyes, surrounded and corrugated by laughter lines. Black jeans. Black cowboy boots, yes, with spurs. A red shirt. In his pocket, a pocket history of Ireland — for an even more pocket-sized summary, see Appendix II — the prodigal son returned, fanatically embracing all he had once renounced. Reminding me of James Joyce's Citizen:

> broadshouldered deepchested stronglimbed
> frankeyed redhaired freelyfreckled shaggybearded
> widemouthed largenosed longheaded
> deepvoiced barekneed brawnyhanded.

"Not a bit like your dad, yeah, but the brainy one." His English accent re-surfacing.

We all sat at the table. The room bright and warm. Steam still percolating upward from the electric kettle. A smell of toast. A sound of the Maestro snoring melodiously.

"So, what says you, Maeve?" said O'Neill, turning toward her, his great big maw tugging at his tyro beard. "Should have of course asked your counsel the last time. But time pressure so it was. Ridiculous situation, nauuw. Just a decoration the presidency is. Give it some power, some steel."

The office of the president of Ireland having little real power.

My mother nodded. Rubbed her newly exposed neck. Was that a little smile before she said, "What does Donal say?"

Donal, The Queen's younger but politically eminent brother.

The Toll Queen almost strangled his beard.

It *was* a smile. My mother the mischievous.

"Och, only having you on, Rambo."

Rambo, his footballing nickname. Which he would leverage, at least initially, for not just the presidency but a presidential referendum, to fortify the ornamental office with real, wieldable power. Or so he said.

The Toll Queen hammered the table with his huge fist. The table shook. The chairs shook. Even the shop downstairs shook. "Always catching me with that wit, yeah. So dry, Maeve. Mother said the same of ye."

And then he laughed that awful laugh of his. A three-stage, chimerical affair. First, a nanny goat quiver of teeth and tongue, which would unfortunately broaden, expand, and elevate to a hyena screech, and proceeding, would distressingly acquire depth, bass, an elephantine volume. So Goat-Hyena-Elephant. An abomination.

A mirthful glance from my mother, who, understandably eager to obviate an encore, continued, "Aye, strong president, makes sense. Especially militarily. Take back the North."

Northern Ireland. Still under British control. Her great murderous passion.

"But the wording, Maeve? You're grand with the wording?"

Which she seemed to be, my mother suddenly the arbiter of constitutional referendums, and whose company and counsel he now sought … but what last time? When? Where? And she had met The Toll Queen's mother. When? Where?

"Aye. But what's the job you have here for Finn?" asked my mother.

The Toll Queen eyed me dubiously. What did he see?

A pale, cow-licked, blue-eyed, chipmunk-cheeked boy, perched between Boston and Ballygall, but determined to "lift to importance" the town of his father, if not his mother. But not navvy material.

"Same job as his father would have done, gas character he was," he said, but flinching at a cross look from my mother, her arms folding. A quick remorseful sup of his tea, after which he looked straight over at me, his hard blue eyes softening in the bright morning light. "Sorry about your father, lad. Terrible."

I nodded. Unsettled by his sudden sympathy. He had lost his own father a year before, a death which had only made the headlines when O'Neill's younger brother, Donal, had been preferred for the eulogy.

"We'll do the Wall your father's way. The old way. Elbow grease and sleeves rolled up." He stood up. Rolled his sleeves up his monstrous forearms. "Need to get in shape, yeah." He rolled up his red shirt and grabbed collops and collops of sunburnt belly flesh." If I'm going to be president. A real president, don't you think, lad?"

I nodded.

"And what's more presidential, in Ireland anyway, than re-building the first Catholic wall, innit." Which prompted him to lower his shirt and reminisce on the lost power and prevalence of his precious-again church. A born-again Irishman pretending to be born again. "Mostly, Aisling. Very religious. What's the word? Not staunch. Devout. Devout."

His wife, Aisling O'Donnell, also allegedly from the Great O'Donnells. Abducted by criminals in a Tiger kidnapping. Ransomed so that her loving husband would commit a crime on behalf of her captors. Which he wouldn't. Her fingers cut off, not both at once, but twice, one at a time.

O'Neill turned and stared out the window. His hand at his beard. It was trembling. "Devout, she is. Have to meet her, Maeve. Amazed at your church here. Cathedral really."

My mother freshened his tea. Sweetened it with sugar. Which seemed to revive him. "Gas man, your father, lad. What was it he would say to me? At Trinity. With that one Aedeen."

Here, a glint sparkled in his royal eye.

"Grave Licker," said my mother, lowering herself to her cup, sucking toward her the vapor from her hot tea. "A boggin' bitch, if ever there was one."

Which startled The Queen. Re-directing him to his huge phone, a text he had been ignoring. "Hope you don't mind, Maeve," he said, at the sound of hurried footsteps up our Causeway. A photographer. A presidential photographer, brisk, quickly congregating us into a lightning storm of photos.

"How bad like," said O'Neill, his giant arms around us. A strong piney smell of beard balm. "Photo with Maeve McAliskey."

Her maiden name. Never actually enunciated Upstairs, and never with such reverence. What had she done to deserve it? Murder, of course.

"Come with us, Maeve," said O'Neill, unclamping us. "Watch your boy put to work."

"I'll not but thank you."

"Thank you," said O'Neill, warmly. Was he about to genuflect?

"Go on away with ya," said my mother, returning to the kitchen.

"Hi-Ho," he said to me. "As your father used to say. Off to work we should go, nauuw."

Down our Giant's Causeway he strode. The structure quaking. A limb of the banisters collapsing. I reluctantly followed.

Our chemist was, as my father would say, jam-packed. Dozens of ulterior customers, even among the lice, scabies, and laxatives in aisle one. All of whom stopped, inexplicably applauded. Even Janowski the chemist, who normally reserved his veneration for St. Palladius (allegedly) of Ballygall. O'Neill took this and a bag of Monster Munch in his stride.

Outside, the sun greeted his royal emergence, already warming a refreshing, salty breeze. The Toffs, led by Teresa 'Tidy Town' McAnteer, stood straight and proud outside O'Donohue's pub. Beside them The Townies, led by Dirty Doherty. In between these two groups, stood Garda Michael, his hand on his new gun, recently legalized and supplied by the Germans, Heckler & Koch. A little bit further south congregated The Estaters, led by Chioma "The Writer" Chijindu and in front of them ran a cordon of Black and Blue, the Black a private security force hired by O'Neill, the Blue Gardai Siochana. Definitely more Black than Blue.

In front of us stood a giant, O'Neill's minder, Glibb, with long blonde hair cut with a straight and severe fringe like his master. Beside him stood a skeptical-looking, scraggly-bearded wolfhound, a newly acquired accoutrement for the born-again O'Neill.

Who whistled for the hound.

Who was ignored.

"Boru," The Queen called.

Odd name for the dog, given that King Brian Boru was generally antagonistic to the O'Neill clan, Great or otherwise.

O'Neill tried and was ignored again, prompting a nervy rendition of his awful laugh, Goat-Hyena-Elephant. Heard all over Ballygall, to everyone's astonishment and distress. Only a Monster Munch would lure the hound. "Ready, Glibb?" asked O'Neill.

The Giant nodded. He was not big on talking. In fact, until things got belligerent much later, he rarely said a word to me.

The street was closed to traffic, blocked north and south by two monstrous yellow trucks apiece. Smaller trucks, a trio of JCBs, and at least half a dozen vans lined the street, clumping at the commercial end of town.

But a wonderful sight, really. The Wall's time had come at last.

... And what rough Wall,
its hour come round at last,
rises from Ballygall to be born.

But where would we start? East or west? My father had begun in the west, behind our house.

"Hi-Ho," shouted O'Neill, scratching his scratchy beard. Tensing Boru's leash. Heading south.

South?

With his quick, little Queeny steps.

South.

His beard balm piney and awful.

Shite. We were heading south. Toward the Estate.

Boru followed, drawn by the Monster Munch.

O'Neill pulled me after him, a quick peremptory hug, presidential practice I suppose, but leaning in, whispering, "This is cracker, so it is. Your Da would be up for it. Sort those feckers out."

"Don't start in the south," I said, my voice unfortunately high-pitched. "I mean. Tactically. Will only antagonize the Estaters."

"Exactly."

Which stunned me for a second. "It's better, start in the west, where my dad started. Once they see it, impressive and all that, they'll be happy to have it on their side. Can then have an arch in the Wall. Pedestrian. Like my dad suggested."

"Attack, best form of defense, innit." His steps lengthening. "Need this."

"But. This cuts everyone off. Day one. Right away."

"Exactly."

"Hate it, they will. And not fair that —"

He stopped. Looked at me. Held his beard. "Listen, Archie." My hilarious nickname. "Told your mother I'd, well, keep you safe. Just do what you're told. Could get dodgy." He nodded his massive fringe at me.

I snuck a quick bite of my thumb of knowledge but to no avail.

"Fuck the begrudgers," continued The Queen, glancing at The Estaters. "Those there beyond in that boggin' Estate. We'll knock the bollix out of them, got me. Taking no crap in this wee excuse for a town."

"Don't know this town. Making a mistake."

"Enough, Archie, lad."

South, we proceeded. The tip-tap of Boru's paws behind us. His Monster Munch crunches. Followed by Toffs and Townies. Black on our right, Blue on our left. Garda Michael, that mad dog, running ahead, his gun wagging in his holster.

I nodded to Chioma The Writer. Conciliatory. Apologetic. She nodded back.

O'Neill nodded to His Holiness Father Seamus O'Shaughnessy, our parish priest, clad in his usual soutane and biretta. Bestowing extravagant blessings upon The Queen.

"Weirdo" said O'Neill, rolling up his red sleeves, spitting on his hands. "Need this, though. Better than all your Hail Marys and Our Fathers."

The builders applauded and cheered the Queen. A sunburst of yellow, all from the Catholic North, clad in yellow T-shirts and yellow hard hats. Two of them, one east, one west, were already soaking the road with huge hoses. The air saturated. Like a giant, improvised car wash.

A concrete mixer truck arrived in the rear, its yellow, yes, everything was yellow, cone revolving happily, like a giant ice cream. Its driver leaning out, adding his own applause.

We arrived amongst them.

Townies and Toffs congregating on the east side and Estaters on the west side, behind a cordon of Black. But everyone distracted, glancing back up the Dublin road, but at what?

An apparition, right in the middle of the road. My mother. Outside. In the air. In the broad and warm daylight. Standing. Watching. Her hair so short. Church-dressed. Smiling.

All of which seemed wrong somehow. Like an escaped fugitive, standing, brazen, taunting. I had a tremendous urge to run her back Upstairs. The murderer.

And Jesus, Conor, her willowy, pillowy Comforter beside her. Had she just whistled for him?

The Queen waved at her before mounting a huge tractor-like vehicle. It was yellow, of course, equipped at its front with a gigantic circular saw, black and serrated, encased at its height by thick yellow housing. Huge chewy wheels, glistening on the soaked road. Shiny. Was it new? Just bought?

He checked the dashboard, the levers, the dials, knowledgeably. Encircled a yellow pair of ear safety muffs around his neck.

I watched him, apprehensive that he might motion me aboard, that I, as the discoverer of The Great Wall, should be accorded the first slice as it were, the first awful cut. I would decline. I would object. I would point us west or even east.

He did not offer.

He stood up on his yellow slicer, steadying himself for his first presidential speech.

"A wee story, yeah," he shouted, his Derry and London accent intermixing. "Let ye know what kind of clan you're tooling with." A belligerent glance at The Estaters. Answered by Chioma, pushing her gold glasses tighter.

"The symbol of our family is a Red Hand. Not the Unionist shite. Forget that. This is the Great O'Neills I am talking about, so it is."

The alleged Great O'Neills. It was never proven that his twig of the family was connected to the Great Earl.

From the seat, he produced a white flag with the aforementioned Red Hand on it. Palm facing out, fingers straight. And from its wrist, blood dripping, a fresh improvisation by The Queen himself. "The story. A competition to see who would be the king of Ulster. A race, from the isle of Man. Whoever's hand touches our fair land, would claim the crown."

"And skip the toll," an Estater shouted.

"My ancient grandfather, Niall of the Nine Hostages, was amongst them. Now Niall was losing. Falling a bit behind. And what did he do? Was he going to lose?"

A strange cadence, more pantomime than presidential.

"The O'Neills don't lose."

An assertion my mother later confirmed, albeit crediting the younger brother, Donal.

"What did he do, yeah?" An unappreciated pause. "He cut his own right hand off and threw it onto the land. Beating them. Becoming the King of Ulster. With his bloody Red Hand."

A collective gulp.

"That's who you're dealing with here, me boyos. And don't forget it."

I had not heard the story before. It shook me. Recalled to me not the feats of the O'Neill clan but the recent Tiger kidnapping and mutilation of his wife. Her wedding finger and her little finger amputated and sent back to her husband. Both, but twice, one after the other.

O'Neill gunned the engine.

The hoses gushed.

Glibb The Giant handed me earmuffs. Just in time. And a pair of safety glasses. Just in time.

O'Neill revved the machine. Clumps of black smoke erupted into the mist. He spun the saw. Lowered his safety glasses. Just him. No instructors, no operators, no side-saddling for this Queen. A last tug of his beard and off he sliced, due west, a mere fifty feet or so south of the B&B (Braid & Barber).

It had begun.

The Slicing of Ballygall.

Such a *screech*. Such a serration of sound. Which seemed to sweep all before it. A malignant force substantial enough to produce its own weather. Wind, rain, and rainbows. The Irish Sea nervous in the background.

The black, serrated teeth sliced westward.

The Toll Queen bent onward. With his big, yellow ears. Slicing. And not the expected ceremonial jaunt either, not the few symbolic slices before unsaddling. No. He kept going. Large jets from east and west hoses preceded him, tempering the friction, sluicing the sound.

Awful.

The Slicing of Ballygall.

Slicing away the Estate.

The Toll Queen, astride his new yellow steed, slit open The Dublin Road. His right fist raised. Shouting something into that convulsion of sound. Looking a little unhinged, in his bulbous earmuffs.

He did not pause. He did not stand to receive applause. He turned the machine, nimbly, quickly, slicing back toward the sea. Serious. Determined. Slicing up the worn soil of Ballygall.

Two more laps he made. Four lines lacerated in the sand.

Did something scandalous emerge from this Ballygall fissure? From the bowels of Ballygall?

Armada gold?

IRA guns?

Yet another Saint Patrick?

No.

Just muck.

Ballygall the Boring.

O'Neill dismounted. Three JCBs, backhoes, drew toward him, but were refused, O'Neill saying, "Hold it. Old style. And let's Archie here get his hands dirty, yeah."

A wink but also a pickaxe for me. New. And one for the Queen and one for Glibb. Also new. Everything bleedin' new. O'Neill arranging us in a line, facing north, me between him and his Giant. No preamble. No words of instruction. No tease. No taunt. The Toll Queen cleaved the earth with a huge blow. Another. Arching his back to an incredible, almost dramatic degree. "Cam' on, lads." His English accent re-emerging. "Nice one, Glibb," he shouted when Glibb hit his first astounding blow.

The crowds shuffled back a step.

Boru too.

I lifted mine tentatively. My shirt tight under my arms. Brought it down, gently. Surely, my reluctance obvious.

"Ha," said the Toll Queen. "Pipsqueak, but we'll toughen you up, Archie. Promised your mother no less."

There she still stood. In the middle of the Dublin road. Looking amused.

A derisive chorus of "Sls-upp, Sls-upp," from the Estaters.

"Cam' on, pipsqueak," the Queen shouted.

I did. The Queen and his Giant did. Leveraging into the lines cut by the Slicer.

I was soon splattered in muck.

Which was bad, but what was worse was O'Neill's accompanying lecture to me. The importance of family, home, tradition, religion, and mistakes, the importance of not just making mistakes but making up for them.

Such vicious swings of the pickaxe.

THAWACKKKK.

THAWACKKKK.

Pausing to wipe the muck from his eyes. His beard. His hair. Eventually taking his shirt off. A tattoo of a Red Hand over his heart, with its red blood dripping down to his flabby belly. Missing two fingers. The little and wedding ones.

Classy.

THAWACKKKK.

And then he stopped. Called for a JCB. His hands torn and bloody. His beard mashed in muck. "Need a bit of depth, lad."

O'Neill deepened the ravine with the JCB. Awkwardly at first, but his expertise returning. Expanding the digging into a trench of sorts. And into the trench we descended. Even Boru the wolfhound. O'Neill enjoying himself. Laughing now. That terrible-terraced laugh, goat-hyena-elephant. Digging. At a steady pace, but unrelenting. Muttering to himself. Only resting to arrange his new beard. Boru eventually asleep beside him. Glibb the Giant taking frequent water breaks.

O'Neill would not take water. Or a rest. Muttering to himself. Tears in his eyes at one point. Slick with muck. Shouting at everyone not to slacken, though everyone was only watching. Quiet. Nervous. O'Neill shoveling huge clods of earth. Spitting. Stamping. Like a work horse, digging itself deeper. Taking his boots off. His socks. "Toughen them up, so it will," he said. Digging in his feet. Big, hairy feet. Blood soon spoiling the clay. Muttering to himself. Incantatory. The rosary. He was actually reciting the rosary. Penance.

Jesus.

He had chosen Ballygall as his place of penance. To atone for his wife's amputations.

Lucky us.

And so began the Great Wall. The builders eventually dispatched east and west, rousing and refreshing the two ravines to accommodate the wide and curved foundations of The Great Wall. A force of hundreds where once we had previously only been a dirty dozen; by a battalion of JCBs where once we had only a few wheelbarrows; by a work force regimented where we had been improvised, impulsive, with uneven starts, unexpected endings, late hours and lackadaisical lie-ins.

An army, really.

The Toll Queen restricted them to the east and west, retaining the south for his own labor, done mostly, to the exasperation of his foremen, with shovels and pickaxes. And me, always kept by his side, his promise to my mother.

Weeks of it. My job and lodgings in Boston relinquished.

A great pall of dust rose up around Ballygall, as if the town itself were spinning backward, retreating to the era of St. Patrick (or St. Palladius), to a simpler, superstitious time.

And the noise.

Hellish.

The foundations were completed in days. The first stone of The Great Wall a day or two later, delayed to accommodate O'Neill's presidential campaign.

Yes, the first stone, but no pomp or palaver. No band, no speeches. Just O'Neill, his Giant, and his wolfhound.

And me.

O'Neill himself laid it. Beautiful, dense stone, a mottled gray, cut and carved from the exorbitant quarries of Kilkenny. He did most of the South's stone work.

The construction was simple.

Two lines of stone were needed, an inside wall and an outside one, and in between the middle, filled with what would become known as the Filler, which would join, solidify, and unify the walls. The Wall would be built horizontally not vertically, at least initially, nothing more than two stones a day, left overnight to sit and settle. Cute and lilliputian, at least initially. Sectioned into sections. Separated by control joints, those connective parts of the Wall that both strengthened and structurally separated the sections, helping to prevent instability and unsightly cracking.

I heard a lot about control joints.

But where would this Filler come from? What would it be filled with? An implacable refrain all summer. What *is* the Filler filled with?

A question sharpened by the selection of that first Filler, drawn from the rubble of Dirty Doherty's house. Yes, Doherty, the most outspoken opponent of the Wall, the Church, and the Queen. They knocked his house down.

Demolished it via Eminent Domain late one evening. Supposedly obstructing the Wall. It did not take long. A few JCB swipes, a few charges and it was gone. Everyone watching. Helpless. In shock. Doherty absent. In his new house in the Estate. Promising vengeance.

Then they pummeled it. Pebbled it. Fed it as Filler to the Great Wall.

Other homes would be pummeled, pebbled.

Fed to The Great Cannibal Wall of Ballygall.

The B&B (Braid & Barber)

A visit, conciliatory, explanatory. Only yards from the southern Wall and its froth of barbed wire. The poor Estate now excluded from the town, not visible behind the Wall, the Black (private security) & Blue (Gardai), the JCBs, the workers, and the barbed wire.

Did they really need that much wire?

The door to the B&B was shut. Perhaps a first. The noise and dirt or was it the lack of business, their clientele, both local and beyond, discommoded by the yellow invasion.

A big bite of me thumb, a settle of my cowlicks, before – but Kanu the Coach saw me, laughed, ushered me in with a, "Sls-upp, Sls-upp."

Well, not what I expected. Not the usual pandemonium. Just Chioma 'The Writer' Chijindu, my first love's mother, sitting in front of that blunt little kitchen in a high-backed chair. Backlit by the setting sun. She moved the chair throughout the day, following the wheel of the sun, a photosynthetic light required to transform her reading into, and I quote, "the efflorescence of writing." Always with a book, her golden glasses perched on her small retroussé nose, which refracted her gold tooth (molar), which recalled her battered golden slippers. Slightly chubby, a gestatory bump she claimed, the growth of her first book and not her daily indulgence in bowls of The Polski Sklep's Jollof rice.

Something was cooking in the kitchen. A stew. A Polish Bigos stew.

"An American delegation," Kanu announced.

"Come in, come in," said Chioma, sucking her teeth. "Ai, the noise. Shut the door. And the dust." Wiping a chair for me. Resting her book carefully on the tiled kitchen floor behind her. Yes, Yeats, *Michael Robartes and The Dancer*.

The salon was strictly split, women on the left, men on the right. On the left hung photos of well-coiffured, female Nigerian writers, Emecheta, Ngozi Adichie, and Oyeyemi. On the right hung a photo of Kanu, the real Kanu, that famed Nigerian center forward. A vague resemblance but our Coach not as tall as the real Kanu, not as slim, not as sinewy, not as skilled, but the same braids, the same wispy goatee, the same good looks. With the ever-present whistle necklaced on his chest, the Adidas runners, the boundless didactic energy. He limped into the kitchen to make tea. A protean limp, at times stiffly extravagant, at other times deftly attenuated, but genuine, his footballing downfall, the lost fame and wealth, now memorialized in the name he chose for himself. A teenage footballing phenom, he had been recruited from his native Ogbomosho by Crystal Palace F.C. but was abruptly sidelined by a succession of knee injuries. Which produced a right-side limp, which provoked a persistence of arthritis. Shamed by this failure, he did not return home, but stayed in London, then Dublin, and then Ballygall, befriended by Chioma and her husband Emeke, who arranged a straw marriage with Bridie McCarthy — citizenship for him, euros for her. But as the straw turned to the true green and gold of love, Kanu took the precarious step of truly marrying Bridie, a Kerry woman. A flowering which produced three kids, two boys and one girl, friends until I discovered my American birthright.

We sat with tea and a plate of soft, chocolatey Delicje biscuits. Chioma immediately curious about my emigrant life. Always overly polite to me. Happy that I had diverted her daughter after the murderous death of Young Akinfenwa, but not that happy. Wary of my American birthright, my westward determination, which might have, however improbably, waylaid her daughter, Obee.

"How is America?" she asked.

"Ah, it's great," I replied. "Best country in the world."

"Shush," she sort of whispered, "you'll have Mr. Kanu ranting about his Giant."

Nigeria, The Giant of Africa, a common speech of Kanu, who said, "I don't hear you."

Chioma asked about my lodgings, my job, my life, the attractions of which I embellished, conjuring a townhouse, a directorship, and a life populous and popular.

She did not seem impressed, taking an exploratory sip here and there. She put her gold glasses fully on. Pushed them up her nose.

"My office is right in Harvard Yard," I lied. "Director of Finance." Another lie, my job and location being decidedly fluid and temporary. "Cafes and bookshops everywhere." Which was half true. "Ben Okri taught there." I think. And would have added Ngozi Adichie had I been sure of the pronunciation.

Chioma sucked her teeth. She generally evinced little patience for cities other than London and Lagos, reserving a special distaste for American cities, which had, at one brief juncture, drawn Obee's interest. "Obee is doing excellent in London," she said. "So smart. Solicitor. Maybe she will become a barrister. A judge, of course."

Was Obee still betting?

"London is a wonderful, old, historic city. Vibrant. Very vibrant."

Yep, still betting, I bet.

"Legendary writers. Shakespeare, Dickens. And now Zadie Smith, Onuzo, Okojie."

Still chubby?

"And the restaurants. The cafes. The best in the world, Obee says."

Yep, still chubby. Lovely and chubby.

"Fantastic flat in South End. Great community. Even acting a little. Shakespeare. Natural they say."

She was always natural, natural and lovely, O-bee from Bally-G, my first love.

"Visit her soon. Once this nonsense, o." Her little 'o', always a warning, often a prequel to a more energetic arrangement of vowels. A forced smile, a glint of gold. Pausing. Shuffling her golden slippers.

The aroma of stew thickened the air. Spicy. Sour. Smoky.

"I didn't agree," I said. "The south Wall. It was all The Queen."

"Getting married," Chioma said. "Obee is getting married. In a couple of months. Lovely man. Actor. Very happy."

"She's what?" I replied, spilling my tea.

"Yes," said Chioma. "She didn't tell you?"

She didn't. Other than a commiserative text regarding my father's premature passing, we hadn't talked in months. Before that, it had been sporadic, competitive.

"Ah, tell him," said Kanu, pointing his cup at Chioma. "Tell the boy."

Chioma shrugged. "Might be more to it. We don't know."

"Tell the boy."

"Go on, Mr. Kanu, you," she said, stepping back.

"It's straw, Finn."

Ah, straw! Which meant it was not love but circumstance. A straw, transactional marriage, English citizenship for Obee, Sterling for whoever the hell he was. Probably some gambler.

Chioma nodded. "But nice man. Actor. Maybe become like you, Mr. Kanu, not made of straw?"

Kanu smiled. His eyes twinkled. "Maybe. But sometimes straw is just straw. Finn knows that."

I slumped down in the chair, dying to take a good, relieving bite of my thumb.

"Straw's like water," said Chioma, "mutable. Turn into gold but can turn back too." A smile for Kanu.

A pause.

The noise from outside, a JCB turning, beeping, reversing. The expletive shouts of the builders.

"So sorry to hear about your father, Finn. Wonderful man. Wonderful character, o."

Which wobbled me a bit.

"Agree, Mr. Kanu?"

"Super star," said Kanu.

"He did so much for the town. *And* the Estate."

"Man of the people, all the people," said Kanu.

I braced myself: a man of purity, ethics, a man that would never support that southern abomination.

"A library, for instance."

Chioma's holy grail, a library — how is it a town without a library, no matter how many phones you have?

"A man of the books," said Kanu.

"How is it a town without a library, no matter how many computers and such you have?" said Chioma, returning the biscuits to the kitchen. Checking the stew. Wearing her usual jeans and purple dress. Returning. Her mouth full, its corners crumbly.

"Always with a book in his hand," said Kanu. "On the Causeway, yeah, Finn?"

I nodded, though he wasn't a serious reader.

"Good friend of the Super Eagles. Treasure man," said Kanu, coach of the unbeaten U-18 girls team. Nationally renowned.

"Treasure man," repeated Chioma, smiling at Kanu.

"But the best," said Chioma, still standing, pushing back up her glasses which had slid down her nose. "The Wobbly Shamrock. Remember Mr. Kanu. Still have the scar. Show it. Show it, man."

Kanu did, smiling. Unzipping the top of his green tracksuit, pulling his T-shirt down a little, winking at Chioma, exposing a long, jagged scar, compliments of Burke the Butcher.

"Brave," Chioma almost sang. "Wrestled the Butcher. Stuck him in the ground."

Overall, a shameful episode. The sale of The Wobbly Shamrock to Edun and Oluremi (aka Charming and Cinders,) had enraged Burke and too many others, all aghast at the prospect of an Irish pub, on Irish soil! being cast into the hands of "foreigners." A fight between Burke and Kanu marred the opening, escalating, causing injuries on both sides, stopped not by Garda Michael, who watched with relish, but by the disappearance of half of Burke down half a pothole. Stuck like a pig.

"I did, yeah," said Kanu, smiling, embarrassed, proud.

"Victorious," said Chioma.

"I was," said Kanu, re-zipping his tracksuit.

"But that boycott, Finn," she said, still looking at Kanu.

The town, even some of the Estate, had then boycotted the Wobbly.

"Who broke that?" asked Chioma.

"Fionny," said Kanu.

"Fionny," said Chioma. "What did he call it. A Drink-In. Wasn't it?"

My Father valiantly abandoned his Causeway for the troubled tables of the Wobbly. Every day, throughout the day, he sat, defiant, but not too principled to take the free flow of Chianti.

"A Drink-In," repeated Kanu.

"A Drink-In," said Chioma. "What a man."

True.

"Without him," said Chioma, sucking her teeth.

"Without him," said Kanu, sucking his own teeth.

"Not to mention the pitch," said Kanu.

"Super Eagles," said Chioma.

"That pitch," said Kanu, turning, pointing south. "Potholes before Fionny. Drummed up sponsorship."

"Drummed it up," said Chioma, drumming her fingers. "Flattened it."

"Drained it."

"Drained it," said Chioma, her smile fading. "But never, this Wall, would he have, cutting away the Estate."

"Never," agreed Kanu. "But Finn, not his fault. Just arrived. Jet lag, and everything."

Which seemed a nice way of avoiding the usual taunt: that I was not a patch on my father, that I had such big shoes to fill.

Chioma took a few backward steps back toward the kitchen. "This Wall is not tourism, or marks for the competition. Teresa 'Tidy Town' McAnteer is wrong, deluded."

"Wrong," said Kanu.

"This Wall, the southern part, is against us, o."

That ominous 'o.'

Gesturing toward the front door, the construction. "It is to remove us from the town." A pause. "Why not the entrance in the south? Not the north. Why barricade us? And something else." She raised a reader's finger, with yellow highlighter stains. "The shops that have recently, mysteriously closed. Yes? The Off-license. One morning, closed! Poor Olga evicted. The shop was shuttered in a day. Its inventory taken *that* day. Yes? *Boots*, yes, part of a chain, but supervised by Miss Martichenko. The same story. Within a day. A chain like *Boots*, but they are also banished in a day. And still shuttered. The Off-license still shuttered. Even the Bookies, Cantrell's yes, but run by Wole. Same brutal story. There is a pattern here. Yes?"

I honestly hadn't noticed. Not even *Boots*, our despised rival.

"And this pattern continues. Our own shop, the B&B has been harassed. Legally, financially, and also The Polski Sklep. This is a pattern, isn't it?"

Kanu nodded her on.

"The same pattern, like the first Nigerian-Irish pub. I do not say why or who, but we can agree that there is a pattern here. Yes?"

"Yes," said Kanu.

Chioma grimacing. Her tooth (molar) glittering. "But there is another piece of the pattern. It is bad news, Finn. Very bad news. You will be upset."

She paused, pushing her glasses back up her nose. "The Wok and Roll is also closing."

"Yes," said Kanu. "Bad. Very bad."

"The same pattern. They will close soon. We don't know why, we don't know who."

"We don't know why, we don't know who," repeated Kanu.

" Isn't that peculiar? Coerced to sell, I can confirm that. May is very upset."

May Zheng, brilliant owner of The Wok and its food truck. A generous sponsor too. Our first attempt at The Great Wall, in particular.

"So, now we have four of our businesses shuttered. Four. Yes. Our other businesses, the lovely Wobbly, our B&B, the amazing Polski, are also under assault. But the other establishments, Butchers, Supermarket, Florist, they have not experienced this."

"We don't know why, we don't know who," said Kanu, anxiously.

"So, then can we say this is part of the pattern? Yes? Let me continue. Now, to the Wall. The lovely Wall of Ballygall. Fionny's Wall, though I believe Finn was the original discoverer."

Kanu clapped me hard on the back. "Sls-upp, Sls-upp!"

Chioma continued. "We all remember the first effort at the Wall. Didn't we do it as a town, a team, a community? For free! Just the Polski's sandwiches. The Wok's stir fries. Every weekend. Led by Fionny. He in the west, we in the east. In the trenches, wasn't it? The Wall was to be east and west. Never. Never. Never was it said that it would be built south."

She paused. Took a big, uncomfortable breath.

"But let me ask you, who invited this yellow army in?" Gesturing outside, the arrival of a new truck, loaded with that exorbitant Kilkenny stone. "Who authorized them? Gave them permission? Nothing in the law, the zoning approval. The Town Council. What are their plans? The design? The schedule? The budget? Who is paying for this? A huge wall is to be put in our faces. By The Toll Queen. He. That beast. Slouching toward Ballygall. Destroying our town, our community. Not legal. Never asked our consent. And who approved Doherty's house. Demolished. Don't like the man, but he knows, supports us. Who authorized that?"

She paused here. Took a breath. Her yellowed finger pushing her gold glasses back up her nose. Sat. Then stood. Straight. Held her hands. "We need legal help. Maybe I should send for Obee?"

"You should," I said, too abruptly. "I mean, it all must be illegal."

"We don't know why, we don't know who," said Kanu, standing, standing me up too. "But we know we have some of us coming, Sls-upp, Sls-upp. May not be as open, as comfortable, if you were here. We know, we know. We trust you." Taking me by the elbow, leading me toward the door. Leaning in, whispering, "Just straw, Finn, lad. Just straw."

"We don't know why, we don't know who, but we know this Queen," said Chioma, in the kitchen, stirring the Bigos stew. "He destroys. This rough beast. Slouching toward Ballygall. To be born again. This devil, this lion-devil that bit his own beloved's fingers away. Pitiless. What then will he do to us? We who – but we don't lack conviction. We are full of pride. Full of conviction. We will fight!"

Dirty Doherty, My Uncle-in-Error

A day later, I repaired to the Causeway to think, to reflect, to catch my breath. Well-provisioned and with plenty of tea, gazing at that news article, that BC professor poisoned by Dirty Doherty and my mother. The culprits never apprehended. The motive never ascertained.

Jesus.

And who should come along just then. The poisoner. Emmet 'Dirty' Doherty. Besplattered in muck. Carrying his usual avuncular gift, Ferrero Rocher, which I had once proclaimed as a kid and was now condemned to receive forever more. This error was matched by another greater error, when, too young to understand sarcasm, I had accepted him as the endeared uncle he was presented as; a mistake that irremediably connected us.

My uncle-in-error.

Forever.

Taking a pew a couple of steps below me. Always too close. Glancing at the Wall, my father's collage. A grimace. Understandable now. A grind of his sharp teeth. "But here you go, Finn."

I took the chocolates, careful not to touch his gloved hand. He wore fingerless gloves on both paws, not woolen and Fagin-like but yellow and black Izumi biking gloves, which hid his scars, his stigmata or so said my father. Raising one filthy glove in a conciliatory gesture. "Me house," he said.

Which was gone. Pummeled. Pebbled. Gone.

"It's all right, lad. I know. Nothing you knew about. Nothing you could do about it. Not here for that. I'll take care of that. Not getting away with that shite. Not with me. Here, Finn, how is the Big Dig, the tunnel doing in Boston?"

Doherty, small, lithe, was a professional tunneller, veteran of The Liffey tunnel, The Lee, The Thames, and now awaiting employment on

TIS, Tunnel the Irish Sea. And yes, the Big Dig in Boston, all those oft-recounted years ago. Which he always asked me about. The Sumner tunnel. The Ted Williams.

"Ah, the Sumner. Class construction."

And on he went. As usual. Ad nauseam. To warm himself, to settle his nerves, probably. So, did we owe him money? Was that his purpose? My father's inverted form of philanthropy?

But no, a more delicate matter: "Sincere condolences, Finn. Your dad, above everything else, was a great character. Sorry I didn't make the."

The funeral.

Or the non-funeral. The non-invite to the non-funeral.

A tensing of his jaw at this. Probably a glint in his eye, but not discernible behind his tinted glasses. Small and oval. Menacing, even to me, his nephew-in-error.

"Thanks," I said, offering him a Ferrero Rocher, which he always took, always ate in one cavernous gulp.

He inquired about my brother, Liam. Everyone loved Liam, Maestro Liam. "Good lad, he -" but cut short by his usual battery of coughing. All that tunneling no doubt, and often done, per my father, in his own subterranean network below Ballygall. "Sorry, Finn, lad," he said, broaching the real reason for his visit: an invitation to my mother and I to have a wee dram at The Wobbly.

My mother? The Wobbly? Was he newly deranged?

"Do youse good. Terrible business."

Did he mean my father's death, or did he mean his own estrangement from our family? He had been a constant at all our occasions, though mainly invited by my father to irritate my mother. Understandable now. But there had been some feud between him and my father, just prior to my father's mistreatment.

"Haven't seen youse all in a bit."

Estrangement, that was it. I bit at my thumb. I think I did audibly groan. Why me? The conduit.

He leaned upward. The stair groaning.

Not a man you'd easily refuse. That violence, said my father, lurking below that already strained surface. Yellow but black too, those colorful, fingerless gloves. A murderer. Him and my mother.

And so, not a man you'd expect to be wearing a Babybjörn. Which I hadn't noticed. Filthy, and in the pouch a large bottle of Red Bull.

So, I quickly agreed. Sure, I'll ask. The pub. And sure, my mother might even abandon her cell above.

He opened the Red Bull, offering.

I drank tea instead. Repressing any baby-related, Babybjörn jokes. His separated wife, Denise, a gorgeous, gorgeous woman, had deepened their separation with the production of an illegitimate baby girl, additionally vowing, it was rumored, never to return to Dirty Doherty or back-stabbing Ballygall, despite the flight of the biological father. Her reasons were not disclosed.

But, of course, my father must have been involved in all this. His counsel often proved too blunt and unvarnished, drawing on a wisdom obviously accumulated outside his own marriage. He had been friendly and flirty with Denise (among others), and had been, like the rest of us, astounded by the stupendous good fortune of Doherty. Perhaps he had said too much to Denise? He rarely said too little.

His commission discharged, Doherty relaxed. Drank. Turned avuncular. Warning me against the Wall, that it was not the Wall of my youth, that it was not the Wall of my father, that it was now the malignant maw of the Church, led by that awful Toll Queen. That the Townies agreed. Most of them. Gallagher, Costello, and Duffy, definitely. "Haven't they already closed everything. The Off-license. The Bookies. *Boots.* A Church Wall, Finn, lad. Cutting the gambling, the booze, the condoms and that. Not your dad's Wall. And your Father never wanted anything in the south. But Church does. Seal off the town. They have their saint. Palladius. Have that Toll Queen. Have that lunatic, His Holiness O'Shaughnessy. Though it's above him. That Bishop Slattery is a nasty piece of work." He reached out his gloved hand, taking a Ferrero Rocher. "Been through a lot, you have. Eldest. Know what it's like, I do."

I bit my thumb of knowledge. Sat straighter on the hard, thin stair.

Doherty noticed but continued. Flakes of dry muck falling from his Babybjörn. "Ructions in town there will be." He glanced around. Listened for customers in our shop. Quiet, except for our chemist, Janowski, at his Palladiusian prayers.

"Fecking eejit," said Doherty. "But here, not going to go on about it, but like I said they would, they've taken me house. Demolished it. Wouldn't give them the pleasure, watch it all, me arse."

I could only shake my head.

"And *legal* proceedings they called them. *Legal.* Kangaroo court more like. Best of barristers they had. Professional. Ruthless. Vindictive. Typical of the gang taking over this town. Church and Queen."

It did not take long. A few swipes, a few charges and his home was gone. Then they pummeled it. Pebbled it. Turned it into Filler for the Wall.

"Least I'm in the Estate now. Near Kanu. New start. Old house had, well, old, bad memories."

He stood up. Tried to compose himself.

I almost told him then. The demolition. I had participated. Not so much JCBs but sledgehammers. The Queen, his Giant and me. I'd no choice. Glibb insisted. Hammered the place asunder we did. The Queen, his fits of penitential laughter. Awful.

"Here, they are a whole different story to your dad's efforts all those years ago. Stay out of it, Finn, lad. Going to get rough. Don't think you have your dad's stomach for, for all the ructions coming."

A common refrain. I didn't have me dad's stomach, his bigger boots, not nearly a patch on his wit and willfulness. Me bollix. I'll show Doherty. And the rest.

"Well, have work to do," he said.

But he didn't. He was safely on the dole waiting for TIS, Tunnel the Irish Sea.

So, I asked him. "What was the feud, you and my father?"

"Ah, Finn, better to leave it." Wiping his hands on his dirty Babybjörn. "No sense in opening all that up."

"Was it about Boston? The poisoning? You and my mother?"

He stood up. Clenched his gloved fists.

"Me dad told me. Only a few months ago. You and my mother poisoned him." I pointed at the news article. "The professor."

Dirty Doherty glanced above me.

"She's at Brady's. Doesn't know I know."

Which seemed to relax him. Was *he* afraid? "But my dad wanted me to know. The feud I think, upset him. Get it all off his chest. Maybe he knew? What was coming?"

Doherty paused, glancing again up the Causeway.

"Told me to ask you, Doherty. Wouldn't tell me why he was poisoned."

"Yeah, he seemed to have left that part out a lot."

"Sorry. Know it's hard for you."

"It's not, Finn, lad. Obviously, you know the I.R.A. part. Well, that professor, Tim McGregor, was a computer genius. Bit of a boaster, but he was a genius. Me and your mother buttered him up. Dared him to access classified files, British Security Forces, if he could. Well, he could. And to prove it, he showed us the lot of them. Just what we wanted. Fingering five informants. Touts. Scumbags. Assassinated, the lot of them, a week later. Bullet to the head. Bodies left on the Falls road. Warning. All grand. Me and your mother well commended by the leadership. Ah, don't look like that, Finn. Five killed, but dozens saved."

I leaned away from him. Another early lesson, when my uncle-in-error is flowing, lean away, boys, lean the fuck away.

"Unfortunately, yer man McGregor, Mr. Computer Genius, found out. Threatened to rat us out. Not that clever, was he? Hadn't we just taken care of five informants. Well, we couldn't convince him. Not even your mother. Unfortunate. But quick, painless. Solitary bloke. Not married."

"You poisoned him?"

Dirty Doherty nodded. "Unfortunate. But painless. Cup of coffee with me and your mother. God, you were there too. Wee baby. Forgot that."

Would my mother have done the same if it had been baby Liam?

"But painless. Didn't feel a thing."

"Was my father, was he part of the thing?"

Doherty laughed, which set him off coughing.

I waited.

"No. Your father. Not the constitution, had he."

"He didn't know?"

"No. But panicked, the fool. Ran. Should have stayed. Stuck it out. Already thinking it was some student thing, they were. Even says so, in article. But your dad, impulsive. Always got him in trouble. Impulsive." Doherty lifted and took a long, slurping sup of his bottle of Red Bull. Belched. Returned it to his pocket. "Impulsive, your dad. Give him the benefit of the doubt now, that business with Denise."

The poisoning, obviously.

"Impulsive. When he told Denise about the murders. Likely told her the same way he told you. I was just a murderer. A poisoner. No mention of those five informants. Their harm. Impulsive. I'll call it that. Though it looked a lot like revenge, right, Finn?"

"Dad, always talked too much." Though it must have been revenge.

"He did. So, that was the feud, to answer your question. Frightened Denise, whatever he said. She left. Disgusted at it. And really disgusted I never told her."

"I'm sorry. Denise was, I mean, Denise is great. I hope that, you know."

Which seemed to wobble him a bit. Peeling then re-tightening his gloves. Pushing his glasses tighter up his dusty nose. "Some neck on your father. Dispensing marriage advice, and a full-scale conflict going on under his own roof. And him the instigator. Treating your lovely mother like … and running all over the town … the whole town knowing … ah, here, don't get me started." He stood up. Re-pocketed his Red Bull. "Good man, Finn. Go on, we'll have a drink soon. With your Mum and Liam. And that idiot, Conor. Don't bother her with this, sure you won't?"

"I won't."

"Don't get up," he said, turning and leaving, dust parting from both sides of him. Through the shop he went. "Ask me bollix," he said to Janowski's greeting. The door then the bell, but not before he took a packet of crisps.

I sat for a while.

In silence.

I finished the last of my tea. Cold. Bitter. A hard skin on it.

Jesus. Six murders. Five informants, and then the professor. And they had expected my father to stay in Boston, to stick it out. Jesus. My poor dad. And *me*. What about me? I was there. Just a baby.

Jesus Christ.

Wok and Roll, Closed

A few days later, at midnight, on a miserable Monday, the Wok and Roll wokked, or rather wept, to its involuntary end, its mortgage revoked, its premises confiscated, its inventory unexpectedly full.

Of course, not just a business, not just a Downstairs of commerce, but like us, an Upstairs of domesticity. A half-home for the Zhengs. Town neutrals like us, the McCormacks, neither Toffs (the posh folk) nor Townies nor Estaters. Peter Zheng, the eldest, my peer, strangely, coincidentally, also in Boston, having also emancipated himself from the yoke of his family business. We had been close once, an abortive interest in hurling, which naturally lapsed for me on the discovery of my American birthright.

Yes, a Zheng home Upstairs, but what food downstairs! The chow mein. The aforementioned king prawn fried rice. The spring onion and ginger. The curry chips, of course.

Ballygall without the Wok? Like a football team without a pitch. Like an army without feet.

So, like the rest of the town, Estate and environs, I stood in the queue.

The Last Supper.

Cash only.

A long queue. Bunched up against the southern section of The Great Wall, with its Black and Blue guardians and that convolution of barbed wire. A line of seagulls, abrasively shrill, perched on the wire. Watchful. Patient. Like vultures.

The town was now cul-de-sac-ed. Dammed. The once trafficked street now flooded with hungry, bewildered Wok and Rollers. Doherty, my uncle-in-error, vocal and vituperative. Gloved. Tinted. Covered in dirt. Chioma too, with Kanu the Coach. Nervous. The Wok already wokked out of chop suey, beef black bean sauce, and chicken satay, which

May Zheng, the matriarch, the manager, had announced like a gustatory banshee.

Who else was in the queue?

Everyone.

Except The Toffs, especially Teresa 'Tidy Town' McAnteer, who was thought to be responsible for the closure. Not Tidy Town enough, especially with a new, fancy Wall.

Except His Holiness Father O'Shaughnessy, who was fasting. Supposedly.

Except my mother and her Comforter.

Except Liam, at his keyboard in the church. Playing Bach.

Dirty Doherty addressing the throng.

But before the Wok, what was closed?

- The Bookies.

- Boots.

- Off-license.

All shuttered now.

And what have they in common?

A collective groan.

- How in the holy name of Jaysus has the Wok to do with the Church? And with yer man Palladius? Chow mein, is that what they're excommunicating?

Which only encouraged Doherty.

And what are the Zhengs? Are they Confucian? Taoist? Buddhist? Atheist?

Which was not readily rebutted, until,

- They're Wok and Rollers.

- Laughter!

Infidels, aren't they? Not Christian, are they? Can't have pagans in our shrine of a town, now can we? Knock by the Sea.

Which did make me wonder. Standing feet from the reconstruction of what was, after all, an ancient Christian wall.

Someone shouted, "TIS!" "That's what all this is about. The Tunnel. The property prices. Flipping."

Others disagreed. "TISNT."

People were angry. Hungry and angry. Earlier, a demonstration had spontaneously fomented itself outside The Wobbly Shamrock, seeking a target, Garda Michael the obvious outlet, but unfortunately he was armed.

May Zheng broke in. "King prawn fried rice, GONE."

Ah, crap!

The queue began to bicker, to fidget, but it did not move.

Another Zheng cry, "Satay. Bacon. Chicken. GONE." May was standing on tippy-toe at the front door. Her cheeks glowing unhappily. Her hair in a ragged ponytail. Wearing, as always, one of her dead father's (a slow, staccato cancer) button-down shirts, un-tucked, her arms raised, like that statue of Jim Larkin. "GONE," she yelled, trumpet-tongued.

Jump the queue! That was my only chance. And wasn't I still in mourning? Hadn't my father been a prodigious customer? Hadn't he tried to convert the Ballygallians to authentic Szechuan, even sacrificing the ubiquitous chips. Wouldn't a Wok and Roll 'wreath' make his grave more bearable?

Which I explained to my uncle-in-error, who marched me to the front of the queue, the Ballygallians too afraid to challenge him. Not even the criminals, Razor Curran and Sawn-Off Akinfenwa.

But suddenly there was a lull. Silence even. Only Liam's organ at play. The seagulls quiet.

A fox stood in the middle of the Dublin road. Exactly where my mother had stood, watching O'Neill on his yellow Slicer. Its long tail up. Its ears pointed. Its long snout twitching. Its fur covered in Wall dust, a ghostly white and angry red.

It took a step toward us. Its teeth bared.

"My fault," said Doherty, quietly, not explaining himself.

Another step, another aggressive twitch of its nose, but it turned, trotted off, left.

We gained entrance to the Wok. Hot, aromatic, its windows steamed, its interior stacked with boxes, its two green budgies at full song in their golden cage.

"For his Da. For the grave," said Doherty, embarrassing me.

But it took May Zheng by surprise. A quick sniffle into the crook of her shirt before she agreed, she understood, what a grand man My Da had been, what a grand appetite, trying to recall his preferred dish, which I preempted:

"King prawn fried rice, please."

"Gone," she said, which she softened to, "Gone, Finn."

I nodded. I understood. "Whatever you think."

Behind her, behind that beautiful bay window, garlanded by plumes of steam, worked her miracle workers. Who she quickly questioned, cleaving through the clouds and finding two beautiful king prawns.

Showing me. Raising her thumbs. Coming back to the counter. "Good," she said, "your father was, big shoes to fill. Stay. Wait."

Which I did. Moving over as May moved over, the low, red counter between us.

"Boston?" she asked, by which she meant her son, Peter, or Pete.

"Great," I said, my stomach rumbling. "Great town. Met Peter, Pete, a few times." Which I had. "Doing great. Landed on his feet." Which he had. In the building trade. Dry wall. His illegal status not an impediment. "Started his own business too." Which he had. Landscaping. As entrepreneurial as his mother, who had established the Wok, innovating with the simple service of delivery. Free, local delivery, no distance too near, no order too negligible. Which was abused initially, a spectator sport watching Tommy 'Teddy Boy' McDermott, atop his black, suede, brothel-creeper shoes, delivering bag after bag of boiled rice … the novelty eventually fading but the habit remaining.

"Hurling?" she asked.

"Yes," I said. Which he was. Star forward for the Barley House, which had facilitated his way into the building trade, additionally enabling his landscaping.

"Fighting?" she asked, expecting a fib.

Which I supplied. "Ah, no." An atrocious gob on him, and a short fuse. "Doing well." Which he was, though strangely pining for the old country, the old, moldy town.

A pause.

May looked tired. Drawn. Noticed me noticing. "Cabra," she said. "Brother-in-law." Raising her eyes upward to the upper floor, where her husband, Li, was packing their home into half a dozen suit cases. Audibly cursing.

At her feet I noticed a lamp shade, and in the pockets of her red apron a scrum of salt and pepper shakers taken from tables already taken, the chairs already carried away. The giant drinks fridge was already gone, though somehow its refrigerant noise seemed to linger. The place looked bare. Would the same ignominy befall our poor chemist? Eviction? Banishment? Foreclosed by the Teutonic Bank of Ballygall? We owed them a fortune. And what kind of closing sale could we have? Last of the lice, scabies, laxatives, anyone? Which encouraged me, an emigrant returning west, to ask bluntly. Why? Who?

"The bank," she replied. "But it was suddenly. We always, arrears, like everyone else. But it's Teresa McAnteer. Behind it all. With the Church.

His Holiness O'Shaughnessy. Devil she is." May paused, turned, checked on my order. "No choice. That dog, Garda Michael made clear. Fifteen years. We have." She undid and redid her ponytail. "But frightening. Look what happened to Doherty's house. Part of their Wall now. Fifteen years, we have been here." She took a moment to herself.

Upstairs, a suitcase cracked open on thin floorboards.

I handed her a check, a thick, absorbent, italicized check. Settling our sizable debt from my own small savings. Which she accepted after the requisite pair of refusals. Though I did have to force the twenty euro on her for the prized carton of precious Wok and Roll. Patting my hand as she handed it to me.

"Definitely," I said, too obvious in my eagerness to leave. "Definitely will drop in on Peter. Or go see one of his matches."

"That would be nice," she said, nodding, suddenly re-seeing the crowd behind, the line of hungry Ballygallians. But not rushing. "Glad he has a friend over there."

I left at speed, a wave to Doherty, hurried up the Dublin road, into the graveyard, a gap at the rear of the fence I had cut a couple of nights previous. Right to my dad's unmarked grave, behind Palladius' grave site, now additionally enclosed by its own perimeter of fence.

Stood. Took a deep breath. The carton exuding its wonderful aroma.

I would leave it on his grave.

I wouldn't touch a bit of it.

That angry fox could eventually have it.

But I did want a look.

Yum. Not just noodles, but beef, chicken, a spear of broccoli, a rattle of carrots. Glistening. Crowned with two curved, ghostly prawns.

Well, just a taste.

For my efforts. And for that thick, absorbent, italicized check.

Just a smackerel.

I ate.

With my hands.

My two hands.

Soy, of course, and sesame, and girded with garlic, and ginger, but the secret ingredient, once divulged by a tipsy May: Bisto. That horrible, hackneyed Sunday stalwart, which nevertheless bore within it the comfort of Mother and the stertorous slumber of Father. Comfort. Security. Calories.

I ate more.

But reserved some noodles for my father, for the belly of his unmarked grave.

Until I ate those too.

Just the prawns remaining. Two little crustaceans hooked and crooked, bulged in sections by the binding of their veins.

One for me and…

But I ate both.

Immediately full.

Immediately ashamed.

So, I called Peter Zheng, who was on a ladder in Sudbury drywalling a barn. Shouting. "On a fucken wonky ladder in the horse arse of nowhere. This stupid barn they haven't used in donkey years. Oh, yeah, sorry bad manners, Finn. Sls-upp, Sls-upp."

Laughing hard. Continuing.

"Yeah, know all about that shite. Yeah, I know. Tonight. Ya know, if me Ma collected half the money that those wankers, those gobshites queueing up now, we would have sorted out the bank years ago. I know. I hear you. You're a good skin. Knew you'd settle up. Your old fella was a good skin an' all. Jesus, this fucken ladder. Yeah, I know, Cabra. But grand big gaff me uncle has. But not like this one here. Lord Muck himself. Yanks fucken love themselves they do. But here, think I was born yesterday. Me Ma is right. Obvious who's after our grand little Wok. That Tidy crowd. Teresa. Do you have any bleedin' idea who the McAnteers are? Mad powerful crowd they are. Go all the way back to Brian Boru and all that. Mad connected they are. And if Teresa wants the town tidy, that's what they'll give her. A'course we know what tidy means. Didn't you go with Obee for a while, after Young Akinfenwa and all that. Anyway, you know the jackanory. Tidy isn't just the fucken litter is it. Fuck, here's Lord Muck, with another poxy cup of pink lemonade. Jesus."

"Cheers, Peter. But don't you think —"

"But here let me ask you this, Finn, ya think these wankers would be going to all this bother if it was a chipper. Fish and chips! Don't fucken think so, pal."

A Hospital, A Punch Thrown

St. Patrick's Hospital.

Which neglected him.

Misdiagnosed him.

Abandoned him in a corridor.

Left him to die.

Which then offered a mediated conversation regarding our bereavement, regarding our needs at this most difficult time, and yes, a friendly, general, neighborly peek at our grievances, which should not be construed as an admission of…

Surprisingly, my mother the poisoner agreed, with the one condition that Dr. Lathey, that arrogant-patronizing murderer, be present.

Even more surprisingly, she insisted on driving.

Sudden cudgels of speed, sudden cataclysmic stops. But she insisted. A short, shoreline distance to a seashore hospital. Dressed in layers, blouse, cardigan, sleeveless jacket, wax jacket, garlanded with multiple scarves, which hid her new neck, her shortened hair strained upward into a severe bun. Her right hand was knuckled with big, brassy rings, ugly heirlooms from my grandmother, Tasy. Her skirt knee-long, covering her prayer bumps. Calm, if not calming. Without her Comforter, absent, without an explanation, but myself and Liam still exiled to the back of our pharmaceutical van. Facing each other, on the cold, bare, cushionless floor, ignoring the lingering smell of Old Spice.

"Now, just a wee meeting, boys," she said, a ridiculous singsong to her voice. "Many more, so there will."

My mother the murderer, now happy-go-lucky.

An admonishment to herself, but mostly for Liam. Who paid her no attention, immersed again in our father's medical file. Chewing gum, arraigning his case. His left hand at play on an invisible keyboard. Thin. His face scratched. A recent church scuffle with a church-goer unimpressed with his music.

A sudden roar, not the sea but the engine confronting its familiar nemesis, Killiney Hill. In those last treacherous days, my father intubated and ventilated, I had made a bargain: if the van could survive the hill's twice daily gradient, so he too could incline his way back to health.

But no.

Initially, my father had forbade any communication to me, stateside. Obviously mindful of his own American misadventure, he had wanted me, the eldest, to have a free run at my own folly. His request was respected, and so I had arrived late, his turn for the worse already taken. I was angry, but also shamefully relieved, exempted from the hard conversations, the difficult decisions, the impatient requests to remove, detach, turn-off, to allow what must be allowed, to see what must be seen, though they had seen the wrong thing coming. My mother had told that arrogant-patronizing doctor to, yes, resuscitate, but only once. I liked that. Only once. A single, superstitious reprieve against that finality. But not the heart trouble they so diligently misdiagnosed, but the pneumonia, the cough, the fever, the obvious fucking difficulties breathing.

The van prevailed against Killiney Hill again. My mother and her forty layers leaning into the steering wheel. "He'll be there himself, that murderer. But not a word." Glancing at us in the mirror. The sun glinting off her brass rings, round and shiny, like her cheeks, her chipmunk cheeks, reddened, hot, and anxious like mine. I had watched her at home, readying herself, layer after layer, suspicious that she might provision herself with, well, with poison, powder, or liquid, vials or tinctures, and somehow smuggle it in one of those brassy rings. I quickly gave up, unable to follow her nimble hands, her numerous pockets, preserving instead my energy, my vigilance, for the meeting itself. Which would double if there was food, if there were drinks. She could not be trusted.

Liam the Maestro began extemporizing from the files. "The dopes. Simple obvious blood work. Took them two days to …"

St. Patrick's hospital was a modern, three-story, multi-occupant glass building, perched on a picturesque bluff overlooking the Irish Sea. Not tall but deep, its occupants arranged east to west. The eastern side, a glassy curvature of privilege, has been retained by a private for-profit hospital. Well appointed, prodigiously equipped, a credit to any illness, it allowed for a sea view, for sea air, for secured walks along the bluff. Profitable, and also profitably anticipating the construction of TIS

(Tunnel the Irish Sea) and its influx of medical tourists. Subsidized by the state, of course. Grafted onto this vision, like a Supermodel's mole, was a consultant-owned, for-profit medical center. Credit cards only. A sleek showroom of MRI, CT, CAT, PET, EKG, EGG, and other contiguously capitalized letters. Also with a sea view. Subsidized by the state, of course. In the middle of the building, in an interior warren of windowless rooms, ran the Church's not-for-profit charitable hospital, therapeutically dependent on holy water, crucifixes, and a phalanx of Luddite nuns, overseen by a witch doctor. Also subsidized by the state. On its western side, facing the road, sat the state-owned hospital, which consisted predominantly of corridors, studded with lush administrative offices. A collection of once modern diagnostic equipment, but in corridors. Comfortable beds, but in corridors. Surgical theaters, but in corridors. Those fucking corridors.

"Finnegan, meet us there, so he will." A roundabout lopsided her words. Those three roundabouts, too proximate not to seem like a prank. The first she always took carefully, the second confidently, the third concussively. Twelve every day, those last days. She repeated herself. "Finnegan."

A florid, fubsy solicitor, with a leg that didn't seem long enough for its extravagant limp, and who, for now apparent reasons, had long been a frequent visitor to our Upstairs. Usually accompanied. Distant northern cousins of ours, supposedly. And presents. Nuts and Bananas. The exotica of his Belfast youth. An eloquent, vehement man. A well-known Provo (IRA).

Earlier that day, he had outlined those who would confront us at the meeting, not the least of which would be their aggregation, a mosaic of uncommunicative, unaccountable parts.

First the Church, the owners of the hospital, and somehow managerially involved in all of Ireland's hospitals, clinics, hospices and infirmaries. A hand in every ailment. They were represented at the meeting by a prelate, fattening himself on an unspecified probation. A pear-shaped man.

"Finnegan will do the talking," she said, tightening her scarves. "Though when is that there any different," she added, concussively revving over the last of the speed bumps. The leveling sun in her eyes. Glinting off that bulbous coin ring.

"I have something too," I said. "I'll read it. Set out the facts. Calmly."

She nodded. Glanced at the empty seat beside her. Missing her Comforter?

"On a stretcher, for God's sake," said Liam, still reading. "For hours. A corridor. A Jaysus corridor."

Second on Finnegan's list was the HSE (Health Service Executive), responsible for the provision of public health services in Ireland and its non-existent colonies. A behemoth. A country unto itself. Fluent in multiple, untranslatable languages and partitioned into internecine principalities. A banana republic run by pear-shaped men. At the meeting, it did in fact produce a cadre of pear-heavy ambassadors, pale, ample-arsed, who, when it happened, could do little but wobble amongst themselves.

"Not a word on damages, or that there malarkey," added my mother, a sharp glance at me. Even turning around a little.

With poor but surely excusable timing, I had proclaimed our bankruptcy before our late departure, mostly oblivious of its potential connection to the meeting, to such words as 'settlement' and 'damages.'

"Finally," said Liam, still twinkling his invisible keyboard. "Blood work negative, right, but for the wrong thing. EKG negative. And still they wait."

The last on Finnegan's list was, of course, the state-run, corridor-heavy hospital, somehow separate from the HSE who managed it. It produced, in number and shape, a representation similar to the HSE, but two others are worth mentioning. Nurse Fitzgerald. Our sole source of succor and clarity in those last days, until her shift abruptly shifted her. A crafty inclusion by the pear-shaped. And that Doughty Administrator, imposing and interposing, her name still un-retrievable, but whose preventative reflexes at the meeting would prove incendiary.

And security. A battalion of battle-ready security who, when it happened, were not ready.

"There, now. This awful place."

The car park. Its warning sign, *Pay or be Clamped*. Every visit, a different car clamped. It became a game, spot the clamp, guess the medical emergency.

Doughty the Administrator greeted, small-talked, chaperoned. She led us not inward but upward, a private, plush, panoramic room. A pear-shaped panoply. He sat in the furthest, darkest corner. Dr. Lathey. Bald, thin, arrogant-patronizing, a Caribbean tan, a sharp suit. My mother walked past the rising pear-shaped ranks, past Finnegan, past that fat prelate, even past lovely Nurse Fitzgerald and threw a brass-ringed punch at Dr. Lathey, her hand only inches from his arrogant-patronizing … but blocked, pulled back by Doughty the Administrator.

A brief, terrible arm wrestle.

I want to end there, an aborted punch, a collective breath taken, a dignified under-the-circumstances withdrawal. I want to say that at my first consoling embrace my mother succumbed, relented, but she didn't. She – It is too painful to say. Her cries. Her struggle. Can a word match it?

Anguish?

Her grief finally released.

All those lost, ruined, bitter years.

She pulled me and Liam into her. Cried. Sobbed. The three of us. Cried. Sobbed. In that private, plush, panoramic room.

His Holiness Father Seamus O'Shaughnessy

Our Giant's Causeway. Sunday morning.

Sideways l lounged, on the middle stairs, suspended between Upper and Lower, my boots protruding through the now toothless banisters. Provisioned for the afternoon: Ferrero Rocher, a bag of Krowki, and a cup of tea.

Above me, in unprecedented bare feet, my Mother the Murderer, dancing to and fro, opening the east and west windows to a convinced breeze, the radio classically attuned. Her usual admonishment, "Nay slurping," but sung down rather than shouted. Even my keys, jingled-jangled, not bothering her. Whistling. A happy truant from noon Mass. Cleaning and cleansing. A veritable cleaning fairy, in her sleeveless blouse, her hair bobbed, her sun-paned neck aglow.

Not the same woman my father warned me about. 'Watch the shop,' he would say, positioning me on the Causeway, 'watch the shop, but watch your mother.'

Repeated often.

Though he probably had never heard her whistle like this.

I sat and slurped, trying to ignore Liam at play in our Not-So-Small-Church a couple of doors down. Mass. A nice little earner for him, the Maestro at Mass.

"Ciao, Ciao," came a greeting, accompanied by a blessing, 'che Dio vi benedica," annunciating the arrival of His Holiness, Father Seamus O'Shaughnessy. Observing his usual appointment with my father, mid-Mass, with a bottle of Chianti, a weekly rendezvous which absolved him of any liturgical obligation. Father Tas did all the work.

His Holiness was punctual but in his own Roman way: Since his arrival a decade ago, he had stayed on Roman time, an hour ahead, an allegiance which also extended to his punctuality, which added the tardiness of a Roman hour, which mathematically meant that his punctuality was, how you say, perfecto. He was proud of such perfecto.

"Il vino fa buon sangue," he exclaimed, handing me a glass, "or as your father used to say, bloody good wine." Unwrapping himself from a long papal blue scarf, worn in protection against the Ballygall dust. Removing gobs of cotton wool from his ears, worn in protection against the Great noise.

Without preamble or explanation, he sat a couple of steps below me. He poured a glass each, implicitly assigning to me the place and purview of my father. A common, town-wide elevation, much to my satisfaction, and much to my brother's spleen.

"Cos'è quello?" he said, slurping.

"No slurping," sang out my mother, which precipitated a round of reciprocal apologies, hers sent down to him, his sent up to her, an apologetic ping pong in their best sing song. His Holiness did not inquire further of her, preferring to leave the problems of his parish to Father Tas.

"Cos'è quello?" he asked, again.

"Krowki," I said, offering him one.

He demurred, patting his once plump, emperor belly. "A whale no more, no! Fasting. Biscotti and Pellegrino. E tutto!" He sat on his soutane. Removed his biretta. Gulped clean his glass of Chianti. "Preparing myself, no, the resurrection of St. Palladius of Ballygall. Bellissimo. Will change everything, Finn. For sure. Not for physical, this weight loss." Patting again his once plump, emperor belly. "Not aesthetic, Weight Watchers, Basta! No. No. Purification. How you say, atonement."

The skinny gospel according to His Holiness. Purifying himself for Palladius, allegedly of Ballygall.

"Like an enemy, no? Starving your enemy."

"Who's your enemy, Father O'Sausagee?" My father's name for him, O'Sausagee.

"There ya are, Boy. 'Sausagee', from your Papa."

'Boy', from his vestigial Cork accent, which continued its sing-song lilt. "Old Celtic custom there was now. Fasting against your enemies. The holy shame of someone starving themselves right outside your door, your moat, you know, like. Shocking. Mighty effective. Gentry, and the like. Wait."

With some convoluted lifting and swiveling, he pulled his iPhone, a new one, from an inside back pocket. Sat down again, his soutane floating down around him. Intoned:

An old and foolish custom, that
If a man
Be wronged, or think that he is wronged and starve
Upon another's threshold till he die,
The common people, for all time to come,
Will raise a heavy cry against that threshold.

"Yeats, Boy," he concluded. "No Dante, but not bad."

He drank, inclining his glass precipitously.

I joined him.

Ah sweet Chianti, transubstantiating a mere Sunday into something softer. Expensive, I learned later; and expensively part of the debt owed to His Holiness. Which I would partially pay. Via a thick, absorbent, italicized check. The first of many settlements. Simultaneously empowering and impoverishing.

"For sure, for sure," said His Holiness. "But what enemy am I starving against? What threshold?" He paused, pretending to reflect. "So many, I suppose." Another sipping pause. What an odd bloke. Half-forced Italian, half-forgotten Cork man. "Si, si. Sloth? Si. I not a man of action, but scholar. Si."

Another sipping pause.

"Sin? Si, si. But the real devil?"

"Booze," I ventured, as he refilled my glass.

"Ha. Like your Papa. No. Doubt, how you say, apostasy."

He did look, how you say, starved. His face, perennially and artificially tanned, had sharpened, relatively enlarging his papal blue eyes, emerging his cheeks, fattening his lips, and even his nose — his small, pudgy un-Roman nose, the disappointment of his life, which he mercilessly and ceaselessly tugged — had acquired girth if not length or elevation. And had he whitened his teeth? Had he dyed the profane erections of his once graying hair? Had he plucked his eyebrows? His nostrils? His ears? Was he making his aerodynamic way back to God?

"Starve it, si. I am starving away my doubt. My stupid doubt. My enemy. Only Biscotti and Pellegrino. E Tutto!" He smilingly stood, each thumb to each index finger, which he raised and shook.

No doubt about it. His Holiness was happy. Skinny and happy.

But not happy enough for Krowki, which he again refused. But he did take a Ferrero Rocher, until I mentioned its provenance, a regular and regularly unwanted gift from my uncle-in-error, Dirty Doherty.

His Holiness spat it out.

Spat it!

Right onto our beloved Causeway.

The cheek.

He wiped his tongue with a monogrammed handkerchief (H.H.). Rinsed with a swig of Chianti. Spat again. "Nothing from that gobshite."

In his best Cork brogue.

"Why, how you say, gobshite?" I asked, in my best Italiano.

He ignored my jest. "Malefico. Dangerous. Weirdo. You know, his nickname, from your Papa. Dirty Doherty. Si. But not dirt, muck, he meant dirty, prurient."

"Sexually?"

"Si."

"Thought it was the tunnels, his digging all over the world?"

"Si, tunnels. Your Papa told the whole town. Vigilance! Tunnels under Ballygall. For peeping. Watching. Those tinted glasses. Those fingering gloves. And thieving. Bit of a magpie. Your Papa warned everyone. But somehow they friends."

His Holiness shrugged, an extravagant Roman shrug.

"Keep your enemies close, no? Murderer too, said your Papa."

His Holiness knew?

"Si, small animals. Rabbits, badger, even fox. Watch your cats, guard your dogs, your Papa would say. Lock up your daughters. Si. And smells, the gobshite smells. Your Papa say, The Dirty Stinker."

My dad could be vicious.

His Holiness refilled our glasses, retrieving a couple of oblong Biscotti from the voluminous pockets of his soutane. Nibbled. Exulting in the almond crunch, purchased from the Polski Sklep. Probably free. The indulgences of the proprietor, Ola Waclawski.

"Now Finn, your Papa could be vicious. But never unprovoked." Tugging at his too-small nose.

"I know," I agreed.

We took to our glasses. Gulping to the sound of concluding bells from his church. My mother the murderer above, still barefoot, still humming, getting younger every day.

"Had a barney with my dad, too, Doherty did," I said. "Weren't talking. Something to do with his marriage breakup."

His Holiness refilled our glasses, nonchalant, pretending not to listen but he was.

"Something my dad told Denise. Something about Boston, what happened. Something Doherty had done." I gazed at the opposite wall, the article regarding the poisoning. His Holiness followed my gaze, not with any sense of surprise or confusion. He knew.

Above, the stopping of her bare feet. The conclusion of a hum. Was she listening?

"Something bad."

Father Sausagee stood, gesticulated. "Your Papa, si, a blunt man. A favor for him, si, I also talked to Denise. Truth is important, Finn. Veritas. There should be truth in every relationship, like. But my error. That is Father Tas' expertise. Me, I am a simple scholar." Pouring another glass for himself. Shrugging away the topic. Tugging his nose, ferociously.

I drank my own Chianti. Took a Ferrero Rocher. So, His Holiness had helped poison Doherty's marriage. Revenge. Incited by envy. Poor Denise in the middle.

"Your Papa, I say to him, be more like me. Leave the town to Father Tas. Concentrate on your work. Si. Your father's work, his shop, his family, his wife." He raised his eyes to Upstairs. "And DIG, I don't say not to DIG. But home. You boys. Treat you boys like boys, not like soldiers. The war, no?" He again raised his eyes to Upstairs.

I didn't know what to say, though he didn't seem to expect an answer. He sat back down. Put his biretta on and off. "But that gobshite, Doherty. Feckin' glad they knocked his house down. Got him out of the town. Though heard the weirdo moved to the Estate. Beside 77, the Straw House?"

"I know."

The feet above renewed their motion, pursued by a recrudescent hum.

"Bad business, Boy. Stay away from that weirdo." A shake of his olive-oiled head. "Ah, but the Wall, Boy, it will be a grand, shimmering thing. The first bricks. The bambino Wall. Bellissimo. How goes it?"

"Bellisimo," I replied, taking a good slurp of wine.

"Nay slurping," shouted down my mother, laughing.

Which pleased His Holiness, sending a benediction upward.

"Skilled builders they are. Beautiful stone. Easy to add an arch. Obvious. Makes so much sense, right? And already big disturbance for the town. I know the dust and noise are a pain. Everyone complaining. Even your Father Tas, asking for a break for Mass today."

His Holiness wagged his finger in disagreement. "Us Ballygallians are a tough bunch, robusto!"

"True enough, I suppose. Bit like a siege, though. Building on all sides, except the north. And early. Town's running low on sleep. Even Ma 'Run Run' Brady, missing her morning run now and then."

He smiled. "Lovely woman, atrocious husband." From his soutane he produced another expensive bottle of Chianti. Opening it. "Drink to it, Boy. The Great Wall of Ballygall."

I took another heaping glass. Took a long bite of my thumb. "But here, Father, they're saying, all the businesses closing. The Wok even. What do you make of that? The mysterious work of you and Father Tas?"

His Holiness laughed. A big Cork laugh. "Mere foot soldiers, me and Tas. Mere afterthoughts of the great Bishop Slattery." He raised his hands in awe, glancing heavenward for a second, his neck thin, purified of those rolling Tuscan chins. "But, me, no, me that discovered the DIG?"

"Just like me. Discovered the Wall."

"Si. You are a good, how you say, il figlio." He raised his glass to clink mine. "Saluti."

"Slainte."

"Slattery moves, like you say, in mysterious ways. Si, the businesses. Not a word to me, but it is him, no? Understands what we have found here. Maybe. Maybe. A Knock by the Sea. But the promise to your father, to be buried here in Ballygall. It was Slattery, refused. You believe, no?"

I nodded. "Know it wasn't you," I said. "You were a good friend of my father."

"Si," he said, leaning, re-clinking my glass.

"Why the Wok, though? Everyone loved the Wok. The Zhengs. May, all that money for Kanu and The Super Eagles?"

His Holiness shrugged. "This is not little bambino stuff, Finn. We must prepare ourselves. Like me. Prayer. Fasting. Biscotti and Pellegrino. E tutto. Body and blood."

"And Chianti?"

"Certo!"

I sipped. Then gulped. Then asked, "But the Estaters. They're going mad about the Wall. Blocking them off."

"Si, si. But they are good people. Father Tas tells me so. Observant. Honest. Once they realize. Once they see the beauty, no, they will be thus converted."

"That's what I thought."

Another clink of our glasses.

"No, what I worry about, what I can't figure out, Boy. The Toll Queen. Builds the Wall. Catholic, isn't he, but ignores the DIG, ignores St. Palladius of Ballygall. Those rumors of suspension. Cancellation. Right under his big, rich, fat feet."

"Know he's a billionaire, father, but not the smartest. Seems to be only able for one thing at a time."

"Si, one finger at a time."

Which surprised us both into a grand burst of laughter.

"Go easy, you two," shouted down my mother. "You'll frighten the builders." Who had resumed their racket east, west and north.

We settled ourselves, biscotti for His Holiness, Ferrero Rocher for me. Enjoying the woozy, dusty silence, eventually spoiled by an organ grinding back on a few doors north.

"Si, momentous time, Finn. Your father knew, God bless his soul. St. Palladius of Ballygall. The first St. Patrick. A renaissance. Nothing less, no? Sure, listen now, Janowski."

Janowski, our chemist and founder of the Holy Sodality of Palladius was praying down below in the chemist.

"Heathen, he was. Drug fiend, ah, you didn't know, your father helped him, si, but what saved him was the discovery of St. Palladius. Here, in this piccolo town. Of course, Janowski is a Pelegian, believed Palladius was also. The chronology reasonable. The schism speculative. Let me explain. Pelagius was a notorious Irish monk, dissented on the truth of original sin, which amounted to moldy ol' Manichaeism, or so he claimed. Said there was no original sin. Moreover, no need for baptism, which Janowski might be a wee bit prejudiced on."

Janowski, the story goes, had been dropped at his Polish baptism, which left his shriven brow with a definite divot.

"But, Boy, ah, the best of it, this Palladius has proved me right."

His Holiness sat down two rungs below me, his soutane splayed like a slack nimbus. And upward from him came that now familiar, scrutinizing stare: Could I be trusted, an outsider, once an insider, an emigrant probably returning west. His intense stare, infallibly blue. Seeing what?

A pale, cow-licked, blue-eyed, chipmunk-cheeked boy, perched between Upstairs and Downstairs, eager, proud of his Wall, and tipsy, deservedly tipsy, determined to "lift to importance" his town.

"Not anyone I tell, Finn." He tugged at his nose, still too abbreviated for that long Roman variety he so coveted. A glimmer of hesitation.

Struggling, reaching for the safe engagement of his more usual reticence. But he was too happy. A last attempt, a last repress of nostril, but he couldn't. "One thing, make clear. I came of my own accord. Not a papal edict. Those rumors, nervous breakdown, utter nonsense. Summertime, Ballygall, to honor the grave of Saint Ciarán Saighir the Elder. A Cork man. Bit of a wild man like meself. I was standing before his gravestone. Seeking his counsel. Finn, I am trusting your discretion, Boy. In the broadness of daylight. I will never forget it. The air seemed to bristle. To know. To part. I saw this sudden astounding approach of light. Deeper than daylight. Golden. Effulgent. As large as myself. Around it the pale morning. A trio of crows above it, fleeing. What was this? This apparition? Extending itself toward me. Cohering. A luminescence trying to resolve itself into form, into shape. No, not resolve, but attempting to accommodate itself to me. Yes, yes, to my senses, my paltry faculties, but moreover my fear. I was trembling, Boy."

He drank, took a huge bite of Biscotti.

"Never, nothing have I ever encountered. Even in Roma. This incandescence. Well, a vision is the only word commensurate. Afflatus. It configured itself into a face, a body, an expression of such fierceness. Rising from the earth. A man-like apparition. In white. A beard aflame, a beautiful mountainous nose. His hands raised high, commanding a kingdom of light upward from the graves."

Another gulp, another bite.

"Its eyes. Cobalt blue. But not two, just one. The other closed. One eye open. Searing into me."

I met His Holiness' glance. Was he joking? A reference to the burial of my father, our one-eyed, standing sentinel. Did he know about it? But no. He was serious, entranced by his own recollection.

"That terrible eye. That evil eye. That Italian phrase, In un mondo di ciechi un orbo è re. In the land of the blind, the one-eyed man is King. It perceived my terrible sin of doubt. But forgiving, compassionate, exhorting. I understood then. I had been chosen. In the land of the blind, as flawed as I was, what did Hildegard von Bingen say, *O weak mortal, both ash of ash and rottenness of rottenness*, but even so, I could bring forth what kingdom lay hidden in this graveyard, in this Bethlehem, Ballygall. I knew this with certainty, as a fact, a thing unquestionable. Revealed to me, as a truth. From this graveyard, the Church would rise. I knelt. I yielded. Such visions then engulfed me. A world of magnificence, a world of arboreal splendor, now united in our Lord. No longer separate, no longer banished. Such joy, such blessedness. I lay down, outside time and space. Teresa of Avila, her four devotions, heart, peace, union, and ecstasy. All delivered unto me. I cannot describe it. Ineffable. Bliss, Boy. Knowledge beyond knowledge. Tears burst from me. Like a little bambino."

He stood, electrified by his own words. His face red. His hand at his nose, tugging, exultant. "Finn, for hours, I lay there, in Heaven."

I nodded as numerously as I could, still wondering whether it was an elaborate hoax. Surely, my father's burial requests were known to him, familiar to him?

"And who should find me? Si, your Papa. And who should listen to me? I don't say believe. Just listened. Si, your Papa. A debt I will forever owe, God bless his soul. He heard me. Took me seriously. Took my vision seriously. This man who had already found The Wall, God's Wall. That verily, from the graveyard something of importance would rise, something magnificent enough to save our half-blind Church. Si, your papa, he dug the first shovel. I too delicate for shoveling. He found Aedeen. Converted her! He found O'Neill, converted him!"

He drank, took another oblong Biscotti from his pocket. "And such joy, the artifacts first, and when St. Palladius, discovered. Bellissimo. Bellissimo. Bellissimo."

He wiped his eyes. Tugged his nose. Continued. "So similar. Me and St. Palladius. Both of us sent from Roma to save the Irish. Scholar. Mystic. I, mio, the new Palladius."

His Holiness was serious. Close to a new cascade of tears. From his soutane he miraculously produced yet another bottle of Chianti. Opening it. "Drink to it, Boy."

"Gameball," I said, mimicking my father. "The first St. Patrick, here in boring ol' Ballygall. We're going to be Jaysus millionaires."

"Ha! For sure, for sure. Exactly your Papa's words, chase the holy pound. Ah, your poor Papa."

"Papa!," I said, leaning down, clinking his glass.

A clinking which continued long into the afternoon, aboard our Not-So-Sober-Causeway. Which Liam joined briefly. Which Conor joined briefly. Which my mother broke up eventually. Dismayed at our drunkenness, her son transmuted into the likeness of his father.

The Two Murals of Ballygall

The first, a startling composition, boldly colored, conjured from a necessarily restricted and hurried palette, which set forth a narrative of horror - two figures, one predatory, one prey, painted together on the interior curve of the southern part of The Great Wall. A giant mural, featuring a bearded, red-eyed Queen, tiara-crowned, biting, with Wall-bricked teeth, the legs of a black baby. The baby's head turned away from the beast, staring back into the heart of Ballygall, defiant, rings on her fingers, bells on her toes, rounding her chubby hand into a fist, coiling, ready to turn and punch the beast. Other details. The Red-Hand-shaped pupils of the Queen, its three-fingered hand, its wolfhound tail.

Wow.

Ballygall's first mural.

Thickly applied. Impasto. Jack B. Yeats under the direction of Diego Rivera. The Toll Queen biting a black baby. Rendered in broad, swirling brushstrokes. Done under the cover of darkness. Somehow under that periphery of barbed wire. That cordon of Black and Blue.

Wonderful work.

Surely Flora Chijindu, daughter of Chioma, sister of my first love, Obee.

But Sawn-Off Akinfenwa from the Estate was blamed, first by Garda Michael, seconded by The Town Council of Ballygall. Arrested, roughened.

And Ballygall's second mural?

Yes. The same night.

On the interior of the western Wall. Facing the presbytery at the rear of our church. Set in holy chiaroscuro. A pale arse, tiara-crowned, protruding north, indulging the insertion of a brown nose, a distressingly small nose, attached to His Holiness, skinny, his soutane settled high like a skirt.

Done under the cover of darkness. Somehow under that periphery of barbed wire.

The same prolific night.

Surely, Flora Chijindu.

But Razor Kelly of The Townies was blamed, first by Garda Michael, seconded by The Town Council of Ballygall. Arrested, roughened. An eviction proposed from his Townie house.

The murals were erased, sand blasted, the sand extracted from our very own lack of a beach. The periphery of barbed wire was thickened, heightened. Patrols set on patrol. Garda Michael supplied with more ammunition.

News reports, of course, but royally commissioned. A hate crime, a slander on the very heritage of our poor, troubled, and still incomplete nation. The Town Council copiously quoted.

The Queen aghast. The feckin' dope. Told him, told him until I was blue in the face, that there would be trouble.

But what lovely trouble it was.

The Bank of Ballygall

Liam. My one and only brother. Responsible, commanding, even caring, but only when it suited him, only when it could be wedged comfortably between his music and his medicine. (I shall refrain from mentioning his volatility, his tempestuousness, his vindictive impulsivity.) But our Liam was no longer a boy, no longer sheltered by secondary school or the completion of his Leaving Cert. Our Downstairs waited. Younger son and impoverished heir, he needed to be roused from his obliviousness, his indifference, his selective maturity, to assume the McCormack mantle, however meager, however indebted, however vulnerable to the tumult of Ballygall.

So he did, after much virtuosic moaning, agree to accompany me to the Bank of Ballygall. At the behest of the bank, who felt it would be neighborly, perhaps even productive, to discuss in general, uncommitted terms the broad contours and context of our upcoming court date. The Bank of Ballygall, a subsidiary of a German financial giant, vs. McCormack's Chemist.

In a month or so.

Dublin.

The summons hand-delivered to our Upstairs. Well-written, forceful in its pursuit of arrears and remind-full of the collateral committed, not just Downstairs but our Upstairs too. Which I read aloud many times, translating from its legalese, but ignored, belittled by my mother — Och we'll be grand, she repeatedly said.

Not a small loan either.

A quarter of a million and climbing with interest. Borrowed by my dad all those years ago to build a ravine east and west.

On the Causeway, preparatory to our departure to the bank, Liam allowed again that he could understand the loan, its terms, its negligence, but not its connection to its collateral, our business, our half-a-home.

"Doesn't the bank just own the ravines, or the Jaysus Wall now, what's it got to do with us, our lice, scabies, laxatives, and all that?"

"Security," I explained. "If you don't pay back the loan, they keep it."

"Yeah, they keep the Wall."

"Can't keep something that doesn't have any feckin' value, and that wasn't part of the contract in the first feckin' place."

"Exactly," he said, "no value, failed, gameball, we're done."

"Exactly," I said, "we're done."

"Exactly," he said.

On the strength of such clear and brotherly agreement, we proceeded diagonally across the road to the bank. Liam wore his new, long, pinstriped suit jacket, new, ugly cowboy boots, with spurs, and hitched his hair up into a ponytail, a gunslinger walking. Additionally sporting ski goggles against the dust.

A bright summer morning.

Happy to be accompanied, I tried to engage the gunslinger in small talk. What did he think of the murals? Bit much, right? A bit offensive? A red flag to a bull like O'Neill? Cost fortune to fix? A reprisal probably imminent? Mad they blamed Akinfenwa and Curran? And all the new security, battalions of Black and Blue now?

Liam had not been made aware of the murals.

Or the DIG? Closed, Liam, that fence is really electrified. Our dad's grave. No access. Who knows for how long. Obvious, someone doesn't like Palladius. Da would be going nuts at this. And Aedeen. Kicked her out. Haven't heard a squeak from her since. Heard she's started legal proceedings, against Church. His Holiness with her. Strange, *she's* vanished, but Conor is still around.

Liam had not been made aware of the closure of the DIG.

The demolition of Dirty Doherty's house?

No. He had not been made aware of this either.

The closure of the Wok?

No.

The closure of our Not-So-Small-Church?

WHAT? He stopped. Lifted his ski goggles.

"Just joking," I said, avoiding his glare. "Look," I said, raising my voice over the builders din. "Let me do the talking in here. Bit complicated, and big numbers, like I showed you."

"Not sure why I'm even going."

Which was typical of him.

"Went over the stuff last night."

Which was true, nearly a whole night of preparation, and in particular a re-reading of my father's epistolary feud with the bank. Missives and missiles back and forth. Funny if it wasn't so costly.

"Brendan, can't take long," cautioned Liam. "Have to practice."

"Take as long as it takes. If we can just get them to settle or something, or just postpone the court hearing."

Liam had not been made aware of a court hearing.

The court hearing would be tough. Our default obvious and chronic in front of a judge. But my father's correspondence had suggested a defense, or at least an obfuscating tactic that might delay seizure and foreclosure, that might allow enough time for the Wall to entice those holy pilgrims and their sacred euros. At the meeting, I would declare the original indebting contract null and void by virtue of my father's mental incompetence. Which should be easy to illustrate. The sole borrower, being a drinker, a gambler, and a philanderer, and supine on his stairs all day and DIGGING in a graveyard all night, is somehow and incredibly loaned a quarter a million to re-build a Wall which he claims was originally built to protect the first of not one but two St. Patricks.

Odd, no?

For security, he offers half-a-home and half-a-business, and for the rest of his and the loan's life engages in a vituperative, unhinged epistolary feud with the lender. Surely a sign of not only his mental instability but also the bank's, who acted recklessly, negligently, without due diligence or fiduciary oversight, funding two exorbitant ditches, east and west of this tiny parenthetical town.

Surely the loan should be written off, swept under the fiduciary carpet, written off the face of the earth. If this failed, I would bolster our defense with a thick, absorbent, italicized check. Something as painful as five thousand. Euros not dollars.

The red-bricked bank, snug to the northern curve of the Great Wall, had grown a large snout, a thick, protective, windowless protrusion that directed two small doors toward the main street. In and Out, both securely manned by large non-Ballygallians, of big belly and egregious ears. Behind them the structure was elevated on four fat legs to permit an array of subterranean reinforcements, which seemed superfluous to the town's indigence. The bank itself was also being expanded. The belly of the beast widened, fattened, armored, north and south, encroaching on our TD's

(Congressman) Bandy Driscoll's office, acquiring a girth that eventually and unbelievably, like the Great Wall, would find its fill.

We hurried through the new metal detectors.

Late.

Of course.

This did not disrupt nor quicken Helmut the Banker's disquisition on the matter in hand, or the matter of what was not in hand. With German thoroughness, he began at the beginning of Ballygall time, a prelapsarian idyll whence Tasy McCormack, my grandmother, was tempted into teahouse debt, but our Fraulein, not tainted by the sins of her future offspring, remitted and repaid the original and its interest. Prompt, punctual, precise, often delivered by hand. The exact coinage.

At this point, Helmut, tall, thin, thoroughly tanned, and obviously nostalgic for such monetary conformance, rose from his armored desk for an emotional march along the promontory of his narrow office, composing himself before its view of the Great Wall, now eight-plus feet and rising, the envious sea behind it. A decent second-story view really, the offices originally on the first floor, but now elevated, a precursor to what became known as The Ascension of Ballygall.

Helmut shook himself. Blew his nose. Dried his eyes. Picked at his sty. Then invoked my father. His epistolary opponent. "Reckless, Ja. I tell your father. Do not endanger your family, your home, your business. For such a thing. Such an abundance of money. Even my bank. My superiors. I tell them. Do not allow the loan. Never clear how the repayment would be amortized. Ja, a grant should be. From the government. Heritage site. Not a mortgage of a home and business. Reckless. Deeply reckless." His face reddened. He bit at his lip. A brief look of anguish.

A decent bloke obviously, but of a different, straighter cloth than my father.

"A good man, though, your father." An indignant glance, that non-invite to that non-funeral. Surely, he hadn't expected an invite? He blew his nose again and began at a new beginning. McCormack's Chemist, Drugs not Darjeeling, inaugurated… a synopsis he might not have finished by Christmas had he not been interrupted, replaced, ejected. A word in his ear before he was out on his ear.

Teresa McAnteer, Ballygall Councilor and Tidy Town Czar, barged in. Sober, suited, even a briefcase. A tall woman, fit, with washed-out blue eyes, a button nose, scrupulously small ears, and white teeth. Warm, energetic, her heart in the right place but perhaps in the wrong town.

Formerly a financial titan, before irregularities were discovered. Pardoned somehow. Empowered by royal command. Leading this takeover. A takeout. Pushing Helmut by the elbow out of the office. Teresa McAnteer now in command. Behind her, around her, similar scenes were enacted on this upper floor, words into ears, elbows into ribs, the entire staff out on their ears. No resistance, no surprise. Not as much as a squeal. The bank now and suddenly under new ownership. Royal ownership. The Queen's oligarchic funds finding an Irish home, a Ballygall piggy bank.

Teresa sat right down to our poor plop of paperwork. A quick audible surmise. "Jesus, not a penny, years. More. And overdrawn. What was that gobshite Kraut doing? What are all these letters? Jesus. Oh, good, court date. The town. Inside. Good. Perfect. Silver platter."

She lifted her hard blue eyes. Shook her tidy blonde bob. Behind her lay the sea, flat and vulnerable. "And why are we here?"

I stuttered, stumbled, and in a poor mimicry of Helmut, trotted out Tasy, teashops and time immemorial.

"What?" She stood up, obscuring the entire Irish sea. Impatient. A woman of importance returning to importance.. Allowed to take financial reins again, dismayed by our trifling Upstairs and Downstairs.

"Mental incontinence," I ventured, meaning 'incompetence.' "Some compromise. Some amount I can pay now."

"T.T.B.!" she suddenly shouted, raising a thumb, remembering me if not gunslinger Liam. Tidy Town Ballygall! Loud and sonorous. "Archie McCormack."

"T.T.B.!," I shouted, dabbing my thumb at her.

"How much now? Payment," she asked, sitting down, taking time for her own amusement. A bright smile. A readiness to laugh at what could only be paltry, partial.

Deep in my backpack lay my own gorgeous checkbook. Thick, absorbent, italicized. My emigrant's savings. "Five grand," I grandly said.

Liam wolf-whistled, flapping his long, pinstriped coat.

"Ah," said Teresa, glancing again at our paperwork. Pausing to consider our little family, our small plot of debt.

A great and mysterious pause ensued.

And into that great, mysterious pause galloped Liam, astride his own brand of fearless ignorance. Standing. Ponytail thrown back. His ski goggles hanging from his neck. "Here, the money was for the Wall. Those ravines. What's it got to do with us, the Chemist an' that?"

A flicker of irritation from Teresa, disturbed from her reverie. But then that tight, tidy smile. "Ah, sure, I'll just go back in time and repossess those two old ditches."

I almost chuckled.

Liam rose to the sarcasm. In leaps and bounds. "Load of bollox. Tried to build, didn't work. End of story. Have the Wall. Take that."

"Now you want me –"

Liam cut her off. "Ask that baby-eating Queen for it."

So, he did know about the murals. Of course he did.

"And if he refuses to pay for a couple of ditches?"

Liam laughed. "Then we'll give you a couple of our fingers, gameball."

"Ah," replied Teresa, entering a second dry stage of recognition. "You're the bloody organist." She raised a hand to quieten Liam. Then two hands. Informed us, in an unmistakable mimicry of my mother's Derry accent, "Och, you'll be grand."

My mother's new mantra: Och, we'll be grand.

Which instantly pleased Liam.

I asked for specifics.

But more specifically, Devlin the Developer appeared, as if out of thin, sulfurous air. With tousled hair and his big, bully belly. A Ballygall Toff, second only to Teresa. Who stood. Said, "Out lads, a lot to do. Go on. Out."

"The check?" I asked.

"T.T.B!" she replied, laughing, waving me away.

We left. Bemused. Relieved. Quickly agreeing, yes, an early pint or two at The Wobbly.

Which was already full, pullulating my father would have said. A sunburst of yellow, the builders, all from the Catholic North, clad in yellow T-shirts and yellow hard hats. Dusty jeans, dirty boots, dirty stories. Shouting, flinging sausage and such from table to table. Maybe two dozen of them, even the foremen, slumming it until O'Donohue's opened later for lunch. Their late breakfast break. The usual fare, but also the Nigerian ogi and akara (corn and beans), and the Polish kielbasa and rasher pierogies.

A feast.

The owners, Charming and Cinders, that perfect couple, envied by me and Obee, attended to the builders. Happy. Generous. Busy.

But not too busy for my customary greeting, "Sls-upp, Sls-upp."

Which did make me smile. A welcome further improved by the attendance of their favorite, Maestro, who was ushered, with me, to a small northern table on the Townies side of the pub. Townies north, Estaters south. Just below the TV. A daytime program. The Toll Queen himself. All clean, shirted and presidential. Articulate, even eloquent. Far from his penitential Ballygall self. His wife beside him, one hand covering the other.

"Ask him," shouted one of the builders.

"Never'll ask him," answered another.

His wife's fingers. Tiger-bitten.

"There's your boyfriend," said Liam.

"What you having?" I asked.

Once assured of not having to pay, Liam ordered The Full Ballygall, a monstrous, multi-national breakfast. I took a dirty coffee. Hanging above us, on the freshly painted wall, smiled the young Super Eagles football team, U-18 girls.

A few general questions for Liam:

> What do you think Teresa meant, 'Och, you'll be grand'?
> Something to do with Ma?
> Something to do with the Queen?
> Something to do with the Bank changing into royal hands?
> Something to do with Devlin appearing out of thin, sulfurous air?

"Like the dope said, we'll be grand. Ma's well in with the Queen. Don't know. But here, that five grand. You have that kind of dosh, do you?"

I did. I really did. But it wasn't for the likes of Liam.

"No, not for me," he said, scornfully anticipatory. "That murdering doctor. That corridor hospital. Use it to sue the shite outta them. Damages. Get some justice."

Which did surprise me. Putting my dad and justice ahead of his own interests.

Our breakfast arrived, Liam's substantial enough to merit a standing and sunny ovation from the builders. A few who knew me, who nodded, who, having suffered Liam's daily recitals, sympathized.

"Not sure about suing," I said, thanking Cinders for my dirty coffee.

"Can't let him get away with it," said Liam.

"I know, but bit harder now. That punch didn't do us any favors. Have their backs up now. Drag their feet so they will, and every other part of their pear-shaped lard."

Liam tore into his breakfast. "Not bad job they've done on this place. No potholes."

"Don't skip the ogi and akara," I said, noticing his sidelining of them. "Better than chicken balls," which is how Obee had converted me to their soft, crispy deliciousness.

He ignored me. "But fucking hospital cunts. Should get what's coming to them. Crime it is, the stuff they missed. And in a bleedin' corridor."

I nodded. I agreed. "Look, I'm nodding. I'm agreeing."

"Fucking disgrace."

I sat back. Took my dirty coffee off the table. An early lesson. When his fires are flowing, when his cheeks are blowing, lean away, boys, lean away.

Once he subsided, I offered the reassurance of retaining solicitor Finnegan and his extravagant limp, which was a lie: I would not so quickly waste my money on what would now be a long, legal ring-a-rosy.

Liam grunted his full-mouthed agreement, but knew he was being pandered to.

The builders stood, stretched, and left en masse with a massive, "HI-Ho," throwing the pub into a full and welcome eclipse. On their exiting backs a new insignia, a man of muscle, etched in thick, black lines, and an inscription, Rambo for Pres, O'Neill's old G.A.A. (Irish football) nickname now formally reprised for his campaign.

I drank my coffee, exulting in the sudden quiet, the emptied-outness of the place, Cinders singing a song to herself, Charming drying glasses behind the bar. Och, we'll be grand, I thought. The soothing prospect of a court case receding. It fully receded a few days later with a letter from the O'Neill Bank of Ballygall formally withdrawing all legal proceedings, complete with a last comforting line: "Och, Yours Sincerely, The Great Bank of Ballygall."

"Justice," proclaimed Liam. "Otherwise, hospital get away with it."

"What about your own patients?" I asked, attempting a redirection to his Hippocratic rounds of Ballygall.

"Given all that up, Brendan," he replied.

"Nah," I said. "Sure, since you were a snapper. Gouty was asking for you the other day." Gouty O'Donohue of Donohue's pub, often shoeless, comfortable in her white, gout-friendly padded socks.

"Given it up. Better things. Dad is."

Our dad is dead. And wasn't his vulnerability the real reason for Liam's Hippocratic oath, taking up the stethoscope after his heart attack? That awful time. The ambulance blaring outside our home. The paramedics rushing up. The noise, the stress, the horrible excitement, the afterwards of worry. That's why Liam took up medicine. No great insight that, well accepted if unremarked in our family. The filial concern and solicitude for my father, but it was for my mother really. Liam would never admit it, but it was her distress, her pain that so scalded him. Mother not father.

"So many fucking better things to do."

"Don't know, Liam. All this building going on. Respiratory stuff. Everyone coughing like smokers. Made for you. Give the piano a rest."

He put on his ski goggles, took them off again, nodding. "Yeah. Not ideal. Silicosis."

"Sila-wha'?"

"Dust in the lungs. Be rife, it will. But I've given up all that. Don't have the time. Here, where's that pint you promised me?"

A Carlsberg for the Maestro, a Budweiser for me.

"Cheers," said Liam, adding, "septic tank Yank" at the clink of our glasses. "Don't have a Jaysus minute anymore, do I."

I drank, long and dubiously. Busy, Liam? Busy about himself, that's all. No thought for the family, the business, our mother, and Ballygall itself melting down.

I took a long sup. Took a good wise bite of my thumb.

But reddening with shame when I realized, his Leaving Cert., obviously complete, I had forgotten about his Leaving Cert! "Ah, but here, Liam. I completely forgot. Your Leaving. Done, right? How'd you do?" Raising my Bud. Not only a toast but maybe an apology too, admitting that I had ignored it all, an ordeal that he really had endured on his own, in the worst of circumstances. A preamble like that. But he was still stuffing his face with his multi-national breakfast, so, instead, I just clinked his parked glass. "Congrats on finishing, bud."

He did not clink back. Tears. Quick tears, too fast for words. His lip, then his chin, turbulent, trembling. "I didn't," he finally said. "Sure, how could I? Dad. And I had to do all that." He fisted his tears away, scowling, staunching. "I did all the funeral, the burial, the bandages, the … all that stuff. So I didn't. How the fuck could I?"

"You didn't what?" I said, worried. Cinders had noticed, had stopped her singing. Prince Charming now perfectly at her side.

Liam turned to me. His face wet. His eyes red. "Didn't sit the Leaving, did I? How could I?"

Ah, Jesus, the sly prick. Do anything but grow up he would. "Did ya do any of it?" A stupid question. Either you do or you don't, and he didn't. Which meant another year in school. Which meant another year not managing our Jaysus bankrupt business, Janowski fully retained.

"And you, Brendan, you weren't fucking there. Twice they did. In that corridor. Told us, turn everything off, but of course, our choice. Asked us. To let him die."

"I wasn't there because no one told me. As soon as, I did." A morning, an afternoon's delay, to compose myself but no shame in that.

"All that. And how am I supposed to? Study. Concentrate."

Yeah, but you can play your poxy organ all day long.

"Ma knows. She's fine. It's *you* we were worried about."

"Me? We?"

"Yeah, Yankee you. Thinking you'd have to come home and save the day. Take over this, take over that. All the while moaning about missing your American wet dream. All pissy. Sitting on the stairs. In the way. King Muck. Ordering everyone around. Rattling those stupid keys." He caught himself, took a breath. "Wasn't going to tell you, the Leaving, until you went back. But."

He took a large preventative gulp of his pint.

I matched him.

He lifted and, without looking, clinked my glass.

The prick.

But I clinked him back. Surprised by my own tears. "Ah Jesus, Liam. We've been through the wringer."

"I know, bud. We have. We Jaysus have."

We drank fast, keeping ahead of the tears. He shared his breakfast, well, just the ogi and akara. I shared my impressions of Boston, which he encouraged, which he eventually directed to its Berkley School of Music, which he probably hoped would elicit questions, warm-hearted queries, his plans after school, maybe music not medicine, and certainly not the impoverishing chemistry of McCormack's Chemist.

Me bollox.

It was not open for discussion.

He'd made his bed, made his commitment. Take care of the business, our bankrupt business. Take care of our mother, our murderous mother. That was his deal. The family deal. The sly fucker, giving himself another year in school. Another year playing with his stupid church organ.

So I changed the subject. No. Not our mother's homicidal past. No, not her vengeful game with Conor. Liam was too volatile, too violent.

Instead, our favorite subject. Ireland's favorite subject. The case of two fingers not one. Tiger-bitten, not both at once, but twice, one at a time. O'Neill's poor wife. No one believing O'Neill's story about a deplorable ransom, far worse than money. A disbelief that might imperil his presidential election and his anti-ornamental referendum.

A national discussion then, which invariably involved the appraisal of one's own five fingers. Their long, bony brilliance, their easy, lissome movement, but mostly their hard, un-snappable strength. A bone saw, they must have used. A Jaysus saw.

"Fentanyl," opined Liam. "A good dose, and she probably sawed them off herself."

Which is when I again noticed my father's wedding ring on Liam's finger.

"What's the problem?" he said, flapping his finger. "Ma's grand with it."

"Not married to Ma, are you?"

And around we went. It's grand. It's not. It's stupid. It's not. It's weird. It's not. It's fucking stupid. It's not.

The stubborn prick.

He refused to take it off, citing my obvious jealousy, and wouldn't it keep all the women away. Except we all knew Liam was gay, or would be, if he would ever grow up.

He ordered another free-for-him pint. Leaned back. Relaxed. Shook his ponytail. He pulled over a chair for his feet. On his school holidays now. Nothing to worry about. Just a summer of church organ at our Not-So-Small-Church.

Prick.

A Tower House Unfit for a Queen

A bawn, Aisling O'Neill called it, enjoying the word, its repetition, moving her tiger-bitten hand along the top of her defensive wall, her bawn, which partially surrounded her Dalkey tower house. Into its gaps she inserted herself, replacing errant stones, massaging its base as if she might encourage it back to its former and full height. A small, scraggly wall really. Miniaturized by the tower house, four levels high, gray and darkened by the summer rain. Rectangular not round. Its stone cobbled not smooth. So tall, forty feet perhaps, but vertically only three narrow windows, tightly mullioned, far apart, which seemed to stretch and accentuate the building's height. It stood like a craggy, old man at the precipice, the Irish Sea stalking below.

On its canted roof, crenellated like a castle, flew the O'Neill flag, a Red Hand, drops of blood drip drop dropping, which must have unsettled her.

The house was approachable only by a narrow, curved driveway, which, according to Aisling, who now moved out of the bawn, could be straightened and widened to allow quicker surveillance. The vegetation could be cleared. The descent of trees down the crunchy, elevated road could be felled. Bushes dug away. The neighboring and adjacent tower house made invidiously visible. Nothing would be able "to hide, to prowl." More lights could be installed, a flood of them. More alarms. The slightest stalking motion. A gate, of course. Iron. More bodyguards too, to reinforce the two already stationed at the driveway's entrance. Supervised by Glibb the Giant. But would it be enough?

I nodded, unsettled by her anxiety, wanting the security of the house myself, the meeting with O'Neill to begin. The sea seemed to hiss below.

"Like it's going out of style," interjected her sister-in-law, Mary O'Neill, meaning money and its frittering. A harsh smile. Hard, limpid, blue eyes, long brown hair. An Aran jumper, but only to mock her brother's new-found Irishness. A mocking tweed cap too. A wee cuddly wolfhound in her pocket. And Great, big silicone breasts but only to annoy her Great family. The black sheep. An aerobics teacher where her more sheepish siblings were the prescribed solicitors, politicians and professors.

Aisling continued. The bawn would be the first line of defense, rebuilt, if their neighbors, affluent and idle, would only relent. If it was scaled, then quick defensive action from the tower, from its slitted windows, its parapet, its crenellations. Anything. Arrows, bullets, even, she joked, a few wee cannonballs.

She retreated closer to the tower, the blue summer sky now lined with clouds. Gazing down that curved driveway, probably imagining the worst of her imagination. Dressed in a tight tracksuit, with pink runners (gutties, she called them), her once long, bleached-blonde hair gone, a wig, I realized with shock, her hair now tight and auburn, all of which, she said, was harder to grab, to pull.

A welcome development, Mary said later, the Great Mrs. O'Neill finally dismounting from her sartorial high horse. Giving up that race, against those English princesses, all that blonde beauty and blue blood.

Aisling wore at least three gold crucifixes around her neck, circling her back to the devotion of her church-spent youth. Daily observant now. Attended by Bishop Slattery himself.

"Cannonballs against a tiger, yeah," Aisling said, still with a London twang. "It's the neck. How tigers. Strangle. Bleed out."

An extravagant sigh-moan from Mary O'Neill. "Tigger fact number three."

The other two had not been so sanguinary: (1) Tigers have round not slitted pupils, like humans not cats. (2) The markings on a tiger's fur, unique to each animal, also extend to their skin. Not only fur deep but skin deep, a tiger in tiger's clothing. Each fact relayed as a non sequitur, produced from the poor, traumatized trappings of her mind.

Her kidnappers had worn tiger masks. Not the cheap, stringed, plastic variety but real pull-on masks, with cloth and fur, stripes and stiffened ears, orange and black, and with a mane of whiteness. Masks that exposed human eyes and human teeth.

"The bawn, definitely, back up, yeah. Like that lovely Wall, Ballygall." She walked us toward the tower itself, pointing toward a small pillar. "A mounting stone, for the horses."

"Shouldn't you check?" asked Mary, grimacing, nodding back to the straggle of wall. "Only been an hour."

Irritated, but Aisling ran and checked, its exterior, the improbable appearance of a slanderous mural. Another protracted glance down that curved, crunched driveway. Her movements stiff, cautious. On her hunkers, a glance under their yellow armored Ford Explorer for explosives.

"She would have, if I hadn't reminded her," said Mary to me, sighing. "Once in the door, back out again, poor lamb."

Aisling stood behind the wall. Listening. A strengthening sea breeze.

What did it sound like to her? What did it evoke?

She had been held for as long as a week. A seaside town, she said. Her fingers had been severed from the tip of each knuckle, leaving two half-stumps. The mocking cries of seagulls.

My poor, wee octopus, Mary called her, but never to her face. Aisling had refused prosthetics, or cosmetic surgery, leaving the bite, or bites, raw and bare. She now wore her ring on the full finger beside the bitten half.

"Hate that sound, the sea," said Aisling. "Can't hear a thing. Tigers, yeah. They only ambush. Need the surprise, otherwise will back down. In India, wear masks at back of the head, tiger thinks you're looking, won't attack."

"Tigger fact number four," announced Mary, putting her woolly Aran arm around Aisling when she rejoined us. Aisling's hands joined, the good fingers covering the hurt. A tender glance at her sister-in-law.

"Was there any sign of that there mural?" asked Mary. "My brother's oligarchic arse?"

"Scum," said Aisling. "Ballygall scum," she added, a challenging glance to me.

I nodded, reflexively.

"And what would you expect there now," said Mary, amused, thrusting out her chest. "Don't like our good Queen 'Ugh, do they? Who would? All this Great begorrah O'Neill stuff. All new to him, so it is. Not even Paddy's day did he bother back then. And now, barely back in Ireland."

Barely, but fully, his kingdom folded and repatriated completely to Ireland, some of it to the Bank of Ballygall.

Mary continued. "Only history interested him was his own wee self, and even that."

In his online profiles, O'Neill had often relegated the past to the past, citing it as a hindrance to a toll-heavy future, i.e. selling the people what they might expect to already own.

"Left all that to Decent Donal, so he did."

Donal, the preferred, non-prodigal son.

"Och, didn't he want an English princess? Aisling knows all that."

Close on two occasions, minor royals, but neither sufficiently disobedient, unwilling to prickle their matrimony with their parent's disfavor. Skeptical perhaps of O'Neill's opportunistic claim to Irish Earldom.

"And och, married an Irish one instead. That right, Aisling."

Who smiled.

Not love at first sight, Aisling later confided. Its vigilant opposite. Wary of each other. From the same place, the same tradition. Wouldn't they drag each other back to Ireland? To the same-old-same-old. Both successful, she an investment banker intimate with a rung of royalty, suspicious that such intimacy was the initial attraction for her Great husband. They returned to the south not the north. A healthy distance from their families, from the troubled tensions of our incomplete nation.

"Ah. But now everything for him Irish Irish Irish," said Mary, in a sing-song voice. "Especially the Church."

O'Neill's love of Church was new, passionately pragmatic, secured in his momentary and nepotistic apprehension of Irish history. But generous. To expiate his sins perhaps, his near miss with near Protestant royalty, he gave the Church buckets of money.

"Och, he's the worst kind of Irishman, a born-again Irishman."

"A grand door," explained Aisling, leading us to the entry way.

Which was wooden, thick, pointed at its top, sort of bullet-shaped. Which could be further protected by a Yett, a metal grille, a sort of domestic portcullis, if the accursed neighbors would only relent. "And above," she said, pointing upward, a crenellation which would allow a downward volley of projectiles.

"Wait for it," whispered Mary, "Tigger fact number five."

Aisling nodded, stopped herself.

Which made me wonder: Why was Mary here and not one of Aisling's own sisters? Which was later ascribed to the estrangement between the two (allegedly) Great families, the O'Neills and the O'Donnells, the latter unwilling to accept any sort of ransom that would risk the mutilation of their daughter and sister. And the insulting lack of consultation, or post traumatic explication. Aisling's notorious brother, Red O'Donnell, threatening "a sorting out."

Inside the door was a small anteroom, "a killing space," said Aisling, enabled by a murder hole cut above into its ceiling. "Hot oil," she suggested. "Few chips. Curry sauce." Her wit returning, but not yet resurgent enough to humorize the kidnapping. But she was trying. "Ballygall could use a bit of it. Hot oil. Those fucking scumbags. The Currans and Kellys. Drug dealers. Murderers. Were you no terrified growing up, Finn?"

Actually, good protective friends, until my American birthright interfered.

"Och, everyone loves Finn," said Mary, "what is it, Sls-upp, Sls-upp." Done sibilantly, lasciviously, but exaggerated. "Cow licks. Or is it your brother that's the popular one?"

"Empty," said Aisling. "Always the downstairs was kept empty. Most vulnerable space."

To the left of the anteroom, secured by a thick wooden door, was the main downstairs room. Cold, crepuscular, full of boxes, crates, Louis Vuitton suitcases. Dozens of them. Unopened. In no apparent order. The same on every floor, the cluttered remnants of O'Neill's English empire. But why reduced to such a cold, uncomfortable house? Its thick, scarred walls. Its bumpy, cold, uncarpeted floors. Its thin, embrasured windows. Couldn't an Irish billionaire, albeit a Born-Again Irish billionaire, do better?

"Those disgusting murals," said Aisling. "But might be good way to get rid of those criminals. Kellys and Akinfenwas. Nicer place without them, Finn? Wouldn't it?"

She was well informed.

"And that woman Ola. That horrible Polish warren. Such an arrogant, ignorant woman."

I shrugged.

"Better without them. That African hairdresser. All grand, but not in Ballygall. Wee town has such potential, yeah. Know your mother, not a fan of the place, but even she, agreed that the town, few changes could make a difference."

Not only did she know my mother but had talked to her? Recently?

"Your father. Met him once." Followed by that now familiar indignant look, that non-invite to that non-funeral. "Sure, he sold us on the place. What he say. Poem. Wall lift to importance my home town."

"Yes, Kavanagh."

"Tell me, Finn, yeah. Is that Men's Shed used at all? Heard, waste of space. Good space."

"Think it is," I replied, avoiding her glance, thinking of the Sheddies.

"That priest is a gobshite. Father Seamus Sausage Meat. Thinks he's God's answer."

"Och," said Mary, putting both arms around Aisling. "Isn't it time for your nap, Mrs. Cranky Rambo?"

A timely reminder.

And from above came another reminder, a child's cry, a tentative explorative lament, which nevertheless convinced Aisling up that narrow, cold, stone staircase. "Last Tigger fact, Mary," she said, pausing at the first of many fortified doors. "Tigers can't purr, yeah. To show happiness, they squint or close their eyes."

"Och, go on out of that," said Mary. "Leave them, have your salt and vinegar crisps and then get your happy nap." Said kindly, squinting then closing her eyes. "I'll watch the princesses. No charge. After I show this fine young fella to his Born-Again Queen."

An exchange of smiles.

"Salt and vinegar," said Mary to me. "What they fed her, kidnapped. Therapy, isn't it."

The poor woman.

"Take a while," said Mary, wincing.

Upstairs I was then prodded.

The meeting was on the second floor, once Mary, after much urgings, removed herself.

A campaign meeting, expletively explained O'Neill.

Whiskey not tea.

Tayto not toast.

The attendees congregated around a dark, wooden table. TD (Congressman) 'Bandy' Driscoll astride a wooden crate. Bishop Slattery atop a treasure trunk. Teresea 'Tidy Town' McAnteer and Devlin the Developer on two wheezy boxes. I sat on a bony pew, unsettled by my inclusion. Driven here by Glibb, no excuses taken.

Under the dark, wooden table — a long, feast of a table, the only piece of furniture commensurate with the great room – slept the stertorous wolfhound, Boru. Finally at his master's feet. Fattened by ham.

At the head of the table, on a tall, wooden chair, sat Rambo The Toll Queen himself. Spine straight, his upward hair almost strafing the low ceiling, his right foot tapping on the flagstone floor. Behind him a long, narrow window squinted out over the sea.

Another cold, crepuscular room. The great fireplace cold. Ghostly imprints on the hard, mottled walls, where paintings and tapestries must have hung. To O'Neill's right, a domestic altar, where a fresh vase of orchids and a pair of bright, warming candles were offered up to a statue of our Virgin Mary — no doubt hoping she'd turn the bleeding central heating on.

Such a poor refuge for such a rich man, for such a public man, albeit a man with piss-poor presidential polling, both for himself and his non-ornamental referendum. The lowest polls seen.

But Bandy, the seasoned politico, was euphemistic; ground had been gained, but plenty of more ground could be, well, gained. "Country is a profusion of niches, special interests, but amenable, it'll come round. It'll wake up."

"Bandy," said O'Neill, causing laughter, heedlessly applying his nickname in public. Not apologizing. In fact, laughing, igniting that terrible terraced laugh of his. Goat-hyena-elephant. The sound reverberating around the bare room.

Bandy, playing along, throttled his knees, the source of the sobriquet, which, though connected to two straight and at once athletic (hurling) legs, deviated from each other as if biologically repulsed. Very bandy. A roly-poly man, with pale, floury cheeks, a collection of chins, and a fat, inflatable neck, which, like a cobra's, would engorge when aggravated. A town councilor originally, like my father, but now quite powerful, quite shrewd, quite ambitious, attached tick-like to the Queenly pelt of O'Neill.

"What has this country come to? Am I right, Archie?"

Archie, my hilarious nickname.

"Is it a country at all, and held together by what? English football? When I was growing up, all in it together, yeah."

His English accent still malingering.

"When I was growing up, sure, didn't you know your neighbor, know their family, where they came from, who they were, who they weren't, which side they were from? Didn't we have the same history, the same culture, the same stupid programmes. Jesus, the same dinners? One long magnificent row of roast beef down our street of a Sunday. Now, it's everything from everywhere. Am I right, Archie?"

I nodded at the dope.

"When I was growing up, on my side anyway, no divorce. Plenty of bad marriages, but they'd get on with it. Stick it out. Now probably get it online. And Jesus, you wouldn't even mention abortion."

A pause to tug at his beard.

"When I was growing up, pubs not cappuccino shops. A couple of breweries, now it's everything from everywhere. When I was growing up, ah, we all knew who was gay, a' course we did, but they kept it to themselves. Not a big deal. Nay problem. But now all that marriage malarkey."

Boru sighed in his under-table slumber.

"When I was growing up, sure, the Church. No offence, father, but you wouldn't really listen, but you wouldn't miss. Folk Mass especially."

"Midnight Mass," said Teresa, with a shiny smile.

"And a feed after," said Devlin, patting his big, bully belly. Finally wearing trousers not shorts, his hair cut shorter, more like the adult he wasn't. Throughout the meeting, he and Teresa often stood, stretched, even yawned, rousing their pardoned selves from those long years of exile.

"When I was growing up —"

"Definitely political resonance," said Bandy, interrupting, the creaky crate beneath him assisting his welcome disruption. "People really miss the Church, the centrality of it, the comfort of it. The reliability of it. Our mythical past."

"No myth about it, so there isn't. When I was growing up, the Church, sure, it was in your head, in your boots, in your pocket. As unavoidable as the rain. Am I right, Archie?"

"Finn," I said. "My name is Finn."

O'Neill waved me away. "Quiet you! Only here because of your mother. Should be paying me for babysitting so she should." Smiling. "But what's happened to the Church?" he continued, patting his yellow T-shirt, embossed with *Rambo for Pres*. Tugging on his beard, still tough and tufty. Directing himself to Bishop Slattery, who slid himself back up the treasure chest only to begin the slow, irrefutable descent back down. Digging his cracked nails in. A wry smile. A formidable man, but uncomfortable, dismayed by this slippery treasure chest. Ascetically thin. A disarming stare. "With your generous assistance, we are renewing our ministry. We are —"

But Rambo cut him off. "When I was young, such a part of our wee home life. Not just the sacraments, and the Mass, but here, that simple thing, fish on Fridays. What happened to that? Such a simple thing, Church and the community through a bit of fish."

"Ray and chips," said Devlin the glutton, salivating. He chewed into his chewing gum, as did Teresa, who added, "With nice bottle of Sancerre." two addicts still battling their addictions, her hand shaking, Devlin's belly rumbling.

"Know why it's Friday?" asked O'Neill, keen to exhibit his newfound learning, the prodigal student returned. "Most think it's fasting, but then why not Saturday before Sunday Mass?"

Bishop Slattery interrupted. "Our Lord's sacrifice. Died on a Friday. Commemorated on a Friday."

"Correct," said O'Neill, throttling his beard. "And no other sacrifice on the same day can ya have. Warm blooded animals, I mean. So either snake or fish is the choice."

"Had snake once," said Devlin. "Skinned it right at the table. Tasted like old fish fingers. Ate a ton of them there. Hold the record still."

"Intelligent animals," said Teresa reproachfully.

"Could be good messaging," said Bandy, rubbing his bald head. "Fish on Fridays. Back to basics. Make Ireland Ireland again."

"At least call it Fish and Chips on a Friday," said Devlin, who drew the salivating support of an under-tabled wolfhound. Still asleep.

Bandy stood up with his idea. "Cooking segment on *Midday*. You and Aisling. Fish. Be great to bring Aisling into the campaign."

Which had proved difficult. Which had impaired the campaign. Which no one had the neck to explicitly address, except maybe Bandy.

O'Neill also stood. "Och, no bad. Could fillet it meself. Ash do the actual cooking."

"I'd stay away from knives," said Devlin, the box wheezing beneath him. "Any sort of cutting really."

Which ushered in a tense silence. Even the sea below seemed to pause.

The Toll Queen sat down.

"I agree with Devlin," said Teresa. "But would be great if Aisling could get more involved. Polls are way down."

Devlin concurred. Two allies allied, which illustrated their independence, their power. They were not lackey sycophants, but members of powerful families, well used to the accouterments and privilege of power.

"I'll suggest it to her," said Bishop Slattery, now ensconced as her spiritual counselor. "At an apt moment."

"Thanks," said O'Neill, tearing up. Actually tearing up. Which was to prove common. Which was also to prove to be a mimicry of his great, great etc. (alleged) grandfather, The Earl of Tyrone, who would tear up at pivotal, even confrontational moments.

A re-seated Bandy intervened, asking Slattery if the "personnel changes" were in place.

A purge, really, the evisceration of the upper echelons of the Church. Cleansed. Renewed. Ready.

"Indeed," replied Slattery, easing himself back up the treasure chest, tensing his fingers, digging in his nails, but still sliding back down. "An announcement has been approved. The gallows are under construction."

"Happy Days," said O'Neill. "Do it on Friday. A sacrifice. Though, are they warm blooded?"

To which Devlin added, "Reptiles most of them. Depredations of some of them."

"Timing is important," said Bandy, interrupting. "First, Hugh, I mean, Rambo."

A round of smiles.

A snort from under the table.

"Rambo criticizes the Church, calls for significant change. Return of Church to its cherished place etc. No response from the church, until the announcement. Expulsions. Credit to Rambo."

"Good man, Bandy," said O'Neill.

A round of laughter at his continued use of the nickname.

"Agreed," said Slattery, "per our agreement." A pause before he added, "Our quid pro quo agreement with Rambo." The appellation seeming new but pleasing to him.

"Already in your collection plate," said O'Neill. "This morning."

Cash not religion. Business not faith. O'Neill merely using the Church.

Devlin the Developer then stood, producing from his sports bag a laptop, which illustrated a lengthy and broad array of property transactions, the Church selling, the Devlin family acquiring, finances arranged by the McAnteer family, with a percentage to the O'Neill family, a finder's fee. Not churches but playgrounds and playing fields, parks and farms, convents and a few shops. Funds to offset legal and other fees. Though it was clear O'Neill would acquire one or two of the better properties.

"Here's another thing," said O'Neill. "When I was growing up…"

A repetition which produced two things: a terrific under-the-table snore from the under-tabled wolfhound, and a small knock and the bold entry of O'Neill's eldest daughter, Elizabeth (royally named), striding in. Blonde, aged eleven, a proper royal accent. Something held behind her back. A mischievous smile. "Daddy, one could hear you scratching upstairs," handing him a small, curved comb, which, until he worked it through his beard, until she bent to pet Boru, until she gained a ticklish Rambo kiss, she did not depart.

A teary O'Neill resumed, as did the under-tabled snores. "Me kids, love them to pieces. And, Jesus, when I was young, the country, a united Ireland. Whether for or against. Och, it was part of the talk, a slice of every topic. Lost, so it is. Swamped we are. Am I right, Archie, lad?"

I dutifully nodded, still mystified at my inclusion at such a rarefied and tactical meeting. But good information to relay back to the Estaters, becoming that thing, an informant, that drove my mother to murder.

"Not an issue, for the election," replied Teresa, raising a shaky hand, missing her Remy Martin. "No votes in it."

"None," agreed Devlin.

"Exactly," said O'Neill. "Let's make it one. I want to be president, yeah, president of all of Ireland. 32 not 26. Or at least make a Jaysus effort. "

My old sense of rivalry was thereby revived, an insecure son against an incomplete nation.

O'Neill continued. "We've lost the sense of our history, our long struggle. Different concerns now, multicultural this multicultural that. Nothing against immigrants, well, most of them, but they've no sense of the country, not in their blood, is it?"

Everyone agreed, said they agreed. Everyone took a minute.

Better to hear another tiny-knuckled knock on the door. The appearance of the younger daughter, Anne, also blonde, aged seven, carrying a tin case of Mountaineer Beard balm. "Three times a day," she said, wagging a finger at her father, unwilling to leave before the completion of its second application of the day.

"Now, Anne, tell your Aunt Mary that that's enough. OK? No more interruptions." Said over a thin flow of tears.

The departing girl shrugged, well acquainted with the incorrigibility of both her father's tears and her Aunt's taunts. Boru traipsed after her. Wagging. His tail inlaid with slivers of ham.

"Now the money. What have we got, Teresa?"

Teresa produced a laptop, at which she typed, cautiously, imperiously, her dissolute hand shaking. "Health, next on the list. Rural and inner city."

"The vans?"

"All arranged."

"Like food trucks," said Devlin, salivating.

Family Vans they were called, The O'Neill Family Vans, freshly painted white and Red Cross red, re-purposed from the Order of Malta, as were some of the volunteer staff, and yes, the same insignia for each, a Red Hand, thankfully not bloody. General family health in the cities, with a generous supply of medicine (or tablets as my father would say), and in the countryside the alleged addition of anti-abortion counseling. To Rambo's credit, the fleet was sustained well after the election.

"Maybe a role there for Aisling?" suggested Bandy.

"I'd stay away from Health," said Devlin, who, having heroically resisted, now converged down onto the pile of Tayto. Scarfing a bag a minute, the glutton.

"Back to the money," said Teresa. "Target the female vote. Lagging hugely there. Schools and pre-schools first."

"Rural and inner," said O'Neill, rubbing his freshly balmed beard.

"And after-school initiatives."

"Poor feckers," sympathized O'Neill.

"School lunch supplement. Organic and all that."

"Poor feckers," sympathized O'Neill.

"Sports programs."

"Rural and inner," said O'Neill. "Make sure G.A.A. is the top."

"And yoga."

"Poor feckers," he sympathized.

And so went the list. The Toll Queen sat back, exultant in his own largess. The one time I really did envy him.

"Thanks, Teresa. Really appreciate it." Said sincerely. Tears welling up again. O'Neill downed a packet of Tayto, smoky bacon, to compose himself. "A' course I know why the polls are against me. Nobody will say it to my face. Except maybe Bully Boy Devlin, here. The kidnapping, isn't it. Poor Aisling. Her ... I know. I know. Not one but two, or twice, whatever the saying is. Everyone dying to ask me. Even Archie's mother. God, she's looking great. Wasted in that dump she is. But every TV program, every journalist. Radio. Dying to ask me. Why did you no pay? Haven't a clue, so they haven't. Worse things than money. Got Ash back, didn't I. Taking the wrong tack the lot of them. Should be saying, how in the world did you get her back? From the likes of them. Without … Aye. Ask me that. Thinking I'm a miser, for God's sake. Money. Me bollix." He paused, his eyes teary. "But what can I do, make up for it in their little eyes? Atonement, the Bishop here says. Think a few prayers will get me to the presidency? Change people's little minds? Need something else. Something to shut the lot of them up. Something an O'Neill would do."

Silence.

A few more moments of silence.

The Queen thinking hard. His forehead creased. That outrageous plan forming in his largenosed, longheaded brain.

Then Devlin said loudly, "Let's switch to Ballygall."

"Ballygall," said everyone.

"T.T.B.!" added Teresa. "Tidy Town Ballygall!"

"Father," said O'Neill, shaking Slattery's hand. "You need to leave, but before you go, that Palladius shite. Buried right, no pun intended."

"The Church is considering the matter at great length. Great, great length."

"And O'Shaughnessy, His Holiness, whatever he calls himself?"

Slattery merely nodded.

"Thanks father. I really appreciate it." Also said sincerely. Tearily. "Please don't look in on Aisling, napping now."

With splintered, abraded fingernails, Slattery blessed everyone and departed.

"Now Ballygall," said O'Neill. "The town I loved so well, right, Archie, lad."

I dutifully nodded, taking a pack of Tayto before Devlin finished them all.

"God, those Jaysus murals," said Devlin, laughing, crisps all over him.

"Gas," said Teresa. "Skillful actually. A good hand, whoever."

"Scumbags," said the Queen, not amused. "And don't remind Ash, not even in jest." Glaring at Devlin. "But, aye, could work out nicely. Get rid of a few them. And the rest? Businesses, I mean. All lease holds, yeah?"

Devlin nodded his big, bully head. "Yes, except that Braid & Barber, African shop, and of course, Finn here. Proper property owner, isn't he?"

Which animated Teresa. "Though we won't mention the jumbo mortgage, Finn. We won't mention it at all. Or the debts. Or the sheer, unadulterated lack of payments."

"OK, leave the lad alone. Let's proceed with it, Devlin. Per discussions. And that Men's Shed thing? Can't believe me brother is into that malarkey."

"All under way."

"What is under way?" I asked.

"Told you," said O'Neill, "quiet."

"The murals?" ventured Bandy. "Could get plenty more play out of it. National heritage, attacked by, well, by those that don't understand our history, our past."

"Och, let's go easy," said The Queen.

"Light touch," agreed Devlin.

"Out of the spotlight," agreed Teresa. "Given what's coming."

What was coming?

"Fair enough," said Bandy.

"Aye," said O'Neill, "but we'll not let it go unanswered. Spent a fortune fixing it. Get a bit of craic out of them yet. Sure, isn't August 14th coming up, yeah."

A date seemingly pivotal to the myth of his great, great etc. (alleged) grandfather.

"Here, Archie, what would be a good reprisal? The feckin' Estate. Hit them where they hurt. Reprisal then bit of a parley."

That was the reason for my invite. To snitch, to inform.

"Didn't you go out with one of them?" said Devlin.

Did I growl? I think I actually did.

"Ah, you're a hard man, Archie," said O'Neill, laughing. Tearing up again. About to wax lyrical about August 14th or something as obscure when there thankfully came another tiny-knuckled knock on the door, which preceded the entrance of a daughterly delegation, bearing comb and balm and Boru the Wolfhound, singing some sing-a-long song. Provoking not the expected annoyance, but the open arms of O'Neill, who gave way to full tears yet again. Asking us, in that babying voice, "Och, would they no break your heart," as the girls attached themselves to his beard. Playing. Laughing.

Such enviable warmth.

But broken up by an inrushing Mary O'Neill, pretending to be flustered.

"Och, sure all done here, sis," said O'Neill. Standing, shaking our hands, even mine, ushering us all out. "One of you take Archie, Glibb is off gallivanting."

I lied and said I had a lift, my brother, a pharmaceutical van. But I walked all the way home. Peace The traffic quiet. But then past that horrible hospital, round those three roundabouts, the first carefully, the second miserably, the third with a queasy, queasy, queasy stomach.

What had the Queen said? 'A reprisal and a bit of a parley.' I didn't know what a parley was, but I knew what a reprisal was, knew what he was capable of.

I would warn everyone, though they probably knew.

Everyone knew The Queen was mad.

My Mother Gains Non-Murderous Employment

Our Giant's Causeway. A few days later. Late afternoon. Outside, the knick-knack knocking of trowels on Kilkenny brick, the Great Wall now ten or so feet tall, unhelpfully reverberating back the carouse of The Wobbly Shamrock.

I bit hard on my thumb. A bit stressed. A bit bewildered. In need of peace and solitude.

But down in diminuendo my mother descended, once called Benandonner, my father's giant adversary, but now transformed into a young woman, growing younger every day, and singing a song to herself.

Not a rebel song but a pop song, and bearing gifts, a cup of hot tea and a plate of boxty. Dressed like a waitress, white blouse and black skirt, her prayer-pocked knees healed. Her hair lightly highlighted, her neck now remembered by the sun.

Happily, I took her gifts.

But unhappily she stayed, sat, a rung below me. Her own cup of tea, and, God, no, our stacking game.

"Och, a wee break," she said, preempting me. "Go on, ate."

Which I did. The Boxty was delicious, crunchy on the outside, fluffy on the inside. The tea wasn't bad either.

She gulped hers before setting up our stacking game on the step between us. A sort of medieval *Jenga*. A wooden figurine, a Celtic warrior, the height of a pen, with two huge, raised hands on which wooden helmets, swords, spears, knives, and the like could be balanced. She began with a flat, easily balanced shield, unusually conciliatory for her.

On it I stacked a pointy helmet, positioned in a non-conciliatory direction, her presence, her solicitude unsettling me.

Unsettling her too.

A sly glance at her. Could I see the murder in her? The mass murder. No, not this younger woman. Bright, melodious. But yes, her other self, those forty layers, her boots, her long, tangled hair, her voice cracked and irritated. Yes, that one I could see, murdering.

She gulped more tea. Looked up at me. Her pale blue eyes meeting my pale blue eyes. Hers widening, warming. "Och, the tower house. What did you think? Insisted, I did, you're included. Lavish. Cracker, no doubt."

"Absolutely cracker," I said, summarily. But she persisted. Demanding the exact location. And its height. Its dimensions. Its thickness. The number of windows. The number of levels. And och surely, a gleaming kitchen, a golden library, bathrooms to beat the band. Surely, a whole room for a whole wolfhound.

My poor, envious mother, imprisoned for so long in our half-a-home, atop a bankrupt business.

So, I lied. I agreed with her. Luxury and art, not cold rooms and unpacked boxes, a ground floor bare and abandoned. An early lesson. When her eyes are glowing, when her cheeks are showing, give away, boys, give away, and she'll soon blow over.

My mother swooned down into her tea, consoling herself, gulping, even slurping!

Below her, in the shop, the exasperated growls of Janowski, confirming again our lack of inventory. Our cash flow was not flowing.

My mother caressed her hand round her neck, its bareness obviously still a novelty. "Och, be careful of O'Neill, like I said. Not the ethics of his brother. His businesses abroad for one. And now his plaything of Ballygall. Benefit us all so it will, but at what price? Ha, good price hopefully."

A laugh which she quickly suppressed, taking her turn at the stacking game. Avoiding my stacked helmet, adding a flat shield to the other hand of the Celtic figurine.

"Och though, the main thing, be careful of Ballygall. This wee slip of a town. Exciting now, all that brouhaha, all the businesses closing, that God-awful Wok, thank God. Heard even the Men's Shed, closing, might be. And. Those shocking murals, disgraceful, mark my words. O'Neill's a vindictive man."

Said my vindictive mother.

"Won't take kindly, messing with his town, his toys. Didn't Mrs. Ward see him go loopy. Sledgehammering at one of those new JCBs. Bran' new, it was. Cursing a blue streak in the church itself he was."

Ward? A new friend of hers?

"Reprisals. There will be reprisals. The O'Neills, not ones to let things go."

Which was true. Even the little I already saw.

"What's a parley?" I asked.

Such a quick answer. "Negotiation." She paused then continued. "It'll all die down. O'Neill will get his election. The town, the Wall, a grand pawn in it. Go back to its own quiet miserable self, this place, it will. And all that talk of tourists, the holy pound, the Wall and graveyard, not a bit of it. That TIS nonsense. New businesses, same ones that were there before, maybe a few more Toff-nosed."

I stacked a flat shield atop her flat shield, slowing, stabilizing the game. Despite myself, I was enjoying her wee rant. Her voice rising, but not dry, cracked, lacking its usual hoarseness.

"And those sleeveens, Teresa and Devlin, back on the prowl again. Teresa in the bank now. Although that nice note about our loan."

Which *was* nice.

"An' that 'Tidy Town' lunatic. Teresa. Be worried if I was poor Chioma. On the chopping block, I'd say. Those businesses. Foreign. Of course, they hate the Wall. Och, can't blame them, though just a bit of a walk really. But, mark my words, it'll all die down. Back to boring ol' Ballygall."

Though her lively, blue eyes seemed to suggest otherwise.

"And then, where will you be, Finn?"

'Finn?'

"Made your start in Boston. Lose all that. For this wee awful town."

Sincerely said. But was she talking to me or to herself? Wee and awful for who?

She stacked a broad, easily stackable sword, which I answered in kind. She then dunked her boxty into her cup, producing in it a slurry of tea-borne crumbs. Such a nice smell. The tea blooming the crispy, biscuity smell of the boxty.

A pause between us.

"Life awfully short."

Why the sudden solicitude? And on our Causeway? Perhaps the preamble to the disclosure of her poisonous, murderous past? Her poisonous affair? Or was she actually being nice, maternal even?

"Now, fair play to you on the bank thing. We'll be grand, nauuw. The court action canceled."

Which was a real relief.

"Really appreciate it."

Said sincerely. Just like The Toll Queen. 'Really appreciate it.' Delicately adding a dagger to the stack.

"Arrears, can negotiate, nay problem. Probably forgive. But I can take it on from here, son."

Take it on? My mother? The finances?

Curiouser and curiouser.

"Get it off our backs."

Was she trying to get rid of me? Using her warmth and charm? Is this how she appeared to that poor, doomed BC professor back then? Beguiled by her. Baby me on her lap?

"Teresa can be a soft touch."

Which I doubted. "Och," I said, teasing her with her own 'Och.' "It'll also give Liam a bit of time. Get his act together. Finish his Jaysus Leaving."

She pointed northwards, a gesture which somehow retrieved the sound of Liam's organ from our church.

I scowled. "He'll then run the shop. But maybe a different business? With the tourists? Tea shop like the old days?"

A shudder. She actually shuddered. Quickly changed the subject. "Meeting Finnegan. Suing that arrogant-patronizing hospital so we are. No need to worry. We'll nay include you. And relax, Finn. I'll not try to clatter him again."

Such a malicious smile.

She had often clattered us as kids. Boxed our ears, said my father. Those memories rose up, raw and painful.

"But not getting away with it," she said. "Though Finnegan thinks our chances, not so great, and the length of time might take. But did say you should stop antagonizing that administrator woman. The fat one."

Ha. My epistolary feud via e-mail with that Doughty Administrator. My father would be proud.

"Och, I didn't tell you." She stood up, smoothed her clothes. She hung her bag over her shoulder, her earphones protruding. Good ear-covering earphones too, Bose. "Got a job, so I did."

"A job?"

With our Downstairs sinking beneath us?

"In town. Restaurant. Tomahawk Steak House. Waitress."

"How?"

Which she bristled at.

"Myself. No help at all. Off my own steam."

I then lurched into all sorts of misstatements. Suggesting I provide more money, or we cut back on expenses, or that she concentrate more on the chemist.

"I'm away off. More boxty there if you want, love. But rest up. Take her handy." Putting on her earphones, wearing new Ray Bans against the dust.

"Our game?" I protested.

"Won't be late."

But she was.

The restaurant, set in tourist-terrible Temple Bar, looked commercially respectable, a purveyor of expensively dried steak and over-buttered, badly salted sides. A middle-aged clientele, slacks and blouses, served by a young wait staff, already familiar with my mother, who bussed not waited. Expertly, I thought. Her clearing was brisk, brusque, even savage, but her setting was poised, precise, finalized with a pause, a review, and always some terminal adjustment, the nudge of a glass, the rebuke of a napkin. Needless but stylish. And that odd, quaint nod before she moved on.

Obviously not her inaugural night at The Tomahawk Steak House of Temple Bar. Perhaps as long as a week. The Boston Poisoner, at your service. Convivial with the staff, even the customers. Glasses of iced coke throughout the night. I sat opposite, at a coffee shop, stooled by the window.

A glass of wine at clean-up, another at close-up. Such a chatterbox!

I waited. Wondering if her Comforter would…but she left, a skip to her step, throwing herself onto the bright, warm streets of Dublin, sauntering up Grafton Street, her bag swinging, nodding to her earphoned music. She pulled her new suede coat to herself, as if she were pulling the whole bright city in with it.

She took a couple of slow laps of Stephen's Green. My mother, the flaneur.

Which was all well and nice, but what about Ballygall, what about *our* business, *our* home?

Och, what about fucking that?

Razor Curran the Alleged Muralist

Days later, on a bright and breezy morning, an irresistible force of Queenly Black and Garda Blue descended from the south upon the conjoined, criminal compound of Razor Curran and his sister, Pennies Kelly. Some of the Blue noticeably armed and rifled. Some of the Black more primitively armed with hurleys and hatchet handles. All led by Garda Michael, similarly encased in SWAT helmet, shield, and shin guards.

An expeditionary force?

No, an eviction force. Approved by the Town Council of Ballygall, now meeting in secret.

I watched from the open back window of our Upstairs, with a cup of tea, freshly made by my brother, the Maestro, who joined me. Both of us standing, leaning against the sofa. The radio off. The TV off. My mother still asleep, Tomahawk-tired. Downstairs was quiet, two hours until opening, though Janowski seemed to be later and later…

We watched.

Liam, in his gunslinger coat and boots, his ponytail freshly formed, looked interested but confused.

I explained.

The murals.

Yes, I was aware that Liam had not been made aware of the murals, an understandable oversight given his Maestro immersion at our church, yes, but come on, he knew. Done in protest against the southern Wall, which the Estate had called exclusionary. Remember? O'Neill eating a baby, and the other one with a nubby nose and a royal arse.

"Ah, remembering now," said Liam, ruminatively revolving my father's wedding ring around his own finger, the prick. "But why come after Curran?"

"Arrested Sawn-Off Akinfenwa for the baby one and Curran for the arse one."

"Ah," said Liam. "Why…didn't the real culprit…ah, because they are criminals. Ah." He whinnied his ponytail in comprehension. "Your girlfriend, the Queen, is after the criminals?"

"Correct. Arrested them both, but only evicting the Curran and Kelly gang. Leaving Akinfenwa alone. He's in the Estate."

"So, that's the jackanory," said Liam. "But here, heard Finnegan is representing both Razor and Sawn-Off."

Finnegan, our fubsy, Provo (IRA) solicitor, but how did Liam know that? And why?

"Finn, have we hired him yet? Not letting those wankers at the hospital get away with it."

"Ma is dealing with it. Let's watch. The Currans and Kellys, going to be some battle. Here, get your first aid kit ready."

"Done with that, told you," said Liam, taking a large, affronted sup of his tea.

"Watch a bit," said Liam, "but have to get to church."

The Black and Blue advanced, spreading their formation across the road, across the path, Black first, then Blue, through gardens, over walls, under trees and brush, their sticks hammering against shields, their boots sonorously crunching. Had they brought their own gravel?

We supped and watched.

The neighbors did likewise, spectating from the safety of their own upper floors.

Our back window provided an ample angle for observation. Beyond our stubby back garden lay the 'borough' of The Townies, two parallel streets, six houses on each, actually no, only five now on the first street, with the demolition of Doherty's. Gallagher, Costello, Duffy and the rest. Detached but modest homes, of various spirited hues, but burdened with an arse view of the back of the town, especially The Wobbly Shamrock, with its crates and kegs, bottles and boxes. The Currans and Kellys, well-known criminals, perched on the far northern section of the nearer street, enjoyed the better and exhortative view of the church and graveyard, which they shamelessly littered.

Beyond the Townie houses, rose ten thick feet of Great Wall, its periphery already cleared of vehicles and machinery, which matched the evacuated emptiness of the two parallel streets.

Everyone knew.

Everyone waited.

Everyone watched.

Precautions had been taken by the Currans-Kellys, blockading their conjoined side-by-side compound with their old Hiace van, piebald colored, encircling it with a selection of motorbikes, bikes, prams and scooters. Ramshackle rather than repulsive. Half-hearted, I thought. Perhaps weakened by the precautionary arrest and detention of Razor Curran himself, an alleged and unlikely muralist.

Strangely, his family hadn't formed a defensive formation, congregating instead around a small, spindly tree, centered in their joint front garden. Talking. Mildly smoking. Gesturing profanely at that approaching force of Black and Blue, but with no great animation. Armed only with long, unwieldy shovels. Their three Bullmastiffs missing. Standing awkwardly. Around the tree. No PLO scarves, or gloves, masks or balaclavas. The Curran twins, play-girlfriends before my American birthright, wore their Aldi uniforms. Even Young Curran, partner-in-crime with poor, murdered Young Akinfenwa, looked indifferent.

Strange. More like a funeral than an eviction. All standing around the tree. Or was it a ploy? A feint?

"No," said Liam, with Hippocratic authority. "Tree, remember, Razor's wife.

I did.

The tree had been planted by Razor to commemorate the tragic passing (lung cancer) of his wife, Sharon, who, during her treatment, had become an ardent gardener. Despite the initial collective negligence, the tree had survived, annually producing small white flowers, convincing Razor of its value, both commemorative and arboreal. Rowdy anniversaries were conducted round it, encircled with photos and keepsakes, and it was gradually embroidered into the sometimes sanguinary rituals of the combined families. It became a place of comfort if not contemplation, especially for the insomniac Razor, a summer armchair often set in the long Savannah grass beneath its shady canopy. So, it was expected that it would accompany the two families on their migration (eviction) south, to the Estate, planted anew in a newly conjoined garden, roots an' all.

But Razor, newly infatuated with his new Polish girlfriend, Margaret, had defied all expectations and abandoned the tree. Even prohibiting its migration, or any sort of grafting. The families objected but understandably did not defy him. Even his sister, Pennies Kelly, did not risk his wrath. She leaned against the tree, smoking, ignoring the harm crunching its way toward them, batons raised.

Surely a ploy by the Currans-Kellys? Surely, others, armed and dangerous, were concealed in the houses?

We leaned in.

The neighbors leaned in.

The Black and Blue charged, led by Garda Michael, barking; I think he was actually barking.

But a minor skirmish, a modest scuffle.

Disappointing.

An almost palpable and collective disappointment. The breeze sighing in from the west. A darkening of clouds. Even intrepid boos from next door, the Estaters congregated outside The Wobbly, Chioma, Kanu, and others, and further north, at the back of the church, the Toffs tutting, Devlin the Developer shaking his fat, bully head in annoyance.

Even Liam seemed disappointed. Hoping for blood and guts.

But no.

A comeuppance denied.

Which illustrated two interrelated things: the astuteness of the Currans and Kellys, and the formidable forces arrayed against them, roused and directed by Queen and country and sanctioned by the Town Council of Ballygall.

The leaderless, treeless Currans-Kellys were frog-marched north, then south to the Estate, retreating under the disconsolate cover of cigarette smoke.

Defeated.

Routed.

But were they gone?

Tentative Townie steps were taken down collective Townie stairs. Doors peeked open, feet cantilevered over doorsteps.

Were they really gone? The criminals. The Curran-Kellys.

Myself and Liam descended to our back door. Opened it. Cantilevered ourselves.

Were they really gone?

That gang of good-for-nothings. Lounging, loitering. Thick-necked and thin-skinned. Like a pride of lions. Noisy, nocturnal, internecine, a law unto themselves. Vicious. But somewhat restrained in this, their domestic habitat. The Curran-Kellys. Only playing with us, their easy, proximate prey. Reminding me of that Woody Allen observation that the lamb may lie down with the lion but the lamb isn't going to get much sleep.

They often kept us awake.

Kept us on edge.

Kept us in fear. Even my father, though he was always on excellent terms, perhaps facilitating their prescriptive needs, their painkilling needs.

But yes, they were gone.

From their doorsteps, people stepped. Breaths were taken, arms unfolded. Thumbs-up to the Black and Blue. Exultant. A dance-around of children. A slew of phones sharing what was just recorded. The notorious gang of Curran and Kelly, banished.

Yes, gone.

But not far. A stone's throw. The Estate.

But the Wall, we realized. They would now be behind The Great Wall, which now encircled the town. Safety at last. Protected by that thick, Kilkenny stone.

But.

The poor Estate.

Which was not lost on Coach Kanu, issuing a formidable 'boo' at the turn south of those frog-marched lions. The Estate would now be unfortunately burdened with two criminal gangs, led by two criminal kingpins, Razor Curran and Sawn-Off Akinfenwa, the Ballygall Two, convicted but framed muralists.

"Someone is waving at you," said Liam.

Garda Michael, our SWAT hero, surrounded by Blue.

"Blow him a kiss," Liam added.

The remaining force of Blue surrounded, then entered the conjoined lair, searching, ransacking, too reckless to be investigatory. Breaking and emptying, obviously expending that superfluous scuffle-free energy.

All satisfyingly loud and violent.

"Go on," shouted Liam. "Knock the shite out of it."

Which they did.

"Some operation that," said Liam. "Bleedin' arrest anyone they want. Drug kingpins, Razor and Sawn-Off, and they have them tagged as graffiti artists. Locked them up. Evicted them. *Some power that*. Wouldn't mind a bit of that. The hospital would be first on the list."

"Who's behind *this*, do ya think?" I asked. "Why the big frame-up?"

"Your Queeny boyfriend, of course. With all the other parasites. That Bandy fucker too." Shaking his ponytail. "Question you should be asking, seeing as you're one of them, is why? What's the big idea?"

"Not one of them at all, I'm not. Only for Ma getting me in. Sure, he calls me 'Archie'. Doesn't even know me name."

"Three names you have now. Anyway, all to do with the Church. Not a fan of Dirty Doherty but agree with him. Knock by the Sea. O'Neill is one of those opportunist Catholics. The Wall. That saint bloke, Palladietis or whatever. Like Jesus in that story. Throwing out the money lenders, the drugs, the gambling, the criminals, the lepers."

"Don't think he threw out the lepers, Maestro."

"Know what I mean. Betcha they do up the church next. Renovate. Organ could do with a good tune-up."

"Don't think so. Was at his Tower House and —"

"Gawd, Ma won't shut up about that. Them tower houses are the business, she says."

"Anyway, obvious it's about money," I said. "Gentrifying the place. Poshing it up. Town close when TIS comes in."

"TIS? I am not aware of TIS?"

"The tunnel. From England. Tunnel the Irish Sea. Anyway, prime real estate."

"Such a Yank, 'prime real estate.'"

"It's all financial. Not religious. McAnteer, Devlin, all big money families. And Bandy in cahoots. But you're right in a way, Church probably gets a share. Do up the organ."

"Would ya look at that mad dog gobshite," said Liam, pointing northward.

Garda Michael, with an axe, swinging into the poor tree. Howling, I could swear he was howling.

The final climactic blows against the Curran-Kelly lair?

No.

Behind him arrived three yellow JCBs, exhausts fuming, shovels lifted, bristling in the now blazing sun. Attended by an infantry of yellow-vested builders, armed with pneumatic drills and sledgehammers.

Which deterred me and Liam and our Townie neighbors not only inward but upward, back to our upper living rooms. Re-stationed by the window. Shocked.

The JCBs encircled the compound. Revved their engines. The smoke blending with the dust, with the sand.

They knocked the compound flat.

It did not take long. A few swipes, a few charges and it was gone. Then they pummeled it. Pebbled it. Turned it into Filler for the Wall.

"Jesus," said the Maestro, marveling at the speed and coordination, reducing two family-sized houses into immediate rubble, the structures pulverized, including the poor tree.

Each JCB was then loaded with the pebbled rubble and bumpily and happily dispersed to the west, south and east sections of the Wall, freshly manned by yellow-hued builders. We followed the western JCB. All of us. Speechless. Mesmerized. Holding our phones out ahead of us, to record but also maybe to separate us, protect us. Followed then overtaken by a force of Blue which established a cordon ahead of us. Barricading themselves needlessly with rolls and rolls of concertina wire.

But we got close to The Western Wall. Really close. It was huge. Sheer. Ten feet. As tall as the JCB, but thicker, formidable, bright in the bright sunshine. It seemed to lean and loom. Its scaffolding, front and back, like black metallic teeth.

The JCB was cheerily welcomed by the builders, some on the scaffolding, some at the base, all clapping when the pebbled rubble was emptied. Quickly mixing it with mortar and transferring it to buckets hoisted up the scaffolds. And then, without much ceremony, the buckets were emptied into the great maw of the Wall, the gap between its inner and outer, already filled with eight feet of Filler.

Bucket after bucket.

Thrown in.

Fed.

A couple of homes only an hour ago. The Wall fed.

"Jesus," said Liam.

Bucket after bucket.

Which the builders, leaning, balancing, troweled flat.

Chioma The Writer stood beside me. Grinding her teeth in shock. Her gold glasses held in her yellow-highlighted hand.

I couldn't think of anything consolatory to say.

The Great Cannibal Wall of Ballygall. The poor town once again shortened, two more of its toes bitten away.

Chioma looked at me, her gold tooth glinting in grimace. "And what rough beast, its hour come at last ... " Shaking her head. Putting her arm around her daughter, Flora. And around her other –

Obiageli Chijindu!

Obee.

O-Bee from Bally-G.

My first love.

Back in Ballygall, the town she left so cruelly.

It's *not true* I didn't recognize her, no matter what she says. Dressed formally, in a black business suit and white blouse, wearing sensible, solicitor shoes. Hat-less. Scarf-less. Her brindle-colored glasses now tempered to a more professional black. Her ears bigger without her big earrings. Her nose bare without its stud. Her hair chemically straightened not braided, its color lightened. Her locket, ugly and bulbous, still around her neck. Heavier, but attractively so. Like a good bread she had risen, from her bony beginnings to a more natural bloom, a flourishing which more naturally accommodated her undoubted effervescence.

A gruff greeting. "Mr. Brendan," she said.

I rose above it, saying how great, how good, how well she, and how well her mother was …

A shrug in response. But then she remembered, offering her commiserations, and instead of the usual indignant glance for that non-invite to that non-funeral, she asked, "Was there no funeral?"

"No," I said. "His last request."

Which drew that skeptical frown of hers. Well-acquainted with my father's self-regard. Shaking her long, straight hair.

Changing the subject, I asked if she could believe the madness in Ballygall.

Such a withering glance, but within it the vestiges of her own shock. Her eyebrows elevated. Her hand reaching for the now-missing nose stud.

I withdrew a little.

"Where's your friend, The Queen," she asked. Which stung. But she added, "Munk," her nickname for me, aka my chipmunk cheeks.

"On his throne somewhere," I replied.

"A bag load of questions for you, yeah," she said ominously, but left, walking carefully on her sensible shoes. Her Mum and sister following. Coach Kanu too, but whispering, "Only Straw, Sls-upp, Sls-upp, only straw."

A straw marriage. English citizenship for her, sterling for whoever the hell he was.

The Yellowing

The following article appeared in the Irish Press's midweek sports digest, written by Eamon Houlihan, cousin of that famed journalist, that colossus from Castleisland, Con Houlihan:

The Super Eagles Surrender

The Ballygall Super Eagles, unbeaten in all competitions for five consecutive seasons, have finally surrendered their national record-breaking run. The U-18 champions were defeated 1-0 by their nemesis, Rivermount Girls F.C. of Finglas.

It was a stout performance by Rivermount, aided, it would appear, by the general tumult surrounding the town of Ballygall, which is in the midst of constructing what the locals are apt to call The Great Wall of Ballygall. This is a replica of a medieval town wall. The consequent dust-bowl of dirt and noise seemed to discommode the home team, who were already unsettled by the recent closure and withdrawal of its legendary sponsor, The Wok and Roll, whose famed spring rolls were rumored to be the true source of the Eagles' invincibility.

The first half, begun with a minute's silence for the passing of the Eagles' beloved treasurer, Fionny McCormack, was restricted to defense, each jittery team favoring the long ball, the vertical clearance, the 'give' rather than the 'go.' And were it not for the silky skills of the Super Eagles' maestro, Flora Chijindu, the large crowd might never have been enticed away from the beguiling rise of The Great Wall.

Both teams also struggled to accommodate themselves to the conditions of the pitch, which had been vandalized overnight with a veneer of yellow paint. Splotches of it splashed all over each goal area. A terrible slander on what would prove to be a momentous game.

It was to be settled by a lone goal. Not surprisingly a break-away by Rivermount, via their less-yellowed left wing, with a quick cross to Rivermount's center forward, Denise Rogers. Her shot, a low, hard, daisy-cutter, found cover in the yellowed pitch, blinding Ballygall's keeper, Brenda Thorp, who, like the unfortunate Icarus, knelt too close to that sun-colored grass. For a crucial, unfortunate moment, she lost the sight of the ball.

Ballygall were suddenly behind.

On a normal day this would be an accessible deficit for the mighty Ballygall, but whether it was the noise and dirt, or the loss of its treasurer, or the withdrawal of its sponsor, or the disfigurement of its pitch, it did not prove to be a normal Ballygall day.

The Eagles succumbed.

The Record Breakers were broken.

The tears and recriminations flowed.

****

A shameful day.

The pitch nocturnally and vindictively yellowed by O'Neill, a mural at each goal, though their images were indecipherable.

His revenge for the two murals of Ballygall.

The fucker.

But there was worse to come.

The Ascension of Ballygall

One peculiar effect of the turmoil came to be known as The Ascension, which prompted, where feasible, the collective domestic ascent from ground to upper floors. Sitting rooms were elevated to bedrooms. TVs, lamps, carpets, coffee tables, ornaments, all lifted, Sherpa-like, on backs that could only shrug in explanation. Even armchairs were lifted. Even a sofa or two. Kitchens, too: cutlery, plates, bowls, and of course kettles and toasters and microwaves.

Our own family was not immune. Liam had migrated to our attic, taking a box of Monster Munch with him.

Was it the dust, the noise, the debris that caused this Ascension? Or the inundation of the local fauna — badgers and foxes — or the unsettled peregrinations of rats and mice? All travelling two by two. Securing a berth on the Ark of Ballygall?

Or was it safety? The fear of eviction? Homes so easily pummeled, pebbled.

Liam's response was typical: "What are ya supposed to do when a mad Queen is building sixteen feet of Wall around ya?"

Doctor Lathey, Attacked

A couple of evenings later, my mother the murderer convened a financial summit: just me, herself and Conor her Comforter — but not Liam who was a few doors down tormenting that poor church organ.

I sat at our teak table, in my dad's place, waiting for her to finish the first of her Purges.

Her bedroom. First.

Which was a mess, as if the narrow room had recently returned from turbulent flight. Its door flung wide, its wardrobe winged and tilting, its chest of drawers askew, its bed overrun with clothes, shoes, hats, a storm of books, and declining from the ceiling fan, like oxygen masks, my father's collection of ties.

He wore ties?

And in its midst, my rejuvenated mother, stewarding the room to order, to a widowed sense of spaciousness. A pretense at equality, purging both hers and his, but mostly his, ultimately to the bin but only after a compunctious interval in the attic, now occupied by the Maestro.

Conor sat beside me. Checking his phone. No doubt reading about his estranged wife, unseen since the closure of the DIG, but frequently in the news, popularizing the notion of Palladius, the first of two St. Patricks, buried in Ballygall not Scotland. Now vehemently rebutted by Bishop Slattery. Quite the argumentative pair.

Outside, the sound of builders finishing their day's labors, packing and parking. Loudly wading toward The Wobbly.

"I read it, so I did," she said, returning and dropping from a satisfied height our folder of colored bank statements and financial data. The landing split its spine against the kitchen table, spilling everything, especially those letters from my father, his epistolary feud with the Bank of Ballygall. "Read it all. Your father, sure, he was a..."

An accusation she didn't finish. Showing a belated respect, her purge shaming her a little, perhaps.

"Not a penny. Just transfers from one empty account to the other indebted account."

An impressive synopsis.

Which impressed her Comforter.

I mentioned the collateral, the commitment of our Upstairs and Downstairs, the risk, less now with Tidy Teresa at the bank, the cancellation of the court date, but still, payments should be made.

Which she understood and agreed. "Any money at all? Yourself, Finn?"

"I have a check. Five thousand, maybe." A thick, absorbent, italicized check. A boast not an offer.

"Not at all. We'll be grand. With The Queen, plenty of time."

I promptly agreed with her.

The golden, corpulent folder sat in front of her, foolhardy, fat, and expensive.

"Such a lot of money, though. What about a VAT (sales tax) refund?"

That surprised and impressed me. How much did she know? But I demurred. "Done enough of those dodgy returns."

She extricated the returns from the folder, looked, nodded, her own writing now scrawled on the documents. A glance toward the west window. The sun withdrawing.

"Have to economize," I said.

She nodded. Continued nodding as she walked toward the eastern window. She gazed out to sea. "Economizing, well, we know about that, don't we?"

"Have to at least start paying something, bit of the interest," I said.

She sat at the table, facing me. "Och, I know." She poured herself a full glass of wine, before advancing a regret which seemed to have the benefit of a rehearsal. "Pity we didn't settle with that there hospital. But that doctor, such an arrogant-patronizing."

As if the punch thrown but blocked had not been hers.

"Awful shame. A grand wee settlement, and you'd be on your way back."

On my way back? She really was trying to get rid of me. And this show of financial competence.

"Not until the Wall's finished," I said.

"Ay, it will finish. The O'Neills tend to finish. Of course, there's that offer. The Toll Queen."

"What?" I said.

"O'Neill, I'd say. Not personally. From Devlin the Developer. Has offered to buy us out. Well above what it's worth, so he said. Well above."

"Didn't know that," I said. So, that was it. A firm offer for Upstairs and Downstairs.

"What do you think, son?"

Son?

Leaning back, her hands on her tanned neck, supporting the shortness of her shortened hair. Direct and sincere. Allowing me my thoughts. Which did not run, did not compute. Sell? Why would we sell our home and business, the only thing left from my father? Wasn't she purging everything else?

"Ay, it's a lot to think about, Finn. This town, it gets its claws in. But would have to be soon, I think." Tidying our corpulent financial folder. "Could have a figure for us easily."

"Family, though," I replied, looking at the folder not her. "Isn't it. For generations." Jesus. O'Neill, Devlin, McAnteer, they must be buying the whole town. Something to do with TIS, the tunnel.

"Ballygall, not what it used to be, Finn. Dangerous. Divided. Those demolitions. Vandalizing that pitch for God's sake." Standing. Smiling her new persuasive, patient smile. Taking the folder. Returning it to the bedroom, renewing her purges, removing those matrimonial years from her bedroom.

But.

Downstairs, a knock on our front and commercial door. The bell jangling at the knocker's entry. Liam?

It was Garda Michael.

Up he came, preceded by his rust-brown mustache, an overgrown brambly thing, interwoven with leftovers, matched in girth by his thick eyebrows. His usual half-a-uniform (jumper instead of jacket) emerging into our half-a-home. A friendly greeting, his hat withdrawn, his breath slowly catching him up. Pointing quickly to his holster, empty, unarmed, trying to set our minds at ease.

Standing. Sniffing. His nose wet.

Startled by my mother, who, exiting the bedroom, a swag of clothes over her shoulder, also startled.

My poor mother. That look of terror. Caught at last. Her murderous patriotism.

Garda Michael, at our unsolicited service.

We sat at the table, our three facing his one.

My mother quickly asked, but Garda Michael, perhaps guided by his Garda manual, insisted on small talk, accompanied by a little snack of biscuits — Hob Nobs are grand. Sleepily, he lamented the lack of a summer, the lack of a breeze, the lack of a break in the ring-a-round construction. Not to mention, which he did, the loss of that unbeaten Super Eagles run, a shame, and a scumbag who did The Yellowing. Which of course reminded him of his late brother, Brian, a detective, who mastered much worse cases before his tragic death many years ago. Murdered.

Ah yes, his idealized brother, preserved in perfection by his untimely death. And his poor posthumous children, often brought to Ballygall to partake in the spoils of their uncle, daily sustenance from the pubs and restaurants. Garda Michael was indulged by everyone, like your friendly neighborhood Labrador, fed and petted, grown chubby, tame and sleepy.

Until he was given a Heckler and Koch, which seemed to roughen him.

"What do we owe the pleasure?" said my mother, cutting him off. "And you having to come so far."

A joke, since his station, or kiosk, lay just across the street, beside O'Donohue's. My mother was obviously nervous.

"Just a quick natter with Finn here," he said.

My mother exhaled beside me. Already exonerated.

"A word in his ear," he added, pointing a big thumb toward me, though his late brother's thumb was bigger. Bright blue eyes, though his brother's were bluer. And so on, everything bettered by his late brother.

"Your dad was gameball," he said, still obviously indignant at that non-invite to that non-funeral. "Covered for me those times."

By which he meant those weeks after his brother's murder, when my father had aided and abetted his understandable torpor, even, rumor had it, impersonating Garda Michael with the wearing of his actual uniform. A tight fit. Patrolling the mean streets of Ballygall. I believed it. A reliable example of the theatrical altruism peculiar to my father.

"A saint," he added, before divulging the shocking news in his brilliant Northside accent. "That doctor, you kno', from the hospital up the road. St. Patrick's. Treated your dad, or didn't, heard abo' that. Awful. Not official this, righ'. I'm not here officially." He gestured to his empty holster, and less persuasively to his jumper. "Unofficial capacity, righ'."

We understood, righ'.

"Well, there was an assault. Bollix knocked right out of him. Still in hospital, righ'. Blunt object. No interview with him yet. What was … Dr. Latte, I think."

"Dr. Lathey," said my mother, correcting him. "He was attacked?"

"Yeah, he was."

"Where?"

"In the car park. Only got just wind of it meself."

My mother snorted. "Probably some poor soul, car clamped."

"Not sure about that. But a' course they're going to go through his recent cases, kno' wha' I mean." Garda Michael forced a smile, his large teeth parted down the middle, a sizable gap, which over the coming weeks would widen, would sharpen.

"Och, treated private, I'm sure," said my mother. "No corridor for him."

"Not sure. But thought, give Finn here a heads up. Least I could Jaysus do. Be questions an' all that. The eldest, you kno' wha' I mean."

My mother retrieved her mobile from her skirt pocket. Texted solicitor Finnegan.

Conor stood, actually stood, to our defense. "Nothing at all to do with us, Inspector."

Us? Conor the Comforter was part of *us* now?

"Not an inspector," said Garda Michael, delighted.

"Good enough for that arrogant-patronizing so and so, so it is," said my mother, gleefully.

"Grief," explained Conor, patting my mother on the shoulder.

"Appreciate it, Garda Michael," I said, also standing. "Didn't know. Taking the time to come over. Unofficially. Fair play."

Garda Michael nodded. Sniffed. But didn't stand. His nose wet again.

So I rounded him up some more Hob Nobs.

Of course, he refused, but only once and not the usual twice. Down he hungrily went, adding a crinkle of crisps to his departure.

"Did you do it?" my mother asked, still sitting at the table. Was there a glance of expectation, a glimpse of maternal pride? Or was it mischievous, the exultation of her own vengeance? "Wait," she cautioned. A precautionary swirl of our Upstairs, checking for the paraphernalia of surveillance. Satisfied, she sat before me, a certain relish in her repetition of that question. But was it my answer she relished, or the question reciprocated to her? I was tempted to lie, to be that kind of vengeful, impulsive son. But a lie would foment all sorts of other lies. So, I answered and asked. "No. Did you?"

"Ha," she said, standing. "If it were me, he'd be dead so he would."

Which I believed.

Which she repeated. "Dead so he would."

The exact words Liam used later that evening, with a supplementary expletive. A quiet, soggy dinner, the happy family four of us.

I asked my brother directly. "Was it you, Liam?"

"Ha," he said, spewing spuds and onions. "If it were me, he'd be fucking dead so he would."

A youthful guffaw from my mother. Unrestrained, unchecked. Full of pride, I thought. Conor adding a comforting laugh.

"All funny," I said. "Except me. They'll be after me. The eldest. Garda Michael wanted to talk to *me*."

Liam waved such concerns away. "Sure, you're a Yank now. Like de Valera. Won't execute ya." Still wearing my father's wedding ring, no matter what I said to him.

"You'll be grand in America," added my mother, standing, refreshing everyone's wine, her Comforter's first.

Jesus, such a mindless comment. From my mother of all people. Who fled America. Who hid out in our poxy, parenthetical town. Upstairs.

"Simple," said my mother, mindful of her mirth. "That man wronged others."

"Simple," said Liam. "That man wronged others."

"Someone rightly took justice into their own hands," said my mother.

"Into their own hands," echoed Liam. "Rightly."

"A good right is as good as a bad wrong," said my mother.

Which didn't make any sense.

"As good, if not better," said Liam.

A pantomime, but was there some underlying collusion? Conor? But he wouldn't return my gaze. Liam, in singsong now. My mother, so youthful and happy.

The three of them, all so bleedin' happy family.

My Father, in Flashback

Just one. A quick flashback to him, himself.

In the final furlongs of Trinity, I had announced to my father my surely not unexpected decision to emigrate to America.

A late summer evening. His favorite time. Post dinner, a night of graveyard troweling with the Gravelicker ahead of him.

A propitious moment.

Lying lengthways on our Causeway, his dirty monkey boots protruding through the banisters. Wearing a white granddad shirt and dirty digging jeans — my father the gentleman archaeologist, the Indiana Jones of Ballygall, fattened from the summer.

His long black hair lounged on his shoulders, curling upward. Tanned. His blunt nose sunburnt. His face cobbled in stubble. His dark brown eyes bent into a habitual book. More of a pamphlet really. *The Two Patricks, a lecture on the history of Christianity in fifth-century Ireland,* by T.F. O'Rahilly. Which I had read, once, agreeing with its premise of two St. Patricks, Palladius being the first and more deserving.

Humming to himself. Always at hum.

Annoyed at the interruption, but then he was happy to see it was me not her. Ring-rattling his big bunch of keys. His deep, brown eyes twinkling. "Sls-upp, Sls-upp," he said, laughing, which made me laugh. He meant it so warmly. "Och, what about cha'?" he said, mocking her accent.

Immediately, the retaliatory stamp of her foot above.

I took his offer of a Krowki.

"Can't let you, tonight," he said, referring to The DIG, the graveyard, though I had stopped asking to go years ago.

"Not that, Da. Have something to tell you." Loud enough for my mother to hear — our family announcements, giant or otherwise, were always made on the Causeway.

"Jesus, you've got her pregnant."

She being Obee, my first love. But we had broken up by then, Obee preferring the gambling charms of Ola Waclawski's son, Aleksy.

"No," I said loudly and quickly before my mother came running down in flames. "I am going to America. For good. Have a job." Which was not true. "Recruitment fair at college. Harvard University. I'm emigrating to Boston." Which made the job sound true.

"Boston?" yelled my mother from on-high.

My father stood up. A slight wobble. Tears already standing in his eyes. His chin trembling. Grabbing me. A big, wounded hug. Which confused me. I had expected toasts and teasing. An impromptu wake at The Wobbly. The whole town invited.

My mother stamped down the stairs. Joined in. A family hug! Which really confused me. But nice. Together for that brief moment. Embraced. Just the three of us. And then we separated, my father for America, my mother against America, and especially Boston.

Which now made more sense. My father's grieving, envious tears. My mother's understandable fears; her eldest son returning to the city of her crime. My not unexpected decision unexpectedly dividing our already divided family.

But I will always remember his quick standing tears, that wobbly hug. Which he held for a few lovely seconds.

The Charge of a Yellow JCB

I was standing outside of the town, in the no-man's land between the Estate and the Wall, waiting for Dirty Doherty, my uncle-in-error, a rendezvous, urgent, the Battle of Ballygall upon us. "Punctual. Don't be late. Ten o'clock."

But a Yellow JCB.

Stolen, diverted, roaring diagonally from the barricades of the Estate to the southern rise of the Great Wall.

Dust and dusk.

Its front shovel lifted, brandished, glinting beneath its blaze of bouncing white lights. Its mirrors detached. Its glass removed. Its exhaust at full fume. Its rear shovel raised — a scorpion's sting, sparkling.

Two drivers, but really a whole militia, hanging on, protruding east and west, yelling. Bouncing past me. Their arms left, their arms right, waving. Like outstretched wings, flapping the JCB toward the center of that twelve-foot Wall. Not a JCB but a ship, a galley of oarsmen, at ramming speed. Maybe an actual shout of, "Ramming speed!" Obee? But flags not oars in their hands. Tricolors. Speed-whipped. Their faces hidden behind the scarves and hats of The Super Eagles. And tiger masks for the two drivers. Those plastic party kind, elasticated with string.

Now feet from the exterior wall.

From its barbed wire perimeter. Its scaffolds.

The many arms gave one last flap before jumping east and west — a unified shout of "Super Eagles" — running past me, back to the Estate. Definitely Obee.

The two tiger-masked drivers remained. Bent aerodynamically to their task. A bulging moon above them.

Who were they?

A scream of engine.

Which prompted the flight of the co-driver, who flung himself awkwardly west, his arms akimbo, his fingers spread and braced, wearing, Jesus, fingerless gloves. Dirty Doherty. Who landed heavily. Who staggered backwards. The JCB roaring on. Doherty stopping beside me. Tiger-masked, without his tinted glasses, laughing, saying, "Sls-upp, Sls-upp." Standing beside me. The crowd behind us cheering, calling him back. "Start walking, Finn, lad, keep you safe," he said. And backward we walked, watching.

"What the hell, Doherty," I said.

The JCB roared on through the barbed wire, through the scaffolds, shredding them like wrapping paper — a gift that released the remaining tiger driver, who jumped, who hit the ground running, back toward us, his arm raised in defiance, clad in green and striped with gold.

Coach Kanu.

The JCB slammed shovel-first into the outer wall, into the Filler, into the interior wall — a collision stupendous enough to create its own weather. Thunder. Staffordshire steel against Kilkenny stone. Lightning. Hail. A hail of splinters - bright, incandescent.

The JCB did not stop. It barged through the Wall and staggered up the Dublin road. Its front shovel crushed, bent sideways. Black smoke pluming. Bouncing along. Glass everywhere. Its shovel driving sparks from the ground.

Finally stopping.

In the middle of Ballygall.

Dust and Debris.

Sirens. Shouts. Cheers.

Laughter.

The laughter that launched The Battle for Ballygall.

The Purge of Ballygall

Ballygall became a battleground. It drew more Black and Blue, more yellow, more wire, more scaffolds, and in the middle of the street, opposite the B&B, that nose-broke, battered JCB. No longer a harbinger of resistance but of royal revenge and retaliation. The bellicose Queen. Who would he accuse? Roughen. Pummel. Pebble.

Ballygall was afraid.

Anxious, contrite, their lower floors already abandoned, the good burghers of Ballygall (excluding the Toffs, of course) chose to purge.

The Great Purge of Ballygall.

Huge piles left on the street. TVs, computers, and printers; occlusive structures within which were hidden the many articles of vice; the usual drugs, alcohol, cigarettes, gambling, and porn, but also hatchets, knives and worse. It prompted an inundation of treasure seekers, which was to foreshadow other inundations.

A personal cleanse also. Fiber, purgatives, castor oil, followed with the comfort of crisps-chocolate-coke — good business for our chemist. Plus ablutions. The regime of daily showers. Sometimes twice daily. An epidemic of handwashing (The Pontius Pilate Syndrome), a hurried quest for purity. For redemption. For retention in the holy town of Ballygall.

All of which interrupted the famed seaside sleep of Ballygall. Sedatives and caffeine became its twin pillars, the former useless, the latter merried with Irish Cream. But still the noise, the dirt, and the dust rankled beds and pillows, producing poor sleep and gritty nightmares.

Of course, The Wall itself worsened these ailments. Its forbidding height, its width, the thickness of its morning shadow. Dawn just a little later, sunset just a little sooner. The once breezy air stagnant and stultifying. The strange inundation of wildlife: mice and rats, of course, but also rabbits and badgers, as well as the usual enterprise of foxes. And one evening, a doe and fawn — which briefly terrified everyone.

No snakes, thank God, or was it Palladius the first St. Patrick we should thank?

The Ark of Ballygall, declaimed His Holiness.

All of which further disturbed our sleep.

Ballygall had taken a turn for the religious. Everyone, except the Toffs. A sudden ubiquity of rosary beads, crosses and crucifixes. Mass thrice weekly. Confession daily, the air musky with incense and rendered sin. People crossing themselves like it was going out of style. The Angelus gone viral. There were brief shortages of holy water, which incited absolute panic. People also became reticent, fearing the resonance and amplification of the Wall. Whispering became de rigueur. Many believed Doherty and his religious hypothesis, that Ballygall was transforming itself into a place of pilgrimage, a new Knock by the Sea.

Ballygall had found religion.

Again.

Born-Again Ballygall.

It did not surprise anyone when the Men's Shed was closed, padlocked, a security force of Black if not Blue.

We nevertheless assembled. Garda Michael before us. His Heckler and Koch aiming. His fangs bared, savage-looking.

The Ballygall Lock-Out.

There, under that blood-red sky, I suffered my First Temptation. To leave Ballygall, to leave what I had left before. For Boston. Good ol' Boston. Which lacked a monstrous Wall, a penitential billionaire, a town sacked and sieged, and, of course, a murderous mother. Just pack up and leave. Who would miss me? Sls-upp, Sls-upp and I'm gone.

But, Obee, Obee from Bally-G stood up to Garda Michael. "On what legal basis, Garda Michael, are you locking The Shed out?" But over-shouted by shouts: "You're only a prick, Michael. A pawn. A Jaysus tampon for that Queen of yours."

And then someone shouted, "Your brother would be ashamed."

Garda Michael crouched, aimed.

We withdrew a little, retreating awkwardly on the new cobblestones.

He advanced after us. With reinforcements of Black and then Blue.

We dispersed, ran.

Obee taking me with her to the B&B, tea and biscuits, which strengthened to Vodka & Lucozade, our usual salve against danger. Which turned a little nostalgic. Our history recounted.

We had become romantic in a sudden, traumatic way. Both sixteen or so, the world at our delusional feet, me bound for my birthright city, Boston, she for hers, Lagos via London, and both appalled by the death of Young 'Sawn-Off' Akinfenwa. Killed in Dublin, fighting for turf, his partner, Young 'Razor' Curran, injured but surviving the gangland shooting. Obee, much younger but precocious, had dallied with Akinfenwa, a minor scandal.

So, she sought me out. In history class. Seeking revenge.

Me?

The thin, cow-licked, chipmunk-cheeked Yank-to-be.

Yes.

Hadn't I less to lose, given my transatlantic future?

Happily, her vigilante vindictiveness dwindled during a cold, wet autumn. We became romantic, both eagerly practicing for our future loves in our future countries. Often in the Ballygall graveyard, the DIG, forbidden to me by my father.

She called me 'Munk,' per my chipmunk cheeks.

I called her Obee, which she liked, her more formal honorific being O-Bee from Bally-G, the culchie, redneck resonance of which she sometimes liked. But Obee was city not country, suave in her leather jeans, her porkpie hat, her PLO scarf, and shoes well-heeled enough to rival Tommy Teddy Boy's. And her nose studded, her ears multiply pierced, her glasses brindle-colored, and her tooth false and golden.

She was fandabbydozy.

I should also mention her locket, a gift from Young Akinfenwa, thought to have contained heroin at one point.

But stellar students, we studied together at the church, unwelcome in our respective homes. Obee's mother, Chioma, tolerated me, a 'harmless' diversion, unlikely to endanger her dream of returning to Lagos via London, already passed intact to Obee. Her father, Emeke, strict and formal in these matters, was not informed. My own mother ignored us, save for her sole and sorely repeated comment, 'And what sort of nationalist would that there she be?' My father wholly approved.

Our town and our bumpkin Wicklow school were not as reticent. Not as acquiescent. Preferring to see something exotic, untoward and insincere in our relationship. Ascribing all sorts of motives to me, Prince Boko. The usual racist ones. Some of it subtle, some of it shouted. But always that look, that query, that suspicious squint. Directed at me but slandering Obee. Unable to see our simple affection for each other. It was nothing new for Obee but nothing she ever missed.

We did our best to ignore them, to rebut the innuendoes, but we did shy away. Preferring the nocturnal privacy of the graveyard. Our favorite night consisted of study at the church (powered by Ritalin borrowed from Downstairs), a Chop Suey at the Wok, and a bit of thievery at Brady's Supermarket before a frolic in the Forbidden Graveyard.

Yes, Obee, like me, liked a bit of thievery. Not for the thing itself. For the fun of it. The lark of it. The relief of it. Usually Brady's, but sometimes *Boots* and The Polski, and especially the Off-license on Fridays. Obee was often the diversion, clumsy with her big elbows and her mother's wrappa (shawl), while I, of angelic and cow-licked innocence, stole. It was fun, pressure-relieving, we were both studious students.

Obee also liked to gamble, her under-tabled bets at our Bookies, Cantrell's at a Canter, regular and regularly rewarding. She had a knack. She had an interest. Which I didn't share. The place too tawdry, too slothfully symbiotic with The Wobbly. That mire of whiskey and wagers. Or maybe I was leery of my own genes, my father, barred from the place 'for his own good', his debts cleared in good part by his wagering buddy, Burke the Butcher.

I also didn't like losing.

But Obee won a lot.

Ah, we had a great, inseparable year.

Until decisions needed to be decided.

Which university and where?

I favored Business in Dublin. Trinity College — my application abetted by one Professor Aedeen O'Reilly. Near but far. Good pubs, good flats, good music, good betting shops. She favored Law in London. A step on her mother's path back to Lagos. And a nice path too, London, cosmopolitan, sophisticated, vibrant, diverse, theatrical. And business, could there be a better city for business? And Dublin, too small, too provincial, too narrow, she said.

Losing the argument, I had speciously invoked my parents, their enmity toward England if not the English. I couldn't go to England.

She did not yield.

I did not yield.

It's only now I see another motive for my intransigence. Not my fear of never leaving London and thereby forfeiting my American dreams, but a sense that Obee might be transatlantically persuadable from Dirty Ol'

Dublin but never London. I think that's right. I wanted to steal her away to Boston. But what was Obee's scheme? Was it really Lagos via London? Or a more far-flung freedom from her family and its B&B? Did it involve me at all?

We broke up.

A shared decision.

Its mutuality compromised a month later by her dalliance with Aleksy Waclawski, son of Ola of The Polski Sklep. He was a noted gambler.

That rankled.

It was he, in his tattoos and studs, who gave her away to England at her farewell party in The Wobbly. The fucking dope.

Obee, but no longer in BallyG.

Teddy Boy Filler

One warm evening, Tommy 'Teddy Boy' Taxi Driver McDermott was arrested by Garda Michael for the destruction and desecration, via a nose-broken JCB, of The Great Wall of Ballygall.

Yes, Tommy.

Erstwhile delivery driver of the Wok and Roll.

A wholly preposterous allegation. Alleging that Tommy would deign to use his black, suede, brothel-creeper shoes on anything as uncouth and uncool as a JCB.

Ridiculous.

And weren't the culprits widely known?

And his motive?

Anguish at the closure of the Wok and Roll, The Town Council asserted. The loss of his delivery business. His loss of income. His consequent and desperate need to sell off part of his priceless vinyl music collection.

Arrested, roughened.

Tommy pleaded guilty, accepting their terms, which provided for his immediate release, conditional on the relinquishment of his house and his prompt relocation to the Estate.

He complied one breezy afternoon.

Dressed to the nines.

A new, black pair of suede brothel-creeper shoes. Sea-blue socks, exposed below black drainpipe trousers. A high-necked, loose-collared, white shirt hidden behind a rosacea-red waistcoat, which might explain his Presley Vegas sunglasses.

His bachelor belongings — records, clothes, and wedding album — were easily accommodated in his blue Ford Cortina, freshly refurbished. One trip was sufficient. The turntable rode in the front seat. A rice cooker, microwave, kettle, and provisions in the boot.

His hair, freshly dyed, stood up stupendously. A tsunami-sized quiff, girded in gel.

His trip was quick. He kept his taxi meter on.

The streets were crowded. Mute with shock. Waving only because Tommy waved. We followed him, as if it were a hearse. Through the northern 'gates' of Ballygall and into the Estate. Taking a back row house, near that Yellowed field.

Once his belongings were unpacked, he paused before the huge crowd at his new front door. He asked for privacy, answering only one question. "Devlin the Developer took the house. Paid me. But they will knock it down. Feed it to the Wall."

It did not take long. A few swipes, a few charges and it was gone. Then they pummeled it. Pebbled it. Turned it into Filler. It had stood behind the Curran/Kelly compound. Its disappearance forging a gap at the north west side of the town. The poor town shortened again, another little toe nipped away.

Teddy Boy raised his fist, his sea-blue drape jacket lifting with it. "Long live The Wok and Roll!" he shouted.

"The Wok and Roll!" we answered, weakly.

He strode inside. Barricaded himself behind two locked doors, and for weeks fed himself, with rice and broccoli, the entire catalogue of his priceless music collection.

Professor Aedeen O'Reilly & Burke the Butcher, Separately

Alone on the Causeway. Just me and my rattle of my keys. The family and the Comforter dining at the Queen's cold Tower house.

I was surprised to see Professor Aedeen O'Reilly. "Hi-Ho," said in greeting, standing at the bottom stair. It's not true I didn't recognize her.

I did.

There just seemed to be parts of her missing. Her muscular arms missing beneath a businessy blouse. Her beautiful, short black hair missing beneath an ugly fedora. Her boots usurped by a pair of black pumps. Her youthful sheen also missing. Her skin dry, her eyes baggy, her jaw tightening around those dry, lumpy Grave-Licking lips. She seemed to be the Wildean portrait of my mother, aging while my mother rejuvenated.

But not completely changed. Under her nails that lovely curve of consecrated clay. Still. Though the DIG has been long suspended.

"Hi-Ho," I replied.

From her briefcase, large and luggage-sized, she produced a thermos. Opened it. "Have a wee dram, Finn. Laphroaig 30. Your father's favorite."

I took a long, sumptuous sup. The molten flow melding me more comfortably to the Causeway.

Aedeen easily matched me. Refusing to sit. Taking another prodigious dram, which seemed to soften her mouth, moisten her eyes. Extending the thermos back to me. Refusing the reciprocal offer of a few Krowki.

"Surprising what our Professor Plod has been concealing all these years." Her name for her husband. A pause. Anticipating a response, but I was still adjusting myself to the Laphroaig. "For one thing. A friendship with your legal acquaintance, Finnegan, that old Provo solicitor."

Finnegan?

"Obvious you don't know. Well, our intrepid and suddenly grown-up Plodness has applied for divorce. Quick one too. Attesting that our marriage has been in abeyance for at least the requisite four years. Myself frolicking in the graveyard of Ballygall, him in the poor, neglected loneliness of Killiney. I am not jesting. Such a tool."

Divorce?

Aedeen and Conor divorcing?

Which meant a complete victory for my mother. The marriage now broken, poisoned, as hers had been.

Aedeen fortified herself with another sup, shortened it seemed by a glance upstairs. Her lip trembling. "Won't let him have a damn penny."

Poor Aedeen. She had lost Palladius, lost my father, lost the DIG, and now had lost her plodding ol' husband. But this was not a conversation I wanted. So I redirected her with questions. The burning questions of Ballygall. "What *is* going on, do you think? What is the town turning into? The closures? The evictions? What is the Filler filled with?"

All of which she waved away. She took another swig, not offering the thermos. She took off her fedora. Her face red and angry. "Church would prefer not to have someone with a bit of basic intellectual competence looking over their shoulders. Finn, I'll tell you something." A cautionary glance backward to the chemist.

This was still proving common, the confiding of confidences confidentially to me.

"It *is* the resting place of Palladius, from Gaul, sent from Rome. The first St. Patrick. I have no doubts. The paper I am writing now – God, should have written it a year ago. Stupidly listened to Professor Plod."

She put her fedora back on. An angry Indiana Jones.

"Our findings, our scholarship, represent a level of certitude that even the Church may struggle to accommodate. But beyond that, there is something even *more* ancient, more profound in that graveyard."

Which conjured for me that one-eyed vision of His Holiness. An ancient bearded figure rising from the grave.

"The early Church were strategic in their choice of ecclesiastical sites, often supplanting pagan sites of worship, displacing but also leveraging the traditional connections of the populace. Palladius would have been no exception. Ballygall may, I would conjecture that it has, have much more archaeological significance than that first colony of Christians. Of course, we have fuck-all leverage now."

Jesus, never heard her curse before.

"Surrendered his body to the Church, didn't we! Another capital idea by His Plodness. Your father strongly, strongly opposed. On this very stairs. Not trustworthy. The Church. None of them. He said. Except His Holiness. Independent scientist, that was what we should — God, I should have listened."

Another aggressive glance up our stairs. Her hand on her luggage-sized briefcase. Was she about to bound up there?

"Gone out," I said, unable to be more specific without being inflammatory. "We could go up? Make a fresh cup of tea?"

This seemed to fluster her. She had to go. Visit His Holiness. Seek his help. Then a visit to Bishop Slattery later in the week. "But here, Finn, a gift for your mother."

For my mother?

From the briefcase, she handed me a small package, gift-wrapped with Valentines' wrapping paper. Smiling. But as quickly frowning, fretting. Maybe regretting. "Now, for your mother, Finn." Said harshly, maternally. "Don't open it. Promise me."

I promised, feigning indifference.

We drank to this. A last, strong drink before she left.

Was that actually her luggage? I wondered. Had she sold the conjugal house in Killiney? Not homeless, but peripatetic?

After a respectable interval, I delicately unraveled the wrapping to reveal a bottle of tablets. Medication. Prescribed to Conor O'Reilly, otherwise known as Professor Plod. Sildenafil citrate, otherwise known as Viagra.

Which was funny.

Half a bottle left.

Which was sort of sad.

But should I give it to my mother? Wrapped and anonymously dropped? Or bin them, protecting my mother and Aedeen from their worst impulses?

I wasn't sure.

But then I thought, well, what would the London-Lagos girl do? What would O-bee of Bally-G do?

She would take one. That's what she would do.

So I did.

I took one of the little blue pills. Chalky, with a hint of blueberry. Threw the rest away later. Made another cup of tea. Had a couple of Krowki.

Waited.

But not long.

But not the segue I wanted.

Burke the Butcher barging in. Loud as ever, "Sls-upp, Sls-upp," he shouted in greeting. Dressed in a green T-shirt, studded with TISNT stickers, and his bloody, butchery apron. With his holster of knives.

"Pay up, pay up," he shouted, his huge chest heaving at Town Crier volume. Pausing to catch his formidable breath. "Pay the fat man," he intoned, always an advocate for his own corpulence. Pausing again to allow a sweep of sweat down his fat-cheeked face. His head shaved bald. His ears floppy and pink. His large nostrils cinching a likeness to the pig's head that hung ceramically over his butcher's shop.

He brought two things: a chair that he drag-scraped from the chemist and a large package covered in brown butcher's paper. He sat himself on the chair, and the package in his lap.

"Sorry, Finn, lad. Calling all me debts in." Wiping away another downpour of sweat. "Bad timing for youse, I know. Your poor aul' Da." Said with such indignance, that non-invite to that non-funeral. "Have to. With what's going on in mad ol' Ballygall. Need the spondoolicks."

"How much was it again?" I asked.

"Five."

"Five thousand."

I couldn't believe it at first. Five thousand. For a few pork chops. A turkey at Christmas. A goose at Easter. Never forgiven, but never dunned either. And no interest added. Burke was generous, especially to the old Ballygall Guard. An old argumentative friend of my father, they had been a reliable opposition for each other.

"Ah, just give me four. Don't tell Sinead."

His wife, who did much of the butchering. As physically tumultuous as her husband, but only half as generous.

I wrote out the check, thick, absorbent, and italicized. Handed it to Burke. Months of scrimping and saving gone.

"Dollars wouldn't it be, ah, don't worry, I'll take the exchange thing difference." This double generosity set him off on a sweaty series of inquiries about Boston, which wound, as we both knew it would, to the question of Irish pubs, and more precisely their ownership. Aren't they owned by the Boston Irish? Aren't they?

So, I answered. The Abbey. Grainne O'Malley's. The Druid. The Phoenix Landing. The Field. All Irish-owned, but I Americanized half in my answer.

"See," he said, leaning forward in his chair, ignoring half my answer. His bleached blue eyes blazing. "Irish-owned. Ours. It's our culture. Like if the Wok and Roll were run by The Bradys, God help us. I'd be as thin as a whistle. But wouldn't be Chinese then would it? Cultural appropriation an' that." He shook his green shirt. "You should be with us. Protect your Da's Wall. The fucking cheek of them, knocking it down. The charge of that JCB. And murals on it before that. No appreciation. No respect."

"Have their reasons," I replied.

"All started with the Wobbly. Emboldened them. An Irish pub should be Irish-owned, Irish-run. Obvious. Even your Da didn't disagree."

Except he had.

"Could understand, ya know, Timbuktu or something, foreign ownership, but not here. Not in our own Jaysus damn country." He stood up. For his country, or maybe to allow his sweat a less mountainous cascade. He bent over, but unable to stretch to an agreeable angle, he hunkered, opening the package with quick, nimble fingers. A bevy of sandwiches. Created in his likeness. Thick pallets of bread. Collops of butter. Planks of meat, thickly marbled. Fat woozy tomatoes. Matchless onions.

"Here, try this one. Irish cheese, Irish tomatoes, Irish beef, and a bit of Irish brown sauce."

"Lovely," I said, after a bite, handing it back to him. "Something crunchy and sweet, isn't there?"

"A sprinkle of sugar on it, like me Ma loved. God, disgusted she was when the Wobbly, bought by that Charming and Cinders crowd."

Except she had died years previous. Cancer of the kidney.

"In our own country, can't even keep our own culture."

Channeling Obee, I retorted, "Except in Ireland, it's not an Irish pub, is it? It's a pub in Ireland. Just a pub. Millions of them. And they also happen to be Irish."

Burke smiled his porcine smile. I had taken the bait. He swallowed the remainder of the beef sandwich whole. "Look, I'm a patriot, not a racist. Everyone is equal and all that malarkey, that's obvious, color of skin and all that bollox, but everyone doesn't need to be in the same place. The same backyard."

I leaned back as he leaned in. Lean away, boys. When the sweat is flowing, when his cheeks are blowing, lean away, boys.

"We're a small country. Tiny. Barely any room. Sure, just got the place back to ourselves, haven't we, after eight hundred years. Well, some of it. Could we enjoy it for a minute before everyone piles in?" He offered me another sandwich. "Need ya to taste, Finn, lad. Get the sandwich shop roaring again. Get ready for the tourists. Business enough for everyone."

His first sandwich shop had been bested and beaten by The Polski Sklep's finer offerings. A bitter loss for the Burkes.

"Irish ham, Irish cucumber, Irish cheese, and tomato, slice of beetroot."

"Crunchy?"

"Few Tayto in there. Good though. That's the thing, Finn, lad. We're not even a country yet. The North. Barely, well, haven't really got back our language, our culture, our sports, our food. Our amazing agriculture and meats. Our religion. The Church is on its arse. Barely got back to ourselves and all this other stuff comes barreling in."

"But isn't that the reward? We're rich enough, stable enough, enough opportunities, attract all this great variety and stuff. Like America, it should be."

He swallowed the ham sandwich. Produced an already open can of Harp from his bloody apron pocket, gulping. "Ah, Finn, we're nowhere near America. We're like a man barely able to walk, brought by force to a stampede. Ballygall, for example. Before the Estate. Great café there was, The Rasher."

"The Rasher was crap. Not a patch on The Wok."

Burke laughed. "'Twas. But good example, Zhengs are a good example. Don't take over whole streets, whole neighborhoods. Shops and barbers. Here in small numbers. Chinese. Don't integrate. Not Irish, never will be Irish. Know that. Accept that."

Bollox. The Zhengs were Irish, and weren't shy about proclaiming themselves so.

"Just like the Africans. Never be Irish. An' refugees me arse. No war or famine just the usual ructions over there. What about eight hundred years of persecution? See how they'd do with that. A hairdressers and a pub. The problem with Africans, different with the Poles and Liths, is it's far. Africa is bleedin' far. It's another bloody world. They'll never go back. Ryanair don't fly to Africa. They're going to stay, Finn lad. Stay and grow."

"Good."

"Ah me bollox, what do you care, you're going back to Boston. Here, try this one."

Chicken curry salad, with apple, raisins, green onions, and a splash of lime juice. Tasty but over-proportioned, the recipe clearly purloined from The Polski.

"Lime juice is the sauce, wha," he said, taking the sandwich back and finishing it whole. "Wife wanted little fishy sandwiches, sardine, salmon, mackerel. More pious, fish on Fridays an' all that, but the smell in the shop was already atrocious." The memory of which he drowned with a long sup of Harp. Wiping his mouth with his bloody arm. Pausing. At last allowing his body time to digest. Looking around. Grimacing. "No Mary Poppins meself, Finn lad, but this place is filthy."

"Me Ma has lost interest."

"Grief, understandable."

"Or relief."

He laughed. Such a big, dirty laugh. His huge chest heaving. "Anyway, can't afford the immigrants. Simple as that. Economy, national debt and what have you. Sponging on welfare. Taken what little jobs we have. OK by the rich. Diversity and all that. Doesn't affect them. Lowers the wages, even better for them. Houses painted and whatnot."

He hunkered down for the last sandwich, a Kielbasa on rye bread, wholly plagiarized from The Polski and coyly not offered up for evaluation.

"An' we get gangsters like Akinfenwa."

"Yeah, but also the good ones, like Chioma, Kanu, Charming and Cinders, Ola. All good eggs as me dad would say."

"Talking like a Yank, Finn, lad. This is not America. Get that Yankee Doodle shite out of your head."

"Bollox. Don't we just have to grow up? Join the world? Be part of it?"

"Have your United Nations hat on now, you do."

"Make the country better. Akinwande the Taxi driver. And Ogunleye the Good-Looking."

Burke lifted the entrails of his sandwich in appreciation. "Beautiful woman, though prefer Gresham meself."

I preferred Ogunleye. Tall but not too tall. Long black hair, braided. Fit but not too fit. Always dressed to the nines.

"And Walsh," continued Burke. "The other night in the Wobbly. Jesus. Wearing these pair of jeans."

"Who? Walsh?"

"Yep. Pair of black heels. And this blouse. Tight as...and up and down to the bar. Even Charming taking a gander."

Ogunleye always wore this black skirt. Not short, not tight, but so sexy. Swaying. Sometimes with ankle-high leather boots.

"But here. Something up with yer Queen. And with the Super Toffs. All stand-offish now. Up to something. Something else. Wankers. Too good for us. After all we did. Guarding the Wall."

Ogunleye was friendly, not flirty-friendly, just friendly. Happy in herself. I loved to see her out running. Sculptured arms, scrumptious arse. Sweating.

"No gratitude. Stab his own mother he would. Ha, his own wife. Two fingers for Jaysus' sake. Two! Are you listening or wha?"

I wasn't.

I had become uncomfortably aware of a certain arousal, compliments of that earlier tablet. Something I preferred not to share with Burke. Something that was presenting with its own unique urgency.

I pretended a glance at my phone, pretending the sudden imminence of an online meeting.

I made my excuses and left him to the last of his sandwich, still grumbling about The Toll Queen.

"Up to something else, that dirty Queen. Mark my words."

A Sell-Out

A family night out.

Instigated, organized and enforced by my happy, youthful mother, perhaps to celebrate her triumph over Aedeen.

But I was happy to get out of Ballygall, anyway, away from our Not-So-Clean-Causeway, happy to swap the usual two buses and a DART train for travel in Conor's plush, comfortable Volvo, a slow, smooth drive to the gastronomic center of Dublin.

Baggot street.

A luxury matched by the restaurant, Daisy's Steak House, Daisy perhaps being the inaugural sacrificial cow, her ceramic and diminutive likeness now nailed above the busy bar, a huge heave of oak and mirror.

But for us a nice corner table, far from the cow-maddened crowd. A well-appointed table with glasses of all dimensions and ranks of knives, forks and spoons, overlaid with ecclesiastically thick napkins. Meself and a well-dressed Liam on the interior, facing the bar and Daisy's winsome face, my mother and a suited Conor on the exterior, and around us spun the quickest, friendliest waitress in the world, Marion from Waterford town.

We eagerly perused the menus.

Erroneously assuming Conor, the divorcé, would foot the bill, meself and Liam ordered magnificently, preferring size and expense over variety. Porterhouses, please. My mother added a plethora of appetizers and side dishes, family style, with a couple of château'd bottles of red wine. Happy. Even standing up in her new sleeveless, sun-yellow dress. "Happy Days." Often said but never sincerely.

"Och, listen now there," she said. "Not a bit of it can ya hear."

Sitting down. Enjoying our puzzlement.

"Builders. Not a one," she said.

Which was true. Just the sound of a happy, hungry restaurant.

"Or that mad one praying down away in the chemist."

Janowski our chemist, ardent devotee of Palladius.

"None of that dust, from the Wall. None of that sand, from that so-called beach."

"Amen," said Liam, double fisted with wine and prawn cocktail.

"None of that reek from The Wobbly. All those shenanigans." A gulp of wine before adding, "And none of that awful, minging Chianti."

By which she meant my father's Chianti, already finished by her and Conor the Dirty Comforter.

"None of those Ballygallers, always dropping in. Better class here. Your crowd, Finn."

By which she meant Americans, overstuffed in beige and brown.

"You can hear yourself think," she said over the noise. "Take a breath on to yourself." Which she did, before exchanging half her chicken liver parfait for half of Conor's calamari.

"Sick of seeing those all shuttered up," said Liam, swishing his ponytail.

By which he meant The Wok, Boots, the Bookies, and the Off license. And now The Shed.

"Don't miss that cold, big church either," added my mother. "That awful fence around the grave, the graveyard. Or His Holiness the skinny-malink."

Which drew a grunting round of agreement.

"And always hated that sea breeze, freezing, even in summer."

"No offence, Finn," said Conor, eager to participate. "But don't miss that Wall. Always think I'm going to forget and drive right into it." Happily demonstrating, ramming his knife into the bread.

"And those dozy birds, crashing," said Liam. Meaning the magpies.

"Don't miss that one, Teresa. What a wagon."

"Don't miss that Devlin the Developer chap," said Conor. "Sell his own mother." Shivering his pillowy shoulders, happy to demonstrate.

"Or that one, Chioma," said my mother. "The Writer. Won't miss her. Always looking down on you from her book."

"Or Kanu," said Liam. "Blathering on and on. Nigeria the Giant of Africa."

"Or Charming and Cinders. Too good to be true those two," said my mother. "Mark my words."

"Or you know who I won't miss," said my mother, nodding to herself, taking a long savor of wine. An anticipatory gurgle. "Won't miss him at all. Full stop. Dirty Doherty."

My poor uncle-in-error.

Which drew everyone's approval. And which drew Conor's hand over my mother's for a brief consoling moment.

"Nutcase," pronounced Liam. "Absolute nutter. Those gloves. Those x-ray specs."

"Won't miss him a bit."

They all sat back. Satisfied. Satiated. The parlor game over. My mother the winner, scathing in victory: "Ballygall," she began. "Everyone pretending it's close to Dublin. It's not close to Dublin. That it's like Dalkey. It's not a bit like Dalkey. Not in your wildest dreams. No matter if you Tidy up here and there. It'll never be Dalkey. Even the idea that it's a town. Not a town. Just a few shacks hanging on to the Dublin road. And what sort of town has only two pubs? Even the Chinese left, May Zheng had more sense, eventually. Won't even talk about the Estate. Not an Estate. Not even named. Not even a proper road into it. And all these groups, Townies and Toffs and all that. Not groups at all. All pretending they like each other. And pretending a big ugly Wall will make a difference. It's not going to make any difference. And from St. Patrick's time? Ridiculous. Wouldn't it just be a few banks of mud then? And that saint, pally-whatever his name is. Another Saint Patrick? There in Ballygall? In that kip that's not even a town? One mongrel Gardai. One crooked politician. Ah, Jesus wept."

The second bottle of wine was uncorked.

The dinner then arrived in John Wayne proportions. Marion the waitress quickly dispensing the dishes, extolling our choices.

"Enjoy yourselves," chirped Marion.

Which drew another "Happy Days!" from my mother, entirely directed at me. "So." Looking directly at me. "Answer to our prayers we have, Finn." Still looking directly at me. "Offer for the chemist, as I said before. But firm now. And Upstairs, of course. The whole thing. Huge offer. Devlin the Developer. Half a million." Which she repeated. "It's a cracker. Half a million, Finn. Happy days."

An offer which Conor fleshed out, pointing out that the generous terms and conditions of a quick sale would clear our mortgage with enough remaining for another well-placed property.

Well-placed far from Ballygall.

"Get us well out of that there circus," said my mother triumphantly, adding broccoli to Conor's plate, accepting his reciprocal transfer of asparagus.

"Live in Dublin, close to Academy," said Liam.

By which he meant the Royal Irish Academy of Music.

"Nothing to worry about, Finn, when you go back to Boston. Few bob in your pocket too. And pay you back, all those debts you've cleared. Of course, we will."

An answer. I think the three of them expected an immediate answer.

So, I resorted down into the expanse of my Porterhouse. Watching Conor pour another full glass for my mother. Such fucking nonsense. Sell the only thing left of the McCormack family, the only thing she hadn't wrecked.

Yet.

"Aye, chew on it," said my mother, buttering bread for Conor, accepting a tumble of potatoes with a laugh. One adding salt, the other taking pepper. My mother removing his tie from the peril of his potatoes. Conor even cutting the fat off her steak.

Such intimacies.

A veritable dance.

But a reciprocal dance, I now saw. My mother no longer pretending, no longer intent on what I had thought was revenge. Sincere. Even swooning. Right in front of her fatherless sons.

"Half a million," she intoned, buttering more Jaysus bread for him.

So tawdry. My father barely cold.

More wine for him from her, and from him to her.

Would they be slurping spaghetti next?

The tramp.

Had she no shame? My father was no angel, but she could show a bit of dignity. A bit of class. Jumping on the first eligible ticket out of Ballygall. Worth half a million. The sale would set them up. A place for *them*. Conor's money now probably lost in his grave-licking divorce, but sell the chemist, that would do it. Set *them* up lovely. Probably a flat for Liam. Love nest for them.

Disgusting.

So stupid I didn't see it, my mother capable of something more than revenge.

"Half a million," she repeated.

"But why is Conor here?" I asked, my anger obvious. "What's it got to do with him?"

Which surprised her. Which softened her voice, extolling Conor's negotiating prowess against the devilish likes of Devlin the Developer. "Fantastic deal, so it is."

Marion the waitress was quickly upon us with offers of additional wine but withdrew, sensing the darkening mood.

"Conor's a grand help," said Liam, his cheeks full of steak, swatting a fly intrigued with his ponytail. He already *knew* about Conor. The dirty affair. Already approved. The wanker.

"Of course he is," said my mother, patting Conor's knife and not his hand for some reason. A hard glance at me. Realizing. She now realized that I knew her tawdry secret.

So I said, "It's *our* family home, why does he have to be involved?"

"Just told you why," she said, pointing her knife.

I put down my fork. Spat out a piece of steak. "Mad selling. Town is finally on the up. Flipping it, which is why they're giving you that price. Next to TIS. Property prices through the roof. The holy stuff's just a Jaysus smokescreen. And it's our family home."

"Lower your voice, Finn," said my mother, her voice rising. "That there town is a pit. Worse with all this Wall and Queen business. Half a million. When would we ever?"

Conor tried to interject, but I ignored him. "Been in the family for generations. Generations. Not for **you** to sell. Or *him*." Not lowering my voice.

"*Catch yourself on*," she shouted.

Startling Conor and Liam.

Briefly drawing Marion, who thought better of an intervention.

I was not intimidated. "*It's a family decision*. And what have you ever done for the place? *Not yours. Never was.*"

She jabbed her fork at me. "And what sort of a shite did you give? Off to America, so you were. Since you were a wee snot. Place falling apart, but och, you didn't care. Off to America, so I am. And no coming back. Drowning in debt we were, but off to Trinity you went, your poor brother left to the chemist. And now you're all high and mighty. Generations of this and that, *me wee arse*."

"And why would I *stay*, do ya think? Miserable you were, half-dead Upstairs. Barely a word half the time. No wonder me dad stayed on the stairs."

"Let me tell you about your father."

But I didn't let her.

I got up. "At least he was a bit of craic. Bit of life to him. You were Upstairs just —"

"Your father was a good-for-nothing waster. Do anything, join anything except his family. Chasing skirt all over the town. Owing money everywhere. In that graveyard half his life. No offense, Conor, with that *dirty bitch*."

Marion the waitress accompanied me out, apologizing for the sour turn of events. Thrusting a mint into my hand. "Feckin' mothers," she whispered.

I walked quickly down Baggot Street, toward Stephens Green, nervous of my mother's pursuit. Eventually down Grafton Street and a quick left into Neary's. Turned my phone off. A couple of quick pints.

Calming myself.

Promising myself.

Over my dead body would she sell.

Her and her Impotent Comforter.

Selling everything to set up their love nest.

Disgusting.

Fucking disgusting.

Save The Shed

The next day or so, and eager to avoid her, him, and him, I finally thought of an excuse to visit the B&B, The Braid & Barber.

A lame excuse.

A crossword puzzle.

The town seemed quiet, its recent tumult tempered by the rain. The super-sized cobblestones slick. That huge cartoonish padlock on the Men's Shed sparkling.

I glanced before entering the B&B. Yep, Obee was in the chair, having her hair straightened by her sister, Flora. "Kanu, a crossword for you," I said, entering, as obvious as the obvious laughter that greeted me.

"Sls-upp, Sls-upp," said Flora, laughingly echoed by Obee, who did not turn from her mirror's image. Again, legally dressed in a black suit and crisp white blouse. A book of legalese in her hand.

Ah, the B&B, such a warm, comfortable place to laze and linger.

Three female chairs on the left, three male on the right.

Obee and a woman called Margaret Akunyili, also attended to by Flora.

Chioma sat in her high-backed reading chair, but a different kind of book in her hand now. A new MacBook, with golden sleeve, holding the beginnings of her book, secretly entitled *Things Fall Apart in Ballygall.* Not looking up at my entrance. Just rolling and cracking her reader's neck. A glance at Margaret.

Kanu, appreciating my embarrassment, offered another haircut in return for the crossword.

"Not the cowlicks, yeah," cautioned Obee, catching my eye, mirror to mirror, her back to my back when I sat in the chair.

My face did flush.

A new round of laughter.

"Even the ears, red," said Kanu.

"And give him Jollof rice," added Obee, sounding like her mother. "Boy only bones. Too skinny."

"From the start," said Chioma, loudly, nodding at Margaret. "Everyone soon here, o."

Margaret was thin, young, a giggler, and a nail-biter. Recently married without pageantry or pomp to Finbarr O'Carroll, a Kerryman. A business arrangement. Money for Finbarr and finally citizenship for Margaret. Arranged by Chioma and Emeke, the pro bono matchmakers. The couple, Straw Couples we called them, would cohabit sporadically in the Estate, at 77 Seaview Court, the Straw House, preparatory to their series of immigration interviews.

"Meet?" barked Chioma.

"Sir, we meet at The Wobbly Shamrock," said Margaret. Dressed nicely, conservatively. A long black skirt, a sleeved black blouse, which served, per her matchmakers, to lighten the complexion.

"Put them on."

Margaret dutifully put on her superfluous glasses. Rounded her shoulders. Slouched. Crouched. Bit at her nail.

"Like an old nun," said Chioma, approvingly. "Meet?"

"Sir, we meet at The Wobbly Shamrock," replied Margaret.

So began the rehearsal for her first post-nuptial citizenship interview. Her, first. Then her straw spouse. Then both. And in between, unpredictable, uncommunicative swathes of time. Followed by many more rounds.

"Where the Jaysus is that?" said Chioma in a convincing Northside accent.

"In town of Ballygall."

"Where the feckin' Jaysus is that?"

"Dun Laoghaire, near," said Margaret, rubbing her tiny wedding ring. Flora stood beside her, pausing the straightening of Margaret's already straightened, shoulder-length black hair. Obee sat beside her, still immersed in her legalese, familiar with such rehearsals. Thumbing through other papers too. Bank statements, I noticed, the Bank of Ballygall.

"Love at first sight, wha'?" chirped Chioma.

"Not very. Finbarr is from Kerry, so not very…wears glasses."

"God love ya, a fucking culchie he is. Even worse. A Kerryman. First date?"

"The Wobbly Shamrock."

"The same bleedin' place?"

"Finbarr is from Kerry. Not very…likes the same thing."

"I'm sure he does. Second date?"

"The Wobbly Shamrock."

"Jesus Christ. Third date?"

Margaret giggled.

"Why the short engagement? Your bleedin' Permission to Stay running out?"

Which it was. Margaret, on arrival in Ireland, had prevailed over the Kafkaesque monotony of its Direct Provision program, which quarantined all applicants from the indigenous populace. Mosney, in Margaret's case, that erstwhile residential theme park much beloved by my father in his modest youth. After a long stay, Margaret had made it through, eking a year's Permission to Stay from the authorities, a year that, mired in the challenges of immigrant life, had passed quickly, unproductively. Her quarantine had ill-prepared her for Irish life.

"Finbarr's family are farmers. Traditional. Want us to live on the farm. Sheep and ponies."

"God love ya. Living in the bog."

This was the main tactic. To arouse the scornful sympathy of the Dublin inspector, a Northsider whose antipathy toward Africans was matched, perhaps surpassed, by his animosity to those beyond the pale of Dublin. Yes, only one inspector. For the whole of Ireland. Who holidayed in Courtown for the month of August. Yes, the whole month.

"They've seen you, righ'? In daylight?" continued Chioma.

"Yes."

"Know where you come from?"

"Yes."

"Suppose they say love is blind. Here, what's his favorite program?"

"Ballykissangel."

"Ah, God love ya. His favorite dinner?"

"Boiled the bacon and cabbage."

"Jaysus. What'd the bogger buy you for your birthday?"

"Box set of Ballykissangel."

"Jesus. Here, ever had an abortion?"

"No."

"Sex life? Heard you're all a bunch of goers. Tribal style and all that."

"Regular."

"And here, what's so bleedin' great about Ireland? Aren't we all a pile of pale eejits?"

"Beautiful country. So green. The Shannon river."

"No," said Kanu, interrupting. "Liffey, always the Liffey, keep it Dublin." Pretending to snip away at my hair.

Chioma consented with a laugh, then an admiring wink, a flash of her gold tooth.

"Beautiful city," continued Margaret. "Dublin. Amazing. The people. The Liffey. And missionaries, so nice. Come to our Akura from Ire- from Dublin."

"Gobshite missionaries," said Chioma, back in character. "Those geebags have a lot to answer for. Where do youse live?"

"Ballygall. 77 Seaview Court."

"Ah, the Straw House," said Kanu. "But no sea view. And very little plumbing. Desperate heating."

"And no sewage, o," said Chioma, wearily.

Kanu began to wax querulous about his stay at number 77, a litany of criticisms that couldn't disguise a fondness, a warmth, recollecting a testy incubation that proved fruitful, loving, genuine. He had been a straw husband, mercenarily married to Bridie, also from Kerry, but they had blossomed together. He wished the same for Margaret, that during her time at number 77, she might come to appreciate her Kerryman, that in the confines of a small, Straw House in a neglected Estate, in a bedroom community too far from Dublin, she would come to observe the growth of a shared affection, sparked in those quotidian exchanges, those daily kindnesses, and that from such forced intimacy something would emerge, fully formed and resilient — love, woven from straw.

"Ah, thanks," said Margaret.

"Eloquent," said Chioma. "The man is eloquent, o. Now again. Time for just one more."

Another iteration.

Another giggle from Margaret. Such admirable insouciance.

"Tea?" asked Flora. "We'll need gobs of it."

"I'll make it, sister," said Obee, rising, stuffing her papers in the back of her skirt. Which drew my mirrored attention, her glance catching mine. But scowling. A tsk tsk from Kanu.

Again, I reddened.

Obee made tea in that small, blunt room.

Ola Waclawski from The Polski Sklep arrived, in her usual patriotic assemblage of red trousers and white blouse. In dilapidated sandals. Her hair scrambled up into a bun. Her hands dirty. Carrying a trove of Polish goodies. With her son, Aleksy, thin, tattooed, pierced and perforated, who joined Obee in the kitchen, both quickly on her phone. Gambling together probably.

Then many of the Townies, and Doherty. Then the Estaters, even Charming and Cinders, never friends of Chioma, came in, all ushered upstairs by Flora.

What was going on?

"Meeting," explained Obee, handing me a cup of tea, but ushering me outside to drink it. "Council of War, really," she added, handing me a Delicje biscuit. "Mum's idea. Rally everyone around the Shed. Save the Shed. Not sure that will work. But she'll try."

"What about me? If my dad —"

"Queen's bum boy, ain't ya."

Margaret passed us on her way out, turning right but then remembering, the Wall, laughing, giggling.

"I can help," I said.

"I'll drop over after this," said Obee. "Won't take long. Promise."

But it did.

I lollygagged on our Not-So-Clean-Causeway, relieved to be alone. My mother off with her Impotent Comforter. Liam at church.

But she kept her promise.

She came, bearing, well, bearing a briefcase. Ruffled, tired, sweating. "Ha, Munk," she shouted, "like your ol' fella, on the stairs. Here." She pulled from the briefcase a naggin of vodka and a small bottle of Lucozade, our very own cocktail, V&L. Papers letterheaded with the Bank of Ballygall fluttered from her briefcase. Which she left. Littering the bottom stairs.

"A couple of glasses?" I asked, so happy to see her.

"Me arse," she said. "Never needed cups have we?" Her prolonged gulp of vodka was followed by a quick swig of Lucozade. Proportions I copied. "Robbed it from Brady's, yeah. Himself was there. Gawking at me cleavage as usual."

Her top button *was* open. Her unadorned, glistening skin…but ah, that heart-shaped locket, from Young Akinfenwa, ugly and bulbous.

She untucked her blouse, took her shoes off, clipped to her ears a giant pair of earrings. "And these."

A few bags of Monster Munch. Obviously stolen from Downstairs.

She paused. Her hands on the hips of her skirt. Her tongue playing with her side gold tooth (left premolar), gilded in honor and mimicry of her mother. Looking at me. Looking at the papers around her. "You're the same Munk, yeah? America hasn't, or that Queen bitch, or those Toffs, haven't?"

"The same," I said, gulping another round of Vodka and Lucozade.

"Sure? This Wall business not gone to your cowlicks, yeah?"

"The same. And you, O-Bee from Bally-G? The same?"

"The same," she said and, perhaps convinced of my trustworthiness, wriggled out of her tights. "Before I forget, text me that Finnegan solicitor's number."

Which I did.

Which seemed strange. Wasn't she more adept than that old Provo?

"Jaysus, I'm bollixed," she said, sitting lengthways on the bottom step, her bare legs, her bare feet cantilevered. Parallel to me. Looking up. "I've a barrel of questions for ya, me ol' Munky." Her voice a strong, sticky mixture of Dublin Northside and Cockney London. Friendly. I had not expected her so friendly. And inquisitive. The questions.

"What the Jaysus is going on?"

"What happened with the Wok and Roll?"

"To the Bookies, yeah?"

"His Holiness, anorexic now, wha'?"

"That shit about Tommy 'Teddy Boy'? And Razor, in the Estate. A mural?"

"And Kanu and Dirty Doherty, in cahoots? That's bloody odd."

"Kan-WHO?" I called out, pleased when she answered in kind, "Kan-U."

But as quickly back to her exasperated questions.

"That Yellowed Field?"

I took another gulp of V then L.

"Bank like Fort Knox, yeah."

All of which prompted her to numerous slugs of V&L, glancing up at me. Like an old couple we were, lying in a bony bed, passing the bottle. "And righ', Charming and Cinders. That perfect, perfect couple. Yoruba. Coming to us, Igbo, for help."

The Igbo tribe were, according to Obee, the Northsiders of Nigeria.

"Fackin' weird. Here, what do you know about The Shed, Munk? Closing it. Tell me. Just cut all the shite."

"What? Nothing. Know nothing about nothing. Just in it for the Wall. Me dad's Wall. O'Neill only tolerates me because of me Ma."

"Must know something, bum boy. You're paying off your Da's bills all over the place?"

"That's me own money. Doing quite well, don't you know." An upward skeptical glance, so I added, "Shit has hit us too. Me Ma's thinking of selling. Offer. From Devlin."

"That Devil."

"It's the gang of them. O'Neill, McAnteer and Devlin. With Slattery the Bishop. Lot of them in on it."

I took the bottles from her.

"That's it, drink up, Munk. Talk. Keep talking."

Which I did. "They don't tell me anything. Obvious, though. Financial. Clearing everyone out. Flip the town. TIS. Tunnel the Irish Sea. Except The Toffs."

"I don't know. All this holy business?"

"Just a ruse."

"A ruse?" She tore open a pungent packet of Monster Munch, threw me mine. Ate them quickly, sucking her fingers before eating another packet. Monster debris everywhere.

"Well, what else could it be, then, Miss Legal Beagle?"

Such a dirty look upward from her.

"Nah, I'm with you, Munk. Money. The root of all wankers. Gated community, Ballygall Gated Community. Paid for by the government. And you, you pawn, blocking off the Estate."

A scolding look upward, admittedly mitigated by a mouth of monster crumbs.

"Anyway. Money. Fight money with money. Which is why I'm here, Munk." She paused to adhere a silver nose stud to the side of her nose. Which seemed to calm her. Lull her. Her eyes drooping for a second. Starting to resemble her old Ballygall self. "Collecting for The Shed. Save the Shed. And know you're doing quite well, don't you know."

"Collecting?"

"Yeah. Campaign. Fundraising. Save the Shed. War chest. Legal, political, all that."

"How much?"

"As much as your dad would give." Smiling. A glint of her gold tooth. "Of course, Kanu and Doherty want to rob the bank. Fought the Law and all that."

"Kan-WHO?"

"Kan-U."

I donated two hundred for the cause and asked for a receipt but was rebuffed. My donation seemed to further lull her. She pulled her briefcase behind her as a pillow. "Not raking up old stuff, but ya would have loved London, Munk."

Wisely, I bit my thumb. Not mentioning her upcoming straw wedding.

"Such a buzz, yeah. Diverse. Creative. And banking for you, loads of opportunities."

I continued to bite my thumb.

"Ya know, started acting. Just amateur stuff." She waved the bottles of V&L down to her. Took a smiley, syrupy sup. "Modern. None of that Shakespeare malarkey. Even in an ad. Had to straighten my hair, o."

"Nice balance with the law stuff. Could be dry I'd say."

"Bunch of twats the legal lot of them. Irish, they think I'm stupid. Black, think I'm wild. Have me own portfolio now, though."

"Still gambling?" I asked, knowing the answer, and glancing at her heroin-powered locket from Young Akinfenwa.

"Bloody right," said Obee. "Pays the rent, innit. Building an app, an' all. Jaysus, I'm tired." Yawning long and loud to prove it. "Jet lag, wha'." Laughing her lovely laugh. "Any more Monster Munch?"

I retrieved half a dozen more from the Chemist but she was asleep when I returned. Her arms folded, her ankles crossed, one of her earrings on the floor amongst the Bank of Ballygall papers. Her mouth, crumbed and orange, was open, a gentle snore. Her tights and shoes in a tidy pile. The vodka bottle clutched to her hand.

My lovely O-bee from Bally-G.

Who I covered in a blanket and watched.

But unfortunately not for long. Her younger and amused sister, Flora, retrieving her far too soon.

Doctor Lathey & A Passing Samaritan

The B&B a few days later. Waiting for Obee. Late, as usual. It wasn't a date, we were far from such things, but a bit of afternoon nostalgia, shoplifting at Brady's supermarket. Lucozade hopefully, the vodka already hidden at Kanu's feet.

And in she came, rings on her fingers, bells on her toes, but right behind her that feral dog, Garda Michael, his steps still too big for his boots, and confronted immediately by Chioma, a strong cup of Lipton tea in her hand.

"And what are you wanting?"

Garda Michael did not retreat. His nose wet, his mustache, well, no, his mustache, that brambly thing that had matched his furry eyebrows was gone. Shaved. Pale. Severe. Like my mother's neck.

Had he shot it off?

His Heckler and Koch.

Fully uniformed, not jumpered in half.

Staring at Margaret Akunyili. Sizing her up. Staring.

"What?" repeated Chioma.

"A word with the lad, private," he said, ushering me outside. Behind us, but audible, Kanu, "Not a patch on his brother, that Guard," received with a growl.

He led me across to O'Donohue's, standing under its Red Hand flag.

Faithful to his Garda manual, Garda Michael insisted on small talk. Chatty. The gap between his front teeth seemed to have widened, the teeth sharpened, his tongue between them like a rabid Jack Russell's. "But Kanu and yer man Dirty Doherty up to something. And yer one, Obee Chij-whatever is back, bold as brass. Ructions, Finn lad, as me brother used to say, there will be ructions." His hand on his holster.

Behind him, in the distance, rose the Great Wall. Blocking all glimpses of the sea.

"Here, Finn," he said, leaning in conspiratorially, his breath rabid. "Don't have a lot of time. Some news about the case. The Doctor. Ah, ya don't know. I see. I had an idea ya wouldn't, that he wouldn't. Doctor gave his statement. As expected, corroborating all the details we knew. But something odd. Said whoever it was gave him a good thumping, ya know, also gave him first aid. Broke out the bandages and plasters an' all that. Stuck them on him. You get me?"

"What?"

"Bloke that, t'was a bloke he said, heavy-set, gave him a good hiding, also did the good Samaritan thing. Fixing him up."

"Jesus."

"Ha, wasn't Jesus. But maybe someone closer to home. Someone who seems to live, breathe and sleep in the church, wha'. Now Finn, your dad was gameball, covered for me those times."

I nodded.

"So, not rocket science. Your family. Someone who flies off the handle a bit. But good lad. God awful ponytail, I have to say. Get me?"

Got him. It was Liam. He did it. Attacked that arrogant-patronizing … and then did the Order of Malta on him. What a dope.

"A' course the lads from Killiney, what with your Ma throwing a punch an' that, are all over youse. Zoned in on Liam. Told them it was far-fetched. Only young lad. Hippocratic oath an' all that. More likely you."

"What?"

"Ya know, the eldest. Work for a medical crowd an' that over there in Boston, don't you. An' was closer to your Da."

"What?"

He pulled a piece of Jerky from his pocket. Offered before chewing. "Sure, you're leaving anyway, pal. Soon, I heard from your mother."

Heard from my mother? Was she now, on the eve of her own sellout, forcing me out?

"Least a brother could do. Take the brunt." Which provoked him to his usual fraternal eulogy, which I will skip. "Anyway," he said, chewily concluding, "Bleedin' obvious not you. Not exactly a hard chaw, are ya?"

Which stung.

"Wild goose chase, you'd be for the Killiney crowd. An' keep Liam safe. And then you skedaddle back to Amer-i-ka, they lose interest, get me?"

Sort of.

"A' course, Liam, bleedin' Maestro, decides to take it into his own hands. Come on. There he is. Heading into the station."

By which he meant The Garda Kiosk, diagonal to our chemist. Liam striding in. Wearing his long, pinstriped, gunslinger coat. Wholly indifferent to the tumult around him. Preceded by his invisible keyboard. Playing.

I will confess to a moment's hesitation, tempted to leave him to his own mess.

"Come on!"

But he was my brother.

So I followed Garda Michael, who bounded over the oversized cobblestones, his tongue hanging out of his mouth.

The Garda kiosk was small, hard, like a recalcitrant tumor. Inside, crouched around a small, oblong plastic table were three Killiney Gardai, male, uniformed, armed. Giants. The room seemed to fit tightly around their shoulders. But friendly Giants, making themselves at home, withdrawing hats, opening buttons, loosening their Batman belts, eager to set everyone's mind at a confessional ease. One of large ears, one of large eyes and one of large mouth. The well-eared winking at the tea pot already warm and cozied on the table.

Behind them the extension, The Garda Immigration Bureau, a brown, rectangular carbuncle completed but not yet joined to the kiosk. It would later frighten poor Margaret Akunyili, who would flee, leaving behind her straw man and her Straw House, but also her friends, her supporters, her chance of a dignified life after her long detention at that Mosney purgatory. Poor Margaret.

Liam sat brusquely at the table, his back to and almost out the door.

We squeezed in beside him, forcing the large-eared Garda to rise and stand.

Liam laughed, seeing me. "Och," he said, in my mother's accent. "Me brother. The Grand Protector of the family jewels."

Prick.

Adding his own, "Sls-upp, Sls-upp."

The 'little chat' then began. Three 'Good evenings' followed by two forgettable names and one not so, Garda Woods, the clear, big-blue-eyed leader. All at our unsolicited service.

Garda Michael poured the tea, deferentially exempting himself due to the lack of cups.

"Just a little chat with Liam McCormack here," said the big mouth.

Liam happily gulped his tea and took another cup from the pot. Still Jaysus wearing my dad's wedding ring.

"And Liam, what would you have been doing the evening of July 5th?"

"A Wok and Roll dinner, at home, family. Prawn and everything."

"And what would prawn be now?"

"King prawn," I interjected. "The best."

"King of the prawns, now?" repeated the big-mouthed Garda.

"In fried rice, onions, mushrooms, the lot," added Liam.

Garda Woods, the large-eyed, intervened. "Witnesses. Who was there?"

"Me brother, me mother and friend of the family, Professor Conor O'Reilly, Trinity College."

All duly noted in a giant notebook Garda Woods produced. Large writing, lengthy words.

"And what would you know about a Dr. Lathey?" asked the big mouth, regaining control.

Liam bristled, which was noticed by those large blue eyes. "That arrogant-patronizing…" he said, censoring himself.

Obviously they knew, so obviously I told them. "Treated my father. Passed away in the hospital."

"My condolences," said Garda Woods.

"And what would you know about a certain meeting with Dr. Lathey?"

"Arbitration," I said, interjecting, encouraged by a nod from Garda Michael, now standing beside the large-eared Garda. "Our assertion of his negligence."

"And what would you know about a certain incident at this meeting?"

Liam replied, mimicking his Kerry accent. "And what would you be wanting to know about that for?"

"And what would you know about," began the large-mouthed, but stopped, flummoxed. But began again, gritting his teeth. "And what would you know about a certain violent act at that particular meeting?"

"So what," said Liam, his ponytail shaking. "Ma was grieving. Upset."

"And would you have been upset yourself, now?"

"No."

Woods the big-eyed intervened. "As you know, on the evening of July 5th, Dr. Francis Lathey was assaulted in the hospital grounds."

"Couldn't happen to a nicer fella," said Liam.

"Suffered lacerations, contusions, a nasty concussion," continued Woods, his eyes growing larger, bluer. "The weapon a hard, blunt object. The victim had to be hospitalized,"

"Private," said Liam. "No corridors for him, betcha."

"Strange thing. In an interview with Dr. Lathey." A perceptible wince from Garda Woods. The charms of that arrogant-patronizing doctor, no doubt. Or maybe the awful tea he just tasted? "Claims assailant attended to his injuries. First aid."

Garda Woods leaned toward us, his eyes unblinking and mesmerizingly blue. He talked tonelessly of the difficulty of a loved one's death, particularly at the hands of someone so trusted. He understood Liam, his situation, the sometimes violent nature of grief. "Particularly for the youngest. All that emotion. And the legal, the arbitration process can be a long, a frustrating one." He compassionately leaned back in his chair, as did his colleague, as did the large-eared Garda standing.

Garda Michael hovered nervously. Anxious glances at Liam.

Garda Woods then leaned back in. "You know, Liam. I've been a Guard a long time. Seen a lot. Always better to be straight up. Trust me. " He leaned further forward, curling his powerful body around the corner of the table, his eyes large, inviting, mesmerizing in their own monstrous way. "Sad, sad story this." Their blue circularity seemed to sooth Liam, the deep, dark pupils seemed to lull him. "Sure, an honest statement, before Lathey submits a more detailed description. A line up." He advanced his elbow on the table, immediately lowering and sidling after it. Almost touching Liam's arm. "Trust me, Liam. A statement, with remorse, but good reasons, and you only the youngest, surely, you see. Makes so much sense." Liam seemed to slump a little. "Believe me. Makes sense. And surely everyone will understand." His eyes blazing blue now.

"And what would you be doing with the Order of Malta?" asked the big-mouthed, perhaps breaking the spell.

"Is that all you Jaysus have?" said Liam, rousing himself. "Someone gives that gobshite a few smacks, some stupid Samaritan slaps a few plasters on him, and you put two and two together, and here we are? Is that it? How many cases, negligence and Jaysus worse, has that fecker been in? Senile he is. So me Ma throws a punch, who wouldn't? Been to a hospital lately?"

"But you do have medical training. You're not disputing that?" asked Garda Woods, annoyed at his big-mouthed colleague.

"Look, if it had have been me, here's what I would have done, so pay attention." Liam took a large sup of tea, pretending to relish its thin, scalded hide. "First, none of this out in the middle of the bleeding car park business. People, clamped all over the place there." Another sup, quicker. A flick back of his ponytail. "I'd be in his office. Late. Balaclava. Syringe. In he comes, on his fancy phone. Headlock, quick stab into his arrogant neck. Not instant of course. Bit of a struggle. Big fucker he is. But already I can see you're wondering the same thing he'd be wondering." Another sup, slurped for effect. "What was in the syringe? So write this down Garda Woods, check it with the prick if you value his expertise so much."

Liam paused.

Woods nodded, hovering his large pen over his large pad.

"Succinylcholine. Spell it for you, later."

Woods scribbled something down.

Garda Michael glanced at me, impressed.

"So what is Succinylcholine? Well, it's a paralytic. Used in surgery. Paralyses from head to foot. Everything except the heart. Visible too. Starts with the face. These mad waves of twitches and spasms, then bang." Liam clapped his hands in glee. "You're frozen. And it hurts." Another clap of hands. "It's your body cramping up. Down the body it goes. Ya can't talk. Ya can't breathe either, but I'll get to that. But you can feel it. Brain is fine. Heart is fine. Feel yourself turning into stone." Liam laughed with theatrical volume. Affected I'm sure, but still unnerving. "And there's our good Doctor, looking at me wearing a balaclava. Can you imagine the terror? And his breathing goes too, so I'd have to bag him."

He took a long, gulping drink of tea.

Waited.

Waited.

"And what would bag him be now?" asked the large-eared Garda.

"Good question," replied Liam, wagging a finger. "Now remember, class, our poor incompetent doctor can't breathe. So we bag him. What's a bag? It's an oxygen mask, with a bag. Squeeze the bag, air goes into his arrogant-patronizing gob. Don't squeeze, then there's no oxygen. Doctor's lungs start burning. Suffocating. Ask me: how many squeezes a minute?"

I asked him, but not out of solicitude. I wanted to know.

"Six to seven a minute, for survival. For comfort, double that. Fourteen. Now, remember class, the dopey doctor can feel all this.

Succinylcholine is a paralytic not a painkiller. His brain, even his little brain, would still be working, still registering all the lovely levels of pain."

"And where would you be getting this Succ-in-colleen?" said the big-mouthed.

"Wouldn't say a thing to him. Just watch the terror. Burning for breath."

"And where would you be getting the oxygen, the bag?"

Another gargantuan slurp of his tea, but surely Liam's cup was empty by now. "Squeeze," he said, squeezing his hand. "Stop. Wait. Watch him change color. Pale. Gray. A nice bit of blue, there."

"Wait."

"Wait."

"So blue now."

"Wait."

Liam starting singing. "Blue is the color, Succinylcholine is the game."

The room hot, close.

"Arse blue, now. Give him a little squeeze. Then start the game again." An exaggerated swish of his ponytail before concluding, "That's what I would do, big-ears. Not some handbag shite in a poxy car park."

Garda Michael offered a helpful summary. "So a man of your technical skills, Liam, something more impressive than a daylight assault and battery."

A final fake drink of tea, held aloft for seconds. "That's what I'd do, Mad Dog."

"Bit far-fetched for me," said the big-mouthed Garda.

"That's 'cos you've no imagination," said Liam, leaning back.

Silence.

The thick absorbency of silence.

"I'll make more tea," Garda Michael finally said, smiling.

"Don't bother," said Liam.

And he left.

Striding out in his long, gunslinger coat.

Everyone stood up, sat down, adjusted themselves before a large rush for the last word. But Garda Woods prevailed. "We will continue our investigation. Just the first of many interviews and … "

But it wasn't. The Gardai did not return. They made their inquiries elsewhere. Half-hearted inquiries, I learned later, proof of their shared disdain for that arrogant-patronizing prick.

What a performance by Liam.

But Jesus, what kind of family did I have? My mother a murderer, my brother a thug.

Jesus.

The Battle of The Yellow Ford

August 14th: never an auspicious or commemorated day on the Irish calendar, usually nothing more than the middle of a rainy, middling summer, but to O'Neill it recently recalled the year 1598 and The Battle of The Yellow Ford. A triumph important enough to be recalled and annually celebrated, or so his majesty thought. On that date, in the middle of the Nine Years War, his alleged great, great etc. grandfather, Hugh O'Neill, Earl of Tyrone, routed, via a boggy, yellow ford, a sizable English force — infantry, artillery, cavalry – from his kingdom of Armagh, killing their ignoble leader, and thereby coalescing sporadic fits of rebellion into a countrywide revolt.

In honor, The Toll Queen convened a commemoration at our Not-So-Small-Church on the 14th, despite the tension in the town, despite a growing and coalescing Shed-powered resistance movement.

Actually, more a party than a commemoration. Begun at dusk, invoking the Celtic tradition of day beginning with night.

For the occasion, the interior of the church had been swaddled in yellow, the walls plied with flowers, the floor softened with yellow petals, and looping diagonally from the roof, like monochrome rainbows, yellow ribbons. It resembled a belated, guiltily overblown Easter party.

I preferred not to attend, but Glibb the Giant preferred otherwise, almost carrying me there.

On the altar, a temporary stage had been constructed, made from broad beams of pungent new pine, strong and hefty, but obviously not tempered enough to restrain the saintly, ethereal form of Bishop Slattery, who was now floating in the air. And perhaps ascending.

The miraculous ascension of Bishop Slattery?

But not floating.

Balancing, or balanced on, a sword of some sorts, a pike. The holy Slattery finally forked. But not ascending. Descending. Deeper onto the pike. A purgatorial moan from him. Screams from the kids. Adult laughter. Liam the traitor playing along on the organ.

A tall, caped figure stood over Slattery, wearing a tuxedo, top hat, gloves, bow tie, all entirely and sickeningly yellow. And a mustache and monocle.

Asking the crowd, if he should?

Yes, he should!

Should I?

Yes-yes-yes.

And yes he did; with both hands of yellow, he leaned, he pushed, and straddling a foot for leverage, he forced His Excellency down onto the pike.

Slattery screaming. Pale, impaled.

A last agonizing yell.

Screams from the screaming crowd.

A last death cry.

Then sudden darkness. The church lights extinguished.

Then suddenly back on.

And there lay the bishop, on the floor, dead, perforated, cooked. Over him, that famous magician, The Great Harry O'Halloran. All quiet. Absolute quiet. Then laughter, applause, appeals to be next. Me-Me-Me.

Two questions. How did O'Neill persuade a man of Slattery's sanctimony to be so forked? And how did he inveigle the fame of O'Halloran from the infamy of Las Vegas?

Money, I suppose. In both cases.

The magician did not permit subsequent forkings, but instead produced a mint of money from ears and noses, particularly from the O'Neill princesses, who stood delighted in their English accents, Boru the Wolfhound awag beside them.

A big crowd, swelled by the ranks of the builders and their families.

The town itself was Toffily represented. Bandy, the McAnteers, the Devlins, the O'Donohue's, but no butcher, florist, or supermarketeer.

O'Neill's wife, Aisling, at the vivacious center of it all, seemed happy. Genuinely happy. Exuberantly introducing my mother (bitch) and her Dirty Comforter (bastard) to all. Her siliconed sister-in-law, Mary O'Neill, beside her. Glibb the Giant protectively hovering.

The Toll Queen loved it all. Laughing his terrible terraced laugh. At the rear. Dressed in a ridiculous yellow, button-down shirt. Long haired and bearded. Like a hippie lost at a badly risen Easter party. Friendly, but distracted. Excited. Agitated. But I insisted. Confronting him finally about the offer for our chemist.

"Go on, now. Isn't it your mother's decision?" Brusque, an edge of aggression. Aware of my sojourns at the B&B, no doubt. "Wasn't it her practically running the place?"

"Not her family's, is it? Shouldn't be her. The eldest should. You of all, should understand. Family and all that."

"Ah, Archie, lad, it's a wee tit of a shop. And I mean that. And hasn't she earned it? All those years. Ah, don't mistake me, your father was a character, a man after…charm the knickers…but can't have been too rosy saddled with him. In such a wee town. Wagging tongues. The Gravelicker for one, though I wouldn't have minded meself."

"And what about her; what she's doing," I said, a few drinks on me. "He's barely cold in the grave, and she's off…"

I didn't need to finish. He knew, nodding to himself, but distracted, spiraling out from his pocket his handwritten speech. Scanning it, satisfied. "All right, Archie, lad. Your poor mother, impoverished. After all she done. At least now, bit of comfort. Least I can do."

I repeated my legacy argument.

"Ah, lad, go and have some fucking craic with your family. At least yours is here. Not one of mine has the decency to come. August 14th for God's sake. Except Mary. Jesus wept, her tits, what size are they now!"

He strode away toward the altar. But turned to say, "Lad, stay out of that there Estate. Not your people. Not your kind. I'm serious."

On the altar, The Great O'Halloran produced a magical wardrobe. A wardrobe of evanescence. A demon of dematerialization. But first a speech by The Toll Queen. From the pulpit. Clear, audible, understandable groans.

A structured speech. First a welcome, then a historical lecture, without a Red Hand, thank God, and then a reminder of the ancestral victory of the O'Neill clan blah blah blah … boring…

But then he was disappeared!

Ushered into a yellow wardrobe, pulling Boru the Wolfhound in with him.

O'Halloran slammed closed the door.

"ABRACADABRA!"

Pulling open the door. But O'Neill was still there, Boru panting and wagging in his lap. Both full of pantomime smiles.

But with the encouraged help of the audience, everyone shouting, "ABRACADABRA," The Toll Queen and his wolfhound did disappear. The wardrobe re-opened. Empty.

They were gone.

But so was Glibb the Giant. Through the normal egress of the church door, with a bunch of builders. Silently. Sneakily. Weaving unremarked through the magic.

I followed them. Stopping outside our chemist.

The cobblestoned street of Ballygall was quiet. Lit golden by the westering sun.

That nose-broken JCB stood growling at the far end of the town, its engine rumbling. Black smoke pluming from its engine. Two flags flying, the Tricolor and the Red Hand of O'Neill. Facing the B&B, which was dark, closed.

The Toll Queen ran toward the JCB, followed by Boru. A race. O'Neill shouting. Boru growling. Such a feral growl. Pursued by the builders. Their formal shoes slippery over the sandy cobblestones. Their weapons glinting in the sunlight. Hatchets and hammers.

The street was hung with its usual shroud of dust and dirt, held in by the surrounding Wall. Empty, except for a small smoking group outside the florist. Burke the Butcher and his minions. Who startled at the southward charge of The Queen and his men. Shuffling backward to the butcher's, congregating tightly beneath its pig's head.

The Toll Queen mounted the JCB. Revved it. Reversed it to the padlocked Shed.

Boru jumped up beside him. Standing against the dashboard. Panting. Wagging. The builders climbed aboard, many arms to the right, many arms to the left, eager to propel the JCB.

But to where?

A raid into the Estate? Revenge for the desecrations of his Wall?

The Toll Queen petted his wolfhound. Unbuttoned his yellow shirt. Pointed the JCB directly ahead.

But at what?

Speed!

Such speed. The JCB's broken nose raised for battle.

A yell from O'Neill, answered in kind by those to his right, those to his left, "YELLOW FORD!"

He roared into the B&B, erupting glass, splintering wood, obliterating the door, the front of the shop. Shelves collapsed. Counters staggered.

Mirrors smashed. Chioma's reading chair lifted and pinioned against that small tea room.

O'Neill reversed, dragging the chair into the street, which was set upon by Glibb and the rest with hatchets and hammers. Magazines and newspapers, brushes and combs strewn to the ground. Countless jars and aerosol cans flattened underneath. Shards of mirror everywhere. Posters floored, of Nigerian footballers, of Nigerian writers. The tinkling sound of glass falling.

Scared, I backed deeper into the doorway of our Chemist. My hand on its handle.

He reversed back to The Shed. A preparatory pause. Nodding to himself, to the sixteenth-century reenactment in his head. The lunatic. His shirt shredded by glass.

Burke and his cronies ran into his shop under a cloud of cigarette smoke.

The JCB tore in again, its big wheels bouncing on the cobblestones, a weasel lunging into a warm rabbit hole. Again. And again.

Jesus.

The sound reverberating around The Great Wall. Cries of delight from the builders atop that poor chair. The Toll Queen laughing his terrible laugh.

He dismounted, ran, the others running after him, a truancy of mischievous schoolboys, dashing back to the church. Boru wagging after them.

I ran inside, tried to steady myself on the Causeway.

Not long, but a text from Obee, the understandable profanity of which I won't disclose. But I didn't hesitate. I got up and ran. Hoping she would see me exiting our chemist and not the church.

But she didn't.

Jesus. The damage, the debris, a mess of glass and hair covering the cobblestones.

Obee stood in the road with her mother and Flora, their arms around each other's waist. Looking. Trying to accommodate themselves to the sight. The damage. The absolute lack of a shop front. Teary-eyed. All in golden slippers. Taking tiny steps. Circling the battered writing chair. Emeke, husband and father, behind them. I stood behind him. Followed him as he followed them. A circular procession, moving slowly.

Joined by Kanu and Doherty, both filthy, covered in dirt.

Joined then by an outpouring from The Wobbly Shamrock, Estaters and Townies. Joining our circular procession. Quiet. Silent. Wondering. Not only what and who, but how?

The nose-broken JCB was gone. The hatchets and hammers were also gone.

Chioma, with the help of her daughters, righted her writing chair, somehow managing to stand it in the street despite its damage. She sat into it. Steadied by her daughters, assisted by her husband. We congregated around her. Beneath us magazines turned and fluttered. Obee picked up a hairbrush, glancing back at me. A look of fear.

"Burke," said Chioma. "Laughing in there."

Which prompted us all to look across at the Butcher's. The lights off, "But," said Chioma, "he's still in there, grinning, like that pig over his door."

"Yes," said Emeke.

"We should go and…" said Kanu, but was restrained by Doherty.

"We should clean up," said Chioma. "From upstairs."

And from upstairs came sweeping brushes and pans, which encouraged other brushes and pans, from the Wobbly and the Polski, and from the Estate.

I brought cleaning supplies from our chemist.

The street was swept by us all. Even hoovered by Ola. A brisk clean-up that could not assuage the structural damage. Which was eventually covered by clear tarp and blue tape. A small door carved and taped in its middle. Kept until three ancient but operational Hiace panel vans could be acquired later that week to defend the shopfronts of the B&B, The Wobbly Shamrock and The Polski Sklep.

"Lift," said Chioma, lifting with her daughters — no one else! — the writing chair into that small tea room. Returning to the cobblestones, foraging for combs, brushes and scissors.

"Wasn't Burke though," I said. "The Toll Queen. Did it himself. With the, with a JCB, drove it."

"He?"

"Him?"

"Himself?"

"Not Burke?"

"The Butcher?"

"The pig?"

"No. It was O'Neill."

"Why?"

I didn't answer. I didn't want to embarrass Doherty and Kanu, the retaliatory targets.

"Jesus Christ. Himself, o."

"He's mad," I offered. Glancing toward the church, the party still in progress, his Yellow anniversary now cruelly commemorated.

"A man as rich and powerful as," said Chioma, but did not finish. She didn't have to. Everyone knew. Everyone understood.

Our work slowed. We dawdled and dreaded. But we were revived by Chioma, her resilience, her imperturbability, that night, and the days that followed, and within a week or so, the B&B, though badly scarred, though tarped and tenuous, would re-open for business.

Brisk business, actually.

Everyone suddenly wanted their hair done.

Me and My Mother Get Into It

Sideways, I lounged on the middle stair, suspended between upper and lower, my boots protruding — but no, these stairs were too narrow, their bones too creaky, their banisters too solid. Not the broad, bare stairs of my youth.

These were new stairs.

The stairs of 77 Seaview Court, the Straw House, in the Estate now obstructed by The Great Wall of Ballygall.

So I sat facing downward instead, the evening light frosted by the front door, which was ajar.

I had abandoned my home.

Again, I suppose.

I had moved out. South not west. To the Estate. Still unnamed. Its streets unpaved. Its houses newer but thinner, terraced — quickly, haphazardly assembled by Devlin the Developer, spitefully facing north, not east toward the sea. But boldly and variously colored. Treeless, but well-flowered gardens. An early source of envy for me, all these homes not halved by a business.

The Straw House was nice. Comfortable. Unfortunately available as Margaret Akunyili, her marriage despicably revoked by Garda Michael and his Garda Immigration Bureau, had to urgently leave.

Poor Margaret.

Poor me.

I had fled my mother, who had confronted me on our Causeway. Telling me, without specifics, to 'like it or lump it.' An edict that reprised our earlier argument, at Daisy's, that Baggot Street steakhouse. Her standing at the top of the stairs, me confronting her midway. Red faces, raised voices. Both angry, but a prepared anger that did not lack precision.

I knew about Conor, I told her. Her Dirty, Impotent Comforter. Had she no shame? No decency? Her husband barely in the grave. Her sons in grief. And in comes this gobshite. And what a dozy, dopey gobshite she picked. Not a patch on my father. And then she cuts her hair like a little girl, and some stupid job at a Tomahawk tourist-shite restaurant. When we have a decent business right under her adulterous feet. A business she neglected. But it's not hers, not her family's, keep her thieving hands off it. Only wants to buy a sleazy little love nest God knows where, with her fancy man. That dope.

Go on the fuck with yourself, Brendan, she said. The cheek of you now. Off in America and you're still dictating to us. Your royal highness. Never did anything for the business, you, just like your lazy father. Peas in a pod. On those sulky stairs. Left to me and Liam. And now, you're all high and mighty about your ancestral home and some such shite. What did your father do with it? This great heirloom? He never did a boggin' thing. Just borrowed on its back. And for what do you think? For the God-awful Wall? Not at all. The money all went to that there bitch. Her DIG. Her summer salary. Her students. Her stupid trowels. Aye, or so he said. For her, of course. Get into her knickers. This wonderful ancestral home, you're the big defender of now. Sold it all for her knickers, and God knows who else's. Never put a penny toward Downstairs. Or toward me. Or toward you lads. That the kind of pride and heritage you're talking about, is it, Brendan? At least I had the decency to wait until he died. He. Your honorable father. Chasing skirt all over Ballygall. The wee, dirty coward."

Which I rebutted, calling her a depressive, toxic… and up and down we went, but don't ask a son to describe such things.

Out, I went. Screaming at her. Dragging luggage and knocking shelves as I went. Marching northward to Dublin, but rescued by Obee, who arranged a temporary tenancy at 77 Seaview Court. Providing milk and teabags. Sympathetic.

77 Seaview Court.

The Straw House.

Luxurious in a way, an upstairs and a downstairs of domesticity. Couches and carpets. Even a back garden. A little Shetland shed too.

Real neighbors too. Not holed between a pub and an Off-license. Doherty on one side, Kanu and Bridie on the other.

Narrow but nice stairs.

I slurped tea with impunity. Tears, but of anger. It was a terrible argument. An awful scene. Climactic, surely. The end of a lot of things. Toe to toe with a mass murderer.

I took more tea. Turned my mind to my legal options. An injunction somehow. Declare her insane? Her decades of reclusiveness? That thrown punch at the hospital? Or declare her fiscally incompetent?

Or.

Declare her crimes to the Gardai?

That would slow her down.

No, I wouldn't do that.

I would retain a solicitor. Avoid my mother at all costs. Interact via intermediaries, at arm's length…someone else's arm.

I might never see her again. Except in court. Which gave me a new sense of safety on those Straw stairs. For a minute, anyway.

Before she burst in. Throwing my bunch of keys at me, half of them bent sideways.

"Good catch there, Brendan, forgot them so you did," she shouted. "Forgot these too."

A ball of paper, which, when I opened, contained all my father's Causeway articles, including that poisonous one.

"Nauuw, cope yourself on back to Boston, Brendan. Far from your father you are. That gobshite. If he had spent half the time…" and off she went, defaming him.

I unwrapped the news article. Unwrinkled it. Smoothed it. Raised it at her. This younger woman, in a black Tomahawk skirt and sleeveless shirt, feigning surprise, incomprehension. I scooched up a step before saying, "I know all about it. Doherty told me. Two of you. The five informants. Then the professor."

"Och," she said, holding her chain, "that was centuries ago." Her nonchalance a little betrayed by a clench of fist, a narrowing of her eyes.

"What? That doesn't even make sense. That's all you have to say?"

"Och, you're so smart now, Brendan. Big new secret for you."

"Have you no remorse?"

"You've no sense of it, Brendan," her voice softening. "Grew up, different time."

"Poisoned him."

"Och, he was a blowhard. But, unfortunate. The other ones." She looked straight up at me, her blue eyes bright, her chipmunk cheeks pursed. "Deserved, so it was."

"Jesus. Poisoned him. But you poisoned us. Barely a family we were. Never even a holiday. Even a trip up to Dublin. You hiding out Upstairs."

"Ay, me, so it is, and your father so available. Not stuck on those stairs, or in that boggin' graveyard. Or chasing skirt around the place."

"Can you blame him? Married to a murderer. A terrorist. What sort of marriage is that? No wonder he was always out, or on the stairs. No wonder he was no angel. But at least he tried to do something. The Wall, the DIG, and all the other stuff he did for the town. Put it on the map. At least he tried. Let me finish. At least he had a bit of life to him. Ruined his life you did, at least you tried to, and now, now that you couldn't, you're going to sell everything he had."

She moved up a step in her new Puma runners. "Go way the fuck, Brendan," she said. "Always the know-it-all, even though you never see the half of it. Of course he knew. The IRA. Wee thrill for him so it was. Not the extent, I grant you that. Physical force. But deep down, his dirty secret, he was relieved we had to leave. His research over there not so stellar. Not so well received. What was the word? 'Banal.' His cuteness only getting him so far. Great excuse to leave. To lick his wounds here. Back to being the wee boy in the wee town. A' course, blamed me, but could have gone back to Trinity, he could have. Other colleges. But spineless. Coward. And running away from his family too. Running out of our marriage. Aye, running. The coward. Dragging you kids into everything. And off chasing anything around town. That graveyard. God, her nickname. Grave Licker. Mortified, I was. This wee town and his antics. Embarrassed for you boys. And throwing money away. On the Wall. On every stupid town nonsense. And on her."

I moved up another step, away from her. "Sure, sure, his fault, always his fault. But what about *me*?" My chin wobbling a bit. "Did you think of me? Just a baby. And you, my mother, out risking life and everything. And for what? For the North. Jesus. Poisoning and murdering. What if you'd gone to prison? Or worse? What would have happened to me?"

She laughed. "Your precious father, all to yourself. But fair point, Brendan, let's consider you, nauuw." She spat her gum out.

"Och, my wee boy Brendan, aye, let's nay forget yourself in all this. Your own behavior. Your own mischief. Always a disappointment to me it was. Your choices. Harmful. Mediocre. America and money. Not Ireland and its history, its culture. But that's your own life, your own choices, your own harm to yourself. But what about here, at home, with us? What did you do? Organize a holiday, a trip to Dublin even? No. You joined him on his sulky-boy stairs. Backed him. Supported him. Only half the sense of Liam you had. My dear husband wouldn't have lasted without *you*, so he wouldn't. Didn't have the backbone. Let *me* finish. Without his precious wee Finn. Up he would have come crawling. I told you. Making matters worse you were. Told you till I was blue in the face, but och, you knew better. Think on that so, Mr. USA. Wouldn't have lasted, this sulk of his, without you, my wee traitor. On the stairs with him. Out for the Wall with him." Pointing at me now. "Though, gave you the hump when he barred you from the graveyard, so he did. You almost saw sense then, you did. Saw the real man there. Think on that a bit, Brendan. All you did. And you *did* a lot for the wee coward. And he stabs you in the back. What was it, he would say, the graveyard too dangerous. Laughable. His own son. My own wee traitor. You got a bit of the real man there."

"Bollocks," I shouted. "You murder six people and you blame him, and the audacity," my chin wobbling badly here, "to blame me. Blame anyone but yourself, you do."

"Bollocks yourself," she said, stepping back, turning. "Think on that, Brendan. What you did." Putting on her headphones.

Sauntering out.

The lying, murdering bitch.

A Fu-Fu Fight

An evening or two later, I surprised Obee with a thank-you dinner: Jollof rice. Surely the way to a woman's heart.

Rice, of course, Brady's finest. Bags of it, an unnecessary, ostentatious volume which perhaps betrayed my desire for more Obee dinners. Spiced with nutmeg, ginger, cumin, garlic, complicated with dollops of brown sauce, which Obee saw, and a flick of curry sauce, which she didn't. She lounged in the sitting room, dividing her attention between her phone, her Star lager, and my culinary efforts. Surprisingly well dressed, despite our long day at the B&B clean-up. Her black barrister suit. Shimmering white blouse. Her hair long and straight. Even in heels. Her nose stud the only frivolous concession. Perhaps the outfit kept her in a litigious state of mind, better to repel the assaults on her family and business. A topic that we, along with my mother's execrable behavior, had excluded from the evening's menu.

So, big, ugly onions, cut and fried in palm oil. A few bell peppers. Yes, a few surreptitious Monaghan mushrooms, the Chef's prerogative. Once it was sizzling in a Cookstown way, I added the spiced rice, the aforementioned brown and curry sauce, the cans of tomatoes, and the toothpaste-like tube of tomato paste, all of it.

What a racket!

Then the stock, which should have been chicken-flavored, but I preferred Guinness, supplemented with mugs of Ballygall holy water.

Meat?

Rasher, of course. Cut into soldiers.

I looked around.

And such a nice, bright, ground floor kitchen, well-equipped but somehow missing a sink, which was to be found in the toilet under the stairs which itself lacked an actual toilet. The Estate had been built shoddily by Devlin the Developer.

But, ah, the aroma. Pungent, tangy, acidic.

Which did not entice Obee over. So, I offered her a secret. A fresh one. "Got evicted today." My landlord, Abby O'Connor, happily apologetic, had been delighted by the return of a prior and lovable tenant. Who paid in full. Who assisted in moving my meager possessions to basement storage.

With an endearing alacrity, Obee came over, taking the stool at the kitchen counter. Careful of her sleeves. "Sorry. Munk, Not real Irish, is she, then. Stick together we do, London, Sydney, New York, whatever."

"Not the O'Connors of Boston."

"Well, brighten up, yeah, get to spend more straw with me."

That deserved a kiss, which I deservedly ventured. But she ventured only her hand, which I pecked with an obsequious volume.

"Looks good," said Obee, meaning my hair cut, its cowlicks preserved.

"Thanks," I replied.

A little run of silence, while I ruminatively poked the rice around. "Never been evicted or anything like that."

"Ah, it's the immigrant's bag, innit. Rejection. Nativism. Nepotism. Too dark, not dark enough. Too big, not big enough."

"Since when is the legal profession concerned about bigness?"

"Concerned about everything, innit, Munk," she replied, pausing for a deep, Starry gulp. "Now, don't get your knickers in a twist. Would have told you."

"What?"

"And not a word to them." She paused to check for obvious recording devices. Rubbed her ugly, bulbous locket. "Don't do corporate law, do I. Criminal. Much more fun. Glamorous, really. Some colorful characters, yeah."

"Tsk. Tsk. Your mother'll cut you from her book." A joke to hide my surprise, and, yes, my disappointment. I imagined her a corporate high-flyer, above petty crime and criminals like Young Akinfenwa.

"You know she started it. Yeah, I know, right, all these years. But not a word to anyone."

"She hates me anyway."

"No! Just keep her some Jollof."

"What about Fufu?"

"You haven't, have you?"

"I have. Got it from Moore Street. Bought cassava. Pounded it myself. With mortar and pestle. The traditional wood kind too. Look, molded with me very own hands. Wasn't easy. Had to pound and mold at the same time. Bit of water to the cassava, bit of kneading, bit of pounding. Bit of craic, really." From an upper shelf, I produced the Fufu, a lavish dozen arrayed on an ornamental plate. Small, dough-like balls. White, sticky, slappy.

A delicious moment of gullibility before she said, "Me arse you did, Munk!"

"Ha! Look at the relief on your face."

A pause, a puzzlement about what I meant by relief. But she knew. Such an arduous act of devotion would have unnerved her, exposing her preference for romance, not love, for companionship, not commitment. A skittishness, I suppose, I shared.

"What's her book about?" I asked.

The puzzlement yielded to a smile. "Right, it's about a great hero, working title is, told you before, *Things Fall Apart in Ballygall*. And who is this great man?"

"Kan-WHO!"

"And what does this great man wear?"

"Green tracksuit?" I replied.

"Close. A yellow tracksuit. Get it, yellow, like his yellow vandalized field."

Bastards.

"Ya know, not that terrible, the writing. Took a photo. Here, starts. Let me read it. 'Kanu was well known throughout the nine Estates, and even beyond their unlit streets, their unmarked roads, their yellowed football pitch. His fame rested on three feats: his football team, the Super Eagles, unbeaten for nine years; the overthrow of the Great Wall of Ballygall with nine JCBs; and the creation of nine tunnels, from Dublin to Lagos via London. A tall man who wished to be powerful, a talkative man who wished to be articulate,' and on it goes — Kan-WHO this, Kan-WHO that, definitely the hero of his own tale."

"Love it!"

"Based on Achebe's *Things Fall Apart*."

"Strange time to start."

In a high, theatrical voice, Obee declaimed: "Oh, it's the muse, the muse. Can't calendar the muse."

I poked the rice. Refreshed myself with a Starry sup. Thought of addressing her impending nuptials, however straw-like, but didn't. Wouldn't.

"We're a creative family. Mother and her words. Flora and her murals. And me, what's so creative about me, Munk?"

I would not be baited. "Everything."

"Acting. Remember that group in school. Yeah, well, kept going from there, didn't I." She shook her Star.

I attended to the Egusi soup. Obee's favorite.

"Yeah, been lovely. In this amateur group over there. Even got an ad. Paddy Power. Nice earner."

"Awesome," I Americanly replied. I added dried smoked catfish to the simmering soup. And yes, a sly splash of brown sauce.

"Thanks, Yankee Doodle. Might open a few doors." She curled herself around her drink, the stool wobbling.

I worked in silence for a few minutes. Adding rasher, shredded spinach leaves, and a fistful of Irish cabbage (instead of bitter leaves) to the soup. And a dash of curry sauce. I shuffled the balls of Fufu. Needlessly prodded the Jollof.

"Yeah, a few doors. Have this audition, yeah. RTE."

"RTE!" RTE being a big deal, the BBC of Ireland.

"Chill. Haven't got anything yet. New soap. Modern-day Ireland. Which means immigrants, yeah. Nigerian character. Solicitor. Bit one dimensional, railing against Direct Provision and what have you, as if that's the only thing in our lives. Probably some grisly murder along the way. But could be good. Could develop her. Be great, actually. Even if it is only Ireland."

"Solicitor. Right up your alley."

"Anyway, doesn't work, have this as a back-up plan, haven't I." Lifting her left hand, bringing into shiny prominence a ring. "Engaged," she said, laughing.

"Your Mum told me, actor fella," I said, trying to sound brave.

"Yeah, right." She paused, took another excessive gulp.

"Congratulations," I said, trying not to sound too happy. "We should have a Vodka and Lucozade."

"Twenty-fifth, October. Camden Town hall. It's independence, Munk. You should come. Nice bloke too, you'd like him. House on fire you two." She produced a photo on her phone.

A friendly looking bloke, big goofy smile, silly Dr. Who scarf wrapped around his neck. But Black not White. "Wouldn't White straw be better?"

"No. Too suspicious now. And he's from Lagos, his family is. Yoruba, even. Never mind, Munk. Only straw. Here, help me; let's rehearse the RTE stuff."

We did.

It was fun. She was great. Confronting a panel of pear-shaped civil servants about the Kafkaesque cruelty of Ireland's Direct Provision program. Strident. Eloquent. Humane. Obviously, channeling poor Margaret Akunyili. She was great. Surely a shoe-in.

Twice we did it.

Each twice as good.

A fresh can of Star to celebrate.

In return, I told her the tale of my father's exhumation and reburial.

"You dug up the coffin, yeah? Liam, yeah?"

"Yeah, Liam organized that part of it."

"Bloody hell. What a nutter, that boy."

"That was the easy part."

Obee looked doubtful.

"Was. Had to bury him standing up. No coffin."

"Wha'?"

"Like a Celtic king. Looking out to sea. Bodyguard for his saint. Yer man Palladius. I did the burying. Liam, can't blame him, got pretty upset."

"Facking hell, my mother would eat this up."

"Not a word to anyone."

She nodded. Smiling.

"Not a word. Only the family know, and of course that gobshite Conor. Though means fuck-all now. Since she wants to sell." I took a long Starry sup. "Sorry. We agreed not to talk about all that." I poked the Jollof. Lowered the Egusi Coddle.

A commiserative clink of cans. A nice warmth between us. Sturdy enough to absorb a few other details. "Not that me dad worked in the chemist that much. Well, yeah, hardly at all. But not right, my mother selling."

"Ah, your father had Ballygall in his blood."

Another clink of cans.

"Here, Obee, why don't we buy it? The chemist. Hold out against the wankers. Betting shop. You in charge. Keep me mother upstairs."

Obee ignored the question, veering instead into her love of gambling "Ah, might as well, telling you everything now. The betting. Ah, you must have seen me always on the phone. Paddy Power and all that. Football just started, hasn't it. Group of us. Bet professionally. Well, seriously. Done well, we have. Especially the summer cricket. Always a blind spot for the touts. Have a gander at this great app. In development. The dog's bollix." She pulled out her phone.

I tried, but couldn't quite follow the app. Data, definitely. Odds, betting volume, crowdsourced something or other. Some sort of live feed. Once optimized, a boon to the bettor. Impressive though. Bells and whistles, graphs and graphics. "Seems a little bit too flash for the likes of Ballygall."

"Exactly. Iron it out, bit of luck, could be worth a fortune."

"We could then transform the chemist? Bookies. Call it The Holy Wager?"

"Telling you, Munk," she said, still ignoring me. "App worth a goldmine, could be."

"Let's eat," I said, worried the food and my gastronomic feat would be forgotten.

"Fufu fight first," she said, putting on an apron.

A duel.

Back-to-back we stood. Armed with a ball of Fufu each. She paced east (toward London), I paced west (toward Boston). A count of three.

One.

Two.

Three.

Turn.

Fire.

Fufu!

Two flesh wounds, but we revived ourselves with a Starry drink. Laughed at ourselves. Such nonsense.

Not much later, I announced, "Dinner is served."

"What about," she said. "Take it down to me Mum's. Down in the dumps, they all are, right."

"OK," I said. Better her family than mine.

So, down the bumpy, fissured path we walked, dark, unlit by streetlights, to the Chijindus, a corner house at the most eastern section of the Estate. Only a few feet from the curve of the Dublin road. Our lack of beach beyond that, and beyond that the salty darkness. Their garden was big, wrapped generously around the green colored house but lacking in flowers or grass or any sort of greenery. It had been converted to a practice ground for Flora, with goals and bollards and even a wooden wall, built by Kanu the Coach.

The Chijindus weren't exactly sitting there with knife and fork in their hands, but they were expecting us. Plates and cutlery squared on the coffee table. The telly off. The ornaments separated and polished.

A compliment really.

And a warm welcome too, not always offered. Hugs and a hearty handshake. A fake-surprised delight at the food. Happy questions from Chioma. Quick answers from Obee, but with a smidgen of pride maybe.

We then arranged ourselves around the coffee table, sitting on the sofa and two armchairs, Her father, Emeke, on the floor, allowing Flora to rest herself on an armchair. Beside her the cat, Piscin. Old now, its fur stiff and startled. The conversation quickly veering toward O'Neill, but redirected by Obee to the great topic of the Chijindu household, football, and in particular, Flora at football.

"Peamount Utd," said Obee, "when are the trials?"

Peamount, the elite football team.

Which initiated a collective conversation about Flora's preparation, her diet, her exercise regime, even her sleeping habits. The richness of the mantelpiece endorsing such collective interest, adorned with a plethora of her trophies, golden, braided figurines airborne and acrobatic.

When the conversation ebbed, Obee directed it toward Flora's music, her upcoming concert, her recent TikTok post, an aptitude reflected in the array of musical instruments hanging on the wall opposite the mantelpiece. Fiddle, tin whistle, bodhran, even a lap harp.

"And Liam," said Flora to me, "isn't he brilliant, at the church."

Nice try, but Obee directed everyone to Flora's art, which took up the last remaining wall. Reminiscent of Ballygall's first two murals.

"We won't mention the murals," said Obee. Nodding. Everyone nodding. More than a smidgen of pride.

As previously directed, I then asked Chioma about her writing. Her book. Her answers notably lacking the usual effusiveness. Everyone was tired. Nursing bruises and abrasions. Everyone devoting a few hours a day to the renovation of the B&B.

"That meeting, what The Queen call it, a parley," said Emeke. "Soon."

Which tensed everyone. Quiet. A stiff breeze in through the window, unsettling the instruments on the wall. The sea audible.

Chioma sucked her teeth. “We must watch out. A ceremony of innocence, he will drown the lot of us.”

A Parley at Our Not-So-Small-Church

The Toll Queen's name for it. A parley. The term supposedly originating from his great, great blah blah blah. A week or so after August 14th.

The Estate and Townies invited by O'Neill, who appeared from the rear of the altar, monstrous Glibb on his left, angelic O'Halloran the Magician on his right, introducing himself by way of that terrible laugh. He himself did not descend to the pews, but stayed amid the altar, arrogating to himself the authority of the divine, its bully pulpit. Tears (replicas of his alleged etc. etc.) already in his eyes. Another reenactment obviously re-enacting in his mind. He seemed composed, assured, amused. Boru beside him, equally composed.

He now inspired fear in all of us. Which may have been due less to his beard or wolfhound than to his subsequent production of a severed head, a pig's head, ceramic, decapitated from the front of Burke's butchers. Cheers from the Estate, which were immediately rethought but not retracted. Then an expectant silence, which was when O'Halloran began his distracting show of magic.

But before all that, there were conciliatory words from The Toll Queen, words of compassion and warmth. But Chioma would have none of it. Standing. Accusing. Pointing heavenward, well, altar-ward, at his majesty, accusing him of the B&B, which was when O'Neill produced that pig's head.

But before all that, The Toll Queen offered a list of inducements to the Estate – bribes, Chioma shouted – but which did nevertheless evoke a sense of awe, a sense of the miraculous: a paved road in the Estate; an entirety of streetlights; a level, un-yellowed, floodlit pitch; a rezoning to allow shops; a functioning sewage system; free Wi-Fi (cheers here). All for the simple acceptance of The Wall, south and all. But Chioma was having none of it. B&B, isn't it. What about the B&B?

Descending a magnanimous step, The Toll Queen said, "Burke the Butcher. Arrested, so he is. Full confession to Garda Michael for the attack on the B&B." Replica tears refreshed in his eyes. "Won't have the likes of him bothering you there anymore."

Jesus, Burke the pig-faced butcher, offered to us on a platter.

But Chioma would not be persuaded. The B&B. You, of course! You did it. Not Burke.

Which resulted in the aforementioned production of that pig's head.

But before that there was another inducement, wildly, madly popular. The provision of an air conditioned, heated bus, Wi-Fi enabled, not free but free of stops, an express, which was to proceed from the Estate to the gates of Trinity College. An express C.I.E. bus, boarded from the Estate *not* the town. That did not stop in the town. But the downside? Quickly understood by Ola Waclawski. Isn't it just like the Wall? Keeping us out of Ballygall? An unpopular and derided insight, which only hardened the celebrations, the handshakes of good fortune, the yelps and yahoos. Even I cheered. An express to Dublin!

But that severed head could not be completely forgotten. It had to be disappeared, dispelled. Enter the Abracadabra of Harry O'Halloran, who, for his final trick, produced out of that hot, dusty Ballygall air the actual bus, the actual Express, parked outside. New. Resplendent. Ready to take the Estate out of Ballygall, never to return.

Such a rush up through its shining doors. A back seat for me and Obee. Don't judge us. We are young. Gullible. Tipsy. A bottle of V&L between us. Enjoying a comfortable jaunt back to the Estate. The bus stop, with a shelter, already in place. Even an electronic timetable.

But not everyone boarded that reverse Trojan bus. Chioma, Emeke, Ola, Kanu and Doherty, the leaders, stayed away, wise but now isolated. Or to quote O'Neill, "Divide and fucking conquer, Archie, ya little, traitorous, cowlicked bollix."

Our Half-a-Home, Sold

Decorum would have warranted a slow, melancholy procession through our Upstairs and

Downstairs, beginning in 'my' room, the battered bunk bed, its toaster and kettle that pretended at independence, followed by a tour of the main room, the sofa, the dear ol' dining table (the bizarre pathos of furniture), that battered bread bin. Maybe run my finger along the kitchen counter, pat the stove, salute the sink, a last look out the window, the town now changed, now captive. Followed by a lachrymose march down the stairs, to the once heaving shelves, the indelible aroma of crisps-chocolate-coke, maybe saunter down aisle four, my first kiss with tongue, Obee. Maybe steal the door bell, break a small window. All that kind of mawkish stuff, but I preferred the stairs, our Giant's Causeway, my happy and extended family above me, moving out, selling out. Erasing the last of my father.

Debt, the utter invincibility of debt, my mother had lamented on my arrival, an opening that only deteriorated into a disparagement of my father's extravagance and irresponsibility. His fault, entirely.

Bitch.

So, I stayed on the Causeway, with hammer and saw, removing the slat of stair that had provided such succor for my father. A simple, softened plank of wood. The only memento I wanted.

The wall opposite had been slashed and gouged. Even burnt. Flame marks everywhere.

And down came Liam, an unlikely ambassador for the family. Still gunslingered up. Bright and happy. Whistling even.

The prick.

So, I told him about Boston. About the murders.

He knew. Of course, he knew. But when?

"Right after Dad, when you had swanned back to America." Offering me tea and a Twix with the insult.

"Ah, come on with us," he said. "All blow over. She'll be grand. Plenty of room."

"Me bollix. It's not her —"

"Ah, don't start all that. We all need a fresh start. Just like *you're* getting in America. Here, I'll even visit ya."

"Maybe I won't go back."

"That one, Obee," he said, smirking such a sleazy smirk. "Sure, her lot, think they'll be let stay?" He withdrew up a step, supping the tea meant for me. "Wouldn't hang around once you're done with the stupid stair. She's not in the best." Another sup. Then a gulp. "For Jaysus's sake, wanted out of this kip since you were two, haven't you? An' here you are sulking on the bleeding stairs."

Clearly irritated that I was spoiling his day of emancipation. His now unencumbered run at The Royal Irish Academy of Music.

"Made your bed years ago. What would Dad care? Happy where he is."

I returned to my hammering and sawing. Tears blurring my work.

Downstairs in the chemist, Janowski, that stubborn Palladiusian, was noisily ridding himself of a job. Carrying out the last bits of inventory, the door slamming, his farewells already said.

Upward Liam finally retreated.

But down she came. A downpour of perfume. Sleeves rolled up in exultation, a stupid yellow bandana of all things on her head. Sunglasses perched jauntily over it. But worn-looking, marred by the puffiness of poor sleep, and a scab on her chin and knee-scratches below her non-bumpy knees. But preceded by two bestial Ulstermen, hewn from granite it seemed, each carrying a pair of those high-table chairs, one front, one back, awkward but laughably light. Like errant Monty Python knights.

Our poor half-a-home. So laughable to everyone.

The Ulstermen departed to the street, dismembering the chairs on the cobblestones.

"Move," she said.

Behind her stood Liam and Conor the Impotent Comforter. All eager to begin their new step-family-adventure.

"Ah, come on with us," said Liam. His voice actually trembling. "Plenty of room."

Which was true. The Queen's tower house had plenty of room, plenty of cold and vindictive room. Loaned temporarily to my mother while O'Neill repaired to palatial lodgings in Dublin. A whole hotel floor, if you don't mind.

"Plenty of room," agreed Conor.

"Bad enough," I said.

They braced themselves.

"You sell my father out to that cunt, after all the damage he's done to the town, but now you and your fancy man go and live in his house. Sleep in his bed. Have you no shame at all?"

She tried to maneuver around me.

I stood in her way.

She tried again, her new Puma runners screeching on the Causeway.

I grabbed her wrists. Shockingly cold. Pushed her back up a step. Ducking her punch, and the next one, Conor restraining her around the waist but unable to stop her fist-swinging.

"Get back up there," I yelled, blocking her, weaving when she weaved. Feeling for my bunch of keys, a weapon perhaps, those Ulstermen.

"Ya wee cunt," she shouted.

Behind her, her Comforter stood in shock.

I threw my own punch. A smack, really. Right into his willowy, pillowy gob. Such a sound. Such a face he made. His lip bloody.

I advanced up a step. The keys jingle-jangling in my pocket.

But was lifted,

into the air,

like a toddler,

my arms and legs flailing,

funny if it weren't for the thump that thumped my head. As hard as granite. Stupendous enough to create its own weather. Thunder, lightning, a flash of stars, a concluding darkness. Knocking me almost unconscious. Though I could feel them, *her*, step over me, a Puma kick to my belly.

Many minutes later, I lifted myself from the stair. My head thumping. My eyesight clumsy. Tears, but tears of rage. The place empty. Quiet. The dust settled.

I went carefully back to my hammering. But too upset, I left it. Tempted to go Upstairs but didn't – I wanted to remember it as it was.

Checking, yes, the keys still in my pocket. I gave them a miserable jangle. Gave my thumb a good bite. Stayed for a while, detained by a question: Am I an emigrant if the place I emigrated from has fucking disappeared?

The Estate With No Name

An afternoon or so later, I sat on those straw stairs, jangling those jingle of keys, the only memento of my half-a-home.

Alone.

Obee working, I mean, gambling at home, a few doors down. The others in Ballygall.

The Great Wall was almost finished. A noticeable diminution, a paling of that yellow-hued brigade. The Southern section was definitely finished, its Filler filled with Burke's butchers, including that pig's head, dropped in by a Giant.

Yes, they knocked Burke's down. A few swipes, a few charges. Gone. Justice for his supposed assault on the B&B. Shock, but also belief, some magically believing that Burke was the true assailant.

So, Jesus, what was next?

There was always something next.

Surely The Wobbly, The Polski. Maybe even the Supermarket, the Florist, Burke's misfortune now universalizing the calculus.

I slurped my bowl of Onugbu soup, in quiet if not peace, no longer admonished from Upstairs.

Tired.

Visited by my Second Temptation. To return. A new job. A new apartment. Just pack up and leave. Sls-upp, Sls-upp, and I'm gone. Do what everyone wanted. Except Obee from BallyG —

And in she barged through that frosted door, rings on her fingers, bells on her phone. Another good day at the races or the football field. Huge bets on huge favorites. Nerves of steel. Fist-pumping me, our greetings still relatively formal. But sitting beside me, refusing Onugbu but taking a handful of McVitie's.

A cloudy day, the sky low and pensive.

The Straw House, 77 Seaview Court, sat on the first row of the north-facing Estate, affording an obstructed view of Ballygall, hidden now behind the arse-side of the Wall. A nice little garden, with orchids, a lawn, enclosed by a wall and an iron gate. Kanu's on the left, Doherty's on the right, Chioma's further down, closer to the sea.

The Estate quiet.

But look closer.

On the street.

An unprecedented sight.

Workmen. Not yellow-hued but from the Corpo', the government, installing streetlights.

Work.

Progress.

A Queen's promise.

Well, bribe.

All this, or most of it, visible right from the straw stairs.

"What a facking piece of shit," said Obee, meaning the Wall, adding, "Mum be here in a bit," meaning that all commentary regarding Queen, Shed and Butcher and so on, should be kept "in abeyance." Which she actually said. In a posh Dublin 4 accent. "Have a gift for you, Munk." Extricating from her white blouse a wad of warm bills. A couple of hundred. My share in her bets, though she had fronted me the money. I took it. Sat on it. It did not kill me to take it.

"A favor?" she asked. Which I granted, a rehearsal for her RTE audition. Done daily on the stairs. And then she asked another, a typical Obee tactic. Asking me, looking outside, the street quiet, everyone on that free Xpresso bus to Dublin.

"The grave?"

Young Akinfenwa's, in that Wicklow graveyard that temporarily held my father.

"Aki's," she said. "Wouldn't. But can't ask the family, you know."

Aki, her name for Young Akinfenwa, unused by anyone else. Seemingly a famous comedic actor, though Young Akinfenwa was never a bunch of laughs.

"Have never been, since."

"Of course," I said, wanting to end the discussion. "Kanu, already said, could borrow his car."

"Thanks!" she said. Quickly straightening up, brushing down her hair, her legalese clothes, removing her nose ring, wriggling more securely into her heeled but scruffy shoes. Standing solicitor straight. Her costume, barely changed since her landing in Ballygall. "Let's rehearse some lines. In the mood, yeah."

Scenario. Obee's client, male detainee, Mosney, languishing in Direct Provision. Me, Sargent Brendan, in charge. Facing Obee.

Behind me, the noise, the whoosh of the Xpresso express bus sweeping past. A cry of seagulls in pursuit.

Obee above me, shaking out her nerves.

I called out, "Quiet on set. Roll sound. Roll camera. Action."

"My client," said-shouted Obee, "has been left in the dark, Sargent. A veritable prisoner. No authorization to work. No timeline. No countdown. No visits. He has been told nothing."

"And what would he be wanting to know? The weather? The news? How much the dole is?"

"His future. What is being done with his future? And who is doing it?"

"And what would he be wanting to know about the future for? Sure, can anyone know the future at all, at all?"

"What the bleedin' hell is that," said Obee, dropping her Dublin 4 timbre. "Do Garda Michael."

I did. Snarled, barked, pulled an imaginary Koch and Heckler or was it Heckler and Koch. Extemporized. "Up to me, put all youse against the wall. Shoot youse."

"Is that right, Sargent?" replied Obee, waving me on.

"Fucking righ'. Wasted space ya all are."

He storms off. She storms after him.

Yes, that kind of script …

"What do you mean by 'ya all?' Oh, don't make a face like that. Have you no compassion? No warmth? A poor man. Trying to make a life for himself. For his family. Us Irish, how long have we suffered ... Ah, me arse. Let me just say it. You are a disgrace, Sargent Brendan. An absolute disgrace. To your profession, to your class, to your country." Storming off, or at least up and down a few steps. Returning. Saying in a quieter voice, leaning into me, "Just tell my client what the story is. Just a bit of information. That's all, one bloke to another."

"Bravo," I said, in a posh RTE voice.

We fist-pumped, yes, still that kind of formality.

"Grand," said Obee, glancing outside, expecting her Mum any minute.

But it was His Holiness O'Shaughnessy who arrived, refusing Obee's offer of tea and biscuits. Standing below us. Refusing a stair. So thin! His cheekbones bulging. His eyes big. His teeth visible under his skin. His soutane loose, sizes too big. Stern. Pointing at me. "Ya langer." His Cork accent strong, shrill. "What are you like? Sitting on the wrong stairs, with ya."

"Calm down, Father," I said.

"Your own father turning in his grave. Selling him out. In the family for generations, that chemist."

Finally, someone with the right reaction. "I know. That bitch sold it. To that other royal bitch."

This seemed to confuse His Holiness, who took a moment.

"Some soup, Father, Finn here made some lovely soup. Or a drink of water, yeah?"

"Why would she do that, boy?" he asked softly. Unsteady on his feet. "Town has gone to fuck. Pure fuck. Church. Mass canceled. That cunt is ruining the place."

"Which cunt? There's so many."

"Slattery. Denying, the man is denying our own saint, Palladius of Ballygall."

"Thought you meant that Queen."

"Just a pawn. But here, Boy, that money you, well, your father, the bit you still owe me. Would you have it? Not now, a' course, but can come back. Maybe this evening. Have the motor."

His papal blue Vespa, leaning against the garden wall. Still running.

I handed down that wad of still-warm cash. "Think that should cover it," though I had no clue. What did he want it for?

"Aedeen," he said, perceptively. "Legal avenues."

Why did everyone give that lady, that Grave Licker, money?

"See yis," he said, leaving, barely able to wrest the Vespa from its leanings.

"Should he be driving?" asked Obee, echoed by her arriving mother, saying, "That skinny man, should not be driving, o." Barging in as His Holiness wobbled away, with sudden cudgels of speed, with sudden cataclysmic stops. The children delighted. A couple of dogs in pursuit.

In Chioma came, highlighter on her fingers, TIS' stickers on her phone. A daily intrusion, commandeering the sitting room for her golden Mac and her book in progress, keeping an intrusive eye on us. Settling herself now on the sofa. Moving cushions, elevating the coffee table on coffee books, no longer comfortable writing in the war zone of Ballygall.

"Tea?" she asked, imperiously, unable to see us from her work station.

The tea provided by Obee, re-settling herself a step below me.

"Funny you two. Stairs. Come into kitchen."

We didn't. We never did. So, she shouted today's research questions from the sofa.

"How did The Queen know my father? Know my mother? Why did he not attend the funeral? There must have been a funeral? Why the Wall, of all things? Or was it your mother not your father that interested him? This book. Finally coming."

Then a request for Onugbu, with Fu-Fu. And pen and paper. Another cushion. Another coffee table book. Rolling her neck, such a thunderous creak.

"And what was it that Kanu drove against that evil Wall."

Which she knew, but we had to answer. "JCB."

"Alone," she said.

Which I corrected, adding my uncle-in-error. And then more tea, and a few McVitie's. Which made her thirsty and in dire need of water.

In other words, a pest.

"Show me," shouted Chioma, having finished her tea and biscuits. "Again."

Obee dutifully did. Happily, too. Her wedding invitation. A mock-up. Her name and his name. A mischievous background of straw.

"More straw," suggested Chioma, weddings, she liked weddings, expatiating again on her own Giant Lagos wedding, eloquent enough to draw her husband, Emeke, arriving outside in his new, gold, secondhand Land Rover.

Striding in, slacks and shirt barely creased, a nod to us before greeting his wife, "The writer! Maeve Binchy, isn't it, at work," almost running up to her. Obee behind him, overtaking him, bringing back a Star lager for him (and two for us). A family embrace.

I was not invited.

"An hour," Chioma said.

Another meeting. The business leaders of Ballygall. And Gallagher, Costello and Duffy.

Chioma and Emeke strategizing, but in Igbo.

"Tense mood they are," I ventured.

"Wait for it," said Obee, rolling her eyes. "That shitty word. You'll hear it."

I did. Finally. "Dublin." Emeke. Repeated a couple of times. Their voices tensing, pausing, then launching. But ultimately restrained, I thought. The barbs pulled. "What it's about?"

"The usual."

Money. Or the relative lack of it. Relatively lacking in Ballygall but not Dublin. The B&B, though popular, did not yield much of a profit, and even less from its tenant, Kanu. Whose name was invoked by Emeke, his platonic intentions not completely trusted.

"Kan-WHO?" I whispered.

"Kan-NO-DO," whispered Obee, back on her phone, testing her gambling app. "Hasn't worked in weeks. There, but not working. Off gallivanting with his sidekick, Dirty Doherty. But listen. Here's the latest flavor." A pause. "My father, yeah, thinks he's so smart. Casually mentioning this Dublin house, for sale, reasonable, adjacent to shops, even a bookshop, and even closer to the offices of this publisher, Maeve Binchy's, don't you know." She sucked her teeth.

Chioma The Writer did not want to live in Dublin, a lesser metropolis to her eventual home of London, feted and fawned as an acclaimed writer.

"And my mother, think she's so smart. Listen for it."

"London."

"The only reasonable city," translated Obee, "outside of Lagos, for a man of *real* ambition. Not some flea bag hotel. Money the problem, then earn the real money. But nicer than usual they are. Frazzled. Scared. Wait for it. Wait."

"Beer, Obee," shouted Emeke. "Two. Yes, two. A ceasefire. Start again. My fault. Start again."

And he did. Emeke got up and left. Even got in his Land Rover. Started the engine. Turned it off. Strode back in. Nodded to us. Smiling. Striding in. Embracing his wife, the wonderful writer. "The writer! Maeve Binchy, isn't it, at work,"

"Not bad," said Obee, up to retrieve four more beers.

"Yes, one for Finn," said Emeke, not always as generous.

We sat in silence, two on the sofa and two on the stairs. A salty breeze through the open window, a dusty breeze through the open door, which eventually brought the worried ranks of Ballygall.

A frank, honest discussion ensued.

A council of war?

No, a council of worry.

Everyone talkative. Everyone in despondent agreement. Business was terrible, even The Wobbly. People *were* avoiding Ballygall, preferring instead the Xpresso bus to Dublin, departing every hour, as punctual as its electronic timetable. A double-decker, with seats for feet, and room for bags and prams and even bikes. And free now! No fares for the foreseeable future. A bargain which made Dublin prices an added bargain. And the simple, complimentary joy of joyriding, everyone lollygagging back and forth from Dublin, with feet on seats.

But fear too.

Burke the Butcher, once an ally of the Queen, his shop pulverized into Filler. No one, absolutely no one, was safe now.

Which briefly silenced everyone. Drinking their tea with thirst. Kanu and Doherty asleep, snoring, obviously up to something at night. Tunnels, perhaps.

Outside, the yell of kids bouncing on that trampoline set between the Wall and the Estate. The boing of a pogo stick beside it.

The church had been abandoned too. Masses canceled. Confessions canceled. Even the Maestro canceled.

Others had left. Permanently. Fled. The stress, the anxiety. Ogunleye the Good-Looking, from the Estate. Walsh the Good-Looking, Townie. Aleksy Waclawski, Ola's son.

All fled on the Xpresso.

Terrible. But worse had arrived. Well-bribed and incentivized officials. The Food Safety Inspector. Harassing everyone. Even the B&B. And the VAT man. And the tax man. Audits for everyone, except the florist and supermarket.

And Garda Michael, of course. His Garda Immigration Bureau. Insistent. A dangerous development for the newly Irish, their conditional citizenship, which was revocable, easily revocable.

But money too. Offers for all the businesses, from that devil Devlin. Everyone honest, sharing the terms, the amounts, the urgent timeline. Tempted. And all collectively gobsmacked at my mother's luck, half a million for our lowly chemist.

Such a lot of money, individually and collectively, which could only impoverish the town, eviscerate it. Which was obviously the intention. A campaign accelerated, everyone felt. The Toll Queen more fully aligned with Teresa and Devlin. The Queen's wife now seen often around the town. At the church, closed to everyone but her.

What could we do? To rally the people? To wake them up?

"Ideas," said Chioma. "Ideas, my fellow Ballygallians."

The Grave of Young Akinfenwa

I borrowed Kanu's car, an old, roomy, comfortable Toyota Camry, redolent of football boots and moi moi — an inexplicably favored snack of his — beans mashed and balled, not sweet, not savory, not at all tasty. At Obee's request, I drove, in stiff suit and pressed tie, our early evening departure timed to circumvent her parents, and even her sister, all of whom would not have approved of our trip.

Wisely, perhaps.

Obee wore a black dress and black shoes, brought with her from London, a premeditation that worried me. But also her nose stud, her big, gold earrings, her brindle-colored glasses, her hair up, the Obee of old. She brought flowers, a vase, and a wreath. And a full, unopened bottle of Jameson, obviously their tipple of choice.

But she was composed, grateful to me for agreeing, for borrowing, for driving, worrying that locket rumored to have once contained heroin. Touching up her makeup, her lipstick.

But lovely.

I drove south out of the Estate, taking the abandoned Dublin road until it met with its own diversion further south. I drove slowly, wary of Garda Michael, who had acquired a squad car, often tailing the Xpresso to Dublin and back for some reason. Maybe he had a strain of collie in him?

Obee rarely drove, too easy a target for Garda Michael and his assiduous ilk.

A bright summer evening, we were often preceded by a squall of seagulls, their noise a thankful reprieve from the silence in the car. Obee refused the radio.

I parked where we had parked our van. On the path but not a parking space. The car turned, ready for a quick getaway.

From the far reaches of the graveyard came the caterwaul of cider drinkers, the same medley of song and slur, a standing appointment obviously. The beginnings of a fire too, a belch of smoke. "No respect," said Obee, scornfully.

My father's grave sat blank, anonymous, empty, its ground still a little churned.

Obee didn't notice.

She was still. Very still. Stiff really. Then tiny reverential steps to his grave, stepping over its little plastic fence, badly cracked. The grave was flowered, wreathed, its vases full of water. With a six-pack of unopened Red Bull. His headstone was inlaid with a photo. Smiling. Handsome. Which ill-prepared you for the epitaph below. Murdered but Avenged. Which was true, which had furthered the alliance between Sawn-Off Akinfenwa and Razor Curran, whose son had survived the shootout.

"Lovely, the flowers," said Obee. Looking small, standing below that leviathan angel. Taking a moment. Closing her eyes. Then trampling right into the flowers, making room for hers, the vase, the wreath, clumsy, knocking things over, throwing bouquets out. Jettisoning the Red Bull onto my father's grave. She snuggled the Jameson at the headstone, covering it with flowers.

Serious. Standing back. Evaluating her flower arrangement. Making quick adjustments. Brisk, brusque, even savage. But finally finalized, just one last adjustment, the nudge of a vase, the rebuke of a wreath.

She stood back. Behind the plastic fence. I joined her. But at arm's length. Not wanting to crowd her.

"Will you pray with me, Munk?" she asked, serious, sincerely. "Out loud?"

Shocking. She as secular, as skeptical, and as sarcastic as myself. Taking this too far, she is. For an ill-advised fling. For a bloke who was rumored to have had many simultaneous girlfriends. Don't ask an ex-boyfriend like me to do such things.

"Please? For me?" she said.

I nodded toward the cider heads, but she asked again.

"OK," I said, taking a small step back toward my dad's grave. "You start, I'll join in." Maybe the cider heads will join us too. Probably friends of Young Akinfenwa's.

"Thanks."

"Video," she said, "won't get you." Pointing it at the grave. Recording. A preamble. The date, the place, his name, or her name for him, Aki.

> Our Father, who are in heaven, hallowed be
> Thy name.

Her voice so London.

> Thy Kingdom come, thy will be done,
> On earth, as it is in heaven.

I joined in. She smiled. Turned the phone toward me, despite her promise. Briefly.

Together, we prayed.

> Give us this day our daily bread
> And forgive us our trespassers as we
> Forgive those who trespass against us.

But said slowly, not at Mass speed. So slow I forgot the words now and then. Imagined of course, but I thought I heard cries and laments from her. Which reminded me of the inquisition of my father's corpse. Were you a handsome man? Young Akinfenwa was. Were you a man of wit and utmost sophistication? Young Akinfenwa was witty, but maybe not so sophisticated. A man of brawn and strength? Definitely. He could be a force.

> And lead us not into temptation,
> But deliver us from evil.

"Thank you, Finn," she said, stopping the recording. "Could you give me a minute? I'll join you in the car." Edging back, not inviting any sort of physical contact. Her hand on that locket, rolling it between her fingers.

"OK, you sure? You OK?"

She was. Turning away, back to the grave.

God, the relief. The reprieve. I ran back to the car. Starting the car, it started! Revving it, it revved! Checked the radio. Checked the lights. Saw her coming. Jumped out, opened the passenger door for her.

But she demurred. Sat in the back, in the middle, slumping, her glasses removed, ignoring my lame taxi meter joke.

I drove fast. A sharp turn out of the graveyard, onto the Dublin road. Suggesting some food, a drink, something to refresh us.

But she was crying. Her face in her hands. Her body convulsed. Rectangled in the rearview mirror.

I kept driving. But slowed. Didn't say anything. Let her be.

And she did subside. Apologizing, sitting straighter, wiping her eyes, finding tissues in her handbag. Offering me one, which was sort of funny.

"Didn't realize," I said, sympathetically. "The extent."

"No one did. Couldn't. My secret life, yeah." Trying to smile. "Remember that summer fellowship I had, Trinity, theater."

"Oh yeah," I said, lying. Pulling into the slow lane of the dual carriageway, behind a big articulated Dunnes Stores' truck, which seemed to yield a semblance of privacy, its shade and tremor.

"That was when it kicked off. My Father too busy to check on me. My mother far away in far off Ballygall. Ah, Munk, it was sweet. Our own flat. A whole flat. En suite and everything. You would understand, yeah, your family, your small home. Anything to drink?"

I did. V&L, stowed in the smelly, goalie-gloved compartment. Passing it back, our fingers touching. A glance in the rearview mirror watching her gulp, gulp, gulp. Passing it back to me, gulp, gulp, gulp. Securing it on the passenger seat, safe beneath the seat belt. We were drinking a lot by then.

"Intense. But won't lie to you. Was the real thing." Rubbing that ugly, bulbous locket. "Me and Aki. We had a plan. I'd go to Trinity. Move to Dublin. Good student. The arts. Have pretend digs, hoodwink my father. Live that rich, peaceful life."

"Peaceful?"

"It *was*. Nothing ever happened. Until. You know. But, then yeah, you don't know it all. They murdered him in the flat. The other drug gang. Shot him and Young Curran. How Curran survived, I don't know. Treat the white bloke first, probably."

"At the flat?"

"Yeah, bastards. Got their comeuppance though. All four of them."

Her voice hardening. Reminding me of my mother, justifying the murder of those informers.

"Where were you?"

"Lucky, wasn't I. At class for once, had sent a truancy letter home, hadn't they."

"Jesus. Could have been there."

Silence.

I took a strong bite of my thumb. Focused on the road. Just the Dunnes truck trundling ahead of us. The sea on our right, a curdling pewter. Another round of V&L.

"Mad craic," said Obee, wiping her eyes, righting herself. "Until."

"And that's why," I said, realizing. "Dublin, you wouldn't come to Dublin with me. Trinity."

"Yes."

"That makes so much sense to me now. Arguing over Dublin, the best compromise. London so far. And I always felt there was something hanging over us. Obvious now that you're telling me this, though at the time, thought it was nothing serious between you and him."

"It was serious."

"Should have told me."

"I just did. Only *you* know. The full thing. Of course, Young Curran knows, but he's got his own problems. And Flora knows, probably. Sixth sense, that one. But no one else. Ha! Not even my straw groom."

"Makes sense to me now," I said, speeding up, overtaking the Dunnes truck, swerving back to the slow lane. "Always felt, never measured up, or something. Me not tough enough. Compared to him, that was it. Yeah, suppose I was afraid wouldn't measure up. Put me off London even. But how can you measure up to someone, like him, I mean, after, he's sort of a ghost for us." Yeah, a ghost, perfected and perpetuated by death.

"You're a whole different kettle of fish," said Obee, warmly.

"And there was America, of course. Wanted to get back there, my birth right."

"A whole different kettle of fish," she repeated.

"That's what I mean. Know you don't mean it now. But the comparison, there, unsaid mostly. But like a ghost. Haunting us. Does that make any sense?"

"No. But I get your point. Aki the ghost. He would have laughed at that. But not the only ghost that's haunted us, is it? You have your own ghost, Munk. From your own family, yeah."

"Me? Oh, you mean my dad. Now. Buried. Murdered by that —"

"No, not your dad. That ghost that lived Upstairs."

"What?" I said, slowing, the Dunnes truck blaring behind me.

"Your mother. The ghost. Living that dead life upstairs. Like a corpse. Never leaves, never seen."

"Yeah, yeah, she had her own trauma."

"I betcha' she did."

"Sold us out now, she has."

"Ah, good for her," said Obee. "Getting out there. Getting a life for herself. I mean it." She sat up. Scooted forward. Her face looming in the rear-view mirror. "She's come back to life. Calm down, Munk. I'm just telling the truth. *She* completely haunted us. Yes, like Aki, I'll maybe give you that. But look, you think you didn't come to London with me because you'd miss out on America, but deep down you knew you wanted to stay close to Ballygall. Yeah, I get it, I get it. The official account. The Wall, you discovered. The DIG you were forbidden from. And your dad, descendant of Finn McCool. On every committee imaginable. All that. You thought you wanted to be close to Ballygall because of him. Inherit his mantle, yeah. Popular as hell. But it's not true. It's your Mum. That ghost that lived Upstairs. That's why it was hard for you to leave. Knew you weren't serious about anywhere, other than Dublin. Her. Not him. What I don't get is why? Why does she have so much pull, so much power over you? It's her failed marriage, not yours."

Suddenly in my mind, my father's wedding ring on Liam's finger.

"She was our ghost. Without her, we would be in London. I am telling you. If she was happy and everything. We'd be there. No matter how many committees your Da got on. No matter how many walls he built. No matter how many moldy saints he dug up. You banking, me litigating. What I don't get is why. Now don't get mad, Munk."

I pulled over. Parked just past a chippy van. An evening line of sunburnt customers. Got out of the car. The sea behind me. Obee followed me, standing, the car behind her. Bringing the bottle.

"So, if we're saying everything," I said, "what's in your locket, then?"

She laughed. "Not heroin." Lifting it up.

Ugly, bulbous thing.

"What then?"

"You'll laugh. Safety pin. Piece of it. His as a baby. His beloved grandmother."

I did laugh, nerves probably. I took a gulp of V&L. "Anyway, mad to think it's my mother, somehow implicated, with us, with me. Her happy? Fat chance. And barely said half a civilized word to her most days. Stayed on the stairs, I did, studying, rather than Upstairs, her up there in all her layers."

"Yeah, that's what I mean. This strange ghost Upstairs. Never leaving. Never showing her face. Always in the background for us. No background for your dad, always out in front he was. But she. Up there. You sitting on the stairs. Close to her but not too close. Your dad on the stairs too, close but not too close."

"I know, sort of screwed up. But love the stairs, I do. The tea, the treats."

"Not the same with Liam, she isn't?"

"No. They are a pair. But if she was happy, would I have gone to London? That's sort of mad. Stayed, stayed for my dad, if anything. Build the Wall. Maybe he'd get me involved in the DIG. That I see. But not her. Not her unhappiness. Always unhappy, wasn't she."

"Look, we should talk more. But somewhere else. Maybe not dressed as fancy. But. Finn." Taking my hand. Her brown eyes steady and clear. "I want to say thank you for coming with me today. Taking me, working it out with Kan-WHO." Looking at me expectantly.

"Kan-U," I said weakly.

"Driving me. Listening to me. Supporting me. Now. *And* back then when he died. You were warm and wonderful, and funny. Never should have taken up with Aleksy. That was vindictive. Hurt you. Sorry. So, let me make it up to you. Let me buy you a bag of chips."

I shrugged, my head spinning.

"And curry sauce?"

"Grand," I replied.

The Great Wall, Finished

We were woke by silence. By absence. Dawn arriving without its usual tumult.

I was roused from the floor of the B&B. Wriggled out of my watchman's sleeping bag. Sentinel for the night, my turn, then Doherty, then Kanu, then the Chijindus, even Emeke. The same precautions taken at the Sklep and the Wobbly.

Outside looked like the usual outside, though my view was impaired by the Hiace van, three of them parked protectively outside the B&B, The Sklep and The Wobbly.

A cloudless sky.

But not a sound. I took my hammer, took a protective bite of my thumb and went outside. Joined my fellow Ballygallians. Confused. Discombobulated by the silence.

The absence.

The tidiness.

The cobblestones, shaved and downsized, had been swept clean. Polished possibly. No dirt, debris, sand, or Filler. No litter. No bird shit, which had become a bit of a plague. The air similarly refreshed. Pure. A smidgen of salt. A nice breeze easing over the east side of the Wall.

What probably confused us, in addition to our somnolence, was the Southern Wall. Still the preliminary of that diminutive security wall, its froth of concertina line and its sleepy Blue line. Nothing different there, nothing absent, when everything else was different if not absent.

We massed in the center of town, between Boots and our erstwhile chemist. Some in pajamas. Some with pillows. Looking sleepily around.

Searching for what was absent.

The nose-broken JCB was gone.

But that had been gone a while, hadn't it?

The Maestro at the church organ, gone.

But he'd been gone a while, hadn't he?

Burke's Butchers was gone. A gap, but no rubble, no dirt, a huge tarp in place.

But that had been gone a bit before, hadn't it?

Hadn't it? Looking amongst ourselves, yawning, nerves and sleep. But missing. Some of *us* were missing.

Ogunleye the Good-Looking. Gone.

But she was gone before this. On the Xpresso.

Walsh the Good-Looking. Gone.

Before this. Also on the Xpresso.

The Good Lookers leaving.

But there were things previously missing that now were not missing. Improvements. Marked improvements. The polished and right-sized cobblestones, but also new lights and plant boxes hanging from them. The pavement smoothed, its cracks and crevices soothed. Trees! Baby trees, coddled in wire. And the businesses. Unlocked, cleaned, tidied. Even our chemist.

How had we missed all this? Done when? Done how? Without us noticing? Were we too distracted, too stressed, too anxious?

No.

We were too Xpressoed. Riding the Xpresso bus day and half the night. Feet on seats. Its schedule (suspiciously) escalated to half-hour departures. From the Estate. Its cost still free.

On time, and in mockery, the bus swept past on its western descent to the Estate, blaring its siren.

Which recalled to us other modes of transportation. Particularly and euphorically one.

The JCB.

Missing. All of them missing. Wasn't there hundreds of them in banana yellow?

Missing.

And the vans, the trucks, the mixers, the cranes, the shovels, the wheelbarrows, the hard hats, the yellow-hued shirts.

All missing.

Were the builders gone?

Rubbing our eyes, pulling up our pajamas, we looked, we scanned. We saw what was missing. And it was good.

The builders.

All of them.

How had we not noticed that? Their diminution over time. Surely, over time. Yes. The more we thought, the less they seemed. Over time.

Their encampment?

Kanu climbed the B&B's Hiace van, and confirmed, gone, even cleaned, charred, but empty, returned to the land.

Gone.

But why are they gone? Why are they missing?

Confirmed east and west, and yes, south, behind that Blue Garda line, missing, the scaffolding was missing. The requisite ladders also missing. The tables and workbenches. All that symmetrical string missing. Mortar and trowel, shovel and pickaxes, all missing.

As a group, perhaps even as a town, we headed east, through back gardens, approaching the Great and unencumbered Wall. Stood before it. In awe. In admiration. Stone, not bricks. Beautiful, exorbitant Kilkenny stone. White. Cleaned. Polished. Shimmering. Fronted with grasses, even tiny, yes, yellow flowers. Bees amongst them. A Great Wall. But perhaps too great, too tall. Sixteen feet, each foot an ancestral century for O'Neill. But too great. The creak in our necks. The sun in our eyes. Seagulls lording above us, some perched, some walking, a real walkway, for the Mad Queen?

Could we touch the Great Wall?

Yes, we did.

East, then the west Wall, but not south.

Cool. Smooth. Thick. We patted it. East and west. We petted it. East and west. Measured it. Rubbed it. Tickled it. East and west but not south. Leaned against it. Pushed against it. Listened to it. My uncle-in-error even kissed it. East and west. We walked along it. Jogged along it. Sprinted along it. Interior and exterior, east and west. Hugged it. Sniffed it. Ah, the marvelous quarries of Kilkenny, east and west, interior and exterior, but not south.

The Great Wall of Ballygall was complete.

Done.

Dusted.

Delivered.

Everyone burst into tears.

Which perhaps drew that mad dog, Garda Michael. In his squad car. Panting. Reinforced by that roused Blue line. "Have you no beds to go to? Go on, out of that. Disperse." Drawing his gun, of course.

Which prompted a question for him. “When is the ceremony? The opening? The hoopla? Maybe the Queen cutting his arm off, and bashing it, like a bottle of champagne, against the Wall? His stupid Red Hand speech?”

Garda Michael already knew. Such a smug smile. “No speech. No ceremony. No nothing.”

A nothing that told us all something.

That something else was coming.

The Wall a mere milestone. A part of something more. Something worse.

A Ghost Tour of Dublin

A day out in Dublin. The Big Smoke. Just me and Obee. Just what the doctor ordered. Tired after a night's watch at the B&B, separate sleeping bags unfortunately. But nice. Chatting into the night, anticipating the dawn, the return of the Builders, but no, they were really done.

We took the Xpresso.

Boarding from the Estate. Free. A real express, straight to Dublin, St. Stephen's Green, no stops, not even in Ballygall, our walled-off town.

Upstairs, at the back, feet on seats. Well, mine, anyway, Obee did not take such liberties in public, taking her sup of V&L with extreme stealth. The bus packed, yes, a chorus of 'Sls-upp, Sls-upp' and our old nickname, "Zebra," which we acknowledged, knowing the more scabrous alternatives. But everyone quickly lulled and lullabied by the shushed push of the bus.

We awoke to the verdant splendor of the Green, the ducks fulsome in their welcome. Thanked the driver, Gabriel Okara.

We swanned around the Green, and we saw that all was good. Even saw Boru the wolfhound, with two princesses, guarded by Glibb and other giants. Their father on the campaign trail, trailing badly, their mother more frequently on the telly, talking of Church and charity.

Northwest we perambulated, toward our old haunts, Obee well-dressed in skirt and blouse, shoes and even a briefcase, respectable and unimpeachable. A precaution she often took, being black, not white. Though, of course, there were whistles, glances, whispers, thoughts, *why is he… Why isn't she…*

Arriving at the Brazen Head. Big, busy, loud, brazen, full of my favorite people, Yanks, young Yanks, backpackers, and trust-fund babies. Indulged by Obee, who thought it a little lily-white, but persuaded by the betting shop next door. We ordered our favorite lunch. Fish and chips, twice. With Star lager, which they never had, so Harp instead, fortified by

V&L. All covered by Obee, her winnings, especially given my losses — home, father, mother, brother, and so on.

His Holiness O'Shaughnessy was there. Without his Roman costume. Slacks and a blue jumper, his white priestly collar underneath. Melancholy over a full pint of Murphy's. Skinny. Emaciated even. Saw us. Tolerated us for a while. Would only talk about Slattery. "Devil, I'm telling you, boy. Selling us all out. Not just me, dozens other priests. Removed. Punishment. Heresy. Laicization. And what's my heresy? Saint Palladius. That money-grabbing bastard. With his Queen. What am I supposed to do now?" He tugged at his jumper.

I suggested food, a big plate of fish and chips.

"My whole life. The Church. Scholar. Where will I live? What will I do? Without my church? Without my saint?"

"Come back to Ballygall," said Obee, nudging his pint toward him. "We are fighting back. The lot of us."

"I am heartbroken," said His Holiness. "Please, let me alone now. Lick my wounds, boy." He smiled. Briefly.

We left, but not before Obee ordered and paid for a fish and chips dinner for him. Then we hurried away.

The relief.

The reprieve.

We ran back onto our usual circuit: National College of Art and Design (for a nap), then Christ Church, then the Spar (a couple of Moros). All done faithfully. Our mood picking up.

Normally, our Big Day in the Big Smoke would dictate a long walk across the river to Parnell St., to surreptitiously watch Mr. Kanu actually work, cutting hair. Kan-WHO? Kan-U! But Obee preferred tourist-terrible Temple Bar.

By which she meant The Tomahawk Steak House, within which, my mother, my alleged ghost, was working. Promoted to waitress. At Obee's insistence, we sat opposite, at a coffee shop, The Feisty Bean, stooled by the window.

"Just watch," said Obee. "She can't see you with that crowd in there. Bloody hell, getting younger by the day, she is."

Younger, prettier, the Wildean portrait of her true ugliness.

But we sat and watched, Obee gambling on her phone. My mother was efficacious, warm, vivacious, enjoyed by the hungry Yanks. Taking orders by heart, no Tomahawk pad for her. Sipping coke at intervals. Checking her phone at intervals. So, I texted her. A vituperative volley, but Obee deleted it before I could send. She bought more coffee, counseled me to just watch. So I did. My eyes glazing, my rancor ebbing a bit.

Looked at my phone, my texts. From Liam. *"Loving the Tower House. Come on over for dinner, ya big sulk. Living the life we are."* And other provocations, though he probably meant well.

The pace dulled in the Tomahawk. Her break arriving.

"*No*," I said to Obee. "Nope." Pausing. The coffee shop empty, except for the owner on his laptop. "Look," I said, trying to be civil. "You don't really know her. What we, what I have to deal with."

"Tell me, then. I know what *she* had to deal with."

So, I told her. My mother and Doherty, Boston, bamboozling the BC professor, the hacked secret data, the five, *five* informants executed, and the conscientious professor poisoned. Six deaths. My father unaware, and me just a baby.

"Jesus Christ," said Obee. Gazing across, but my mother on a break. Fifteen minutes usually.

"Ruined, well, my father never forgave her. Had to flee. Middle of night. Back to Ballygall. All his research lost, his career. And I was just a baby. A baby! And she gets involved in all this."

Obee cross-examined me.

"Yes," I said. "Doherty and her, yes. IRA. Yes. Doherty was working on the Boston tunnel. Yes. They knew each other from Derry. My dad, no part of it, but damaged the most. He was a professor of computing, artificial intelligence. Genius. Yes. Six people. All that blood on her hands. No. My father never forgave, obviously. Yes. Explains a lot of it. She Upstairs. He on the stairs. Yes. Had that article on the Wall. The BC poisoning. I know. I know. Right there. Her crime. For decades. Laminated, yes. I know. Mad. And did all this, I was just a baby."

"Jesus, Munk," said Obee, taking, squeezing my hand. Suitably shocked. Even speechless. Standing, getting two more coffees, returning, dazed-looking. Asking the same question.

"Yeah," I said. "Had the newspaper article hanging in front of him. Yes, since I was born. Always there. Laminated. Must have printed it out again a few times. Laminate again."

"Your father the laminator," said Obee, trying in vain to be funny. "Why didn't she pull it down?"

"She probably did. A few times."

"Jesus, Munk," taking, squeezing my hand again. "God love you. Must have been awful."

Which wobbled me a bit.

"In the middle of all that."

Across from us, my mother reappeared in the Tomahawk. Her hair brushed. Her makeup freshened. Touchy-feely and chatty with the young waitresses.

"Jesus, Munk, you were living on a battlefield."

"Yeah, that's right. He even called her Benandonner, Finn McCool's giant adversary. Clashing there daily on our stairs. A war, I suppose. Cold when it wasn't explosive."

"Ya poor thing." Gulping coffee.

Me also gulping.

"Jesus, Munk, knew your parents, something must have happened, dysfunctional, but not something like that."

"So that's who we're dealing with. Murderer and a poisoner. And she barely took care of us. Always Upstairs. Barely out."

"Yeah," said Obee, weakly.

"What? Say it."

"Well, you know I'm no wilting flower, Munk, but your father was no saint. I know, I know she did. But *he* was barely at home. Didn't do anything for the shop. Take you or Liam anywhere that didn't suit him. Sitting on the stairs getting drunk with everyone. On every committee. Yeah, avoiding her, but what about you and Liam? Yeah, the Wall, the ravines, yeah, yeah, east and west. But what about the DIG? The saint. Wouldn't even let you in on that, for obvious reasons. All I am saying, not a saint. Blame on both sides. But betcha' your father asked you to take sides. Didn't he?"

"Jesus, only one side to take when there's a murderer."

"But you didn't know that, all the Boston stuff. Dad dragged you in, turned you against her. Forced you to take sides. Admit it. But never even your problem. Bit like me, yeah. My Ma wants to go to London, then Lagos, but my dad's mad for us to move to Dublin. Both of them trying to drag us into it. No. No. I went to London for my own reasons, not for my Ma. For loads of reasons. But yeah, they dragged me in a bit. That's what parents do, Munk."

"Parents, they fuck you up."

"But compared to me, living in a war, you were, Munk. Sitting on the stairs with your dad. Looking at that article, her crime. Jesus. Laminated an' all. Thought I had troubles, me parents all over us, me be a barrister, Flora be a superstar footballer-artist-musician, but compared to you. War. Absolute war."

"Yeah, did feel like a battlefield sometimes. Screaming at each other. But I was looking out for the chemist itself. The building. All we had. That little thing. Didn't know about loan then. But. Look. Not busy. She's going to see us."

"Let's just pop in and —"

I left.

"OK, Munk," she said, catching me up outside the stately Oliver-Buck-Mulligan-Gogarty pub.

"One more ghost," I said.

From there, under her own directions, I bore her south and east, to a well-appointed building on Merrion Square. Modern, metallic, luxurious, columns of coruscating silver, even a uniformed doorman, very Big Apple, who was likely unaware that the building, or one particular flat, en suite, was haunted. That it continued to haunt Obee. To haunt us both, I suppose.

"Just watch," I said, retrieving coffees for us. Sitting at a bench in the park. The perambulations of well-heeled walkers. Dogs and toddlers. Toddlers on dogs. "Just watch."

She did.

She sat and watched. Remembered. Took my hand now and then. Silent. A tear now and then. Annoyingly restrained, so I said, "Your own battlefield, I suppose?"

Which surprised her.

"No, wasn't like that. Others lived, nowhere near, a place like this. Ah, Munk, it was grand. Our own flat. Shower *and* bath. TV in every room. Carpets as thick as your head. One of those espresso machines. Drank so much coffee. Super-caffeinated bets, yeah. Shopping at Brown Thomas. But main thing, not like where we come from, had the place to myself most of the time. Drug business is a street business, always out and about, yeah. Such peace and luxury."

"Peace?"

"Yep, peace. Just me most of the time. Coffee and TV. Endless afternoons. Takeaways delivered to the door. Even did some studying."

"But him? The gang?"

"I know. But I never saw any of that. Don't think there was much."

"Really?"

"Yeah, but he kept me well out of that."

"And great bloke, don't get me wrong, Obee, only a few years ahead of me, but not the wilting kind either, is he, turf war and all that? Battlefield, surely."

"OK, OK, I hear you. Let's just sit and watch, yeah. No, I do. I do hear you. It's fair. Me at you about your Mum, and yeah, it's fair. But can't explain it. Was a peaceful time." Rubbing that ugly, bulbous thing of hers.

So we sat, drank our coffees, the clouds passing high above us. Quiet. Feeling sort of proud of ourselves. Mature. Composed. Steering toward our mutual pain.

I want to end there, a wise vigil, a collective exorcism, a dignified under-the-circumstances observance. But we didn't end there.

We went back to the Brazen Head and drank our heads off.

The stress, of course.

Atonement by Amputation, both, one at a time

Election night, all sorts of elections, but mainly the presidential election, with the associated referendum to elevate the office beyond its ornamental function.

Me and Obee watched from our straw stairs in our straw house. Via computer. Watching the polls a bit, the pundits a bit, but mainly watching yesterday's news, which began three days ago. The Toll Queen being the news, the whole news and nothing but the news.

At an undisclosed location, offshore perhaps, due to Hippocratic concerns, O'Neill had his wedding finger surgically removed. Atonement by amputation, it was suggested. Political gimmickry was further suggested. The operation perhaps performed by his Giant, Glibb, or the fanged work of his wolfhound, Boru. Without the aid of anesthetic, it was claimed, just Jameson and Nurofen. Verification performed by an erstwhile UN inspector.

Photographic proof was produced.

Medical records, somewhat redacted, were produced.

The Queen himself was produced, his finger missing.

His missing finger, however, was not produced. Perhaps it was posted (mailed) to his wife, or to one lucky, rural voter.

Legal concerns were also produced. Was such recreational amputation lawful? Was it sinful? Was it covered under the public health services (HSE) of Ireland? Was it likely to encourage copycats?

The Queen held a press conference the next day. Flaunted his lessened hand. His wife by his nine-fingered side. Tears, of course, but restrained. No questions allowed or answered, just a statement. Which promised both fingers, but twice, one at a time.

The second digit would be amputated the very next day.

The very day before the very election.

At an undisclosed location.

Likely offshore.

Was there a general cry and hew to save his pinkie? A protest, a campaign of civil disobedience, a sit-in, a sit-down, a finger vigil by candlelight?

No, there was not.

But there were a lot of tweets, #FingerLickingGood being a fair representation.

Everyone waited. Pleased when unofficial reenactments of the first amputation were released. Drawings, cartoons, and puppetry.

No one really believed he would do both. Political gimmickry, isn't it?

But he did.

The day before the election.

At an undisclosed location.

Likely offshore.

Verified by that UN inspector.

His little pinkie amputated. The Full Monty Atonement.

Perhaps mailed to his wife, or a lucky, inner-city voter?

Then his appearance on RTE that night, the very night before the election. Brave and bandaged. With his wife, together, holding what was left of their hands. The picture of love. O'Neill useless, a complete bag of tears at every question, besotted with his own sacrifice. But wary. You could see his wariness. Braced for another #FingerLickingGood.

But Ireland and its non-existent colonies were touched. Impressed. Proved wrong. Perhaps it had misjudged him? The polls tightening. Sentiment softening. Opinion turning.

But Thanks-Be-To-Jaysus, he lost. O'Neill lost the presidential election.

By a finger or two.

Opinion suggesting that perhaps another finger might have made the difference. Or maybe an arm, or a bit of a leg? A head, even.

The poor, lessened Queen was disappointed, but expressed consolation at the accompanying defeat of the associated referendum, Ireland preferring to keep its presidential office small and ornamental.

"Fackin' hell," opined Obee, on the stairs. "Lost. But does that mean Ballygall also loses?"

"Explain yourself," I rejoined.

"President," she said. "Job, innit. Something to keep him away from Ballygall. This is going to be bad."

And as usual, Obee was right.

Our Church Taken, Our Holiness Taken

In the beginning, God knows what we thought.

It began in the dark. Ballygall still without form or shape, its harassed homes and shops barely distinguishable from the darkness. The boozy spirit of The Wobbly still hovered over the town.

But then.

The mahogany pews, bitten and scratched, were lifted-dragged-screeched from the church and arranged like elongated coffins on the cobblestones. But a reckless, haphazard arrangement. Some overturned, revealing mosaics of gum and dried, ancient snot. Some bent, broken, snapped. Perhaps to be repaired, cleaned and arranged for an opening ceremony for The Great Wall? No —there really was to be no opening ceremony. The pews were hammered and chopped, right there, in the cold blood of morning. Drawing the entire town.

Then a shout, "Let there be light," from a yellow-shirted builder atop a ladder. Laughing, before he thumped his lump hammer into a stained window, shattering light and glass. A colleague beside him, also laddered, also laughing, lumped the next window, and so on. Then from the interior came a procession of builders carrying marble and wood, candles and gold paneling, holy water lapping their blasphemous boots. The church now punctured and parched. Two others carried out the pulpit, throwing it atop the chopped pews.

And that was the first day.

The Toll Queen and his wolfhound arrived and saw that it was good. Very good.

Pointing next to the firmament, to the heaven-scraped bell tower, which was de-belled. Extracted through the forcibly enlarged window and swung like an autumn chestnut out and down. Set on the back of an open trailer, its copper taken away to be melted and plundered. An outward procession of statuary followed. A leviathan angel, a St. Patrick, a Virgin Mary and child, a solitary Jesus. Taken. Placed on the cobblestones. Sledgehammered. Our Lady's head into smithereens. The others powdered into pieces.

And that was the second day.

And The Toll Queen saw that it was good, saying, "Let us bring forth the rest."

Which began with Liam's precious organ, removed pipe by pipe and piled on the long back of an open articulated truck. Like sharpened bones. Arranged without bedding, without padding, the breeze conjuring from them a valedictory, melancholy dirge. Out then rolled a large roll of ruddy, red carpet, pushed and kicked, slapped happily along and away, like boys playing with a Halloween tire. Then hymn books, crosses, robes, candles and crucifixes were broken and bonfired. Incensed by incense and a gallon of altar wine.

And that was the third day. And The Toll Queen saw that it was good.

And on the destruction went. Every day.

But on the seventh day, The Toll Queen did not rest. He continued his work and the harm he had done. Continued via his minions the desecration and the destruction of our Not-So-Small-Church. Hateful. Vengeful. Wrathful. Punishing poor Ballygall. And he and his wolfhound saw that it was good.

And then they both left.

We were daily assembled by then, but held back by a uniformed force of Black and Blue and a Giant called Glibb. People were shocked. Scared. Scandalized. Even the new Xpresso bus to Dublin failed to distract. It had been our church. Our preschool. Our Room of Contemplation.

And where was His Holiness Father O'Shaughnessy?

No one knew. Unseen.

I did not reveal his lugubrious apparition at the Brazen Head.

So, the plunder continued.

And then.

Into our sinful midst, His Holiness finally arrived. Defrocked, we learned, an apostate proclaiming the (skinny) gospel of St. Palladius (allegedly) of Ballygall. But still in collar. His soutane billowing around his almost skeletal frame. His cheeks sunken. He did not banter with us. Just Ciao, Ciao. He stood apart, staring at the sacking of his church. Waving away, with fine, gesticulative grace, our questions and queries. Pale, his tan withdrawn. His eyes overlarge, papal blue. His whitened teeth gritted.

We offered Biscotti and Chianti, but he refused. From somewhere, he gathered to himself a bale of straw, standing, an improvised pulpit, but a height he only used for watching. Tears often in his eyes. Mumbling bilingually (Rome- and Cork-speak) under his breath. Taking the saint's name in vain, Palladius, Pally, Pal. Further distressed when the builders converged on his clergical house, ripping and removing.

The Toll Queen and his wolfhound returned, and everything they saw was good, except His Holiness.

"Begone, O'Shaughnessy," shouted O'Neill. "Away with ye."

His Holiness's retort was articulated with a fine, Roman cadence. "Blessed are ye, when men shall revile you, and persecute you, and shall say all manner of evil against you falsely, for my sake."

Which we cheered.

"Ask me bollix," came the royal response.

"Beware of false prophets," His Holiness replied, atop his straw dais, "which come to you in sheep's clothing, but inwardly they are ravening wolves."

"Baa, baa, baa," we sang, meaning them not us, but confused, we stopped.

Garda Michael offered to shoot us.

The sacking of the church of Ballygall continued.

A hydraulic crane arrived. Big, broad, and of course yellow, with those large, chewy wheels. In its metallic cradle a Queen and his wolfhound ascended, one whistling, one howling. One then lifting the cross from the steeple, which he dashed to the cobblestones. Smithereens. The church now secularized.

But what would replace the cross? A pig's head? A tiger's head? Of course not. Obviously some alleged ancestor of O'Neill?

True, sort of.

Think of his favorite story, sanguinary, sacrificial, territorial. Think of a dark, pulsating color.

The severed Red Hand of the O'Neill clan.

Not a chubby, cartoonish hand, but a hard palm, unwrinkled, with slim, elongated fingers, sharpened at their tips, a brief, thin thumb. A woman's hand. Red. And gigantic, probably visible from Liverpool.

Surely, a joke? A prank? To be replaced by something worthy of the holy height?

But no. That Red Hand was now set against the sea.

But missing, someone noticed. Missing the little finger, and the one beside it.

Surely, a joke? We counted. Yes, it lacked the full arrangement of five. The little and wedding finger missing. Just like the royal couple.

Consternation, disbelief, imprecations.

We stayed. We watched the eight-fingered Queen attach his huge Red Hand. Listened to his terrible, terraced laugh.

We stayed. We watched. We withered. Father O'Shaughnessy precipitously. Unmovable as a statue on his straw. Refusing drink and sustenance, even water, though we jokingly proclaimed it holy. He resorted instead to his BIBLE. Castigating the depredations of that eight-fingered Queen. Enlightening us on the deeper meaning of this tragedy, its spiritual exegesis: that Palladius, the real Saint Patrick, dispatched from Rome like himself, a saint equal to the resuscitation of the Church, was being martyred by his own dying Church. And for what? For Mammon. He said, "No man can serve two masters: for either he will hate the one and love the other; or else he will hold to the one and despise the other. Ye cannot serve God and mammon."

We encouraged him to eat, to rest.

His ravings — no, that's not fair; he was articulate, cogent, pulpit-worthy — attracted the media, (not those owned by O'Neill, of course), who evinced more interest in his abstinence than his evocation of Palladius. The Starving Saint, he was called, practicing a contemporary form of that medieval ritual of publicly fasting against one's enemies. Self-immolation, calorie by calorie. His vigil was popular in the media but only briefly, attracting only a trickle of sightseers, gawkers, and tourists. A poem was posted on our chemist door.

An old and foolish custom, that
If a man
Be wronged, or think that he is wronged and starve
Upon another's threshold till he die,
The common people, for all time to come,
Will raise a heavy cry against that threshold

O'Shaughnessy himself considered it less a fast than a trial by temptation.

Our TD, Bandy, concerned by the Saint's deterioration, offered bread and biscotti, cheese and Chianti. Stonily refused. A smoldering cup of espresso? A pizza? A bowl of buttered pasta? Father O'Shaughnessy refused.

The three-fingered Queen found it amusing to torment the poor priest, mocking his skin and bones, his crown of crumbs, his lack of miracles: *Where's your water into wine now? Your walky on the water?*

To which O'Shaughnessy replied, "Do not put the Lord your God to the test."

"Where's your loaves and battered fishes? Sure, that's the real miracle, that you didn't see it coming at all."

His Holiness did not yield. He stood for the Church, the cemetery, the revelation of the first St. Patrick. Not one saint, but two, one after the other.

Garda Michael offered to shoot him.

Archbishop Slattery descended upon him, initially dictatorial but softened by O'Shaughnessy's pallor, his emaciation, his confusion. A new frock was offered to him. And Rome, not a sabbatical, not a seigneur but a position of power, of prestige, of comfort and opulence, and, if not Rome, what about his original Cork, a powerful city, Boy, important?

His response, whispered, was not received well: "The Lord, your God, shall you worship, and him alone shall you serve."

Were the nights unusually cold, dishearteningly windy, irremediably damp? Were we too distracted, too stressed, too anxious? Too concerned with each other? Or, to ask it simply: Were we negligent? Shouldn't we have seen what was obvious? Seen beyond his poor comfort of straw? Seen the true lack of sustenance?

Poor Father O'Shaughnessy died. Underneath that mutilated Red Hand.

I want to say he passed at a poignant, pivotal juncture, overcome by the spectacle, having surpassed all temptations, but the shameful truth is that his time of death was not noticed. It did not register amid that relentless, royal onslaught. And by that point he was sleeping a lot. Mumbling himself into an abyss.

Not our fault, but terrible.

He died on a bed of straw.

Poor Father O'Shaughnessy.

We're On The One Road, Singing the One Song

We congregated inside the warmth and safety of The Wobbly, its windows barred, its door reinforced. Townies and Estaters, intermingled. All dressed in vigil white, per instructions. Bearing candles and crosses. Prayer beads. Posters of St. Patrick over-scrawled with 'Palladius.' Gallagher, Costello and Duffy looking so holy. And even the criminals, Curran, Kelly, and Akinfenwa, even they looked holy.

Obee looked like an angel.

Chioma, atop the bar, addressed us. Easily a crowd of a hundred.

We quietened, which brought to uneasy prominence the noise outside: that Black and Blue force, with their crunching boots on the cobblestones, their walkie-talkies, their attack dogs, their truncheons, and shields, and the arrival of yet another siren.

"A vigil," Chioma reminded us. "For the body and grave of St. Palladius of Ballygall."

Raucous cheers, which only inflamed the barking outside. A massive force. In boots, body armor and helmets. Waiting.

"Peaceful procession. In twos. Candles, beads and prayers." A sentiment undermined by her eccentric armor: a bike helmet, gardening gloves, shin guards, her golden glasses roundly taped to her ears. "Pair up, photo." We photographed each other in pairs, the 'before' picture which we would compare with hopefully a similar aftermath.

The flashlights of our phones flashed. Photos saved and shared.

The vigil for Palladius had been Obee's idea, solving the conundrum of how to rally the town and Estate, all vigorously united in their resistance to the light-fingered Queen but unsure how to express it. Perhaps a vigil for His Holiness, the martyr of Ballygall, spurned by his Church. Murdered, really. Starved to death. His church sold, thirty pieces of Toll silver. But too easily impugned. His Holiness, an odd eccentric, his pastoral phobia, ejected from Rome, clothed in soutane and biretta, his faux Roman, his disappointingly small nose.

Perhaps the Wall? A protest against the xenophobic Wall, excluding a whole Estate, but who cares about a nameless, immigrant-heavy Estate?

Perhaps a protest against The Queen himself, rapaciously seizing the church of a poor, wee town? But churches were sold every day, to cover the burgeoning legal costs of the faith. And hadn't The Queen converted The Shed into a town church, a wee, aluminum cross already planted on its roof? And wasn't the Queen a popular figure now, redeemed by his amputatory atonement.

Perhaps the graveyard, the resting place of so many Ballygallians, also seized by O'Neill? Electrically fenced. Its important and long-standing archaeological work stopped, dismissed, scorned, scourged, ridiculed. But no one cares about a graveyard, about archaeology. But what is *inside* the graveyard? What had Aedeen been telling us for years? And Fionny, too. Saint Palladius was buried in Ballygall. The first St. Patrick. His corpse actually found. Artifacts too, from the disciples. His bones conveyed to the church for confirmation. But somehow misplaced, yeah. Forgotten. A whole saint. Missing. Right in front of us. This is what could unify us, rally us round. We care, and we know Ireland should care about this. Rally around the Saint. A vigil for the return of Palladius of Ballygall! How would this help? How would we save Ballygall from The Queen, already renovating the church for his eight-fingered home? It would rouse the imagination, the publicity, questions in the Dáil, a wee town robbed of its saint, robbed of its church, its graveyard, that something is going on in Ballygall.

Can't hurt, went the popular response.

Might hurt, went a similar response.

"Peaceful procession," repeated Chioma. "In twos. Candles, beads and prayers."

Obee smiled at me. A brave smile. Which I returned. She was wearing a tight, white, hard-to-grab tracksuit, its corners taped down. No jewelry. Her hair tightly pinned and hard-to-grab. With knee pads, gum shield, and rib-protecting cardboard under her shirt. Which many had copied. And swimming goggles, also popular. And biking helmets, which Chioma had made mandatory.

I also wore a white tracksuit, borrowed from Kanu, its oversized flaps and bulges duct-taped down. And a pair of building boots borrowed from Dirty Doherty. Both of whom were missing, on a less pacifist vigil of their own, perhaps.

Outside, those attack dogs howled. Another siren.

"Father Tas?" said Chioma, joined atop the bar by a sprightly up-jumping Father Tas. In civvies, jeans and sweatshirt, its sleeves pulled way up. The real parish priest of Ballygall. From Ghana. Small, fervent, muscular. A prayer in commemoration of His Holiness Father O'Shaughnessy.

> Eternal rest grant unto him, O Lord, and let perpetual light shine upon him. May his soul and the souls of all the faithful departed, through the mercy of God, rest in peace.
>
> Amen.

Followed by a moment of silence.

Followed by a selection of white lies from Father Tas.

"If Father O'Shaughnessy were here today, he would be with us, leading us, directing us against falsehood and oppression. He would be standing here, with brave, brave Chioma, speaking words of support and inspiration."

Nope. He would have delegated it all to Father Tas.

"Wearing his soutane, his dressing gown, you call it. His funny hat. His blue Vespa."

Which was funny.

"Let us go out there, as he would have, in love and peace, to serve our Lord."

Poor Father O'Shaughnessy. His body, like that of his idol, Palladius, had been spirited away by the Church. His final and spiteful resting place was rumored to be Cork, not Rome.

After Father Tas's blessing, everyone checked their armor.

Especially Emeke, who would be our first speaker; *Ich bin ein Ballygallian*, an opening we could not disabuse him of. Then Chioma, Janowski, and then, a surprise keynote speaker, Professor Aedeen O'Reilly, though not yet arrived.

Our vigil to be performed outside the graveyard.

Chioma reiterated the plan: Together, everyone, into the street together, stay in pairs, protect yourselves, but do not antagonize. Peaceful, always peaceful. And in pairs, always in our pairs. Flora will do photos. Weapons, only for defense.

With a defensible ambiguity, we had armed ourselves. Flags because of their poles; umbrellas because of their tips; and hairspray, which included perfume, a poor substitute for pepper.

Sound too. Something to oppose those truncheons-on-shields, those crunching boots, those attack dogs. Whistles, air horns, a trumpet, and a battered bodhran, but it was a Wolfe Tones song that carried us out into that seething night, together, in pairs, arm in arm, two by two, singing, together:

We're on the one road
Opening the one road
We're on the road to Ballygall;
We're on the one road
It may be the closed road
But we're together now who cares;
North men, South men, comrades all
Dublin, Lagos, Lodz, and Vilnius
We're on the one road, marching along
Singing an Irish song.

Out we marched, in intertwined twos, our candlelit procession led by Chioma and Emeke, then Ola and Flora, and then me and Obee, tapping each other's helmet for luck. All of us singing.

We're on the one road
Opening the one road
We're on the road to Ballygall …

What a strange spectacle we must have seemed. A ragtag Tour de France. Surely laughable but not to the three lines of Black and Blue arrayed against us. Hammering their truncheons against their long shields. Their boots stamping. Their dogs barking. Their lights and lasers in our eyes. Garda Michael in front, growling, Glibb the Giant at the rear, waiting.

Waiting until the entirety of us had —

They charged.

Without warning.

Like barbarians. Screaming. Truncheons raised. A legal assembly, but they still charged, without restraint, provoked only by candlelight and song.

> We're on the one road
> It may be —

Clattering into us at full speed. Hammering and slashing. Slapping and punching. Knocking us to the cobblestones. Kicking and stamping. Despite our screams. Our defenselessness. I threw myself on top of Obee, tried to protect our faces, our heads, as Chioma had shown us. But hit. Both of us. Screamed. Obee screamed. Pandemonium.

Then.

Gunshot.

Echoing off The Great Wall.

Garda Michael.

His Heckler and Koch.

A shot heard around Ballygall.

Not in the air.

He had hit someone.

The mad dog jumping for joy. He had finally shot someone.

A woman. Oh no, Chioma. Red already spreading on her white shirt. Screaming in pain. Her glasses cracked. The Black and Blue stalling, retreating.

But goaded back by Garda Michael. Aiming his gun at them. Then at us. The police dogs berserk.

He shot again.

The bullet grazing my head, nicking my helmet.

And again.

Hitting Janowski the Chemist. His shin, splintering.

Turning. Turning. Garda Michael turning. Unable to hear Glibb. Taking his time. Selecting. Selecting. Not able to find his target. Doherty? Kanu?

Truncheoned from behind by Glibb the Giant. Our unlikely savior. Knocking the mad dog out. Reprimanding the Black, forcing back the Blue. An ambulance already upon us. Many others waiting outside The Wall, their blue lights blinking.

Chioma! Taken by ambulance, with Emeke, to that seashore hospital, treated in the same corridor as my father, but surviving. Garda Michael was also brought back to life in the same building but in an actual room, private, overlooking the bluff.

We were commanded to disperse. Pushed and prodded. Obee's face bloodied, mine too. Pushed and prodded. Not back to the Wobbly, which was forced to close, but back to our homes.

A curfew.

A curfew in modern Ireland.

No.

We stood our ground.

We tended to our wounds.

We sang.

The Queen of Ballygall

A number of sore days afterward, myself and Obee sat in the Hiace van, parked protectively outside the B&B, facing north, away from that southern Wall. Nursing a thermos of V&L, tired from our sentinel shift the previous night. She leaning against me, me leaning against her. Still dressed in white, in our ragtag Tour de France gear. Even the helmets.

A lovely morning, excessively sunny, the sun shining for someone other than us. A street cleaner, the size of a golf buggy, was spray-cleaning the blood-soaked cobblestones, its driver whistling. Behind, around and in front of him, an infantry of litter pickers, Mountjoy Prison's finest, chatted and picked. Others watered the hanging baskets of flowers. Others weeded. Others window-washed. Others dusted. Others vacuumed, their Hoovers backpacked to their backs.

Monitored by Teresa, who saw that all was good.

At the north, the Great Wall converged to form a narrow aperture, a door I suppose, manned in Blue, not the more expensive Black. A checkpoint, requiring proof of residency and the statement of your business.

To the east of this, the Bank of Ballygall. Enlarged, armored, its large snout still directing two small doors toward the cobblestones. Closed to the public. Bandy's office beside it, also closed to the public. As was Garda Michael's kiosk, and his Immigration Bureau. The mad shooter transferred to the suburb of Tallaght. His shooting of Chioma defended as self-defense, the matter now concluded, but an investigation (one of large ears, one of large eyes, and one of large mouth) now underway to prosecute his assailant, a blunt object to the back of his blunt but intact head. Mr. Kanu and my uncle-in-error wanted for questioning.

Across the burnished cobblestones, the graveyard sat behind its electric fence, its neglected verdure growing at speed, greening the main chamber and its network of tracks and tributaries. But afflicted with a new shadow, a large, three-fingered hand, set atop the church's bell tower.

Inside the church, the Queen renovated.

Deconsecrated.

Turning worship into luxury-living. A battalion from Waterford at work inside, monitored by the eight-fingered monarch himself, installed in the bell tower, his office and den. Bulletproof glass. Tinted not stained. A Queen redeemed by electoral defeat. Popular. Ireland loves a loser, especially a billionaire loser. Unexpectedly humble. Deprecatory. Not showy at all, except in the exhibition of what was missing.

As a consolation prize, he and his cabal were awarded the TIS contract, Ireland entrusting The Great blah blah…to meet the English halfway across the Irish Sea. The landing site not far at all from Ballygall.

Ballygall. Now the Queen's town. The Great Wall a domestic wall, sort of like a garden wall. Sixteen finished feet of it. And two pubs, a supermarket and so on. Those other empty businesses ripe for an affluent transformation. The Men's Shed converted to a mini church, its roof stamped with a mini gold cross. The town quiet.

All enclosed by the Great shimmering Wall of Ballygall. Its southern section still fronted by a security wall and barbed wire, manned inside and outside by Blue.

"What a fucking mess," said Obee, gulping, handing me the thermos.

"The town we left so well," I replied, taking the thermos, more V than L. Handing it back.

"Wouldn't blame ya, Munky, wanted to head back west."

My Third Temptation.

"Me arse," I replied. "And miss all the craic that's coming. Mr. Kan-Who!"

"You're in?"

"We're in," I replied. "Kanu and Doherty need all the help they can get."

Obee smiled. Nodded. Cute in her helmet. Her white tracksuit, its corners still taped down. Holding the cool thermos against her cheek. Still inflamed. Bruised. Lathered in Vaseline. Honeydew scar cream applied each evening. But too late for the audition, the RTE adjudicators sympathetic, admiring her courageous audition, the pain surely, the aesthetic challenge, but she did not get the part. Someone slimmer, lighter-skinned, someone not burdened with a big, bruised, 'hatchet' face got the part.

Poor Obee.

Her injuries not unique. Similar lacerations, contusions, bruises, breaks, scrapes, aches, and headaches among the Ballygallians. My ears still rang. Tinnitus. Which caused headaches. Which encouraged more V&L.

It was bad all round.

Emeke arrived, finally cleared through the Garda checkpoint. Flora and Doherty with him in the Land Rover. Doherty quickly relieving us of our Hiace shift, Flora opening the B&B.

"Bring Finn," said Emeke to Obee.

Which pleased us both. Obee in the front, me in the roomy back, instantly vulnerable to sleep. Removing our helmets. Roused by those three roundabouts, too proximate not to seem like a prank. The first he took carefully, the second confidently, the third concussively. Driving fast. A box of Ferrero Rocher in his lap. From Doherty. A gift for Chioma, still at the hospital, still in a corridor. In pain. Her right shoulder shattered.

But writing. Her golden MacBook in her lap.

Underminers Unite

Set in the no-man's land between the Estate and the Wall, just west of the sea and our lack of beach, lay a manhole cover, obscured on its northern side by a scraggle of bushes. Noon. Sunday. From frequent use, the cover easily slid off, exposing a narrow drop down into the network of unlit tunnels. I hunkered beside the hole, nervously positioning the cover to the right, then to the left, keeping it easily reachable from within the tunnel. And glancing west, checking. A crowd already forming for the town's first inaugural al fresco Mass, to be given (unofficially) by Father Tas. Everyone working, arranging chairs and raising an east-facing platform, our new mobile altar. Busy. Oblivious of me, hunkered over the hole. Trying to catch my ragged breath. Nervous. Not claustrophobic, but the tunnel was tiny. It was wet. Wormy. What was that word? Vermiculate.

I hesitated.

Violating protocol. Which mandated speed. To lift (the manhole) and leap (down into the dark).

This first section of the tunnel complex was called The Drop. Drop yourself and go. Which I sort of did. Standing. Hesitating. Only my head exposed. My hand shaking. Recalling my father, standing in the graveyard before we…

Against protocol, I turned on my flashlight before pulling the manhole cover over, sealing the tunnel. Such a sickening wobble before it settled, sealing me in. But not all the way. I just couldn't. Leaving a gap. Spider-sized.

I hunkered down, catching my breath. Getting down on all fours, hands and knees, the flashlight on high-beam. Bracing myself for the worst section. The Crawl. A long, northward crawl. Narrow as a coffin. And always wet, which made me worry about rain and water tables, or the salty incursion of the sea.

I crawled, commando-style. On my belly. Slithering, compact and slow, careful of my monkey boots against the soft, giving flanks of the tunnel. So dark. So creepy. Against the roof I wore a Red Sox cap (my dad's). Against the soggy floor, I wore one of his waistcoats. And safety glasses and knee pads. On my back a knapsack full of newspaper, matches and Zip firelighters, but mostly V&L, two bottles of it. And a few paper bags in case of another panic attack.

On I went, slow, as I was nervous of collapsing The Crawl. Dirt already aggravating my neck, dipping into my ears. My elbows repetitively sore, their pads forgotten. And strangely, the fear of falling, the ground opening up beneath me. An earthquake. The Ballygall Fault.

Crawling toward the shaky light.

But admittedly, quiet. A reprieve from the tumult of Ballygall above.

Crawling. A bit quicker now.

Vigilant.

Watching out for animals. Dead animals. Which were often used to ward off interlopers. Mostly dead mice and rats, but once a fox. But pranks too. Last week a Halloween witch, effigy warts and all. Frightened the Jaysus out of me.

Gradually and thankfully, the tunnel widened and heightened into The Hall, its sides and roof ribbed with banks of supporting wood. Its floor swept and smoothed. The Hall was part of the formal network of tunnels, the Drop and Crawl being recent improvisations. Against protocol, I paused for breath. My usual two big breaths. And two more for luck. Marveling at myself. My bravery. On I crawled. Rising onto my padded knees and goalkeeper-gloved hands. Feeling my usual blend of fear and excitement. Did I look back behind me, into that looming darkness? No. Never. I scrambled along, picking up speed, like a demented toddler, following the eerie, downward trajectory of The Hall.

With a good run of knees and hands, I was soon upon the big, open clearing called The Cliff. Sneaking up on such a quiet, almost domestic scene. Kanu and Doherty in the well-lit western corner, on their crossword puzzles. Obee in the east, reviewing a new script, but from the BBC, not RTE.

I growled at them. A tiger growl. A reprisal for that Halloween witch, but up they jumped, welcoming me. Hugs. Our last time in Cu Chi, Doherty's Vietnamese name for his network of tunnels. Helping me with my supply of newspapers, matches, Zip firelighters. Helping themselves to the V&L, one for them, and one for me and Obee, Doherty producing a celebratory-sized box of Ferrero Rocher.

Ah, The Cliff was like a big breath of fresh air. Easily eight feet high, which allowed me to stand. Easily double that in width, which allowed me to stretch. Its sides well supported by a surround of paneling, which allowed me to relax. And well-lit by lights, big and battery-powered, which allowed me to pocket my flashlight. The room was redolent of crisps-chocolate-coke, overpowering the cloying sensation of dampness.

Like a goldmine it was, except that we had prospected up not down for its treasure. Chiseling through clay and then concrete, exposing what we now stood under, the southern curve of The Great Wall itself. Its Kilkenny brick hanging down like a giant set of molars. Held up solely by wooden scaffolding, under which we now assembled a bonfire.

A big bonfire.

Newspapers, sticks, tinder, and Zip firelighters. Then wood, planks, logs, sticks. All assembled. Everyone working. Everyone happy. Especially Doherty. "Good man, Finn, wearing your dad's waistcoat," he said, delighted. "And his cap," he added, with less excitement.

I waited, expecting his interrogative review of protocol. Did I make sure I wasn't seen or followed? Mostly. Did I cover my footsteps? I hadn't. Did I seal the manhole cover? Mostly. Did I stay on the main tunnel, there were murkier branches? Definitely. And so on.

But no. He was too happy. Breaking sticks, halving tinder. Whistling. Gulping V&L. Daubing it all over the scaffolding. Odd-looking without his tinted glasses, his eyes comfortable in this light. Without his fingerless gloves too, which revealed scars but nothing of stigmata size. And wearing the necessary pads and safety glasses but also, on his back, the enviable addition of an oxygen tank, its mask dangling. A subterranean scuba diver, but he had only the one tank. We had asked. Envious of such a failsafe.

"Mass started, Munk?" asked Obee, looking like the Obee of old with PLO scarf and porkpie hat. Wearing shin guards and a bike helmet, crowned with a big, square bike light. Like a lighthouse. Her cheek still injured but not as swollen.

"Setting up, but a crowd. Won't take long."

Which brought Kanu to song. "I fought the Wall and, the Wall fell."

Which he repeated.

Obee joining in, her lovely voice.

"Breaking bricks in a Cu Chi mine
I fought the Wall and the Wall's spine."

Even Doherty humming along.

"I left my town and it feels so bad
I guess my race is run
She's the best town that I ever had
I fought the Wall and the Wall's bad."

All of us eventually laughing. Underground karaoke. Singing as we tidied up. Removing anything incriminating.

Doherty then busied himself just beyond The Great Wall, further collapsing the northward tunnel, which had already been collapsed to a range of ten feet, erasing any linkage to this site. He did not want his tunnels discovered. A precious labyrinth, he had taken us through its southern section after our first week's labor. It seemed to consist of one main artery, of almost walking height, which proceeded north under the main street of Ballygall, branching east and west at uneven and unevenly surfaced intervals. Some murkier than others. Some newer than others, but most were mature and established, excavated by Doherty many years previously.

Why?

A hobby, he claimed. A challenge. A sharpening of his skills. Taking us east on knees and hands down one of the eastern branches, culminating beneath O'Donohue's. Which we verified, hearing the jingles of the cigarette machine.

Doherty only exhibited the eastern tunnels, citing structural problems on the west due to the Wall's construction. A suspicious, lopsided argument that did not make symmetrical sense. I would have liked to follow the tunnel toward our chemist, but he refused. Vehemently.

Later, right after the Battle for Ballygall, I learned from Obee (who got it from Mr. Kanu) that there was indeed a western branch tunneled directly to our chemist. Doherty had planned to use it to set fire to and destroy our chemist. My father's heirloom. A plan made superfluous by his premature death. The objective was fire, not murder, destruction not death. Warnings were to have been issued, my mother, father, even Liam were to be lured out well in advance. A conflagration. A vengeance on my father. For poisoning Doherty's marriage. And freeing my mother from her Upstairs gulag.

I believed it.

Anyway, I helped Doherty with the collapse of the Northern tunnel. We all did, complimenting him again on the elaborateness of his network. His Cu-Chi-Cu-Chi. Taking our time, delaying, I suppose until Obee said, in her best barman tone, "Time, Ladies, and Gentlemen. Have you no homes to go to?"

We were ready.

The lights came down, withdrawn one by one by Kanu, the light fading into his filthy green tracksuit.

The show was about to start.

Not a sound except the fitful unfurling of those balled-up newspapers, ripe for combustion beneath the sticks, the logs, the tinder, and the Zip firelighters.

The stage was set. The Queen's unwanted Kilkenny stone solely upheld by scaffolding. Beneath it our bonfire.

"Add anything else?" asked Doherty, checking his oxygen mask and tank. Smiling. Happy. Jogging. A little zealous perhaps. A little kamikaze. Breathing deeply, athletically.

"What shall ye commit to the flames?" asked Obee, who threw on that old RTE script.

"This," said Kanu. "*Things Fall Apart in Ballygall.*" Holding aloft a well-thumbed, impressively sizable manuscript. Chioma's book!

"What?" said Obee.

"First draft," said Kanu, laughing. "Your mother's idea. Makes way for the second draft. No names on it." He nestled the manuscript atop the bonfire. Patting it tenderly.

"You, Munk?" asked Obee, chirpily.

"No, Obee from BallyG," I said. We were proud of each other. Two weeks of dirty work, not the least of which was the subterfuge, the fear, the anxiety. Miners for a better Ballygall. Underminers Unite!

"Hurry then, Munk," she urged. "Light. Mass will be over. Me Mum, the timing she wants."

I lit the bonfire. Stepped back, past Doherty, already masked and oxygenated, and joined Obee, who squeezed my hand, and Kanu, who was singing softly.

"Will work, yeah?" asked Obee.

A thumbs-up from Doherty. His face squeezed chubby by the scuba mask.

"'A course," said Kanu. "Enough vodka there for Guy Fawkes."

Undermining, Doherty had called it. A tactic of siege warfare. Before cannon or gunpowder. Tunneling beneath and up into the enemy's fortifications, then gradually, carefully, removing the ground beneath it, replacing it, gradually, carefully, and then almost completely with wooden scaffolding. This would then be torched, allowing time for evacuation, before the scaffolding, and therefore the fortification, would come tumbling down, Kilkenny stone and all.

Flames flickered! Spread by the unfurling balls of paper.

Go, thumbed Doherty's thumb. Get out.

A sudden outbreak of fire.

But still we watched, entranced. The Cliff lit up by the sudden excitement of light.

But smoke too. Which drove us away, like kids from a Halloween bonfire. A thumbs-up to Doherty's thumbs-up. Into The Hall, on padded knees and gloved hands we scrambled. Kanu first, then Obee, then me. Always last.

Scuba Diver Doherty would stay behind to ensure the efficacy of the fire. Once assured, he would collapse the tunnel behind him, hopefully erasing any and all linkage.

Kanu was quick. Obee as quick. Galloping on all fours through The Hall. Crawling through The Crawl. Congregating at The Drop. The smell of smoke catching us up. But daylight glinting through the gap in the manhole cover.

"Tsk, tsk," said Kanu, pointing at the gap. "Against protocol."

"Check up there, quick," said Obee.

Kanu checked.

Mass was underway. Father Tas stood, his usual strident self. The congregation kneeling, the dads at the rear, standing.

Up we popped. Storing our paraphernalia in my knapsack. Brushing off the dust. Shooing the scent of smoke. Walking south, taking the longer looping route to Mass, as casual as you like, unperturbed by Father Tas's pause, his eyebrow arched, allowing us to take our seats with our families. No pews, just white plastic chairs.

I had text-invited my mother, hoping she might witness the undermining of the Wall. A feat partially attributable to me, her eldest son, now admirably vengeful and impulsive, just like my little brother. But no, she refused, citing her well-known indifference to Ballygall, sending a reciprocal invite to the Tomahawk, not the Tower.

Feck her.

But there stood The Great Wall, preceded by that small security Wall and the froth of barbed wire. Above it, a papal blue sky, marred by that red hand, raised against the sea.

Father Tas continued, exhorting the Ballygallians back to a Christian life. His words short, direct, muscular.

But no sign of Scuba Diver Doherty?

Perhaps the fire had quailed? Not enough tinder? Not enough vodka?

Chioma was called upon to read. From the First Thessalonians. She wore her golden glasses, her golden shoes, even her shoulder bandage had a touch of gold. Reading from memory, a fine voice, clearly still in discomfort and pain.

> About times and dates, sisters and brothers,
> there is no need to write you,
> For you are well aware that the Day of Palladius
> Is going to come like a thief in the night.
> Amid the quiet and the peace, sudden destruction
> Will fall.

Father Tas, ever the liturgical stalwart, winced at the extemporization, but did not object.

Chioma paused. Turned stiffly, painfully to look expectantly at The Great Wall. Hoping that the sudden destruction might happen. But it stood its sixteen finished feet. So she repeated the incantation,

> Amid the quiet and the peace, sudden destruction
> Will fall.

Disappointed, she turned back to us. Closed her eyes. Continued.

> Amid the quiet and the peace, sudden destruction
> Will fall,
> As suddenly as labor pains come on a pregnant woman.
> But you, sisters and brothers, do not live in the dark
> That the day shall take you unawares like a thief,

Another backward but disappointed glance. Nothing, and no sign of Doherty. She read on, extemporizing at will.

> No, you are all children of light and children of the day,
> We do not belong behind darkness, behind a Wall,
> So we should not go on sleeping as everyone else does,
> But stay wide awake and sober.
> So give encouragement to each other,
> And keep strengthening one another, as you do already.
> We will fight the Wall and, the Wall will fall.

But it didn't.

Something must be wrong. Something must have retained Doherty below. Or had we underestimated the sturdiness of the scaffold? Its lack of flammability?

Father Tas retook the pulpit. Recalled the clandestine congregants of the past. "Hedge Masses," he said. "Under Penal Laws, these clandestine Masses preserved the faith, strengthened the faithful. We are here to do the same thing."

He pulled up his soutane sleeves further, worn in commemoration of his superior if not his mentor, His Holiness Father O'Shaughnessy. "We are both persecuted by a Queen."

A comparison he expanded on.

"Like all monarchs, they take for themselves. Spurn the needs of others, the rights of others. The sustenance of others. Our religion has been banned, our town confiscated and our businesses evicted. The Queen has taken for himself the sanctuary and safety of our beloved church. Thrown down our cross. Destroyed our statuary. He has cast us out. To starve us of spiritual sustenance."

A fitting segue to communion, breaking the bread, saying,

> Take this, all of you, and eat of it,
> For this is my body,
> Which will be given up for you.

And then the wine, which he unfortunately no longer shared with the congregation.

Take this, all of you, and drink from it,
For this is the chalice of my blood,
The blood of the new and eternal covenant,
Which will be poured out for you and for many,
For the forgiveness of sins,
Do this in memory of me."

Which made me worry. Was Doherty staying down there? Sacrificing himself for the cause? Had he misled us about the undermining, the easiness with which a fire could collapse the scaffolding and with it the Wall? It had seemed outlandish to us. Such an immensity subverted by something as soft and lapping as fire. Could the fire be substantial enough? Could it sustain itself? Was there enough oxygen down there to fuel it?

The oxygen tank! Not for his breath but for the scaffold? An explosive, fed to the fire? Doherty climbing into the fire himself? Sacrificing himself? Ending his misery? His marriage dead. His house demolished. His defamers, my father and His Holiness, dead before he could gain revenge.

I listened. Sensitized my feet for vibrations.

Father Tas called the Ballygallians to communion.

Puzzled by our hesitancy, he called us again. Frowning at our giggles, at the light eruption of laughter through the congregation. The plastic seats creaking as everyone turned to look behind.

Doherty had arrived.

Without his tinted glasses, without his fingerless gloves, but with the oxygen tank, its mask dangling. A scuba diver risen from the sea. Smiling. Winking. Shaking a bemused hand or two. Everyone then jumping up to greet him.

Was it this collective jump that proved precipitative? Was it the straw that broke the Wall's back?

A tremor.

A quake.

We stood.

We looked.

Obee pointed, shouted, "Earthquake!"

The ground did quake.

The Great Wall seemed to stutter, to stumble, the ground beneath it giving way. Opening up, it seemed. The ground swallowing a bit of the Wall. The thin Blue line fleeing. Another shudder, another quake. Seagulls in squawking flight. A smell of burning, but surely my imagination. A smell of vodka, definitely my imagination.

The lower stones, a width of three or four, really did disappear into the ground. With a loud landing thump. They sank, noticeable but not exactly cataclysmic. Like a drunk taken to his knees, about to slowly topple over.

Is that all there is to the undermining of a Great Wall?

We walked toward it. The Blue line walking backward toward us. Quickening as the Wall slumped further, the earth shaking again.

Shouts of fright. Fear. Everyone assuming, another JCB assault.

The upper stones began to topple, destabilizing those adjacent. The crack of mortar, the seams ripping.

A huge stone fell. Plummeted. Another. As if they were leaping, Great Humpty Dumpty leaps. Dust shooting into the air. The ground shaking.

"Earthquake!" screamed Obee, wonderfully hysterical.

The Great Wall in free fall.

A collapse stupendous enough to create its own weather. The thunder of toppling stones. The sparks of lightning, stones striking the small security Wall, flattening the froth of barbed wire. A torrential outpouring of dust, debris, giant clouds of it, mushrooming toward us.

WHOOSH.

We ducked under our white plastic pews. Held our noses. Cradled our heads. As if we were diving. Cries of distress. Imprecations from Father Tas. A shout of joy from Kanu.

The earth shook.

The sun disappeared.

The sky disappeared.

A huge crater appeared then, a smoldering grave for the southern section of the Wall. An odor of smoke if not vodka.

For minutes we lay prone. But roused by Scuba Diver Doherty. Removing his mask. Pointing his scarred, ungloved hand. "Look!"

We looked.

The dust still percolating but clearing.

"Ballygall!" he shouted.

"Ballygall!" we recited back.

"Ballygall!" he shouted.

"Ballygall!" we recited back.

We could see Ballygall. We could see *into* Ballygall. So much better than we had hoped. Like dominoes, the entire southern width of the Wall had fallen, the ripple only contained by the control joints east and west. So, not just a gap, but a full and wonderful collapse.

We tiptoed toward it. Astounded. The Ballygallians wondering. What had happened?

A JCB?

No.

A tsunami?

From the Irish Sea?

An act of God?

The wrath of Palladius of Ballygall?

"No," said Obee, holding her wounded cheek dramatically. "An earthquake." Then delivering that well-rehearsed line. "Like San Francisco, yeah. The San Andreas Fault. The Ballygall Fault, righ.'"

The Ballygall Fault.

And we all saw that it was good.

Straw or Gold?

We made love.

Me and Obee.

But don't ask a cowlicked, chipmunk-cheeked lover to describe such things.

And *no*.

Not on the stairs. Nothing as tawdry.

Just the bedroom and bed. And yes, she did take off that ugly locket.

The morning after, we arranged ourselves on the middle stair, celebratory in our Underminer's gear (Underminers Unite!), sipping cooled CVL (Champagne, Vodka, Lucozade). Obee nuzzling, singing, "We fought the Wall and, the Wall fell..."

The front door wide open. A bright, sunny, seagully day, enhanced by a salty breeze, blowing just for us.

The Ballygall Fault still strewn with its own rubble. Cordoned off by yellow tape and a thick Blue line. Dust still percolating. A team of highly sensitive seismologists trying to get the size of it. An earthquake probably. Certainly not an incursion by the sea. Fire not water. An underground fire. Perhaps an old mine? Perhaps a combustion centuries old? No, lava was not likely. But a serious matter. A matter of national terrestrial security. The Fault perhaps not localized in Ballygall. Extensive perhaps. Coterminous with the eastern seaboard perhaps. Questions were asked in the Dáil (parliament). Unfortunately answered by our TD Bandy, skewing the facts. Faulty construction, the Fault not at fault, incompetent Northern builders, that's all.

But an investigation unavoidable. The rubble not cleared, re-construction not begun. A strange pall of vodka.

And Ballygall visible again. Its B&B, its Polski Sklep, its Wobbly, all visible. Its cobblestones, still oversized but accepted. Its Shed, though a mini church now.

But everything was closed. A precaution. The ground unsteady.

But everyone was glad of the rest.

The town at rest.

A hiatus that unfortunately did not extend to the renovation of our church, or was it a palace in the making now? A whole battalion of architects, designers, and builders, sensitive but willing to risk earthquakes and faults. The eight-fingered Queen back on site. Time on his hands. Determined. Pugnacious.

Which tempered our glee a little.

How could we stop the fucker?

Which got me and Obee talking about our own careers. Jobs. Money.

Gulping CVL on our straw stairs.

Obee re-thinking her legal work representing English gangsters. "Defending them, yeah. Sending them back into crime, innit. Should be doing the opposite. Getting them out. What I should have done with Aki." Her chin wobbling a little. "Got him out. So smart he was. No wilting flower, me, could have. Maybe. But, think I enjoyed the life too much. Not the gangster moll shite, not that life. No. The one I had. The peace and luxury. A whole flat. To meself."

"Dunno. That's gangland you're talking about, Obee. Mad world."

"Yeah. But should have tried. Maybe that's what I'll do. Work for some foundation. Get them out of gangs."

"Dunno. Do your own thing. Life's short, innit."

"It is," said Obee. "Wise words. And speaking of wise —"

"I'm not going to talk to my mother. Not yet. Just let it go for a second. But here, been thinking. Why *did* I go to the States in the end? After college. With me dad enjoying all sorts of success. The DIG, Palladius. Why did I just bugger off then?"

"Yeah, surprised me, you did it then."

"Yeah, lived at home during college. Well, not around much, I wasn't. Not a great place to hang out. And my dad was all night in the graveyard. That was hard. Wasn't on his top team anymore. Had the Grave Licker now. Just me and my Ma left. Liam God knows where. And me on the stairs, studying, and she up above."

"Yeah, and decades of that for her."

"Yeah, yeah. She. But I'll be honest. I'd no sympathy for her. Dad told me to sit on the Causeway, 'watch the shop, but watch your mother,' often said that, 'watch the shop, but watch your mother,' and that's what I did. And honestly, I sort of liked doing it. Taking his place. That huge bunch of keys. Rattling them. Watching things. Eating anything from the shop. Antagonizing her."

"Such domestic bliss. Then why you'd head off to Boston?"

My chin wobbled a bit. "No, you know what it was, Obee. Fucking Palladius. The saint. They'd found him. My dad and Aedeen had found him. Success. Celebration. Fame and fucking fortune. And nothing to do with me. Rubbed it in my face, it seemed. There I was, sitting on the stairs, watching the shop, watching my mother, like he told me, and still, never included me. Just her and him. What a dope I was. That was it for me. Couldn't stand all that shite."

"Yeah, and tell me to back off, Munk, but you left your Mum to deal with all that new, additional shite. Aedeen, The Grave Licker, his fancy woman, the whole town knowing."

"No, that's true. No picnic for her. He made it awful for her."

"Made it awful for you."

"Yeah." I took a long slurp of cocktail. "She obviously started the whole mess. But he kept it going. Never let her forget. Remembering now. Always discouraged her. Pick a fight with her when we were to go somewhere. Even just Dublin in the van. Not a shouting fight. Just cold. Could sometimes feel the ice. And holidays. If there was talk of a holiday, Jesus, knew there would be a fight, a cold, silent fight coming. I admit it now. He would start it. Same if they ever were going out. Something at The Wobbly. Or O'Donohue's. Or even The Shed that time. Fundraiser. Never went to anything together. Well, the truth. He went everywhere. Yeah, was a bit of a woman chaser. Knew that. Of course, underneath blamed her, I did. That's why, relieved when I found out about the murders. That was the reason for their wreckage of a marriage. Her fault. But. I know, I know, Obee. His too. Kept the war going. Between them. Persecuted her. Tormented her. Kept her up there, Upstairs. And I believed him. His side of it. That it was her fault. Her against the Wall, the DIG, the saint, and all the rest."

I took another quick gulp. Obee nodding me on.

"All the good he did, for the town and that, he did use it as a rebuke against her. Upbraiding. She, not easy to say."

"Say it."

"She was miserable. Depressed. Sitting on the sofa. Angry. Unhappy. Not this young energetic woman you see now. Then, Liam her only consolation."

"But did she use Liam against your dad?"

"What? No, no, ah, seeing what you're saying. No, didn't. Don't think so. Liam still did his whole Hippocratic thing with me dad. Giving him his daily health check-up. But she was miserable. Always popping down to the church. Was hard to be nice to her. So angry all the time. But yeah, my dad would be out gallivanting. Yeah, no picnic for her. Yeah, awful I suppose. Those trips up north her only escape. Did refresh her, but what was she doing —"

"Yeah, but was no picnic for you, Munk," said Obee, leaning, patting my arm. "Why did your dad drag you into the whole thing?"

"Justice," I said, before I could stop myself. "Or anger. Loneliness. Or make her account for her sins."

"But what she did, nothing to do with you. All right, all right," Obee trying to laugh, "ruined your American childhood, Cape Cod and braces on your teeth and all that, but that whole madness was between them."

"What did my Ma call him? A big sulky boy. Said he was relieved that they had to leave Boston. His research not, well, a bit banal. I know what you're saying, Obee. He dragged me in. Made me choose sides. But the worst. When the DIG, Aedeen. He sort of kicked me away. Enjoy his bogus saint alone with her."

"Not bogus," yelped Obee with faux outrage.

"Abandoned me. The prick sort of abandoned me. No, worse than that. Told me to stay on the stairs, watch the shop, but watch your mother, do his dirty work. Even. God, makes me boil now, remembering. Stupid bogus saint."

"Still not bogus," said Obee.

"Used me. And wasn't I the one that found the Wall. All those bitter cold mornings working with him. Then turns around and flounces off with her. Leaving me with the wreckage at home."

Obee took a long sup, allowed the silence to sit between us.

Unfelt tears had pooled at my chin. It was good to give them a good wipe away. "Anyway," I said, trying to forge a conclusion. "He was at fault. With her. Two of them in it. He was just smarter with it. Sly."

"Your dad was always good with people."

"Yeah, for good and bad. And was good to me. Don't get me wrong. Very good to me. Lots of good times. Together. But what about you, Obee? How did it work, when you left for London?"

Obee nodded. Took a breath. "Different. But plenty of guilt. Leaving poor Flora to deal with both of them. Their full attention. He for Dublin, she for London, and Flora for Ballygall. Asking her to choose sides.

Campaigning they were, always trying to convince her. That girl smart, though. Knows tactics. Knows when to leave. Younger sister, but years ahead. Bit different from your younger, that boy Liam. Eccentric, at least."

"I left him too, I suppose. But he's impervious."

"The Maestro, was odd, even before that ponytail."

I smiled.

Obee smiled.

"Then," I said, "when me dad died. God. All that stuff. But what was it Liam said to me? Worried about me, they were. Him and my Mum. That I'd want to come home and save the day. Sitting on the stairs. Take over this, take over that. Suppose I did want to. Bury me Da. Fix the shop. Pay the loan. Sue the hospital. Build his Great Wall."

"And make your mother live there happily ever after."

"Or unhappily," I said. "Unhappily ever after."

"Yeah. Same dynamic with me in London. At least at the start. Become a rich and powerful barrister. Bring them all over, even the cousins. Install my mother as a famous writer, my father a captain of industry. Hospitality industry. Flora play for United. Eventually return us all in glory to Lagos. Everything fixed and perfect."

"Yeah."

"Yeah."

"Mad how much stuff, just a little town, just a little chemist," I said.

"Not just a shop, is it, though, Munk. It's a battlefield. A war zone."

"A gravestone. You know I thought I would be ecstatic in Boston, all this crap, but honestly I wasn't."

Obee sighed. "Ah, Jesus, Ballygall, the town we thought we left so well, wha?"

"Have a drink," I said.

"I will."

"Underminers Unite!"

"Unite!"

We stayed united, but the fault in the Fault was found. A softness, a swamp, easily fixed, easily filled, or so it was asserted. Which revived the Queen, which re-invigorated his campaign, which sharpened his wrath. Our town in peril. What could save us now? What could rise up and save our poor wee town?

The Winker of Ballygall

The graveyard, once forbidden to us by an electric fence, was now forbidden to us by a smaller, non-electrified fence, protected at its front by a sentinel of Blue. Inside, the graveyard was now lit by a standing assemblage of lights, a blazing ceiling that illuminated the excavation equipment of the workmen — wheelbarrows, buckets, pickaxes, and shovels. Thankfully, no JCBs. At the rear, a line of shoveled men arrayed themselves south to north like a platoon of mine sweepers. Led by a Northern priest, with hiccups. Urging their speed and care. Pointing their shovels toward the line of ancient headstones. An ambulance of all things parked and preparatory on our main cobblestoned road.

Eviction.

Deconsecration.

They were routing the remaining plots. Converting the graveyard into a royal playground. No warning, no notice, no ceremony. Just the secularizing hiccups of a Northern priest.

A process that began that morning, precipitating panic and additionally provoking my own filial dilemma. Should I preemptively disclose my father's unauthorized and possibly illegal presence? No, was the resounding Chijindu consensus. Too incriminating. And potentially a valuable disruption. Grin and bear it. And my mother? Wouldn't she disclose it herself? No. Too incriminating. She'll likely blame His poor Holiness.

Or me?

No, surely not.

But Liam did text me. *Keep mum, we all are. Don't be a hero. Lot at stake.* By which he meant his music, his Irish Music Academy chances.

We stood outside the Bank of Ballygall. A small, exhausted crowd. A brisk evening. Salt on the air. Shadows edging eastward. At the southern end of town, the seismologists retired for the day.

At the rear of the graveyard, the gravediggers dug. Carefully. Lightly. Poking rather than shoveling. Eventually finding something of interest. Something remarkable. Congregating around a small plot, square-shaped, a postage stamp slightly elongated. Two quickly on their knees. Troweling. Brushing.

"Just the magical, mythical Finn McCool," soothed Obee. "Not your dad. Remember. Descended from a fictional character, yeah. Magical, mythical Finn McCool."

"A' course," I said. "Rising to save Ireland, and more importantly, Ballygall."

"That's it, Munk," squeezing my arm. Watching with Chioma, Emeke, Flora, Kanu, and my uncle-in-error.

The two gravediggers stood up. Stood back. One calling the priest, the other on his phone ringing. Consternation. Raised voices. Enough to entice the thick Blue line back toward them. Which invited us closer, across the cobblestones.

"Found something," someone said.

"Doesn't surprise me," another said. "It's that kind of town now."

"A body?"

"His Holiness, maybe?"

"Wasn't he put under in Cork?"

Kanu handed me a pair of binoculars. "Commentary, Finn."

"A body," I said. "See a man's body."

"Just the magical, mythical Finn McCool," whispered Obee.

"Jesus, it's just a head. Buried. Like the beach or something."

Other gravediggers, other lines of Blue and an additional priest converged on the graveyard, sprinting to the rear, blocking my view.

"Jesus, only one eye," I said.

"Good," said Obee. "Keep going. Everyone is texting."

"No coffin or anything. Just. Can't believe it. Buried without a coffin. Buried standing up. Holy shit." Though I wasn't looking at all.

"Buried alive? I mean, before he was dead?"

Others tried but I kept the binoculars, kept up the commentary. "Not His Holiness. Nose not that small."

"Keep it serious," said Chioma.

"Has a radio, right to his ear. Murder. Must be murder."

Three names went whispering through the throng: Curran, Kelly, and Akinfenwa. Criminals. The crowd growing, our exhaustion lifting.

"Buried standing up," I repeated. "Only one eye. Jaysus!"

But the graveyard was crowded now. Impossible to see more, so Kanu and Doherty hoisted me onto the roof of a Hiace van, a much better vantage point to continue my reporting.

"Must have stabbed him through the eye. Whoever he is."

"Must be one of those, Curran, Kelly and Akinfenwa, one of their enemies."

I could see now but didn't look. "No, not stabbed. Actually, winking, the corpse is winking.

"What?"

"Wha'?"

"Just codding us, you are."

"No, I'm not. And radio stuck to him. Jesus, has a mess of wires. Could be a bomb!"

A thumbs-up from Obee.

"Typical, if from Curran and that crowd, there's bound to be bombs. Booby-traps."

The crowd retreated a step. The thick eavesdropping Blue line following us east across the cobblestones.

"Didn't they do it? That fella, that time? At his house? Blew him and the whole gang up?"

Which provoked another step backward. More Blue, and some Black arrived. Another ambulance. The fire brigade even.

"Covering it up," I shouted.

The mythical and magical Finn McCool was covered with a papal blue tarp.

"Blue tarp," I shouted.

"The Shroud of Ballygall," declared Chioma.

"Nice one," said Obee.

We were asked to disperse, but we did not. Our resistance rewarded when the TV cameras finally found the bright lights of Ballygall. We made the RTE news late that night. Here is the transcript in a screenplay sort of format.

RTE NEWS, INTRODUCTORY MUSIC AND CREDITS

DISSOLVE TO MOLLY DONOVAN, NEWSREADER, DRESSED IN A PURPLE JACKET, WHITE BLOUSE, HER HAIR BLONDE AND NEWLY BOBBED.

MOLLY DONOVAN

The body of a middle-aged man has been discovered in the town of Ballygall, Dublin. It is believed to be the result of a gangland feud. The victim has not yet been identified. A number of local men have been detained for questioning.

ESTABLISHING SHOT OF THE GRAVEYARD OF BALLYGALL.

EXTERIOR MAIN STREET. LATE EVENING.

The floodlit graveyard is obstructed by a protective line of Gardai, Blue and Black in color. A huge crowd of locals stand before them, their phones raised and flashing, some on tippy toe, some on other's shoulders and one enterprising man standing on a Hiace van.

MOLLY DONOVAN (Voiceover. V.O.)

The church and its adjoining graveyard have been recently sold to a private buyer. During the renovation of the graveyard by a team of Church-appointed archaeologists, the body was discovered. The prevalence of rival criminal gangs in the town has been implicated in what Gardai are now treating as murder. It has been speculated that this may be related to the murder of Chigozie Akinfenwa, known locally as 'Young' Akinfenwa, who was shot dead in a gangland dispute over drug territory in the Northside of Dublin a year ago.

CUT TO A PHOTOGRAPH OF YOUNG AKINFENWA. SMILING. WEARING A SUPER EAGLES BALLYGALL F.C. JERSEY.

MOLLY DONOVAN (V.O.)

Members of the Curran and Kelly crime syndicate have been detained for questioning under Section 4 of the Criminal Justice Act.

CUT TO A LIVE SHOT OF THE GARDA KIOSK.

The kiosk is a tiny, crowded room, like a glass lift at a modern shopping center. Inside, a surfeit of large Garda hats eclipses what little light is available. At the table, their backs hunched, sit Razor Curran and his sister, Pennies Kelly. Smoking.

CUT TO FOOTAGE OF A PREVIOUS CRIME SCENE. FLASHING BLUE LIGHTS AND HIGH VISIBILITY JACKETS.

MOLLY DONOVAN (V.O.)

The Curran and Kelly gang had also been implicated in the murder of Seamus Boshell earlier this year in the Northside suburb of Finglas. An explosive device, designed to target his gangland colleagues, was attached to Mr. Boshell. Gardai suspect a similar device may be in play in the town of Ballygall. We now join Akwaeke Boladale, live in Ballygall.

CUT TO AKWAEKE BOLADALE, ON-SITE REPORTER, DRESSED IN A RED JACKET, WHITE BLOUSE, HER BLACK HAIR LONG AND NEWLY CURLED.

AKWAEKE BOLADALE

Thank you, Molly. The town of Ballygall is in shock. People are struggling to make sense of this terrible discovery. I have with me the local TD, Charles Driscoll. TD Driscoll, can you tell us anything about the victim and the cause of death?

TD CHARLES 'BANDY' DRISCOLL, SMILING CROOKEDLY.

I can neither confirm nor deny that there is in point of fact a victim, as it were. We are making our inquiries.

AKWAEKE BOLADALE

Can you confirm that a bomb disposal team is on-site? That experts are examining a suspected bomb attached to the victim? That this has slowed the identification?

CLOSE UP OF A NEARBY GREEN VAN WITH THE INSCRIPTION,

"The Defense Forces Explosive Ordnance Team, *sponsored by Dyson.*"

TD CHARLES 'BANDY' DRISCOLL, STILL SMILING CROOKEDLY.

I can't confirm or deny that. We are making our inquiries.

CUT TO CLOSE-UP OF AKWAEKE BOLADALE

AKWAEKE BOLADALE

Other unusual features of the victim's burial have caused consternation in the town. It is believed that the body has been buried vertically, not horizontally.

MOLLY DONOVAN (V.O.)

Sorry, Akwaeke. Can you clarify? The body was buried in a standing position?

AKWAEKE BOLADALE

VISIBLY ANNOYED AT THE INTERRUPTION

That's right, Molly. Buried standing up. His head barely half a foot below ground.

MOLLY DONOVAN (V.O.)

Standing? What could that —

AKWAEKE BOLADALE

Sorry to interrupt you there, Molly, but another disturbing detail has just been confirmed. The victim is purported to have been buried with one eye open, the other one closed. This, and the orientation of its burial, has unnerved the locals. Sorry, Molly, I have with me here Geraldine O'Donohue, proprietor of O'Donohue's pub here in the town.

ZOOM OUT TO SEE GERALDINE O'DONOHUE DRESSED IN A WARM COAT AND WARM BOOTS.

GERALDINE O'DONOHUE

Like you'd see someone buried at the beach. Not that we have much of a beach here in Ballygall, but, we all saw him. The head first. The neck. The bit of shoulders. Blue shirt. This type of radio stuck to him. Like I said, someone buried at the beach. Something everyone should come and see. And have a drink at O'Donohue's while you're at it.

GERALDINE O'DONOHUE WALKS AWAY.

AKWAEKE BOLADALE

I also have here with me…

OBEE PUSHES PAST TERESA 'TIDY TOWN' MCANTEER WHO WAS WAITING TO BE INTERVIEWED.

OBEE CHIJINDU

Obee Chijindu, owner of Braid & Barber.

AKWAEKE BOLADALE.

What can you tell us, Obee?

OBEE CHIJINDU

Buried standing up he was. Execution style. Firing squad or something. With his eye gouged out. Right one we think. Warning to everyone. Everyone calling him The Winker now, yeah. The Winker of Ballygall. And a bomb strapped to his neck an' everything. Mad stuff. Mad stuff in Ballygall. Just south of Dalkey. Express bus from Stephen's Green.

ABRUPT CUT TO MOLLY DONOVAN IN THE STUDIO.

MOLLY DONOVAN

Quite a startling account there, Akwaeke. We can confirm the presence of the nation's top bomb disposal team in Ballygall. We have also learned of a recent death that may now be connected to this gangland feud. The parish priest of Ballygall, Father O'Shaughnessy, affectionately called His Holiness by the locals, died in mysterious circumstances barely a month ago. He was a vocal and outspoken critic of the Church's decision to sell the church and graveyard in Ballygall. There is mounting speculation that his death may be connected to the body buried in the graveyard. That perhaps he knew of the body buried in the graveyard and was murdered to keep him silent. Akwaeke, can you tell us anything more about this?

CUT TO AKWAEKE BOLADALE.

AKWAEKE BOLADALE

I have with me here, Teresa McAnteer, chairwoman of the Tidy Town Commission of Ballygall.

TERESA MCANTEER, DRESSED IN BUSINESS SUIT.

TERESA MCANTEER

Thank you, Akwaeke. I think this has all been blown out of proportion. I think Ballygall is the real victim here. The body was obviously dumped here from Dublin, or Listowel. It wasn't buried. It wasn't even buried standing up. Or had its eye gouged out. It was just dumped here. Maliciously. You know our town has been working hard, you know we were primed to be a real contender for the Tidy Town competition this year.

AKWAEKE BOLADALE

Would you comment on the recent death of Father O'Shaughnessy? Is it connected to what we see going on here?

TERESA MCANTEER

No connection at all. Father O'Shaughnessy was a small-nosed, short-sighted old man. He objected to the quite necessary sale of the church and its grounds. The church was always too big for the town. Lost us countless marks. But the old fool couldn't see that. Right, didn't he starve himself to death. Right outside the church. A martyr in his own deranged mind. Disgraceful.

AKWAEKE BOLADALE

Starved himself?

TERESA MCANTEER

Well, after a month or so of Biscotti and Chianti. Had this weird Italian fixation. Then only drank holy water. The man was a lunatic.

ABRUPT CUT BACK TO MOLLY DONOVAN IN THE STUDIO.

MOLLY DONOVAN, VISIBLY SURPRISED.

Thank you, Akwaeke. Tons more to come, I am sure, from Ballygall. In other news the contract for TIS, Tunnel the Irish Sea, has…

****

The whole town watched it and then followed it online via RTE's Twitter account. Below is the tweet storm!

RTÈ News Now **@RTENewsNow**

An inquiry is underway after the body of a **man** was discovered at a graveyard in Ballygall, Dublin. He is believed to have been the victim of a **gangland execution**. He was **buried in a standing position**, with possibly his right eye gouged out. A **local criminal gang** is being questioned by **Gardai**.

Tweet Your Reply Below

Nico @Nico_Bob072
Replying to @RTENewsNow
Where the Jaysus is Ballygall?

Stop @crimenow1984
Replying to @RTENewsNow
Another gangland killing. Senseless.

Empathee @kindnessNow
Replying to @RTENewsNow
So many lives ruined. So many families hurt.

Nico @Nico_Bob072
Replying to Empathee @kindnessNow
Bollox. Survival of the fittest. #LetTheGamesBegin

PeaceNik @takebackthestreets
Replying to Empathee @kindnessNow
Gangsters ruining the country.

Stop @crimenow1984
Replying to Empathee @kindnessNow
Bring back capital punishment. Guillotine the lot of them.

Maven @Mayoofcourse
Replying to Empathee @kindnessNow
All Dubliners of course.

Beard @FewDollars
Replying to Empathee @kindnessNow
Agree. Senseless. Fighting over a few bags of smack. Bizarre though. Standing.

Home @HeartFire
Replying to @RTENewsNow
Isn't Ballygall in Meath?

Obee @OddsOn
Replying to @RTENewsNow
Weird as F*ck. Buried standing he was. Like in a firing squad. Never seen anything like it.

Beard @FewDollarsMore
Replying to Obee @OddsOn
Must be military Or Paramilitary Probably IRA.

Isis @IsisIsTheCrisis
Replying to Obee @OddsOn
It's ISIS. They're here. We let them in.

Maven @Mayoofcourse
Replying to Obee @OddsOn
Dubliners. Always the Dublin scumbags.

PeaceNik @takebackthestreets
Replying to Obee @OddsOn
It's the breakdown in family and in family values. Setting kids loose on the street.

Roger @ThatYaPrat
Replying to @RTENewsNow
Where is that Akwaeke from? Obviously not Irish. Wakey, wakey.

Wake @The_Hell_Up
Replying to @RTENewsNow
Someone tell me where Ballygall is??????

Chio @ThingsFallApartBallygall.
Replying to @RTENewsNow
Only one eye left on the corpse. The other one shot out. Sawn-off shotgun probably.

Stop @crimenow1984
Replying to Chio @ThingsFallApartBallygall
UVF I heard. Those Protestant terrorists. Starting it up down here.

Paula @feetUpWayUp
Replying to Chio @ThingsFallApartBallygall
Hold on. Shot him through the eye. Then buried him standing up. WTF?

Dan @CablesFables
Replying to Chio @ThingsFallApartBallygall
I'm going to Ballygall, see what the craic is.

Nico @Nico_Bob072
Replying to Chio @ThingsFallApartBallygall
People! The Curran and Kelly gang are from Ballygall!!! Their town. Started a war they have. #LetTheGamesBegin

Empathee @kindnessNow
Replying to Chio @ThingsFallApartBallygall
How many lives have been ruined already. How many are still missing?

Jim @RunForYourLife99
Replying to Chio @ThingsFallApartBallygall
Yeah. Trademark of Razor Curran all over it. Heard bomb disposal there. Body booby trapped.

Isis @IsisIsTheCrisis
Replying to Chio @ThingsFallApartBallygall
ISIS, I'm telling you, it's ISIS.

Bashir @IrishImm.Law55
Replying to @RTENewsNow
Akwaeke is from Letterkenny. Born and bred. Irish. Yes, that's where she's **really from**.

Maven @Mayoofcourse
Replying to @RTENewsNow
Ballygall is in the arsehole of Dublin, just south of Bono's castle in Dalkey.

Obee @OddsOn
Replying to @RTENewsNow
Bomb strapped to his neck I heard. A radio, wires coming out of it.

Teddy @VinylForever
Replying to Obee @OddsOn
Where they'd find a radio these days?

Captain @E-Hab26
Replying to Obee @OddsOn
Probably a wireless. :)

Finn @Sls-upp_Sls-upp
Replying to Obee @OddsOn
Yep. Radio, wires coming out of it. Strapped to its neck. Bomb disposal all over the gaff.

Nico @Nico_Bobo72
Replying to Obee @OddsOn
Exactly. Razor Curran. Did the same. Murder of that Finglas bloke, Seamus Boshell.

Ronan @SubstituteThisForThat
Replying to Obee @OddsOn
Heard yer man Boshell was a right so-and-so.

Declan @Circular-Roundabouts
Replying to Obee @OddsOn
That's right. Took them a week to clean him off the street.

Isis @IsisIsTheCrisis
Replying to Obee @OddsOn
ISIS and IED. Obvious.

Roger @ThatYaPrat
Replying to @RTENewsNow
Yeah but where was Akwaeke *originally* from? Doesn't look like someone from Donegal.

Stephen @InterruptNow
Replying to @RTENewsNow
You're right. Ballygall. Just past Dalkey. Tiny little bit of a town. Only two pubs though.

Finn @Sls-upp_Sls-upp
Replying to @RTENewsNow
Must be tied to death of Young Akinfenwa. Was tight with Currans and Kellys.

Joe @Wrong_Way_Sure_It's_The_Only_Way
Replying to Finn @Sls-upp_Sls-upp
I'm heading for Ballygall. Knowing Curran and Kelly, probably bodies all over the place, like.

Damon @MarmiteMan57
Replying to Finn @Sls-upp_Sls-upp
Bomb disposal, bunch of wasters. Couldn't change a fuse.

Roger @ThatYaPrat
Replying to Finn @Sls-upp_Sls-upp
Nigerians again! Who let them in?

Obee @OddsOn
Replying to Finn @Sls-upp_Sls-upp
So two deaths. This corpse, standing, **shot through the eye**. And Young Akinfenwa. Shot. Killings everywhere.

Nico @Nico_Bobo72
Replying to Finn @Sls-upp_Sls-upp
If Currans on the warpath, get the body bags ready.

Aido @We_Have_The_Gear
Replying to Finn @Sls-upp_Sls-upp
Not Nigerians. They're Nigerian-Irish. Like Irish-Americans. Ireland's finally part of the world. Grow up ya twat.

Ben @Opus_Pocus
Replying to @RTENewsNow
Ballygall last in The Tidy Town comp, #TidyTownComp, and it's not even on the DART.

Flora @iolair_uachtaracha
Replying to @RTENewsNow
Ballygall. Home of The Super Eagles. Unbeaten. National record. Girls!!!

Chio @ThingsFallApartBallygall.
Replying to @RTENewsNow
No. Just heard. The eye is closed. Not shot or screw-driver. Its eye was just closed.

Alex @CommandoContractor
Replying to Chio @ThingsFallApartBallygall
Hold on. They closed his eye. Left or Right? Buried him standing up. With a bomb strapped to his neck. WTF. Why?

Jonathan @BrooklynForever
Replying to Chio @ThingsFallApartBallygall
Wicca. Witchcraft. Satan. Evil Eye.

Obee @OddsOn
Replying to Chio @ThingsFallApartBallygall
Not the evil eye. Winking, innit. Winker. #WinkerOfBallygall.

Carin @MagnusMadness
Replying to Chio @ThingsFallApartBallygall
More like wanker.

Nico @Nico_Bobo72
Replying to Chio @ThingsFallApartBallygall
Gang sign obviously. Currans to their rivals. That Greene gang maybe.

Finn @Sls-upp_Sls-upp
Replying to Chio @ThingsFallApartBallygall
Not the only death in Ballygall. The local priest. Father O'Shaughnessy. Starved himself to death. Hunger strike! Right outside the local church.

Nico @Nico_Bobo72
Replying to Chio @ThingsFallApartBallygall
What? Wha'? ??

Finn @Sls-upp_Sls-upp
Replying to Chio @ThingsFallApartBallygall
Yeah. Starved himself to death. They were selling the church and graveyard, the one with the #WinkerOfBallygall in it. Priest was against it. Hunger strike I heard. Bit of a character he was. Italian accent, fake-tan, very small nose, soutane, like a dressing gown, and drove around on a Vespa.

Gareth @Stone_Wall_V's_My_Head_Everytime
Replying to Chio @ThingsFallApartBallygall
Not just in Ballygall. Church is selling their property all over the place. Pay all their paedo legal bills. Why'd he starve himself? Just over a church?

Flora @iolair_uachtaracha
Replying to Chio @ThingsFallApartBallygall
It's a nice, big church

Kanu @Super_Eagles_Unbeaten
Replying to Chio @ThingsFallApartBallygall
All wrong! Priest death related to corpse they **found a year ago** in that graveyard. Ancient corpse. Thought to be St. Palladius.
https://en.wikipedia.org/wiki/Palladius_(bishop_of_Ireland).

He was first St. Patrick. **Church have been covering it up**. Yep. Found his body in Ballygall. The first St. Patrick. #FirstStPatrick. Some say the real St Patrick. #RealSt.Patrick. Check out article by Aedeen O'Reilly. https://Irishtimes.com/O'Reilly/Palladius

JennieButterfly @SilentlyCorrectingYourGrammer
Replying to Chio @ThingsFallApartBallygall
I have heard about this. Two St.Patricks. And the Church just roped everything into the second one. But the first did most of the hard stuff. Pagan Irish. Conversion. The Lot. #FirstStPatrick. #RealSt.Patrick

DaveM @Zenith_Crash
Replying to Chio @ThingsFallApartBallygall
Hold on. They found the first St. Patrick, 'cos now there's two, in Ballygall? #FirstStPatrick. #RealSt.Patrick.
In the same graveyard that they found this standing-winking corpse? #WinkerOfBallygall
In the same town with those gangs Curran and Kelly and Akinfenwa. Young Akinfenwa himself shot dead a year or so ago? And then the local priest, O'Shaughnessy, starves himself dead in protest? Because the Church covered up Palladius. Mad stuff but clearly true.

Obee @OddsOn
Replying to Chio @ThingsFallApartBallygall
This Palladius stuff is real. They found stuff with the body, thought to be from the apostles. And I mean THE apostles, Matthew, Luke, Roy Keane and those lads. Real artifacts. Not loaves and a few battered cod. Then the Church seized Palladius. No one knows where he is. It's a cover up. Da Vinci code stuff. #ReleasePalladius.

Doherty @TunnelTastic
Replying to Chio @ThingsFallApartBallygall
Priest's body, Father O'Shaughnessy, gone too. Church seized it. No funeral. No obituary. Nothing. Just disappeared. So, there you have it. A missing priest. A missing saint. This standing-winking corpse. #WinkerOfBallygall.
All connected. Not gangland. But the biggest gang of the lot. The Catholic Church. Roman Mafia. #FirstStPatrick. #RealSt.Patrick. #ReleasePalladius.

Ola @BigosBest
Replying to Chio @ThingsFallApartBallygall
Ya, this #WinkerBallygall is connected. He supported #FirstStPatrick. Church killed him to keep him quiet. *Crucified*. Standing up. Warning to everyone! Don't f*ck with the Church. Stigmata but in the eye.

Nick @HipposShouldRuleTheWorld
Replying to @RTENewsNow
Just reading all this now. Is any of this real?

Chio @ThingsFallApartBallygall.
Replying to @RTENewsNow
Here's another twist. Palladius #FirstStPatrick was discovered by a local man, Fionny McCormack, bit of a character, descended from fictional Finn McCool. Discovered Palladius with Professor Aedeen O'Reilly. https://Irishtimes.com/O'Reilly/Palladius.

But Fionny McCormack is also dead. Died under suspicious circumstances. In hospital run by the Church. No joke. St. Patrick's hospital. Died in the corridor. Cretins thought it was a heart attack not pneumonia. Utter negligence. #CorridorCare. So, the discoverer of Palladius, is also **DEAD**.

Geraldine @UpdikeWhatYaLike
Replying to Chio @ThingsFallApartBallygall
Is there anyone still alive in Ballygall?

Cinders @WobblyShamrock
Replying to @RTENewsNow
Newsflash! That private buyer of the church and the graveyard! None other than Rambo himself. The Toll Queen. #Fish Fingers Ransom

Nico @Nico_Bobo72
Replying to Cinders @WobblyShamrock
That three fingered twat. #TigerTollQueenCheapBastard. What's he doing in a kip like Ballygall?

Maven @Mayoofcourse
Replying to Cinders @WobblyShamrock
Looked. Ballygall not even on the DART.

Charming @EntreprenuerExtraordinaire
Replying to Cinders @WobblyShamrock
#RealStPatrick. That's what he's doing there. Doing the dirty work of the Church. Wouldn't surprise me if he did all the killing. Even #WinkerBallygall. Do anything that madman would. Wouldn't surprise me if it was him that bit off his poor wife's fingers.

Chio @ThingsFallApartBallygall.
Replying to Cinders @WobblyShamrock
Not only bought the church. But he put a RED HAND up on its roof instead of a cross. I'm serious. Bought church and graveyard, and half the shops in the town, **AND** he's built this huge Wall around Ballygall. Calls it a Christian Wall.
#TheGreatWallofBallygall.
Built by Palladius. #FirstStPatrick. #RealSt.Patrick.

Know @ThySelfGnosis
Replying to Cinders @WobblyShamrock
HOW DID WE NOT KNOW ANY OF THIS?

Finn @Sls-upp_Sls-upp
Replying to Cinders @WobblyShamrock
And! That Wall was discovered by that man Fionny McCormack. Him again! The same man that found Palladius. The man killed by the Church in their own hospital.

Melissa @CorporationsSuck
Replying to Cinders @WobblyShamrock
WE DO NOT KNOW ANY OF THIS because the rich, like The Toll Queen, #TigerTollQueenCheapBastard own all the media.

Obee @OddsOn
Replying to Cinders @WobblyShamrock
But, that GREAT WALL fell. #TheGreatWallofBallygall.
Some sort of earthquake. Can see the thing yourself, Google Earth, though RTE won't show it because the whole town's owned by The Toll Queen now. #TheBallygallFault.

Finn @Sls-upp_Sls-upp
Replying to Cinders @WobblyShamrock
Have to see all this for meself. Off to Ballygall. Mad stuff. #OffToSeeBallygall.

Chio @ThingsFallApartBallygall.
Replying to Cinders @WobblyShamrock
I'm on my way. RTE and BBC all over the town now. #RealStPatrickCoverUpInBallygall. Am I wrong?

Flora @iolair_uachtaracha
Replying to Cinders @WobblyShamrock
I'm going. Have to see #TheBallygallFault

Joe @SplinterMagnet
Replying to Cinders @WobblyShamrock
Uber giving 40% discount to it.
Kanu @Super_Eagles_Unbeaten
Replying to Cinders @WobblyShamrock
Express bus from Stephen's Green! #RealStPatrickCoverUpInBallygall.

Isis @IsisIsTheCrisis
Replying to Cinders @WobblyShamrock
Holy crap. Ballygall is mobbed. Thousands upon thousands.

• •

It *was* packed. Inundated. Not thousands but hundreds. Arriving by car, bike and Xpresso bus the next day. Amazed, astonished, agape at the town, its secured graveyard, its Wall, its Ballygall Fault, its church and its three-fingered Red Hand. And of course, the Gardai, the bomb disposal unit, the media, and in the center of it all, The Shroud of Ballygall.

A bright and breezy day. Seagulls out in force.

The examination of the corpse, #WinkerBallygall, proceeded slowly, carefully, the bomb disposers in their white onesies unnerved not only by the messiness of the suspected device but the deluge of other suspicious devices reported both in the graveyard and about town (compliments of Kanu and Doherty.) But eventually, The Defense Forces' Explosive Ordnance Team, *sponsored by Dyson,* eventually divined, via their robotic divining rods, that my father's radio, though engorged with wires, was in fact just a radio, and that the graveyard was in fact just a graveyard and not a minefield.

The crowd, mostly young, mostly excited, mostly texting, grew restless, frustrated at the lack of an explosive climax.

Which brought Obee to the stage, atop a van's roof. "Ladies and gentlemen, boys and girls," she shouted. "*I know who the Winker is!*"

A huge cheer.

"He is a local man. You already know his name from Twitter. Fionny McCormack."

A lovely chant of "Fionny, Fionny," initiated by Kanu.

"The man who discovered St. Palladius of Ballygall. You have heard of him, right?"

The crowd loudly assented.

"Discovered by that man in there, Fionny McCormack. From Ballygall. Murdered by those who would deny Palladius. Murdered and buried in this unholy way. Without a proper burial. Without a coffin. Standing up. His eye gouged shut. A warning. For everyone to see."

"Yeah," shouted Flora.

I did have to identify my father later. Under Garda escort, with Bandy. Under that papal blue shroud. A gruesome task. Don't ask a son to describe such things. My mother and brother unfortunately unavailable. But Obee was. Lovely Obee.

Obee continued. "Fionny did not discover Palladius on his own. He was assisted by Father O'Shaughnessy, our parish priest. But he was murdered too. Starved to death right where you all are standing. In front of the graveyard. Poisoned by those that hate Palladius."

Silence. Even from that thick Blue line, listening.

"A little bit of history for you all. Thank you so much for coming to Ballygall, to stand with us. For a decade we have had an archaeological DIG here, led by Professor Aedeen O'Reilly of Trinity College. She discovered the saint's body. Remarkably preserved. Saint Palladius of Ballygall."

A collective shout, "Palladius," led by Janowski.

"It was Professor O'Reilly's conclusion that St. Palladius not only established a Catholic community here, but also died and was buried here. He did not venture to Scotland. He did not die among the Picts. He was not killed by Rangers supporters."

Which raised a laugh.

Obee was enjoying herself, acquiring her rhythm, the bones of her speech scripted by Chioma.

"This Scottish flight was a myth perpetuated by the Church so as to establish their one and only St. Patrick. Now let me invite you to stand on your tippy-toes and look at the front and center of the graveyard. That large chamber, with the adjoining tunnels, was the grave site of Palladius."

Everyone tippy-toed. Some climbed shoulders, some retreated to the Bank of Ballygall and took to its snout for vantage points. But little could be seen above that cordon of Blue. Just the glare of the floodlights, the small, careful steps of men in white onesies scattered around the moonscape of the graveyard.

"Compelling artifacts were found in this grave site. A sacred bell. A wooden staff, its top carved like a snake's head. A wooden box ornamented with silver and gold. And yes, pieces of wood from The True Cross."

A little embellished here, a little confected.

"Important relics which suggest that the person buried here was important, eminent, holy. Palladius of Ballygall."

Obee took a reverential pause.

Dozens of phones were raised, photos taken.

"Others are thought to be buried here. His companions Augustinus and Benedictus. And those early Irish missionaries, Secundinus, Iserninus." Said authoritatively, names she practiced on our Straw Causeway.

"We always knew it was a holy place. When we found Palladius, it confirmed something we've always known. He built something like this beautiful Wall you see around us. Made of beautiful Kilkenny stone, innit. Sixteen feet. Snake resistant. Pagan resistant. Toll Queen resistant."

Another nice, collective laugh.

"Perhaps you can feel it, even with all this terrible noise. The sense of serenity emanating around us." Obee raised her arms, Jim Larkin-style.

"I can feel it," said Tommy 'Teddy Boy' McDermott.

"The sense of power. The sense of healing. Let me give you an example. My Mum was shot right here on these cobblestones. A couple of weeks ago. A peaceful vigil for the return of Palladius. She was shot, on orders from those who deny the saint."

Stunned silence. Many more on their phones, videoing. The TV cameras now rolling, turned upward to Obee, standing tall on the van's roof, then panning down to her mother, raising her bandaged shoulder.

"Her recovery, once she got back to Ballygall, this holy town, sped-ed up. But she also felt the absence of our saint. His presence. His energy.

His aura. We have suffered without our saint. No question. Everyone has gone a bit batty. We all began to live upstairs. Moving our cooking and our telly upstairs. I know, mad. It's like forest animals, when they know something ugly is coming, they climb. And no one could sleep. And we threw all our stuff away. Lost without our saint. If they could just take our dear Palladius, what could stop them?"

The crowd murmured their agreement.

Chioma posed for photographs — early practice, perhaps, for those other photographers when her book, *Things Fall Apart in Ballygall*, was published to great acclaim.

"The brutal truth is that they stole our saint. Killed the two people who discovered him."

She paused for a drink, "Holy water," she joked, but it was V&L.

This stirred the crowd. Salivating at the drama if not the religious poignancy.

"And the Ballygall Fault. This is no Fault, this is the work of those who hate Palladius. They blew it up. Explosives. During the day. Could have killed many of us."

Silence.

"Isn't it strange, people. The Toll Queen, that mighty billionaire, coming to this little town. The Church's own Rambo. Destroying everything. Why? And you can't see, but other homes were demolished, the families evicted. All believers. That's why he's here. The executioner. Persecuting us, who believe in Palladius."

"*How did we not know any of this*?" shouted Doherty.

"Yeah, exactly. Sure, doesn't he own the media now." Obee joined her hands in prayer. "Thank you all for listening. Please support us. Without you we are doomed. Please take photos, videos, upload everything. I hope RTE, the others, will investigate. And I see good journalists amongst us."

Notably Eamon Houlihan, author of the Super Eagles piece, who panegyrically profiled my father in the *Sunday Times*. I didn't read the whole piece, my tolerance for such hagiography waning, but here's a few snippets selected by Obee.

The Winker of Ballygall Revealed

To the relief of the nation, The Winker of Ballygall has been identified. He is Ciaran 'Fionny' McCormack, the local proprietor of McCormack's

Chemist ... Fionny claimed to be the sole corporeal descendant of the fictional Finn McCool, a claim not yet refuted by either law or science. His standing burial and recent exhumation (now paused by a High Court injunction) recall the myth of McCool himself, prophesied to rise from the grave, to save Ireland, or in this case, to save Ballygall from a light-fingered Queen ...

It is, of course, the Church's prerogative to refute the Ballygall claim on St. Palladius, but it is disturbing to witness their obstruction and opacity. It is imperative that it disclose the location of the alleged saint and allow objective and impartial examination by experts in the appropriate fields. This extraordinary claim should be transparently tested.

On a personal note, I should add that Ballygall is a warm, modern, tolerant, diverse town, with two good pubs, a Nigerian hairdresser and a Polish shop. It is energized by an engaged populace, who are friendly, curious and committed. The town has a distinct air of augury, of what might become of our plundered, troubled island. And so perhaps we might broaden #HeShallNotBeMoved to reflect the rich plurality of the town. Perhaps:

#TheyShallNotBeMoved.

I shall leave the last word with Finn McCormack junior — a chip off the old ebullient block:

"Though we Irish are impervious to psychoanalysis, we do believe in magic. If we tolerated a presidential campaign by an eight-fingered Queen, we can conjure back St. Palladius of Ballygall to his rightful resting place."

Not a bad quote — magic and psychoanalysis — concocted by Chioma. Not a bad article either. Splashed across the lifestyle section of the *Sunday Times*, supplemented by the adjoining Palladius insert, which introduced the man, the saint, his Winker, and his alleged provenance of Ballygall. Quite complimentary of Ballygall, quite critical of the Church and The Queen.

Interest in the story, in the town, in our dilemma continued to surge. Perhaps facilitating an injunction against the Winker's removal by a curious judge, the court case nicely delayed for a couple of months. My dad was once again buried, and once again buried without pomp or pageantry.

Questions in the Dáil, of course, but also questions in more important places, at the pub, the pre-school, the lunch table, the supermarket and the hairdressers. Who the hell is this Palladius bloke? All of which did not go unnoticed by a renewed president, primed and invigorated by her recent and relished defeat of The Eight-Fingered Queen. Who suggested a Commission to investigate the authenticity of the saint, and more generally to unravel the mysteries of Ballygall.

A serious Commission. Comprehensive. Diligent. Impartial. Lengthy.

The Last Chapter

A couple of strong drinks after midnight, me and Obee gathered below my father's gravestone equipped with a couple of pickaxes and a sledgehammer, all hidden in a blanket, despite the fact that my flawed, selfish father was a hero now.

And not a gravestone — a statue. Installed per edict of our contrite TD, Bandy Driscoll. Even a ceremony. An unveiling. Speeches, short and laudatory. But I did not speak. I did not unveil. But I did attend, my mother and brother unfortunately unavailable.

The statue was a leviathan. Easily six feet of carved musculature. A warrior. Standing on a great thump of great rock, like Finn McCool atop his Causeway. Completely dominating the graveyard of Ballygall. Which was open again, an attractive iron railing installed around the Saint's grave. Who was still missing. Misplaced among the Church's inventory of saints and saucepans.

Ballygall now enjoyed a daily stream of tourists, eager to see the town once seized and then abandoned by that loveable eight-fingered rogue, The Toll Queen.

Yes, lovable. His amputatory atonement had mesmerized the country. Made him a household name. Well, maybe not lovable, but tolerable.

Yes, abandoned.

O'Neill withdrew. Persuaded by the publicity, the scrutiny, and the persistence of a presidential commission aghast at the deaths, atrocities and irregularities in our small town. Teresa and Devlin also withdrew, their homes now suddenly vulnerable to subsidence and undermining.

The Ballygall Fault was eventually decreed safe, and was promptly replaced by an arch, which further enabled a cobblestoned path all the way to the Estate. With lights. Even a couple of benches.

The Ballygallians were healing.

Darkly heartened at the news of Garda Michael's death. Shot in the rabid line of duty. Additionally heartened when May Zheng returned the town its Wok and Roll. The other businesses also made available for lease. Including McCormack's Chemist.

Which might explain me and Obee's deliberative presence at my father's statue. Yes, himself still below, in his grave, still standing.

We needed to decide. Should we rent the chemist? A nominal amount. From Devlin the Developer.

A clear sky to aid us. A waxing moon. Rabbits and worse among the newly polished graves. Bats through the air.

"Not sure, Obee," I began. "The chemist. It's like you said. Gravestone. Why would I want it back?"

"Let's discuss," she said, taking a sup from our thermos, our favorite cocktail.

"Yeah, and something you asked me before. Couldn't get it out of my little Munk mind." I took my own big sup. "That if my Mum had been happy, I would have gone to London with you. Well, ya know, that's sort of true but only in a different world. Realized, obvious when I thought about it. The whole point, the whole thing, was to keep her unhappy."

"Fight your dad's battles for him."

"Yeah. Battlefield. But worse than that. For her. Upstairs. You know. Her crime fluttering there on the wall. Laminated. Me on the stairs."

"Yeah, your dad put you there."

"Yep, the two of us on the stairs. Blocking her. You know. Sort of keeping her upstairs."

"Her own choice," said Obee, "but, no, I see what you mean. Yeah. Like a jail. And you're the jailers."

"That's it," I said. "That's what I was thinking. Jail her. Her punishment. Maybe, at the start, years ago, she accepted it that way. Penance. Her prayer-pocked knees. Felt sorry. Her mistakes in Boston. Then it became the norm. But yeah, you're right. Jail and jailers. Jesus."

"And you, put up to it by him. Glad we didn't, that funeral he wanted."

I had refused. None of that horse-drawn bier and troubadour shite. Not such a hero, my father.

"Munk, he was to blame. Not you."

"Yeah. Knew I was in the wrong, I suppose. But seemed to be on the winning side, so didn't question it. Jesus, this will take years of therapy."

"Such a Yank," said Obee, winking at me.

"She was right to have a go at me. Right about a lot of that. Even what she said. That's the hardest. That without me, supporting my dad, he wouldn't have stayed on the stairs. Wouldn't have kept the whole thing, the jail, or whatever going on."

"That's a bit much, Munk, yeah. She's completely wrong there. You should talk to her about that. Your dad, like you always said, was a big, fat wheel, wobbling from his own wonky center, yeah."

I smiled. "He was."

"She's gone too far with that."

"Yeah, well, she was ballistic when she said it. That time at the Straw House."

"Good thing to talk to her about?"

"I know. I hear you. I will. Probably go to that recital, Liam's. Dinner afterwards. Probably that poxy Daisy's Steak House."

"I'll go with you."

We kissed, sticky and medicinal.

My mother, Liam, and Conor the Comforter were now comfortably housed in a fully-detached house in Rathmines. Rented. Close to everything — except Ballygall.

"Well, Munk," said Obee. "Are we staying? The town we left so well. Well, not so well. 77 Seaview Court. The Straw House."

"Yep. But I should warn you, O-Bee from Bally-G, that the straw in question is Ballygall straw, a substance known to transform into gold."

Obee smiled. "Duly noted."

We shared another sweet, sticky kiss. Then turned and overlooked our kingdom of Ballygall and saw that it was mostly good.

"Ah, Munk," said Obee, "will we Jaysus hate it?"

"No," I said. "Look what we have now." Needlessly pointing. Declaiming,

> And what lovely Wall, its hour come round at last,
> Rises from Ballygall and is born.

To which Obee replied, "Sls-upp, Sls-upp."

"Here, Obee, what do you think about the chemist, renting it? Instead of the Straw House?"

"Hard to make a fresh start there, right?"

"'Tis. Especially with this superhero lording it over you." I stood up. Faced the statue. Obee stood up beside me. In a surgical type of voice, I said, "Sledgehammer, please?"

"Here you go, Doctor Munk."

I sledgehammered the statue asunder. First the head. Then the chest. The arms. The legs. The ankles. Hammered that lump of rock — like our old damn Causeway. Obee taking a pickaxe, helping.

It did not take long. A few swings, a few swipes and it was gone. Then we pummeled, pebbled, turned it into Filler for the Wall. The Great Wall of Ballygall.

THE FECKIN' END

APPENDIX I

A Historical Glance at my Fictional Ancestor, Finn McCool

Before proceeding, I thought it would be rude to proceed without providing a historical glance at my fictional ancestor, the Great Finn McCool. He was the superstar of Irish mythology, his exploits — and those of his merry band, The Fianna — boldly narrated in the early Irish canon known as The Fenian Cycle.

He was a skilled accountant… no, I jest. He was a hunter-warrior, of course.

His name — Finn, or Fionn — means bright and handsome, just and true. His father was Cumhall, dead before poor Finn was born, and his mother was Muirne Muinchàem, or Muirne of "The Lovely Neck." His essential details are as follows:

Birth

Born in danger. Sought by the murderous enemies of his dead father, which may explain why his hair turned prematurely white.

Boyhood

Given his unpopularity, he was raised in secret by two women warriors in a wild forest, quickly adept at the arts of hunting and combat. His array of adventures have been memorialized in *The Boyhood Deeds of Fionn McCool*, the most celebrated of which recounts his defeat of a fire-breathing giant.

Education

His formal education was brief but comprehensive, outlined in that famous tale, *The Salmon of Knowledge*. The canny salmon, by its ingestion of nine magical hazelnuts, had acquired all the world's knowledge. The first person to eat of its flesh would in turn gain this knowledge. So, quite a catch this fish … caught eventually by the poet, Finegas, and not being much of a cook, he asked our Finn to cook it.

A conscientious chef, he cooked it on both sides, but lacking a spatula, Finn used his hands to turn the fish, burning — and then biting — his thumb. And thereby, and quite inadvertently (our family being mostly honest), gained not only a charred thumb, but also the entire knowledge of the world, easily accessed at any time, day or night, by the biting of said finger. His lowly thumb became The Thumb of Knowledge.

Curriculum Vitae

Using his know-it-all thumb and his warrior skills, Finn became leader of the Fianna, the famed warrior heroes of Irish myth. His feats are too numerous and too impressive to fully relate here, but his battle with the giant Benandonner is noteworthy, illustrating the guile of my great ancestor. Well, Benandonner was colossal, an adversary too mighty to combat by conventional means, so Finn took to his bed. His wife, Oona, dressed him as a baby and put him in a cradle. She then made a batch of griddle cakes, hiding griddle irons in some. When Benandonner arrived via the Giant's Causeway from Scotland, she explained that Finn was out fishing for a salmon of strength. The Giant waited, showing off his strength by breaking rocks with his little finger. Oona politely offered him a griddle cake mixed with griddle iron. The Giant smashed his teeth asunder. Oona chided him as weak (flossing is mentioned in some versions), and to show how weak, gave an iron-free cake to the large baby in the cradle. The baby consumed it with ease. The aching Giant was dumbfounded. Such a strong baby. Such a strong-dentured father this baby must have. Awestruck, he stuck a finger into the baby's mouth. You can imagine the pain. His finger was completely bitten away. Terrified, Benandonner ran away back to Scotland, across The Giant's Causeway, smashing it so that Finn could not pursue him.

Love Life

Finn was unlucky in love. He had many wives, some of whom spent intervals as deer, swans, and squirrels, which would present a challenge for any relationship. His most famous wife was Gràinne, memorialized in *The Pursuit of Diarmuid and Gràinne*. Not exactly Finn's finest hour.

Old, he was promised the young and beautiful Gràinne, daughter of the High King. She promptly eloped with the young and beautiful Diarmuid (who sported a magical, irresistible "love spot" on his forehead). They were hunted by Finn — our family can be a bit vindictive. After many escapades, peace is negotiated and the aged Finn allowed the couple to live in peace, even including Diarmuid on a boar hunt a few years later. Sadly, the boar skewered Diarmuid (via his "love spot" perhaps), fatally wounding him. Even more sadly, Finn did not help him. Diarmuid died. Finn was avenged. Not his finest hour. As I said, we can be a vengeful family.

Death

Finn is not dead at all. Merely asleep. Surrounded by his Fianna band of warriors, ready to rise and save Ireland — and more importantly, Ballygall.

APPENDIX II
A Bit of History Pertaining to Ireland, and The Toll Queen, too

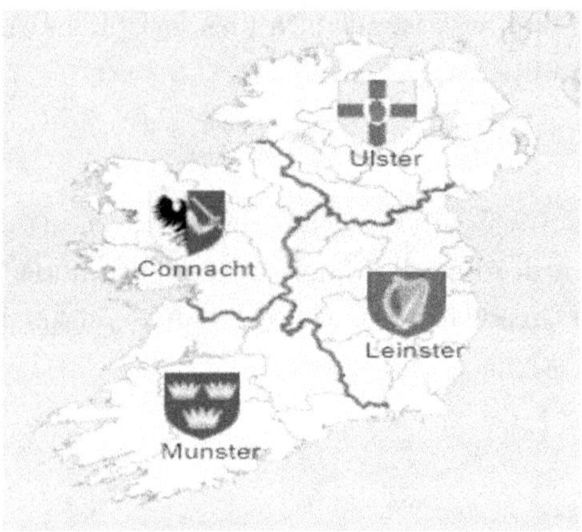

Before proceeding, I thought it would be rude to proceed without providing a bit of history pertaining to Ireland, generally, and The Toll Queen, specifically.

Since time immemorial — and well before that — England has sought to colonize its western neighbor, my very own Ireland. For much of our history their attempts were mainly confined to the eastern province of Leinster, and in particular, Dublin. Ireland's other three provinces, Ulster (north), Connaught (west), and Munster (southwest) were left to prosper.

This changed significantly in the sixteenth century when the English decided on a more comprehensive invasion. This hostility roused the ire of all four provinces, resulting in a coalition led by that charismatic

Ulster chieftain, Hugh O'Neill, the Great Earl of Tyrone. (It should be noted that there is no evidence to support any genealogical link between this Great O'Neill, this courageous Earl of Tyrone, and The Toll Queen encountered in these pages. None. Obviously the cunning work of The Toll Queen's imagination.)

This Irish coalition fought bravely against the English invaders, winning many valorous battles (The Battle of the Yellow Ford, for instance), but were ultimately defeated. Punished. Executed. Their land and wealth reduced or confiscated.

The Great O'Neill eventually escaped this tyranny, along with other leaders of the resistance, a departure known as The Flight of the Earls. A dark time for Ireland, which subsequently suffered intense and cruel colonization of the island. Further rebellion did not recur until 1798, and then again in 1803, and again in 1848, culminating in the Easter Rising in 1916, and the war for independence in 1919. This war for independence was partially successful, bringing three of the provinces (Leinster, Munster, Connaught) and their twenty-six counties under Irish control, but leaving Ulster (six counties) under English control. This is currently the political situation in Ireland, and may explain such complicated math as 26+6=1.

www.ingramcontent.com/pod-product-compliance
Lightning Source LLC
LaVergne TN
LVHW020541100826
845148LV00010B/1558

* 9 7 9 8 3 8 5 2 7 0 5 9 0 *